OF THE STARS

A.M. ALCEDO

ALCEDO
INK

OF THE STARS

Copyright © 2023 by A.M. Alcedo

Published in the United States of America by
Alcedo Ink, an imprint of A.M. Alcedo

Dust Jacket Design by Ibrahim Arfaoui
Inner Cover Design by Amal Dev
Interior Formatting by Evenstar Books

ISBN: 979-8-9884212-6-9

TRIGGER WARNINGS:

alcoholism, anxiety, blood, death/dying, depression, explicit language, fire, hospitalization/medical procedures, PTSD, panic attacks, self-harm, serious injury, smoking, violence, and weapons.

For those who've ever felt utterly alone and unheard in the universe:
You are here. You are alive. You matter. Your feelings are important.

PART I

CORVID

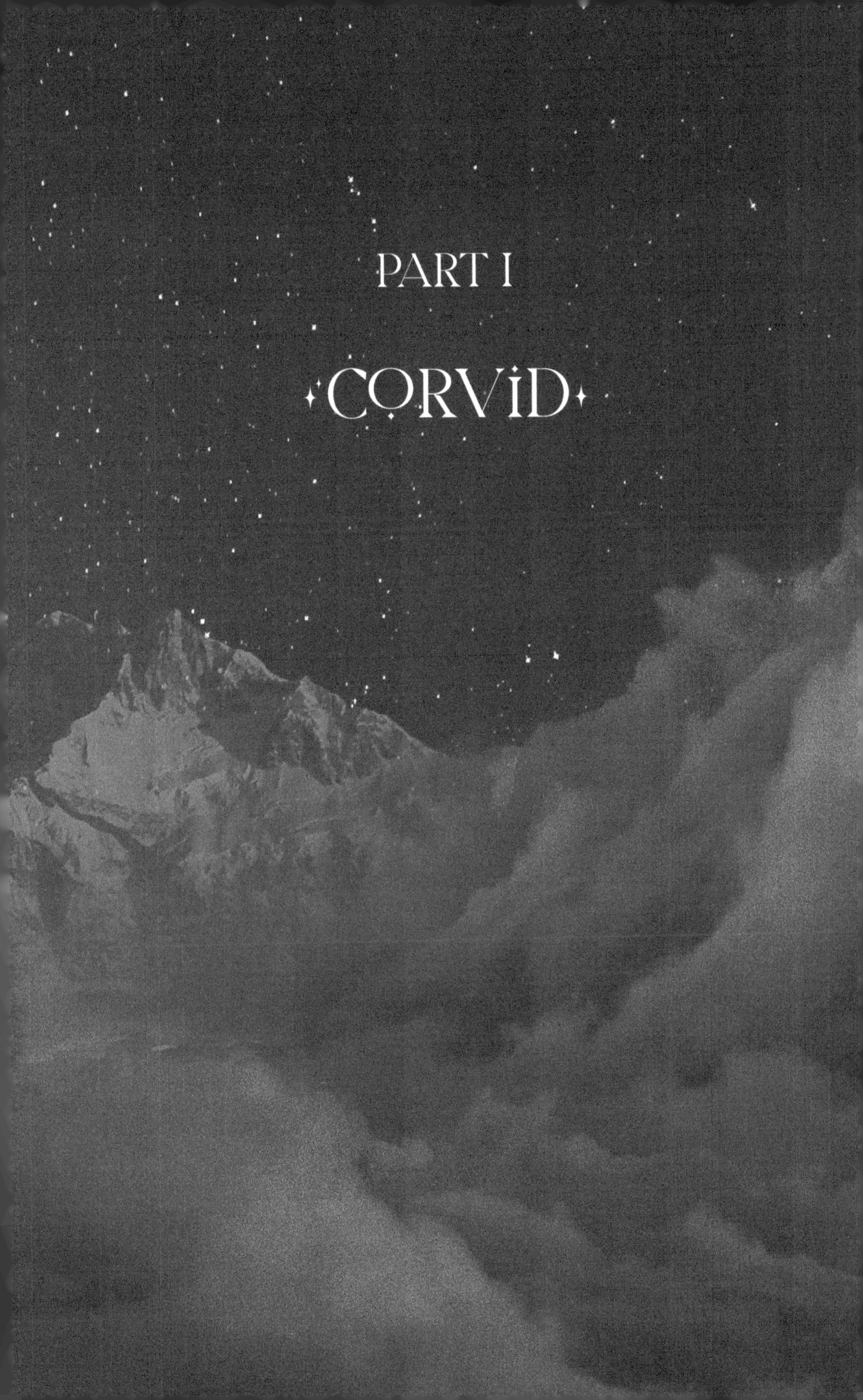

1

✦NORAH✦

THERE'S AN OLD MAN ON THE FUCKING ROOF.

Norah Kestrel gawked open-mouthed into the sky like a useless baby bird, rooftop gravel crunching beneath her as she sat upright. She squinted past storm clouds and smudged eyeliner, sharp face tear-streaked and crimson. Today, she had reserved a particularly horrific meltdown for her usual rooftop hideaway and had hoped to savor its ugliness in private. But there *he* sat amongst the morning fog and screaming birds, perched like a headstone statue atop the building's incinerator chimney.

That had to be what- she huffed, attempting to calculate the distance from her seat on the hospital roof to his. *Thirty feet at least? Surely that's impossible, right?*

But regardless of impossibilities, there he sat, unfazed like a fucking *pigeon.*

Her nose had found him first, hooked by the old man's candied cigar smoke, reminiscent of her father's. It transported her to many moons ago, a time littered with gargled screams and violent outbursts. The tobacco's woody bite in her nostrils reminded her of the red flash of blood on her father's knuckles. The white noise of the broken car radio. Her mother's silent sobs.

Norah blinked hard and shook the past from her skull, eyes finding the old man again. She pinched her arm with biting fingernails and lifted her gaze to the tower once more.

There he still sat. She wasn't going crazy. She wasn't dreaming.

Shit.

The elder above was bowed and bearded, quiet and still like a blue belted Kingfisher. The sun glowed behind his plumage of ivory hair as it whipped and twisted in the wind while he spectated the black asphalt ocean below. At the seemingly insurmountable height, many of his features were hazy, as though he, too, was paling and made of clouds.

How in the fancy-fuck did he get up there?

Norah cinched her coat's gold buttons up to her throat and tiptoed towards the incinerator chimney with the quiet finesse of an ornithologist. Her hands and legs stretched at sore skin, imprinted with the fossils of gravel and cigar butts.

From the base of the smokestack, a murder of crows cocked their heads upon her before springing to the skies. Glossy feathers caught the sun in gemstone green and blue glints as they flapped past the old man's derby boots.

He trailed the birds into the horizon and drew hard on his cigar, thick as the trunk of a sapling. With each movement, the silver buckles of his belt, shoes, and sleeve garters shone. His swinging calves wore patterned dress pants and bright floral socks whose cadence slowed as Norah drew near.

He bowed his head and stilled his old tremors to listen.

Norah stopped dead in the brick tower's shadow, a half-breath caught in her throat.

Then, with the whirring head of a great snowy owl, he swiveled about and found her below. His brows ironed flat in awe as though *she* were the anomaly.

They stared at one another like prey animals in the wood, eyes wide and mouths ajar. The elder glanced over his shoulder as though she might be goggling at someone else atop the incinerator. Finding only himself, his pink lips stammered and his hands rubbed his knees like knobby stones.

How in the actual damned hell.

While there were steel footholds driven into the brick incinerator, they were crumbling and antiquated. Nor's eyes followed the rebar climbing into the heavens to his minuscule perch. The structure seemed far too weak to withstand an old man of his stature.

He was luckier still that the archaic tower no longer steamed with hospital trash and cooking body parts as it had decades prior. There was a time when the entire town smelled as dead and rotting as it often felt to Norah.

Noticing him beginning to shuffle, Norah withdrew a great breath in hopes of calling up to him, to say something, *anything…*

But then, with the casual, uninhibited dismount of leaving a bar stool, the old man shoved away from the incinerator chimney, however many feet above her, and plunged down into the morning mist towards the gravel rooftop.

His button-down swelled and whipped like the beating masts of a ship beneath a bright blue waistcoat, a silk scarf waving like a crimson flare over his shoulder.

Norah slapped her mouth and braced for the gore of his shriveled lungs and entrails to rupture and splatter across the rooftop. Her eyes clenched shut, and she braced for impact.

CLAP echoed a great slap of concrete against the hospital's old bricks. More disturbed crows cawed in the distance.

Then, a throat cleared politely, just feet from her.

Nor dared to peek through narrow eyelids.

He'd landed on his feet, unfazed by the descent just heartbeats from his heels. He winced with seemingly aching joints, but he casually tucked in his loud ascot and approached her.

He's alive.

Holy shit, he survived.

How in the hell did he survive that fall?

The old man snatched the cigar from his teeth and extinguished it between his palms where it vanished out of sight. His round cheeks were red as Nor's and boyishly embarrassed as though she'd caught him pissing in the wind. His wrinkles bunched with shame beneath thick, cumulonimbus hair.

He has to be what, in his late fifties, sixties? she mused. *And that fall didn't kill him. He's alive.*

A multitude of vibrant tattoos crept up his throat, arms, and beneath his blue waistcoat. A small peony was tucked into the pocket. His bold colors and silver trimmings were a striking contrast to Corvid's historic gloom.

"Apologies for the s-s-smoke," he stuttered over the rocky terrain in his neglected throat. His voice rumbled with the lilt of a faraway land, reminiscent of the craggy boulders of some mainland against a distant sea. Its depths reminded Norah of the great, vintage purr of a sports car, like the ferocious V8s that once snarled from her father's favorite car shows on the television. The nearly blown speakers could send shivers across her arms.

"N-no, it's fine," she managed, tearing her eyes from his decorated flesh.

She inhaled the remnants of his cigar on the wind and its sweetness captured her with a hunger, a jealous yearning for its fire in her throat. Her empty pack of cheap cigarillos lay crumpled in the waste bin of her office below.

"No, no, it isn't. Tis' your space and I'll leave you to it," he said with raised hands, avoiding her stare. He rushed for the door with his head ducked beneath his shoulder blades like a scolded sheepdog. Floral socks peeked with each of his long strides.

"No," she called after his heels, pursuing him eagerly. She wanted answers. She wanted to know how in the hell he wasn't dead. "You were here first, really. Hey!"

He spun, eyes gaping at her fingers as though they might scratch and snatch at him. But as she felt him read her wet cheeks and tomato-red features, he softened.

He knows how pathetic you are, Kestrel. You cry more than Mom these days. Pitiful.

"I don't have the credentials to be here, doc," he grumbled, nodding to the badge at her hip.

"Oh God, no, I'm not a doctor," she scoffed, imagining her self-doubt breaching its already critical depths. "Are you a patient?"

"Not today." He managed a weak smile that didn't reach his wrinkles.

"And the key code?" She gestured to the steel door.

"Lucky guess I s'pose." Silver glistened on his jaw, where his empty grin persisted. The handsome senior was stamped with a lifetime of lines, but none of them alluded to an existence of ample smiling.

And the roof's entrance merited a ten-digit code. A "lucky guess" would've been nothing short of *im-fucking-possible.*

But as long as you don't go bounding off the edge, I don't give a damn what you do up here.

"I have to get back anyways," she lied. It was apparent that the pair of them would make for a horribly anxious smoke break, so she put them both out of their introverted miseries. "Enjoy your cigar, really," she said, brushing past him with a smile. He smelled of marmalade and leather polish.

Her fingers reached for the door's handle-

"Are you alright?" he called, age smoothing his words like beach glass on the shore.

She closed her eyes, sighed, and spun.

The wind's fingers tousled their hair, but his shy eyes found hers, shining and blue like a sky far from Corvid. His features were lengthened and sad at her leave, deepening the shadows in his cheeks and crooked nose.

"I'm better now," she lied yet again, "but thanks." Tears threatened to well past her lids. Heat warmed her cheeks and nose.

The ends of his mustache rose, and his bushy brows bent with skepticism. The kind soul looked like the wholesome sort who would've offered her sacred bucketfuls of his time to her. He was likely an excellent listener, capable of accepting and affirming her darkest feelings.

But she was certain that if space were to be offered for her bile, she'd either disintegrate within it like candy floss or harden like cement, incapable of softening for her clients or anyone else ever again.

They exchanged their porcelain grins, balanced carefully atop their inner unease. It seemed they both knew those masks well, even if their peculiar paths hadn't crossed prior. They recognized the mastery, the craftsmanship it took to fabricate such detailed, ornate, and utter bullshit.

Her vision burned and warped with salt, sending her skittering down the stairs. She was nearly quick enough to outrun the taunting of her fact-based prefrontal cortex:

That's right, run away. Run like Kestrels always do.

2

✦DEXTERAS✦

HE CLUTCHED AT HIS HAIR IN FISTFULS, unknowing what time it was or how long he'd lingered on the hospital roof. How long it'd been since *she* had returned inside, nearly weeping as she ran.

I was so sure. I'd been so confident. I swore that this time, I honestly was dead, he mourned. Even as the magpies croaked past and the spitting rain whipped his cheeks, he was confident that none of it was real. That he was a ghost, a damned wraith left to wander Corvid's streets in search of his unfinished business, unable to die. But after decades in this town, it was obvious that he had no business, no meaning, no purpose.

Drifting.
Transparent.
Disembodied.
Unsightly.

Even though the sun was white and cold, his body was warm and without experience like flavorless pit-stop coffee. So warm, he'd forgotten he had flesh or blood or organs at all—tepid nothingness.

If only I sit for long enough, I'll be able to stop being, he meditated. *My insides will match my outsides. This numbing, everlasting rotting will leave me alone. I can truly be nothing.*

His craving for nothingness wrought him with a peace so powerful, he felt selfish for it. For the dreams of its luxury.

But then *she* was there.

She gazed at him as though he were a shooting star.

She saw me.
She.
Saw.
Me.
Right?

He couldn't comprehend which of them was the phantasm. The *persona non grata.*

Her flesh was moon-pale, but her features were as black as the cosmos: cropped hair, coat, inky eyes, and ankle-high shoes. The contrast made it seem as though she'd been dipped in space.

He heard her heart race at the sight of him, thundering like dashing hoofbeats. He couldn't remember a time anyone's heartbeat had changed for him alone. The *th-thud, th-thud* echoed with the timbre of a much older organ, much like his own.

If he had a heart. Did he have a heart?

He heard the pitchy plucking of several scars from her body. A cello crooning poured from her right hand. It promised trauma. It sang of a grief that leaked down her face from dark eyes.

But those *eyes* saw him.

Truly, saw him.

She saw me.
Maybe I am here.

3

✦NORAH✦

TAP. TAP. TAP. TAP.

Beneath her black blouse, a sharp, cold tapping struck above her navel with the rhythm of a pendulum. The force was minuscule and maddening. Her jaw and eyes clenched shut.

Fuck. Leave. Me. Alone, she begged, slapping a hand to smother the pendant beneath her shirt. She pinched the key dangling on its silver chain, piercing her with ancient reminders, dry and clinging like cactus needles.

Mom probably hated wearing it too, thought Norah.

You're just like her, aren't you?

But the day was packed with sessions. Caseloads and crises allowed no time for such thoughts. Therapist Norah Kestrel reaffixed her mask and straightened her spine. As soon as she stepped into session with a client, her brain slapped a summary of their lives across the desk of her fast-working empathy.

Erin Budgie, 18. They/them. Aged out of foster care, no natural supports. Cancer. Alone. Loves stand-up comedy and indie music.

Phoebe Eastern, 55, accelerated atherosclerosis. Adult children won't visit her, estranged. Loves sarcasm and soap operas.

Paloma Garza, 47. Major depressive disorder, moderate. Severe negative-self talk. History of abusive relationships. Loves having her nails done and singing.

Thomas Albatross, 82. Dementia. Deceased wife, Jennifer. Veteran. Loves his grandchildren, cream soda, and carving wood spirits.

Sasha Jacana, 8. Sickle-cell anemia. Dreams of owning her own unicorn-themed restaurant.

James Warbler, 22. Suicidal thoughts following dad's verbal abuse. Loves his partner Whit and tropical houseplants.

Ruby Hume, age 16. Suicidal ideations. Loves hair dye and anime. Wants to design graphic novels.

By the end of the work day, countless stories flapped through her skull like a cage of panicked birds.

But for Norah, the hard part wasn't containing their pain. The hard part was matching their energy. She matched the energy of young clients with their homemade bangs, candy-colored hair dyes, and episodes of dissociation. She bent low in empathy with the old, who slung their defense mechanisms like trebuchets. She sat still with the traumatized, their triggers well-oiled and slick, heavy with the expectation of an unspent firecracker.

The therapist basked in their stories with the casual patience of steeping tea. Once rapport had built between them, Norah and her clients could exchange calls like songbirds.

Norah's song was as predictable as a chickadee's most days:

"What are you not allowing yourself to feel?"

"What did your childhood self need to hear?"

"How much time do you have to authentically be yourself?'"

"When's the last time you had a healthy conversation with yourself?"

"What makes you uncomfortable?"

"Is that a feeling or a fact?"

"What does your self-talk sound like?"

Scabs of the past were torn open to release infections. Stories of survival shattered the sound barrier so they couldn't belong in anyone else's mouth. Fortresses of self were retaken, frayed flags struck into their stone.

"We can only conquer what we confront," the therapist would say. Hypocrisy pierced her tongue.

You're as good at confrontation as mom and dad were, she sneered inwardly to herself.

All the while, that damned key continued its incessant *tap-tap-tap*ping against her like a mocking drum.

✦

She completed her final round of inpatient check-ins, bobbing in and out of hospital rooms with their blinding white walls, lights, sheets, televisions, and plastic cups of pills. Up and down countless squeaky laminate stairs, she toted a thick messenger bag stuffed with writing tools, notebooks, worksheets, affirmations, card games, and art supplies. The pack of resources left her stiff and sore at the end of each day.

Then, as always, she finally made her way toward the second floor, where various conference rooms and employee offices were studded with gold placards. At the very end of the hall, her door in sight, she registered the weight of the day's sessions as one might stand and register drunkenness.

NORAH KESTREL, MSW, LCSW, MENTAL HEALTH CLINICIAN,

shone gold from a nameplate on her door. She remembered with a wince just how many damned phone calls it'd taken to have her name changed from *Lenore* to *Norah* in the hospital's system. She shouldered through, rubbing her eyes, still craving a cigar.

She considered the strange man from the morning, wondering if he'd been a ghost crafted by the overworked cogs of her mind. He'd seemed real enough. But he also seemingly jumped down from the heavens.

But while his voice had been quiet, it was there. *He* was there.

When was the last time you even talked to an adult who wasn't a client or coworker?

Her intrusive thoughts won the day again and dashed back in time, three years prior. She was sitting at a long conference room table with her mother's medical team. A troupe of professionals she'd only met that week after traveling across several state lines and enduring many lonely, dark nights on the interstate.

"Robin is essentially immobile," stated Dr. Fledgling, her mother's oncologist. "She's mentally present, but rarely verbal."

So after a lifetime of drinking and drugs, she's finally lying in the bed she made? thought Robin's daughter. She fidgeted with a vintage quarter in her fingertips. Since she'd received the call about her mother's condition, Norah hadn't taken one deep, mindful breath in weeks.

"She needs full-time care," Fledgling continued. "We have a travel nurse who can come to your home and teach you how to administer medicine, use the lift machines, take blood pressure, and-"

But Norah was already shaking her head. She hadn't even realized she was doing it until she registered the staff's eyes upon her, their gazes bent and scrutinizing.

The small herd of doctors, nurses, specialists, and case managers raised their brows at their patient's sole remaining family member. All of them except for the End of Life Care nurse, Toni Plover, who only smiled her pink lipstick smile.

"I-I can't," Norah choked. "I'm full time here and, and the house, I just...I-I can't, I don't-" She couldn't breathe at all now.

Toni clapped together her thin, wrinkly fingers and nodded. "Then we'll put Robin on the wait list for a residential bed upstairs with us. Her insurance covers all the essentials of palliative care. That's all there is to it."

Grumbles of discontent resounded amongst the small room, but Toni simply took some notes on her clipboard, nodded her approval to Norah, and left the meeting. One by one, the rest of them adjourned.

That had been the last in-depth, adult conversation Norah had endured outside of seeing patients. *Years* ago.

Because you're fucking burned out, I told you this, Kestrel.

And because it wasn't the garish cream walls of her office that bore the burdens of others, nor the shiny laminate, redolent with layers of bleach. Not even her groaning coffee machine could bleed goblets of empathy.

No.

It was clutched firmly within the incessant professionalism and caffeine-infused vigor of Norah Kestrel. Her brain was collapsible, foldable, and equipped with hinges and compartments. It could store lifetimes, ideations, traumas, and the full sloppy spectrum of emotion. Each facet of being a human in a hurting world was filed in the endless cabinets of her mind.

And it was getting to be a lot.

She leaned back into her office chair, its split fabric moaning. The posture rested the tiny key at her navel, biting like an icepick, so she instead draped herself across her desk, limbs lolling like a crash test dummy. She was asleep in seconds.

✦

A knock at the door stole the breath from her chest and dizzily pulled her to her feet. She wiped the nasty smell of drool from her cheek and poured droplets of lavender into the diffuser to conceal the cigar smoke in her hair. She assessed the time and affixed her smile, dusting the sleep from its polished mask. She squinted at her schedule.

Jenna Ibis, 34, grieving dead fiancé, Calum. Loves strong green tea and large dogs.

Rubbing at the desk-shaped dent in her forehead, Nor welcomed Jenna in and snapped on the churning sound machine outside her door.

They settled into her quaint office stuffed with forest green plush chairs, velvet pillows, framed diplomas, canvasses of tranquil forests, and countless fake plants, given there were no windows in the godforsaken office.

There was a time she'd pined for her own private practice amongst the trees with a small garden, maybe a pond. Somewhere lush and green where she and others could find respite. But no matter where she hung a shingle in this town, she would always feel restless and too near to the graves of those she'd once loved.

"There's so much I needed to tell him," said Jenna, her fingernails scraping at a foam cup of tea.

Though the therapist had no love interest of her own, she could empathize with the injustice of Jenna's loss and stolen intimacy. For others, she could always pour her heartache freely like wine.

"Your grief is going to look different from everyone else's. Allow it to exist exactly as it is and hold space for it," Norah affirmed. "Perhaps when you're ready, maybe consider journaling or even writing him a letter. But that needs to be on your time. I don't think it's ever too late to say what needs to be said, though."

Norah turned inwardly for a brief moment, considering her own grief. Commiseration for herself only lay apathetic upon the floor of her consciousness like a beached tuna, gills gasping and odorous. A slug-like trail dragged behind, cuffed to her ankles, heavying her steps. Mentally, Nor toed the creature that was her exhaustion with a grimace.

We've got to do something about that. The smell is appalling.

But now wasn't the time.

It never was.

4

⋆·NORAH·⋆

EVENING AIR GUSHED THROUGH NORAH'S LUNGS as she shouldered through the hospital's glass doors and into the evening. The cold cleansed her nostrils of the hospital's aromatics, a dour combination of cafeteria mashed potatoes and sanitizer. She stripped from her coat, cardigan, and high-heeled boots, tossing them to the back seat of her boxy black truck before she, too, collapsed behind the wheel. She clicked on the vintage CD player in the dash, which shook its crackling speakers with alternative, punkish, and angsty ballads. Once Norah was certain the bass was loud enough to vibrate the life back into her tired bones, the old vehicle shuddered alive and chugged through Corvid's historic downtown.

Corvid's buildings were ominous, sharp structured with old brick, ornate architecture, carved stonework, and embedded with the warped glass of antique windows. Its businesses wore dark, deep jewel-tone palettes shrouded in black awnings and trimmings. Carved pillars and wrought iron jutted from the town's flesh like black bone. Its structures reeked of old money, brownstone, and Gothic features. Its buildings were spindled, stamped with filigrees, Masonic symbols, and brass detailing. Historical plaques and memorial markers bore tarnished tribute for the dead, birth marking each archaic brick within city limits. And it was evident that decades ago, this town was built for the enjoyment of people, not their vehicles, with its chunky, smooth stones.

Corvid Community Hospital and the adjacent church were the largest structures for miles. Norah dipped her head to eye the looming stone chapel as it passed.

It wore the architectural skeleton of a cathedral with massive Gothic spires, arches, flying buttresses, and vaulted ceilings. The groomed landscape consisted of deep violet and crimson buds as though mixed with arterial blood. Their barbed leaves and thorny bushes were dyed sable, like most of Corvid.

Norah avoided the glossy eyes of the saints and angels lurking within the towering panes of stained glass. Instead, her gaze trailed to the monstrosity's pinnacle, some four-hundred feet above the earth. Its spear pierced the clouds in hopes of bleeding them of their holiness. Screaming crows laced betwixt its iron crosses in graceful dives.

Then, her old vehicle jerked to a halt in the middle of West Main Street, resulting in a cacophony of car horns. Vehicles whipped around her with the scornful screams of geriatric residents.

But Nor was far too preoccupied with the black form that sat huddled amidst the church's spires...

It was the crouched lump of a human.

Her arms fell slack from the steering wheel, and she blinked hard. She thought of the strange old man from this morning, but this shape didn't match his tall lanky features. She could have sworn the figure above wore sunglasses and was made of muscles and sharp edges.

CPR is thirty compressions, two breaths, thirty compressions, two breaths. What could I use for a tourniquet? My cardigan. Dad's jacket in the back?

Her chest trembled with the leaps of her heart, ready for carnage, for someone to jump.

Nor blinked again, and-

Her jaw fell even more open.

The figure was gone. A black stone cross sat in its place.

Fuck. She rubbed her burning eyes. *You're losing it, Kestrel.* She breathed a deep, trembling sigh and lurched her vehicle towards home. Her middle finger blew in the wind in eloquent retort to the cussing drivers behind.

The asphalt bled into black silos, fence lines, and tobacco barns. A patchwork quilt of oceanic fields unfolded, shadowed in shipwrecked Victorian farmhouses with deep shadows and old, dark glass.

They matched the sky's eternal wash of slate gray, splattered by laughing crows, whirring weathervanes, and the dead arms of desperately reaching trees that never found proficient sunlight Like a fungus in rotting timber, Corvid leeched life from each passerby.

Aside from the begrudged rich folk and their entitled ancestors, few stayed as Norah did.

Not that she had a choice.

✦

Once parked in her driveway, it took all of her strength to not throw back the seat and fall asleep beneath the glow of starlight from her moon roof. But she shoved her carcass from the old truck and stumbled across the gravel. The untended fields that surrounded her house shuffled with crusty dry crops like whispers and hisses. She preferred the field's ominous muttering to the thousands of dollars it took to invest in the farming equipment to manage it. Her paycheck barely covered the heating bill for the massive home; landscaping was a laughable feat.

The house already looks haunted, she rationalized. Its adjoining land might as well fit the part.

The Kestrel family home was a Victorian farmhouse and a monstrous exhibit of the brain's Uncanny Valley. Coalmine gray with ivory trimmings, its gaudy turret wore a conical topper and a sooty brick chimney. The rooftop was like a flat black top hat held upright by the eggshell spindles of a wraparound porch. Its white-shuttered windows below grinned like teeth whilst those on the upper floor gaped like cadaverous eyes. One of these had been blackened with bruising and smoke damage, darkened by trauma.

There were days she felt pity towards the cold beast and days she swore its jawbones kept her prisoner for grim sport. Despite her best efforts to unload the property, it never sold, because only an idiot would adopt its fiery testimony.

She stretched her fingers, wrinkling and flattening the old scar on her palm as she stepped into the home's open maw. Aromas of Palo Santo and rose water sweetened her senses but would never overtake the sting of fire and cigarette that diseased the beams.

Vincent greeted her with a tall, fluffy bottlebrush tail as he cascaded down the hardwood stairs from an exhausting day of birdwatching. Greeting chirrups bounced from his throat until he collided headfirst into Norah's shin bones.

"Hey, handsome." She rubbed the old Persian cat behind the ears until his shiny eyes closed. His smooshed, fat face twisted for scritches until he was content.

She climbed the twenty-seven stairs to the second floor and kicked at the spare bedroom door beside her own. Though it thudded with the metal slap of locked hardware, she pulled the cold brass key from beneath her shirt and jostled it in the lock. Finding it unmoving and indifferent as always, she returned the key to her chest.

She stepped upon the threshold of her own bedroom and dissociated with a grimace. The bed was firm and its midnight black linens were fresh. Matted paintings of deep forests hung on the storm-blue walls. Dark monstera and hanging pothos swayed beneath the house's circulating warm breath. But still, Norah's face wrinkled as though the neglected space reeked of black mold. She sighed and returned downstairs.

As she pulled a carton of oat milk from the fridge, Vincent gawked up at her with wide green eyes, seated upon the many rolls of his haunches.

"Tea?" she asked politely.

The old cat licked his fat face with a pink tongue.

✦

Shreds of blue cornflower and orange peel swirled within the glass tank of her jumping teapot as she poured her mug of evening chamomile blend. Vince had already lapped at his homemade catnip tea beside her and was rolling around on his back like a fat otter.

Norah revisited the morning's meltdown as though observing a wilting leaf on one of her houseplants. She allowed it no empathy or emotional depth, only scientific deduction. She couldn't risk actually feeling her feelings. The fittings and mechanisms that kept her put together would surely succumb and break beneath the immensity.

You're nearly thirty, Kestrel. Deal with your shit.

She had hoped that the anxious and sobbing little girl that was her childhood self had finally quieted after all this time. Surely, she'd grown up and understood that the love she so craved wasn't hers to have?

Pathetic.

Norah could only consider the woeful child with pity now, much as the old stranger on the roof had today.

Even he saw through your piss-poor façade.

What was maddening was that she'd been fine before. *Content*, even, when she'd lived far away. It was *this town* that had done her in.

Before being dragged back to Corvid, she'd been a coltish, fresh adult. Freedom was hot off the press, and she'd snatched it and ran like a thief.

She once loved researching weird facts about the brain and laughing at dead dad jokes. She'd played ukulele and doodled skulls, wildflowers, crystals, and mushrooms on everything she touched. Past Nor found comfort in

British television and its crass humor, the eloquence of the characters' rage and fury. She'd written quotes on the back of her hand in black ink and read poetry whilst sitting on the roof. She'd once craved art and creative people. And once, so very long ago it seemed, she even sought love in the rich ocean of humankind.

But the childish energy she'd had for such things had bled dry since coming back home.

Norah finished her tea and fell asleep in her father's recliner. Given her distance from the rooms above, nightmares were sparse. But the only one to kiss the young therapist goodnight was the cold key on her chest.

5

⋄NORAH⋄

TAP, TAP, TAP, TAP, TAP.

Norah gave a shaky sigh and smacked the key beneath her shirt. Her spine was pressed against the Two Sparrow's Cafe *Birds of a Feather* board, where random acts of kindness were pinned in the form of free caffeine to strangers. A multitude of push pins dimpled her back.

Her black peplum coat hung below her like the tail of a swallow, matching her dark eyeliner, lips, and soon-to-be morning beverage.

Nor squinted against the gloom of the grungy haunt. It was filled with black-studded sofa chairs, hanging vintage bird cages, and silhouettes of various bird species framed on patterned papers along the walls. Huge ropes of black sweet potato vine climbed black trellises and shelving. A crooning, honeyed voice hummed through the scratchy speakers of a record player in the corner, accompanied by the spitting roar of a milk frother. Nor allowed herself to dreamily saturate in the smells of single-origin coffee beans and baking almond croissants.

"*Dirty Bird*, for Norah," said a pretty barista behind the counter. Sparkling clasps held back their black hair, matching a black skater dress patterned with tiny skulls.

Norah smiled and gave a generous tip for the baked goods and espresso chai.

The barista smiled back with red lips, eyes thoughtfully searching Nor as she left.

The front door jingled with colorful birdcage toys in farewell behind her.

Nor popped a decorated blue cake ball in her mouth and swung towards the cafe's back parking lot, where it was barren and quiet. The space was hedged with Black-Hole Japanese maples and a few trash cans into which Nor tossed her wrappings. Her heeled boots spun in the gravel to return to the street, when a distant, soppy sniff from behind piqued her mental health antennae.

She dipped behind a leafy black tree and peered around its trunk to spy on the back of the cafe. A massive mural lacquered the old bricks there in jewel tones and galaxy hues. It depicted two sparrows flying in opposite directions, wings spread and patterned with stars and Milky Way streaks. Their feathers wore contrasting color schemes, as though one was the rising sunrise and the other was the bringer of night. Both held a colored ribbon clenched in their beak, leading to the other's fanning tail feathers.

It seemed that if they flew in opposite directions, they'd unwind into magical blue and orange ribbons, whipping in the wind. The mural always stopped Norah in her tracks, but today it wasn't the street art that captured her.

At the base of the café in the parking lot gravel, was an old man on his knees in a dapper suit, weeping. One trembling hand pressed against the brick with longing whilst the other muffled his spitting sobs.

As she inched nearer to search him for injuries or wounds, her boots crunched and ground on loose gravel.

With a gasp, the old man spun to his rear with a clutched chest, eyes alert and crimson.

Nor's shoulders fell, and her lips parted. "It's you."

His crumpled features found her beneath tides of white mane and beard. His button-down and thin suspenders were disheveled, his rolled sleeves wet with tears, and his muscular, tanned arms still pulsed with colored inks.

"And it's you," he croaked, cheeks swelling kindly, interrupting his grief. "What a minuscule planet we live on," he said, searching her with the distant awe of stargazing. With another great sniff, he arranged his fallen tresses and tugged the legs of his pants down his inked calves. Today his socks were turquoise with great flapping Blue Jays.

"Oh, oh heavens, I'm s-s-so sorry. I must be a-a horrid thing to come upon…" he muttered, fingers smearing tears from his eyes and cheeks.

"Not at all."

His glossy eyes blinked up at her and his mustache twitched. With a flutter of lashes, he struggled to his feet, gazing bashfully at his toes, wiping the dirt from his knees. "S-s-sorry," he stuttered.

"For what?" He was a tall being that Norah had to tip her chin up to behold.

"I…I s-suppose I don't know," he said quietly.

Besides him, Norah thought of a gentle, heavy-shouldered workhorse, great white head bowed and kind.

"Are *you* alright?" she asked, recycling his question from the other day.

"Oh yes, yes, of course. Thank you. I'm um-I'm just admiring the art." He wiped his nose with a blue handkerchief, gesturing down to the spot he'd been weeping before. He stepped aside to reveal scrawled words graffitied along the mural's bricks, white and drippy with the handwriting of a crude vandal. They were in a language she couldn't read.

"That?" she gestured to the crime scene.

"German," he said, clearing the lingering sobs from his throat. "It s-says, *you are here.*" His jaw pulsed, but he shook his head and shrugged a suit jacket upon his great shoulders. Both it and his pants were pine green, accessorized by a glossy gold tie and a neatly tucked pocket square at his breast.

Knowing there was nothing she could say to improve upon such a reverent statement, Nor nodded and hummed. The concept of being alive and human was powerful news for many. *Being here* meant someone saw you and your pain. Someone beheld you when you'd never been held before.

Her eyes trailed the foreign letters like the following of fish in a tank. Now, they were no longer an eyesore, but more beautiful than the mural above.

"Life has been…foggy for a very long time," he said, eyes sore and low. "It's easy to forget." His hairy, tattooed hands massaged his biceps.

"I'm sorry for interrupting," she said, nodding to the old bricks.

"I'm sorry for burdening your coffee time," he chuckled.

But she remained unsmiling and earnest. "You're a human being with human feelings," she said. "If that were to burden me, it would have nothing to do with you."

Nor sat beside him on the asphalt, procuring one of her business cards and a pen from her bag. She scribbled on it a moment as he sat beside her and watched without question. He still smelled of vanilla bean tobacco and leather polish.

Though thoughts of her father's scream prickled the hair on her neck again, her armor snapped into place before it could puncture her purpose.

She handed the old man the card upon which she'd written the mantra: *You are here. You are alive. You matter. Your feelings are important,* in her wild and bold penmanship.

Taking it with shaking hands, the old man's eyes remained glued to its letters for some time. He ran his big thumb over the ink with pursed lips. A solitary blink polished his eyes glossy. He sniffed and blinked it away, hastily wiping his face. His skin crumpled like homemade paper with divots of scars visible in his brow, nose, and jaw.

"Thank you…Lenore Kestrel," he said, reading her name and title from the card's opposing side, where the text was surrounded by illustrated house plants. "You must be an amazing therapist," he said, an ache in his words.

"It's Norah," she grumbled. It was one of the few pesky misprints that'd found its way into her bag after years of working for Corvid's Hospital. The young admin who'd ordered them couldn't have known that the name *Lenore* made the therapist bare her teeth. "What about yourself?" Norah asked.

His eyes lifted with bent brows, uncertain as to why she'd ponder such a question. But he wiped the residual tears from his cheeks and pulled a navy-blue card from his messenger bag. A stripe of gold foil underlined his name.

"Dexteras Doe, Licensed clinical and business translator," she read, finding it strange the card didn't indicate which languages he spoke.

"Dex is just fine," he added, his baritone tongue again speaking of gloomy islands across the ocean.

"How have we not heard about you at the hospital?" she stated. "Phone translators are always so busy and can make therapy…impersonal. We could use real humans to speak on behalf of our clients."

"I've reached out prior," he admitted, eyelids drooping, "I'd assumed they weren't comfortable with me there."

"What do you mean?"

A tic pulsed at his cheek, bending it towards his large shoulder with a wince.

"I was a patient," he said, eyes avoiding hers.

"Is that why you were there the other day?" *On the fucking roof, might I add.*

"No, no, I was a patient over twenty years ago. I just liked the view. Best in Corvid."

She scoffed. "God, is there such a thing?"

His smile was thin like glass, sensing her disgust.

She yearned to ask him about the immense descent he survived from the incinerator chimney, but felt it would be ageist and ignorantly assumptive.

"So, what languages do you speak?"

"What languages do you need?" he challenged with a wide grin.

Norah smiled, impressed. "And you have credentials?"

He unfolded an old tea-stained certificate from his leather bag as though it were a treasure map awaiting this very moment to be unfurled. The old license was signed by *Dexteras Doe* beside his state-wide credentials, dated decades prior.

What a strange fucking name, she mused. *Wasn't Doe reserved for the nameless dead?*

An unsung loneliness about him plucked a chord in Nor's nearly-orphaned heart. His freely-spilled tears and vulnerability sang out to her like a mournful screech owl in the dark. And despite the fact that her tongue was riddled with fucks and her skull was barren of them, she couldn't deny Dex's pain. She couldn't deny how his call resonated with her own, how his hurt matched her strength, and how her throat burned with a compulsion to answer his call.

"Well," she began, "are you in the market for some work then?"

6

⊹·DEXTERAS·⊹

He had to be real. He had a job now. A real, human job where his hand would shake the real, warm hands of other, real humans.

It took only a week to finalize his contract with Corvid Community Hospital. Norah Kestrel's sweet grace vetted for his approachability and assured Human Resources he would be beneath her close pupillage exclusively. Thus, he would be a mental health translator with her program, The Nest. Norah forwarded him a stack of referrals to review until the day finally came to meet their first client.

The discomfort that stiffened his bones as he walked into Corvid's Hospital was crippling. His polished shoes squeaked, his breath was swollen beneath his sternum, and he felt the scrutiny of professional eyes surveying him like surveying satellites.

Could they possibly remember? he lamented. *Could any of them be old enough to recall the sound of my screams in this place?*

Breath held and eyes watering from the hospital's white light, Dex nodded to the woman at the front desk, who nodded back, but said nothing. He took the elevator to the second floor as Nor had instructed him. Fighting the urge to drop his chin, he instead stared ahead proudly, confidently. A handful of people in muted scrubs passed with clipboards and quiet voices, but none paid him any mind.

And then, he ventured a knock upon Conference Room Seven's fake wood and opened it to reveal Norah Kestrel, beaming and pleased to see him. He hadn't offered up any of his services or benefitted a single soul, and yet, she seemed delighted by his presence.

She slid him a paper cup of coffee and began to discuss their first client, Alina Holub, a six-year-old Ukrainian girl in the ICU being treated for aggressive anaplastic thyroid cancer.

He bent a crook into one of his great tattooed arms and held his face in his hand, beard hairs spilling between his fingers. He gave a great sigh and closed his eyes once the narrative was complete.

"May I possibly have a moment?" he asked, tapping the child's file, "to freshen my linguistics? Medical terminology can be tougher than a two-dollar steak."

"Of course," said Nor, her tall, narrow boots click-clacking from the table. She stopped and spun to search his wide eyes with her dark, green, sleepy ones, painted with narrow wings.

"Breathe, Dex. You're going to do great."

He indeed took a deep breath, air trembling on the exhale.

Though it seemed Norah Kestrel was a perpetual frowner, she gave him a kind nod and smile. Though her presence was petite and packaged, she was not like crystal or porcelain, but rather like a bullet casing, steel filled with gunpowder. When it came to this work, he sensed that her claws were sharp.

She closed the door to the conference room and left him to his thoughts. As she walked further away, an anxious thread tugged at his chest.

He paced around the conference room table, military specificity in his step, eyes following the lines of the green laminate. Chin welded to his chest, he rubbed at his scarred knuckles, alight with shakes.

He counted his steps in an attempt to drown out the unexplained mutterings of The Voices. The merciless echo of conversations in his skull that never ceased nor slept, robbing him of his own rest. On They ranted with Their miseries whilst he aligned his toes and heels with precision.

"One more time just please-"

"-don't let it happen again I really can't-"

"You know I'll do anything-"

"If that's all there is then maybe I-"

"She's dead now. What am I supposed to-"

Despair, desire, frustration, and other unnamable emotions echoed from countless voices in his old skull. While the frail fingertips of empathy could stretch for them from time to time, they mostly littered his skin with goose flesh.

A pang of guilt hung in his chest for the lies he'd already spun for his newfound colleague. His *only* colleague. He needed no practice in Ukrainian. His tongue was always sharp and ready to speak for others, regardless of the language. He'd only excused himself to gather his anxious druthers and corral the mumbling Swarm in his brain.

He pressed his fingers into his eye sockets. *Da mihi pacem aut da mihi mortem*…give me peace or give me death, you bastards.

In the dark cosmos of his head, he saw himself settled on the rooftop's ledge, inhaling lungfuls of murky gray atmosphere into his chest. He could nearly feel Corvid's bitter gales kissing his neck.

He knew it was a strange craving to yearn for the height of a rooftop. It was a grounding but deeply unsettling want. It'd been a need that'd ached within him since the day he fell.

Fell?

Jumped.

Fell.

Tripped, perhaps?

Christ Almighty only knows.

He swung shut the loosely-hinged door of his existential dread. This day was far too important for another mental breakdown.

He drew in deep, sedated breaths through his nostrils. Air whistled out through his mustache. He stuffed his tacky palms into his pockets with a wince. *Heavens, why am I sweating?*

But of course, he knew why.

This was his only chance. A once-in-a-lifetime opportunity to step upon the threshold of normalcy. A job. A sliver of opportunity beneath the door of redemption. In a tight-knit town such as Corvid, fresh starts were as rare as the alignment of celestial bodies.

It was Corvid's hospital that knew him in the most grotesque of details. His shattered parts were scraped from this asphalt and cobbled together within these walls. They'd seen him at his most exposed and ghastly. Each bone was ground to splinter. Each cracked marble in his skull had tumbled upon their doorstep. Each droplet of his blood, each spillage of steaming organ, each incompetent muttering of his heart, and every damaged distortion of his brain was laid bare for a whole community to gawk upon. They peeled him from the earth and toted him in with hope for repair, but they never looked upon him the same way again.

Perhaps that was why he ached for their acceptance, yearned for their embrace: they knew him more deeply than he knew himself. They'd sewn each intimate stitch in his flesh. Just as Frankenstein's monster felt an obligation to his creator, he desired their affirmation of his worthiness, their seal of his validity. He owed them so much. And now, he had the opportunity to repay them.

You are here. You are alive. You matter.

Norah Kestrel's delicate professionalism refocused him. She was witty, determined, and fierce despite the dispiriting environment, but he recalled a brief crack in her spilling light, a leak in her hope. When he'd spoken her full name, she'd grimaced as though there was an ache in her bones.

Though she had to be twenty-eight, twenty-nine, she wore a halo of exhaustion and time. It was as though energy seeped from her cracks and wounds. It was why the traumatized wore such heavy-plated armor, in hopes of slowing the drip.

He knew that cringe, that flutter in her heartbeat, the weight of its charge. He knew a veteran when he heard one, but it didn't seem that she'd paid respect to her valor. It was dominated by another note just atop her breastbone, akin to the crackling of an empty spray paint can. A sharp *tap tap tap*ping....

"So worthless I can't even -"

"Stop it. Why won't you just stop?"

"I promise it's not going to happen like that again, I swear-"

"-giving up, I'm just giving up."

Dex collapsed onto a conference room chair, rubbing at his gold pocket watch. Its shuddering *tick-tick-tick* set the pace for his grounding exercises.

"Vega. Tarazed. Phaet. Gienah Ghurab. Altair. Albireo," he recited, eyeballs rolling towards the respectful location of each star's coordinates in the night sky. He tasted the dialect of their homes in his mouth. Rich consonants struck his tongue with flavor. Soft sidereal vowels seeped between his teeth. Grounded in interstellar peace, he finally found his feet, collected his breath, and sought his newfound colleague.

"Stop it-"

"-happy but I'm not really happy at all and-"

"Seriously, I can't stand"

"It hurts all-"

Please. Please shut it, all of you.

But then, Norah Kestrel's smile distracted him from the end of the hall. His ears burned, and he dropped his chin.

The Voices stopped.

The chaotic Noise within fell as quiet as outer space, replaced instead by the clinician's distinctive melody, a piano soundtrack to a far-flung memory. And still, that mysterious *tap-tap-tap*ping beat from her chest like a metronome.

He'd been hearing not just The Voices, but an assortment of humanity's odd melodies since the day he fell. He could hear a music within others just against the bones in his temple as though he'd been shishkabobbed with a tuning fork. Each song struck and trembled new chimes inside of him. He called them "soul songs' ' to feel less psychotic, but his medical team had diagnosed them as *auditory hallucinations.*

He returned the young woman's smile with strain, noting how foreign it felt stretched across his cheeks. His eye fell on the hand she kept in the pocket of her black coat. It too, sang to him with suppressed vibrations, whirring with muffled energy like a nearby star. Scars often sang to him loudest of all.

Stop staring dead dog, he snarled.

Before he could stifle it, his tic was triggered and his jaw clenched shut with mechanical force, cocking his head with a groan. He breathed deeply and allowed his head to resituate upon his spine, tension spent.

Most flinched at the unsettling knocks of his bones, but the young therapist gave a kind bend of her head. "Ready, Dex?" she asked.

He filed the sound of her voice singing his name to memory, and realized he was smiling again, despite the aches of long-untouched muscle in his cheeks.

"The Cabinet confirmed translating services for Alina, so we're all clear," she said.

Empathy bit at him for the complexity of their small patient's life. She was a stranger to the country and already a ward of the state. He wondered if the tender pianissimo notes he'd heard earlier this morning belonged to the child.

Norah tucked her dark hair behind the multiple gold piercings of her ear and sighed wearily. "While the hospital was attempting to phone a translator, her mother left. The social worker suspects there might've been financial or documentation issues. So we have very little."

"Her mother was trying to save her," Dex observed.

"It just left her with more trauma to process."

A tragic chord of bitterness in Norah's tone flexed the hairs on his arm with a territorial warning. He didn't prompt any further, avoiding its scream like the screech of his hearing aid after its feedback path was interrupted. Oddly enough, he'd found he needn't wear it at all this week, despite Norah's quiet voice.

"Alina," he spoke aloud in Ukrainian, missing its fullness in his jaw. "It means 'light.'"

"It's beautiful," she said, staring up at him.

His chin fell as her glaucous eyes found his, soft, deep like wild woods.

And what does your name mean to you, Norah Kestrel?

7

⟡NORAH⟡

NOR FOUND HERSELF REMINISCING THROUGH THE FAMILIAR HALLS, recalling the seven-fold insecurity of her student years. Back then, she'd never held a caseload, let alone a dying human's hand. And though her fire for advocacy roared with life, the glares of seasoned professionals doused her with unworthiness, even today.

Who am I to talk to others about pain and healing?

But then there was Dexteras.

Despite his vast life, experience, and wisdom, he didn't crush her with superiority. At her side, his fine suit shone with the greens and gold of the Mediterranean Sea whilst his fingers polished the chain of his pocket watch like rosary beads. His subtle limp gave a bob to his wavy mane. His gentle blue eyes beneath drank in everything at all times. He was dashing and lovely, a towering presence that magnetized each eye towards him. But if a staff member returned his gaze as they passed, his chin fell to his chest and his hands found their way to his pockets.

Some beheld him with cold and critical stares, but most were speculative, akin to the glares HR gave her the week prior when she mentioned him for the job. They didn't recall the crippled man in their hospital, nor were they keen on the liability that his blurry history could imply. But despite the past, they had no evidence or qualms to justify the board's skepticism.

So, seeing as his credentials were up to date, they allowed him a trial run beneath Norah, who would provide a thorough report throughout. They'd be submitting a long-term records request to view his medical files of discharge for any "red flags" to ensure the "safety of our patients here." They'd have to ravage the ancient catacombs of hard-copy records, demanding quite some time before they'd surface.

But Dexteras Doe was kind, gentle, empathetic, and communicative. He was perfect. He had a quiet energy that made you want to know him more deeply and speak with him transparently. Even Norah craved to understand him and be understood by him.

But she wasn't there yet. She couldn't even properly navigate his expression most moments. He didn't wear discomfort, but rather, an *uncertainty*… as though he weren't quite sure if he belonged where he stood, or upon this Earth at all.

Having arrived at their patient's room, Nor gave a preparatory nod to her new partner and knocked upon the door frame.

"Alina, visitor!"

A delicate greeting hummed from within, and they pushed past the curtains to reveal a tiny child. Alina was sitting on the ledge of her large window, fidgeting with a bouquet of tubes that connected her body to a mobility cart. Her frail skin was adorned with rose-colored hospital clothes and rubber-soled socks. Her hair was auburn, and her skin was a deep, sandy tone. Her eyes were large, dark-lashed, and somehow smiling despite all they'd known.

They waved with kind grins from the threshold. It always took a brief mental reset when Nor entered the rooms of the children's ward. She blinked against the vibrant colors, a welcome, but jarring shock to the grayscale of the hospital.

Alina's room was catered to childish whimsy and life. The walls and bed sheets were royal, princess purple, and the wall beneath her television was muraled with jewel-toned castles and faraway lands topped with knights and unicorns. A large stuffed unicorn was sitting on the ledge of her window, passing judgment over the gloomy city below.

The glass was framed with sky-blue curtains. The only elements that stood out amidst the candy-colored scene were the blood-red sharps box, the visitor's chairs with their red cushions, and the gray rolling table and drawers.

Norah stepped forward and introduced herself, sitting in a bedside chair. Dex followed suit.

He cleared the nervous gravel from his throat and transitioned to Ukrainian with soft, syrupy tones. His gestures were inviting and kind, and his expression was compassionate. He was a natural at holding space.

Nor nodded to the retractable ID clipped to his suspender with a tall brow, and he hurriedly nodded with a stutter on his lips. She gently pulled it from his chest and stretched it far from him in comic grandeur. The child squinted upon it and then sputtered with laughter, followed by wet, thick coughing.

"This is my friend Dexteras," said Nor, returning the badge. "He's going to help us talk to one another."

The child agreed with a small nod, bobbed hair and eyes shimmering. She responded with a raspy voice, pitched with childish chirps.

Her words then left Dex as though they were his own, delivered verbatim as though he were a ventriloquist dummy of sorts. His timing was measured and patient. His tones were low and rolling like a breeze, just strong enough to sweep your hair behind your shoulders. As the conversation giant, one easily forgot he was in the room. He was good at blending in with the pale fluorescent lights.

"In therapy, you can talk about anything at all. Any feelings, thoughts, questions. It's a safe place. Everything you say stays between us three."

The child's eyes widened, and she sat upright. Then, questions spewed from her chapped lips like an eager stream breaching a dam.

Now that her unashamed curiosity could be fully understood and received, Dex's talents were put to the test.

"Do you live in the hospital?"

"How old are you?"

"Are you her dad?"

"Are there animals here?"

"Did you fly here from Ukraine?" she asked Dex with wide eyes.

"Do you have pets? What're their names? Are they big?"

And as they progressed, the discussion became more sobering.

"Where is Mama and brother?"

Dexteras' shoulders were braced against his ears, likely sensing the room's tangible grief. Norah noticed a pulsing muscle along his jaw as he gnashed on his teeth. For someone who'd been disconnected from clinical work, this was a heavy first case for him.

Nor took a deep and audible breath, modeling its power for her anxious colleague.

"It sounds like your mother was doing everything she could to keep you and your brother safe and healthy," said Nor. "But I know that doesn't change how much it hurts to have them gone right now."

Nor always had a fascination with fathers. Guardians. Protectors, parents. Scolding their small humans, wiping sticky fingers, clutching tiny hands, and pressing children into awkward hugs around their thighs.

She wondered if Alina now had the same infatuation with mothers.

"Am I still sick?" the child asked through Dexteras' translating tongue.

Nor nodded. "Yes. Your body has been battling cancer for some time. I bet you're tired of all that fighting."

The child acknowledged this with distant nods, eyes glued to the artwork that danced up Dex's arms.

"Do you have drawing stuff?"

Nor rummaged through her canvas messenger bag punctured with its enamel pins and inspirational patches. Most of these had come from the incense-saturated hippie shops near her first college when she'd studied states away. They depicted illustrated brains, flowers, teapots, and cats, bearing quotes like, "Your anxiety is lying to you," "Don't believe everything you think," "I didn't come this far, to only come this far," and "Fall in love with healing yourself."

She withdrew a spare sketchbook from the bag's depths and gave it to the child with a handful of clattering, colored pencils, their vibrant wood shining.

"You're always welcome to make art whenever you'd like."

Alina spilled the supplies across her lap, glossy colors filling her hands.

"What do your tattoos mean? Are they real? Did they hurt? Did you cry?" she asked, touching Dex's arm. His muscles bulked instinctively, but he remained still and smiled.

Before he could answer, Alina prodded onwards, "Are we going to talk about dying?"

"I think that would be a really good idea," said Norah. "What about you?"

Dex replicated Norah's confidence in his translation.

Alina nodded before erupting into more bleats of aggressive coughing. Wheezing scraped at her voice box and drew clinging fingers to her throat. Her air strained in squeaks until she gasped.

Norah slid to the hall and hollered for Scott, their attending nurse. He assessed the child's oxygen levels and hung a pumping hose below her flaring nostrils. He ushered in cold water and ice and assured the worried pair he'd notify the doctor of her levels.

As they gave their hoarse patient a moment to settle, Dex hovered with ruffled feathers, fingers massaging themselves.

"How you doing, girl?" asked Nor.

Alina managed a curt nod, ice chunks gnashing between her bared teeth. She swallowed with strain.

Nor turned to the old translator. His brows were bent, but her gaze stilled his fidgeting.

"We should let her rest. The med team will need to assess things. But this was a great introduction."

They thanked the small girl for her time.

"I'd love to see you again tomorrow, Alina. What do you think?"

The child's head bobbed, eyes trailing the line of a teal pencil down her page.

"Can Dex come?" she whispered.

Dex's face fell with that "lost" expression he often wore. "I'd be honored," he said.

Alina extended a tiny fist to Dex.

He presented his own and allowed her to box against his knuckles playfully. He sparkled with life, eyes piled in wrinkles as he grinned.

Norah marveled at their already blossoming therapeutic bond.

The child then pitter-pattered on bare feet across the laminate floor to hug him at his hip.

"Oh!" His bones creaked as he crouched to embrace her fully.

Though his ivory hair shadowed his face, Nor was certain his eyes blinked wistful and wet.

8

✦DEXTERAS✦

Jab-Jab-Cross. Fade.

Jab-Jab-Jab. Fall back.

Uppercut-Uppercut-Uppercut-Duck.

In the basement of his apartment complex, The Aviary, he danced before a heavy bag. His knuckles were bound in tight wraps, mind aflame with The Voices. But the more fervently he flung his fists, the more effectively his strikes could drown out Their pleas.

"Please, I feel so worthless, so empty all-"

Jab-jab-cross-duck

Jab-jab-jab-fade.

Jab-cross-hook-cross.

"Why does it keep burning so much? Please take me away from-"

"How am I supposed to survive this all-"

"*Stercore*," he muttered in Latin. *Shit.* He plastered hairs from his face with a sweaty hand. His arms burned as though they tore through open flames. His lungs threatened to split. Hisses spewed between his teeth.

"Everything hurts so badly and-"

He shook his head with fractious force, trying to shake free of Their words. Sweat sagged his shirt and soaked his wraps. His bones cried out in disapproval. His body twisted and torqued.

But he couldn't feel anything.

Nothing.

He was thirsty for a challenge, a distraction, a worthy opponent, but his only target swung with dead apathy.

1-6-5-2

1-4-3-2

"She never cared about me, she never wanted me to-"

"I cannot change that he's dead, I can't fix-"

He sped like a runaway train, investing each pound of force into his punches, preserving minimal energy for his wheezing lungs. The chains bearing the bag shook like a rattlesnake tail. He dashed outwards, stretching his jabs straight and long. He slid inwards, firing his shots from the hip, tucking them deep and low. His forehead pressed against the bag's vinyl. He begged for it to fight back. To wound him. To hurt him.

"How am I supposed to do this on my own? How can-"

"Are you even listening? Can you even hear me when-"

Sweat splattered the concrete below and squeaked beneath his ankle-tall sneakers. His hits alternated between head and body blows. The breaths from his bared teeth were now reduced to growls and snarls. He circled his opponent with the snapping teeth and dashing feet of a wolf.

"Would anyone notice if I died? Who would even-"

The blaring screams of a woman pierced his skull.

"Placere Deo, nullum…" he begged, *Please God, no.* The screams were the worst part of The Voices. They rinsed his inside with cold blood, upsetting his tempo.

His slick fists slipped across the bag and he cursed for the trifle error.

He pounded harder. Faster.

The bag jerked and jutted at its restraints like a bronco.

Sweat soaked his mustache and beard, sponging his mouth in hot salt.

But The Voices kept pace with his ruthlessness.

"I wonder how long I'd-"

"He's dead, and I can't-"

"Please listen-"

"Is this it?"

"Please, please listen-"

You know The Voices will only die when you do, right? They'll never stop. It was an intrusive thought that snuck up on him often.

A tsunami of jab-crosses machine-gunned from his shoulders, quaking the heavy bag's chain until it shimmied like sleigh bells. He attempted to keep proper form and shift his blows, but his stature fell apart at the seams, as did the bag he bludgeoned.

But it wasn't enough.

Real enough.

Painful enough.

He wasn't enough.

"-must be close, it has to be...."

"Stop, please, make it stop..."

"-die. I know I'm going to die. It just-"

Dust rained from the bag's anchor above, sticking to his flesh and falling into his eyes. His lesser-dominant right hand begged for mercy, riddled with needle-like knife pricks. Lava melted his crushed knuckles.

Yet he forced himself onward. The promise of pain blinded him with craving.

Bones shifted.

Fingers crunched.

The tiny bones in his fingers screamed with white-hot splinters. He pushed them harder.

"Am I alive?"

Jab-jab-step-overhand

CRACK.

With a gunshot pop and burst of searing pain, his knuckle fractured, and the heavy bag broke at its anchor. The boxer and his opponent collapsed to the floor in a cloud of debris.

Crumpled and groaning on his knees, Dex spat concrete dust from his mouth and wiped his eyes with lesser-broken fingers. He rolled onto his spine, squinting through the fine powder. With a loll of his head, he could see the downed bag and its mutilated hardware.

Another one, broken.

Yet another stony crater chiseled in the concrete above, matching the countless holes beside it like shrapnel damage.

His hands were rigid and jutting with fractures, sharp and spiny like rose thorns beneath his skin. Tiny metacarpals crackled with breakage as he spread them for inspection. They sat disfigured beneath their fleshy casing, trembling.

Despite the very real pain, the appendage didn't feel like his. His misery felt eons away, per usual. It was as though his insides were blistered and raw beneath his ill-fitting outsides.

The only pain that was his was the *toska*, the soul-deep anguish in his chest. A headspace that left him wanting and empty for something he could not name. But he'd always felt that way since the day of The Fall. He remembered nothing prior to the eternal hum of nothingness in his flesh.

He shoved himself up on shaking legs and passed a final glare of disdain to the downed bag. He left the stone sanctuary and trudged several flights of stairs to the roof of his building.

✦

His aching bones rested upon an asphalt bed many stories above, staring at the octillions of stars with astrophilic longing. *They* knew who he once was. They'd seen him before he'd forgotten himself. But they'd never tell him.

They were already dead. Dead philosophers whose secrets he could never hold.

Maintaining the waxing moon in his sight, he unwound the wraps from his deformed hands. He assessed the shattered pieces in his fourth and fifth digits with an impulsive squeeze. They popped like bubble wrap. He squeezed harder. His back arched with a blinding sensation.

But even the bolide of breakage couldn't satiate him. It simply whetted his hunger for more.

He wrenched his fingers until they were crooked and riddled with spasms. Until he was forced to confess his cries to the solar systems above. But it could not override the screaming Voices in his head.

He covered his eyes, shaking with emotions that had no words.

Then, within the blackness of his lids, a new voice intruded above the noise.

"This is my friend Dexteras…."

Norah Kestrel.

His pain dulled to a hum. The buzz in his blood quieted. The sinews of his torn joints felt more bruised than shredded.

He clawed through his nothingness to behold her in his mind's eye like an old friend. A scar cratered below her eye, long and complex as the Milky Way. It hummed to him as scars did. But Norah's scars always sounded protected, as though they sang from the confines of a tomb. And he saw beneath the glassy, frozen pond of her clinical language and carefully measured emotion, was a deep, dark lake, churning with life. He wished to understand its depths. To brave its cold.

But for now, he found peace in her calculated aesthetic. Her features were bold and dark on moon-pale features. Her cropped hair was shining. Her eyes were bright like a forest.

And they saw him.

If it weren't for Norah Kestrel and Alina, he wouldn't be so certain that others could see him at all.

But they *did* see him.

They *could* hear him.

Maybe I am alive.

Maybe I am real.

9

✦DEXTERAS✦

"I'VE EXPERIENCED MORE PAIN IN MY LIFE than I thought a heart could survive," said Dex aloud. The words fell from him with affluence, though they belonged to their newest client, Marie Chardonneret.

Nor, Dex, and Marie sat in the quiet of Conference Room Seven, with its fluorescent lighting and generic landscape paintings. While the chairs here were more plush and accommodating than the guest chairs of the patient rooms, his back and knees hadn't been crackling nearly as often as they'd used to months prior. Distant from his pain, Dex reveled in how French twisted and flipped his tongue like an elegant whale in the sea, diving between waves.

Norah explored the heartache Marie attempted to rinse from her blood in alcohol, sex, drugs. But they only rotted her insides, much like the roots of what others had taught her. She believed she was worth what her school performance could do for the perfectionist cravings of her father and later, what her body could do for other men.

A paternal fire burned in Dex's chest for their client's endured injustices. He leaned against the long wood table, finding he was squishing his paper cup tightly.

"I want you to think of each thought, feeling, and trauma as a piece of paper," said Norah. "The things you've learned from unhealthy people and situations. And imagine all of those scraps of paper shoved into a dark closet in your brain." She tapped her forehead.

Dex shared the wisdom in French, attempting to mimic the shared *sotto voce*, hushed quiet, in the tones of both women. Given that they were both seasoned musicians of survival, their instruments harmonized in his head. While their bodies were decades apart, their songs intermingled in a brief concerto.

How he wished they could hear their likeness without thinking him mad.

Marie took diligent, scripted notes in a tiny notebook upon her lap as Nor pressed on.

"When we're stressed, our brain pulls up all of that documentation of the unsafe past and tries to convince us that the future is unsafe too." Nor rested her chin atop her hands. "It's just trying to protect us. But there's so much more to hear. Our desire to be safe and comfortable just happens to be the loudest voice in the room."

Marie set down her pen and pulled a crushed tissue from her pocket. She squeezed it between her glassy pink fingernails, nodding and sniffing.

"So, we need a system for organizing the voices in our head. So we can choose which ones we'd like to act upon. I like using binders." Norah drew a few boxes across the page of her own sketchbook.

Dex and Marie exchanged fragile, amused grins.

"Each binder is a different person or trauma from the past. One might be your dad. One might be an ex."

"What goes in them?" Marie asked through Dexteras.

"They hold the lies we learned from each person or trauma," said Norah, her eyes pacing between Marie's. "So, with time, we can recognize the voices that aren't our own. And with even more time, we can begin to replace them with a voice that is." She poked one of the drawn binders. "Triggers will still hurt, and you will still feel uncomfortable, but we're going to give our brain new options aside from our fight-or-flight responses."

"*C'est ma vie*," Marie whispered, fingertips shredding the tissues as though she were tearing stained pages from her story.

"*My life,*" Dex grinned, eyes twinkling as he translated between the two women.

The therapist nodded. "Exactly. So who might have a binder in your life?"

Marie twiddled faster now. "My ex-boyfriend…"

"What lies did you learn in that relationship with him?"

Marie stared into the shiny checkered laminate below her heels. "I'm only lovable when I put my needs last. When I do something for others. Give them what they want."

Dex watched the magnitude of such a distortion weigh the clinician's eyes and head. But he could also hear the vibrating song of Nor's empathy. It was sometimes so loud, he had to tilt his ear and strain to hear over it.

"Using our 'I feel, but I know' template, how should we reply?" Norah pressed.

"I feel worthless…" broke Marie's quiet voice, "…because he treated me that way for a long time." She swallowed. "But I know he was wrong for treating me like that. I'm worthy of love. Real love."

The therapist tilted her head as she often did. A slight grin lifted one side of her lips with pride and her eyes sparkled like Mercury in the twilight sky. She gave the smile of a corner man seeing their champion victorious in the ring.

10

✦·DEXTERAS·✦

"So weak-"

"-never not tired, please let me sleep-"

"I hate it so much. I just want it to end."

"And what are you waiting for?"

The Voices were brutal during his first few days of work. He avoided going home for fear of being alone with them. Instead, he ambled about the halls nearest the ER where he was out of everyone's way and could keep a keen ear for distant sirens. Should someone need his services, he wanted to be useful and available. This wandering felt more purposeful than his rooftop episodes of nothingness.

Though he missed Nor's company amidst these times, he was the one who shoved her towards home each evening after sessions. She'd otherwise linger, wander, procrastinate for hours in the hospital if left to her own devices. She'd pace the halls and tap at her phone avoidantly like an orbiting satellite, never landing, never returning home.

Though she claimed to abhor the town of Corvid, Dex didn't find it so deplorable. It wasn't polluted or congested. Sure, it was old-fashioned, like Gothic bones dressed in modern attire, but it was pedestrian friendly. Collegiate towns and campuses were distant enough to inconvenience partygoers while still calling to those hungry for gilded art and shrouded history. Its city was alive with dark plant life and landscaping, rumors, ghosts, and an elderly population that was commonly priggish and proper.

And yet, he sensed a fluttering panic in Norah's chest at the end of each day as the prospect of home became apparent. He couldn't be sure if it were the damning quiet of living alone that he knew all too well, or other unspoken secrets that haunted her there. But it seemed she disguised her fear with a contempt so immense, it bled across all of Corvid.

Thus, every evening after their caseload was tended to, before she could remove the old phone from her pocket and get lost in its lights and sounds, he asked for feedback on his progress notes. This often led to Norah completing her own documentation alongside him in the conference room. The pair would complete their paperwork, tired fingers tapping until they'd finished. Then, she could leave her work laptop at the hospital and go home. He hoped it would allow her at least an evening to focus on herself after a day of focusing entirely on others.

As soon as her taillights shook across the thick cobblestone, The Voices grew loud and raucous once more. Then, he was alone.

He stretched his gruesome knuckles, gnarled and knotted in violet. Despite their unsightliness, they seemed more healed than he would've expected. However, his frail body seldom made any sense to him these days.

Dex closed his eyes as he shuffled down the darkened hospital halls, lights dim and humming in his head.

"How long, it's been so long-"

"Why even try, it's-"

"Please don't let me go, I-"

"I don't even feel anymore, I'm so numb and-"

The soft rubber tapping of his soles fell away, and the black ocean of headspace enveloped him. He saw a shape in the darkness of his closed eyes. He squinted into the strange dreamscape ahead.

What seemed to be an ivory statue was partially buried in black sand. A sonar scream wailed from the shape as though it were haunted ship wreckage. It rested on the forgotten ocean floor of his memories, a stony figure with unsettling patience.

The pale form was clothed in charcoal, tall and beautiful with alluring curves, still and dead like a ship's figurehead. Its soul and scars sang with a cringeworthy pitch, cutting him with a cold that sliced clean to his bone marrow.

The long-forgotten creature stood without any sign of life, eyes closed and still. Dex reached to touch the solitary form, but once his fingertips were inches from the silhouette's cheek, its eyes snapped open wide, flashing glowing golden eyes.

Dex cried out and backstroked, choking and unable to breathe, desperately flailing, kicking, paddling. His hot, rushing blood fell into the awareness of his cold flesh, and he tore open the eyes he had forgotten were closed.

Evening chill stung his cheeks and sweating neck. Perspiration sputtered from his lips. A violent wind rocked him on his toes, stealing his attention downwards.

He was on the rooftop of Corvid Hospital, feet peeking over its ledge. The wind pressed him towards the gut-wrenching nothingness below. Arms swimming, he tripped back from the ledge and landed hard on his spine, dropping anchor onto his rear. He huffed at the stars, heart near to rupturing.

And for what felt like hours in the cold, he could only see the luminescent burn of golden irises in his mind's eye.

11

✦NORAH✦

Word swept through the hospital of Alina's uncanny treatment team. The availability of full-time mental health services for non-English speaking clients was pivotal in a hub such as Corvid with its neighboring cities rich in diversity. Thus, they were ambushed with countless referrals.

The handsome old stranger was no longer gawked upon or shied from in the halls. Most now beamed upon his large figure, groomed, combed, sharp, and debonair beneath his blushing features.

The tall patriarch and his dark-haired clinician exchanged conspiratorial chuckles along their hallway commutes, sporting their long black dress coats, chrome buttons shining. Coattails, empty cups of coffee, and calmed clients were often left in their wake.

Alina was in recovery from her most recent round of radiation treatment. Chemo brain could make therapy unnerving for some clients, if not infuriating. Thus Rosella, Alina's nurse, promised to alert her team once the "light" had returned to their small patient's eyes. Until then, she needed rest.

Yufei Yan, 29. Social anxiety. Depression. Enjoys reading fantasy novels and baking. Cat named Ben Ben.

They met for Yan's sessions in the hospital Memory Care Garden, sitting on rusted black patio furniture. The sky was gray, and the garden smelled of freshly churned mulch.

Senior patients would often prune and tend to obsidian coral bells and black dragon coleus whose blooms were cut before their petals could unfurl and sap the vibrant energy from their plum-wine leaves. Just beyond the hedges of black mondo grass, silver feeders were packed with unshelled peanuts for the crows. Plucky, conversational chortles and garbles were exchanged by the massive birds as Dex and Norah met with their client.

"I feel…transparent. Or perhaps I'm…easy to not see…like a shadow," Yan muttered in her native Cantonese. The young woman was just beginning her first week of inpatient care for suicidal thoughts. "I didn't think it was possible to hurt so much and not be seen."

The translated words fell from Dexteras with ease, Norah observed.

"I don't feel anything at all, and I…I still feel like people look *through* me." Consonants rode his tongue like big tires across gravel. His gaze fell distant and shiny with rumination at times, but still, he out-poured praises for Yan's growth.

"May I share something with Yan, Miss Kestrel?" Dex asked Norah gently, professionally. It was the first time he'd ever interrupted the therapeutic discussion. "I promise it's therapeutically relevant."

She smiled, proud of his courage. "Of course, Mr. Doe."

With a groan, he stretched low to rummage through his leather bag, fidgeting with its brass buckles and clasps. From one of its tiny pockets, he retrieved a familiar business card, soft and crumpled like well-worn fabric. He flattened it onto the small table before them and allowed his eyes a moment to twinkle upon the now smudged black ink scrawled there.

You are here. You are alive. You matter. Your feelings are important.

He read this in Cantonese to Yan in slow, intentional words, breathing between each statement as though it strained his lungs with effort. He then scrawled the words in her language onto a scrap of paper and gave it to her. As he did so, he reread them again, wistful and sniffing.

Yan was weeping large, round tears by the time he'd finished.

Norah hoped with all her being that the both of them felt the mantra deep within their bones.

12

✦NORAH✦

FOLLOWING THE MORNING'S SESSION, the therapist and her interpreter returned to the halls, shrugging from their long, black coats as they stepped in from Corvid's dreary cold.

"Hey," Dex muttered, voice crackling.

Nor raised her brow and spun with a fanciful flourish. "Yes, Mr. Doe?"

He grew pink, and his lashes fell to the floor and he stuttered briefly.

His quiet nature made Norah feel confident and energetic. Childish and goofy. Lively and listened to. Experiences she hadn't known in...forever.

"Care to join me for a coffee?" His nervous blue eye found her from beneath his white hair.

They'd shared many cups of coffee, but this was different. This was an invitation for fellowship. "You know, I can't think of anything I'd rather do more," she sang.

In the hospital cafeteria, they ushered brimming foam cups of molten black liquid to an empty table. Years prior when visiting her mother, Norah had tried the hospital's vulgar bean juice and had since made a point to avoid its sour wretchedness. But today, she followed Dex's lead with high hopes and sipped. Immediately she shivered and winced, cursing her optimism.

His laughter boomed with a shake of his large form, rounding his cheeks and crinkling his few smile lines.

"I know. Honestly, it's for the company rather than the potation," he admitted.

"Well, I'm honored," she sputtered, sucking the flavor off her teeth. "This is quite the sacrifice for a conversation with the likes of me." Her eyes roamed the dank cafeteria for foods that might redeem her taste buds.

Dex reached for the plastic saltshaker at their table's center. Casually, he began to tip it above his cup.

"Wh-no!" she gawked, face horrified, fingers outreached.

He tipped but a sprinkle into his drink, stirring it with a wooden stick and sipping. His mustache wriggled, but still, he swallowed.

Norah's cringe was frozen in awe as she awaited him to gag.

"It does help. You should try." He slid the shaker to her earnestly.

She could only refuse with a bitten tongue, certain the drink was unsalvageable.

He snapped his fingers. "You know, I may have something else…" He plunged a hand into the inside pocket of his great, black coat, revealing a small chocolate bar. It was dressed in a blue shimmering wrapper and elegant German script.

"Real German dark chocolate. Crème de la crème," he said with flawless flairs of his tongue. He broke the bar in half, chrome wrapping and all, and slid part to her. "It'll get the acidity out of your mouth."

Nor peeled the blue foil from it and dared a taste. In brief moments, she'd inhaled the chocolate until it left her fingers sticky and coated. Notes of rich cream and vanilla painted her palette and melted down her throat. Thick and milky and filling. She was intoxicated.

"Damn." She sucked each precious finger without shame.

He brushed cacao bits from his beard and button-down. "I have a telephone client I translate for from Leverkusen. Sends me a box at the end of every fiscal year."

Norah shook her head in awe of his talents and was consumed by his winnings.

"Say something in German," she grinned like a child, certain it was an ignorant request the old translator got often.

He hummed and lifted his bushy brows in great consideration.

"My favorite word is *torschlusspanik*," he said, respecting the language with its full mouth of character and valleys of inflection. "It means a gate-closing-panic," he added with fallen lashes. "The feeling that you are slowly losing worth. That your life is slipping away as you age."

Norah repeated the word on her own tongue, paying homage to the great grief it served. She remembered her second time meeting the old man, sobbing, his forehead pressed to the German graffiti behind the coffee shop.

"I can't imagine that feeling, Dex, but I can tell you it's not founded in any truth. You do so much good. You are so needed."

His mustache twisted. "Thank you, friend. But I fear with time, what little I can offer will come to an end."

"Career or not, you're still a lovely human being to know," she said. "Nothing else in nature can always be in a season of productivity." She thought of the bright pink blooms of her Nana Rose's Christmas cacti in her kitchen. "Nor do we expect it to. You're a creature of nature, too, so don't expect it of yourself."

The old man shared one glossy eye with her before it fell, and she watched his fingers attempt to rub a tattooed anchor symbol off his ring finger.

"I have a question you don't have to answer," she began, bending to find his lovely eyes. "But when I saw you at the coffee shop a while back, you said your life was foggy. What did you mean?"

His fingers fluttered to the back of his head, where they rubbed his neck. A tic in his cheek made him shift, but he took a great breath and closed his eyes. He opened them and swallowed.

These self-soothing gestures made Nor feel immediately idiotic for barraging him with such a personal question.

But she wanted to know him. She did.

"I had a traumatic head injury twenty-plus years ago," he said with a meek clearing of his throat, gazing up at other patrons guiltily as they passed. "Quite the mental break, too, I was told. I had to relearn how to walk and s-s-s-speak. How to listen to body cues, thoughts. How to be a human e-s-s-s-entially. Took many months and many, many people." He took another deep gulp of air and slumped as though he'd finished a marathon.

"Jesus, Dex, are you serious?" she gawked. "You went through all of that *here*?" She pointed to the hospital floor as though it were swelling with lava.

He nodded, rolling his shoulders.

She considered prodding further but saw the tired blue shadows darkening his eyes and the returned tremors in his hands. "Do you want to talk about it?" she asked gently, aching to comfort him, to touch his wrinkled hands.

He blinked and considered this for almost an entire minute. "No, no, I don't think s-so," he muttered. "Not now anyways, but thank you for asking Nor."

"But isn't it hard to keep coming back every day? After all of that?"

He nodded again, his eyes finding hers for but a moment.

"You began translating in Corvid *after* that incident?"

He nodded.

She closed her eyes, knowing the answer to her question before she asked it. "So everyone-"

"Everyone knew what had happened to me," he confirmed. "Knew who I was. No one would answer my calls."

She dropped her chin into her propped palm in anguish, but her blood boiled. She could already hear the ignorant stories and myths that'd surely been spat about him.

"Total bullshit," she snarled.

He leaned back into his chair with a small smile, unfolding his thick arms. Colorful birds and fonts peeked beneath his sleeves. The itchy sweater of "lostness" that he often wore seemed less suffocating now.

"I'm sure you understand." Sadness croaked from his throat, made silvery by chocolate. "I can't deny I've heard your name used countless times by the staff. But it's because they adore you. They refer all their most beloved patients to you without hesitation," he said. "Towns like these like labeling their heroes. Their legends, if I may." He winked.

She snorted and had to stop herself from awkwardly drinking from her cup once more.

"Like most legends, though, they're often blown out of proportion. Just as their monsters are." She raised a tall brow and pursed her lips. She prayed she hadn't been too bold.

"*Or* perhaps it's closer to a well-written horror story. Maybe their words don't begin to scratch the surface of what truly lurks beneath," he challenged, brandishing a hand in his direction.

She was certain he expected her to laugh with his jesting, but her heart ached. As so many had gawked upon her survival of "The Kestrel Tragedy," she was certain just as many stared with idiotic unease upon Dex.

It had to be why he clambered about with such obligatory politeness. It was the uncertainty of someone who'd never been truly accepted. It left him to pretend and charade normalcy despite his disregarded pain.

Damned be the masks forced upon us in tiny towns.

"Well, call them heroes or monsters, or what have you. But they're my kind of people," Nor stated, raising her chin.

The elderly pilgrim shed decades of age in his genuine smile and managed to hold her eyes authentically for a moment. It was an effort

Norah knew taxed her friend especially.

When his gaze faltered, she removed the rings from her right hand and slipped them onto her left. She retrieved her father's quarter from her pocket and allowed it to cascade across her barren knuckles. They both watched the coin in lieu of the burden of eye contact.

"How do you *do* that?" he asked.

A joyless chuckle shook her throat. "I'm an only child. I know lots of useless shit to keep me busy. Lots of alone time to practice." She didn't tell him that she used the trick to keep from picking at her scalp when she was a child. It would bleed and scar until tiny, coarse bundles of silver hair poked through. Even decades later, a few long sparkling strands still remained.

"Unfiltered question time…" she said to her hands.

"My favorite time of the day," he replied. "Shoot."

"Corvid. This place, it's…" She raised a brow and shook her head. "Why don't you start someplace new?"

His gaze followed her coin, and he squeezed at the muscles of his forearms, bruises and bright inks stretching. The script of his parchment skin warped and twisted.

"Do you truly believe it's this *place* that hurts you as it does?" he asked with a kind eye. It wasn't judgmental, but caring and inquisitive.

It was her turn to fall quiet and consider. The challenge swelled in her chest until her breath shortened, and her insides felt naked and seen.

Dex must have sensed this unease because he spoke up to offer her relief this time. "I know it sounds… nonsensical. But I've always felt a need to stay. To wait for an opportunity to heal things. To fix things. Even though, yes, it hurts." His lips stammered as though they considered diving deeper, but he only shook his head. Waves bounced loose about his features. A tic pressed his ear into his shoulder. Flustered, he stood with a groan and took their cups.

"Well, good sir," began Nor, hoping to recover from her uncertainty and keep him a moment longer. "I've lived in Corvid for, fuck, a *lifetime*. But you know… I think I've finally made my first real friend here. So that's got to count for something?" She leaned back in her chair and tossed her hands with a grin, anxious for his reaction.

His cheeks rounded like perfect pink melon balls, shining with quiet excitement. His eyes were low but crinkled with their rare smile.

"Well, it's extraordinary, actually," he chuckled, "but I believe I have as well. So who knows, maybe our luck is finally turning around?"

13

✦DEXTERAS✦

CORVID HOSPITAL'S ROOFTOP WAS SOBERING AND COLD. It was harder for him to slip into dreams and dissociation from his numbness.

"Don't let me go please, I need you to-"

"-didn't say it would burn so badly, but it's-"

"-want to thank you, but I'm not sure how to."

"It's always like this. Always so empty and-"

The rooftop wasn't ideal, but he found if he paced the hospital's halls for too long, late-shift nurses and insomniac patients became wary and angsty with his presence. Eventually, he'd writhe within his needle-pricked skin until he was forced to retreat beneath the stars. A baseball swelled beneath his breastbone at the thought of their eyes upon him.

"Am I dead? How long have I been here?"

"Where am I supposed to go?"

"How can anyone survive-"

He rocked on his toes and squinted at Polaris in the sky. It wasn't even past three AM. He had so many hours to go. Tears boiled beneath his lids with ravenous exhaustion, yet The Voices roared onward with Their tragic song.

He moaned.

He tried to think of nothing.

Of lovely things.

Of old poems he'd memorized about the skies.

Nothing made his headspace bearable.

"Io, Europa, Callisto, Ganymede…" he muttered, narrowing his gaze at the skies. "Aladfar, Alchiba, Algorab, Buna, Sterrennacht, Azha…" Despite the yellow light pollution of Corvid, his eyes found the voids in the sky where each star would reside. He chewed on his cheeks until copper coated his tongue and bloodied his teeth.

"Phoenix, Pavo, Grus, Tucana, Apus-ow, dammit, *irrumator!*" Bastard.

He skittered backward in the rooftop gravel with a hiss, hand recoiling from an unseen pain against his fingertips.

He looked down to find he'd dropped a lit cigar, now spewing centripetal plumes as it rolled away. A broken pile of neglected ash littered his leather shoes.

How long had it been burning in his grasp?

"Dammit," he muttered, picking up the cigar and blowing debris from the papery tobacco leaves. Yet another he couldn't recall lighting.

What the hell is that about?

Are my faculties gone to hell so soon?

He smeared sooty fingers across his eyes with a sigh and pulled on the cigar, but his drag was greedy and ash filled his chest. Smoky tendrils dug their nails into his throat, leaving him to choke, spasms, bending him across his kneecaps in the dark.

Eyes weeping, he regained his breath and eyed the crackling ember on his tobacco stub.

His gaze then dashed to his hand, to the ancient tattoo of a faded bird flying across his palm. His fingers twitched, and his dry, dead apathy shuddered with interest. He sat on his rear, hand poised above the ink.

He pressed the burning cigar into the bird's chest until it peeled with sickly white fumes of melted flesh. The smoky stench swirled like a ghost. He gnashed upon his teeth as his skin blistered and blackened.

It'd been ages since he'd attempted such a means of feeling. It warmed his skull guiltily like a drug. He unfolded onto his spine, his blood cold and alive.

His innards bulked, fire wrinkled the thin epidermis, and his limbs convulsed without permission. His moans tore into cries and streaming tears. His teeth grimaced but grinned with fleeting existence.

But it wasn't enough.

He wrapped his fingers around the cigar like a dagger and stabbed it until it was snuffed in soupy, soft tissue and leaking fluid. His skull screamed with panic, dominating The Voices.

Burning and oozing, his spine bucked on the stone roof. The smoking crater simmered into the heavens like the battleground of a ceasefire. Sweat and tears leaked down his temples.

But the euphoric high of feeling drifted, and the blanket of numbness returned to his warm, unfeeling corpse. Droning pleas crashed against the halls of his brain.

You feel nothing because you are nothing.

He clenched his eyes shut and crushed the cigar butt against the concrete. He lifted his head and frowned at the seeping burn. It swelled with white bubbles of putrid flesh. Lava-hot pus and secretions dripped.

But it wasn't enough. It never was.

He was still hollow. Vacant. Unfeeling. Dead.

"Are you there? Can you hear me?" screamed The Voices.

More blood-curdling screams.

They were furious with his brief reprieve.

"Please, no…" he moaned, digging through his scalp for distractions. His wet face was covered by his abused hands.

Why? Why am I here? Why am I here if I can't feel anything?

He opened his eyes and stared at the stars through his shaking fingers. Their burning, radiating bodies, swollen with life. Energy. He swallowed, throat hoarse with unheard cries.

Or perhaps they were simply ignored.

"Alchiba, Algorab, Buna, Sterrennacht, Azha…" he returned to the blinking balls of fire.

The baseball in his throat twisted, allowing more breath to hiss through. His eyes jumped from star to star, speaking on their nomenclature as he did so.

He found Pollux and considered its Grecian namesake, Πολυδεύκης, Polydeukes. *Very sweet.*

"Maybe our luck is turning around…"

Norah.

His hands slid down his cheeks, and he beheld the skies fully, eyes burning with tears.

Those Neptune green eyes actually saw him. A *real* friend.

He'd been fading and falling apart for all of his miserable life, but as of late, he'd observed more cognitive disintegration. He'd find himself craving a cup of coffee or a cigar, and without recollection of the time in between, he'd suddenly be holding it in his grip. Sure, the bodily pains of his mortal coils had lessened, but God only knew what further atrophy would come of his brain.

The hospital would ask me to step down, he grieved. Telephone clients would still satiate his rent and coffee addiction, but he'd lose his chance at redemption. At fixing the untold thing in his life that needed to be fixed.

He'd lose his only friend.

He recalled their earlier conversation about myths and monsters. He had heard whispers of her origin story amongst the denizens of Corvid. They took crude and wild stabs at the events that toughened her heart, but Dex always turned his ear away promptly. If she wished to talk to him about her past, he'd be honored to know her story firsthand. Otherwise, it wasn't his gift to have.

But ruminating about their potentially shared pains rocked him into a disassociation, more powerful and peaceful than the breaks in his bones and the burns in his flesh. He considered the aligned stars in their galaxies and the forces that had drawn them nearer to one another.

What a strange constellation they formed.

14

✦DEXTERAS✦

His nightmares had left him ragged the following day. His thoughts were loose and poorly saddled. His brain was afire with exhaustion. The Voices roared. Scolded. Begged.

From across the small Family Consult Room on the third floor just outside the surgical suites, Dr. Tanager's dark eyes soaked Dex like a coat of paint, suffocating and heavy. He was searching for errors and finding too many to count.

Dex kept his fake smile bolted on tightly for the sake of their clients who shared the space. They were a Chilean family, kinder and more patient than he ever deserved.

Dr. Tanager's lips moved, and Dex tilted his ear to listen, but The Voices were unyielding, demanding his attention. Piles upon piles of lingual tongues filled his skull until nothing and no one could be comprehended:

"-can't handle this any longer, I need to go, I need to die."

"There's just not enough of me to handle this, there's-"

"Of course, he's gone. Everyone leaves. Everyone."

A child screamed, voice trembling with a despondent vibrato.

Dex blinked and noticed Dr. Tanager's expression. It was still now. Expectant. Angry.

"S-s-sorry doctor, could you please repeat that?" Dex admitted, a guilty break in his brows. This time, as the squat man spoke, Dex pressed his thumbprint into the gory crater he'd burnt into his hand, tucking his limbs against him to shield the torture from others. With each pang of pain, he was allowed a moment of clarity to make out Tanager's nasally words. Once Dex memorized the sentence, he relinquished his grip, closed his eyes, and breathed.

"-and when will this stop? Why do I-"

"But she has no one now. How am I supposed to fucking-"

He relayed the dialogue to the waiting family. It was a list of detailed instructions for their daughter's post-surgery care.

Dex squinted with focus as they voiced their questions, pressing into the wound to quiet his head. He spun to share these with the impatient doctor, but Tanager's voice was already overtalking him, barking and irritated.

Ill-prepared for the interruption, Dex hadn't readied his ears and was left blinking against the barrage of voices and overstimulation.

Tanager's tongue pressed about the insides of his mouth as though itching to scream obscenities, not that Dexteras could've properly heard them.

Before Dex could open his mouth to apologize, to ask for yet another chance, Tanager was standing on his feet and opening the conference room door. He spat something along the lines of "get yourself together" and "telephone translator."

Dex raised pitiful brows to the family before him and repeatedly apologized for his struggle.

They were loving and affirmative and watched him leave with worried faces.

He'd thought Tanager would slide into the hall to scold him, but the man only glared and slammed the door as soon as Dex's coattails cleared the threshold.

Stitches pulled apart at his breastbone. His world wobbled with anxiety and blackened peripherals. Louder still, The Voices screamed at him. His fingers shook as they ran along the wall, assessing doors, handles, and curtains. Finally, his nails scraped with a steel *shing* along the metal of a supply closet.

"Dexteras…?" cooed a voice beside him.

He flinched and spun to find a tiny nurse with silver features and a kind face below.

He blinked the hot tears from his eyes and squinted down upon her. He knew that face. He knew her.

The tiny woman smiled up at him with pink lips, wearing pink scrubs patterned in purple cows. "Dexteras, I don't know if you remember me, but I'm Toni Plover, I-"

"You found me," whispered his dry lips before his brain had fully comprehended it. His stomach flip-flopped. Panic swelled in his throat. Toni was the one who'd found him after he'd…

"I've thought of you every day since that day. Every day…" she said in her quiet singsong voice, eyes soft and assessing.

He remembered her fingers being the least cold on his skin. Her words the most loving and calm:

"Hey friend, I need you here. I need you to stay with me. I need you to look at me if you can, alright? Feel my hands. I'm not going to let you go."

She smelled of an old perfume that he couldn't place but felt he could name if given enough time.

"Th-thank you," he said, investing his all just to smile. "I c-can't thank you enough. You were the kindest person I'd ever met during that time." Not that such an accolade was a difficult one to earn.

Her lips parted to ask him more questions, maybe how he was, how life was treating him. But he felt her gaze fall to the sweat on his chest, the burning in his eyes. Then, she simply closed her mouth and smiled. She followed his anxious features, which darted from her wrinkles to the supply closet beside them.

His heart was thudding in his throat. Could she hear it?

Toni removed a ring of keys from her pocket and unlocked the supply closet with an encouraging nod. "It's good to see you, Dexteras," she said. "Be kind to yourself, okay?" She winked and opened the door.

He took it from her and flung himself inside, tucking his body between its metal shelves. The door shut behind him with an affirming click. Yet another gift he could never repay Toni Plover for.

He dropped his head back against the cold brick, pressing the heels of his hands against his burning eyelids. Heat swelled within him, tightening his chest stiff with tension. He wasn't certain if he'd sob or pass out.

Fearful he'd fall unconscious, he spun and impulsively struck the painted brick.

Then again.

And again.

His vision doubled with the pain.

Worried tones mumbled from surrounding rooms as the walls thudded.

His world trembled, but his burning knucklebones kept him tethered to the present. Hot tears blinked from his eyes with shame.

What would Tanager say to Norah?

What would Toni think?

"This isn't going to work."

"Your man is falling apart."

"You're a fool for believing he could do this."

The Voices agreed with their unending screams.

Through the blur of his vision, he eyed the dented, bleeding skin of his fists. Their edges were bone white, divots filled with pools of crimson. The sight of them offered no peace, but The Voices had suddenly grown still.

Silent.

A grateful sigh trembled from his chest.

The quiet was loud and foreign, allowing him to hear his racing heart and the tiny metallic taps fiddling against the closet's door.

A breeze like a seashore rushed over his hot limbs. He drank in the chill, his shoulders fell. The door opened.

And there she was, head sideways and observant.

He was certain Norah Kestrel was eyeing both his inward and outward hurts with disgust, but as his eyes focused, he saw no fury, no disappointment. She was simply there, taking in his corpse.

She stepped in and shut the door with gentle fingers as though she could feel his pounding headache.

He cursed his impulses. His optimism. His belief that he could do this. That he could actually fix people in the way they fixed him. *You foolish, stupid old dog.*

Norah leaned against the brick beside him and gave a small smile, resting her temple against the cold wall. Her gaze was neither pitying nor mocking. It was an *I've-been-there-too* sort of expression.

He pressed his forehead against the wall, eyes pacing the floor below. "It's just been s-such a long time. And s-s-so many people. So much I can ruin." He muttered, knowing he was making no rational sense.

But her eyes brightened like gemstones, and she nodded. Then her gaze fell to his shaking fists. She held up a finger and stepped into the hall, where the rummaging of a nursing cart could be heard. She returned to him in the dark with supplies.

"Nor, please, you don't have to. This is *my* problem, *my* fault, I'll-"

"Dex," she interrupted, voice stern and honest, "as long as you're safe and the clients are safe, I'm never going to take this opportunity from you," she promised. She took his lead fist in her hands and dabbed ointment on its seeping wounds. Her fingers were cold and healing.

"You're giving people a voice in a way no one else can here. You don't owe anyone anything. You have nothing to prove. No one has grounds to judge you," she added, conviction firm in her gaze. "You're important. Your work matters."

She spun a thin web of gauze around his knuckles and examined her work before returning the hand to him.

He held it in his own, hoping to savor the kindness.

"But more importantly, so do you. *You* matter. So, if you need to breathe, to walk away, you leave at any moment. I'll always back you up." She raised a brow, daring him to speak harshly of himself.

He nodded, thoughts oscillating betwixt unworthiness and accountability. She reminded him that his self-care was his charge. His advocacy was his own to care for. But regardless of what others thought they knew of him, he didn't have to be ashamed of it.

"You are the professional of your needs, Dex. Fuck them and what they think, you take care of yourself."

15

⋅NORAH⋅

DAVÍDEK HRDLIČKA, 61. At Corvid Hospital for substance abuse treatment, depression worsening. Anhedonia. Non-responsive to modalities/meds. Loves his younger brother and fishing.

Dexteras and Daví mimicked one another's large gestures and volumes in mighty Czech tongues. They carried big, rolling shoulders and soft-spoken demeanors. She wondered if she'd finally deciphered Dex's heritage in their closeness.

Daví was painted with tawny wrinkles, purple bags beneath his eyes, and a settled droop in his cheeks.

"When was the last time you were happy?" Nor asked.

"I don't know what happy feels like anymore," he admitted through Dexteras. The language was sharp and bellowing, like cracks across a frozen pond.

They gently prodded at his feelings until they shuddered to life and unfurled to their fullest height. From there, they could understand them with more accuracy.

Daví's parents were emotionally and physically abusive towards one another. A countertransference clenched in the therapist's chest as he shared the woeful narrative.

"Mom would drink and get in Dad's face. Dad would shove her against walls, sinks, tables. They'd both scream."

Their mutual pasts panged the heart beneath Norah's breastbone. She was certain she hid these aches from her client, but Dex's glance slid knowingly over her.

Daví's form shook as truth spilled from him in rolling tears and twisted wrinkles.

Nor allowed a quiet reverence so that his story could press against the walls and brush the ceiling with its immensity. But in the silence, she prayed Daví registered it too. This story has always been violent. Devastating. Unspeakable. But now, as it sat, it did not destroy him. It did not tear his breath from his throat as trauma often felt it would. He was weary with the spent adrenaline of survival, but he'd survived.

Despite all he'd known, Daví was still here.

✦

After their rooftop cigars and shared fist-bumps, they returned to the conference room to finish documentation. The ugly shadow that had to follow clinical work with each step.

As she typed absent-mindedly, she recalled a strange interaction she'd had earlier in the week.

She'd strode past a nursing station on the fourth floor and heard various mumbles and whispers.

"-in his fifties, maybe? Sixties?"

Exasperated scoffs and snickers followed.

"-so many tattoos."

"-just weird."

"…not even professional, I don't know HR doesn't…"

The tops of Nor's ears were hot when she spun on her toes with a horrid laminate squeal. She rushed to the nurse's island and hopped up on the countertop in a swift, adrenaline-fueled gesture. Sitting above them, she painted on a devilish grin and set her chin in her hands like an eager schoolchild.

"Spill the tea, girls," she whispered conspiratorially. But her eyes felt wild and wide with unspoken threats.

The nurses went silent with the confrontation. One looked to her clipboard with guilt and the others grinned stupidly. Norah wasn't surprised by the honking geese specific to this particular gossiping gaggle: Jamie Pidge, Kathleen Dover, and Autumn Tula. Their brows were narrow and judgmental. Their nails were coffin-shaped and clacking. For no reason whatsoever, their ignorant, pristine features made Norah's blood boil.

This was why she kept her back turned to the whispers of staff. Why her boundaries with colleagues were always firm and formal. If her memory served her, it was in fact Kathleen who'd once worked as her mother's nurse when Robin's first bout of stomach cancer became prevalent. It was no secret that Robin lied recklessly to staff regarding her substance use history and illicit drug and alcohol abuse. The staff replied with irritable jabs and shameful eyerolls beyond her mother's room. It was Kathleen who referred to Robin as "the wino" in the halls. Norah had even heard rumors of the term "Norphan," in reference to herself along the oncology halls, which Nor quite frankly found resourceful and clever.

But this was vastly different. They weren't wrong about her and her mother. The Kestrels deserved the shame and sneers. But in this moment, before Dex's dignity, she found herself armored, hot, and tempted to pummel faces with the many rings along her knuckles.

Say something, say one fucking thing about Dexteras Doe, I dare you… she begged, eyes nearly watering as she grinned like a madman at them.

The trio exchanged shifty glares that reminded her of the bullshit she'd dealt with in grade school. Norah had been small then, meek and terrified. But she wasn't anymore. She'd barely noticed her father's quarter speeding up and down her knuckles.

It was Jamie who dared to speak up first, her voice brave, yet breaking. "Oh, we-we were talking about y-your translator actually, D-Dex, Dexter-?"

"Dexteras," Nor snapped. But in a blink, she masked the fury with feigned curiosity. She was good at lying. She'd watched her father do it to his wife for years. She knew how to keep her features loose and unthreatened. She knew how to wrinkle her brows in surprise and hurt. She knew how to look emotionally distant, yet interested. "Oh really? Anything I should know?" she dared with a syrupy-sweet croon, tilting her head with masked concern.

Their eyes dashed to Jamie beneath their fake eyelashes, breaths held.

"We-we heard the ER staff say they've seen him translating for clients through all three shifts, days at a time," she added with a careful dash of admiration, reading Norah's face for tells of how she felt for the old man.

But Norah only blinked and dropped her shoulders, offering them nothing. Her chest hurt at the mere thought of Dex working for days on end.

But that wasn't humanly possible, of course. Nobody could do that for days on end.

Heavy keyboard taps from his inked fingers returned Nor to the present. She considered him while her own hands hovered above her laptop, concern stitched in her brow.

Then, an evident tic seemed pulsed in his cheek. His eyes scrunched with pain. His bandaged hand gripped his head with a scowl as he attempted to rub the wrinkles from his face.

"Headache?"

"No… not quite," he muttered, seemingly listening to *something* in the stagnant hospital winds.

Before Nor could prompt him further, the old man was mobile. In seconds, he was spinning on a polished boot, sending his chair aside, and was out the door and down the hall. He rounded corners at a healthy clip.

"What the shit," she mumbled, scrambling from her seat. "Dex?"

But he wasn't listening. His head whipped about in search of something beyond them both.

She sought after his heels as he bolted for the elevator.

His massive arm held open the shining door for her but didn't speak as they ascended. Then, the elevator chimed and pried ajar, he dashed into a new hall, limbs long and reaching.

Norah's hip vibrated as she gave chase. She snatched her phone from her pocket to see a text from Rosella, Alina's nurse:

AH missing from her bed, alert has been sent.

Then, an announcement shook the halls through its booming intercoms: "A code pink has been placed until further notice. Code pink."

Well, shit.

Dex's pace quickened. Jarring turns and hurried shuffles brought him to a fork in the road, where his leather boots squeaked to a halt. His chest heaved, and he tilted an ear to listen.

Before she could inquire, he was ablaze with fresh fire, hot on the trail once more. He stopped, spun, and then shouldered his way through one of the many stairwell doors.

At the top of the stairs, a small gasp escaped him.

Norah peeked around his great, heaving form to behold the steps below. And there she was.

At the bottom, Alina was burrowed into a corner with her knees to her chest. She was clutching something in her tiny hands.

Dex jumped the remaining few stairs and slid to his knees beside her, cooing to the child with his thunderstorm deep voice.

"Ohh, Lina, Lina. Shh." Ukrainian saturated his words as he scooped her into his arms.

She wept between hyperventilating breaths, unfolding like a paper crane onto Dex's chest, sobbing and whimpering.

He inquired with low whispers.

She returned them with broken cries, clutching to his shirt.

"Is she okay?" asked Nor, wide-eyed.

He stood with a groan, holding the child close to him. The nostrils of his crooked nose flared with strain. He nodded slowly, heavy with sadness.

Norah finally saw what Alina clung to in handfuls: clumps of thin, dark hair. Her balled fist was pressed against a pink, balding spot on the side of her skull.

"Oh, Alina," Nor cooed. She tapped a prompt text to Rosella:

Bringing the bird back to the nest.

Seconds later, an announcement concluded that the "Code Pink has been lifted."

They trekked to Alina's room, Dex carrying her all the way. He spoke warmly until she was limp with sleep, cheeks glistening with tears.

Seeing the weary caravan treading home, Rosella jogged towards them. Anxious moans bobbed from her with each heavy-breasted sigh. She rubbed her face in her hands, tears welling, and embraced Norah.

"She's safe, no harm done, Ella. She's safe."

"Norah," she whispered, words breaking. "She'd finished treatment and was sleeping like a bear. She was so tired… I got called to cover Eric's hall a moment and forgot to set her bed alarm, and just…it was my fault. Entirely my fault."

Norah laughed, squeezing her tighter. "El, stop that. She's alright. Dex got her."

Dex rubbed the child's back. "She's grieving some big things right now," he muttered. "But she's safe."

Rosella's eyes sparkled at the old man as she clutched her cheek and smiled up at him.

They laid the child on her purple bed sheets, where she muttered inaudibly and sank into the linens. They slipped rubber-soled socks up her shins and tucked her in snugly. Tiny oxygen hoses were looped around her ears. Her monitors were reset. Her swinging tree vines of tubes and cords were restrung. Dex and Nor hugged her tightly. They wiped away her tears. They told her she was beautiful, because she was. She was asleep before they'd backed softly from the room.

Dex whispered a Ukrainian farewell and followed the triage of professionals into the hall. Rosella snatched him into a massive hug, making him laugh and groan simultaneously. His lashes fell low, and his cheek twitched. His hair was slick with sweat.

✦

They returned to their floor to gather their things. He was still huffing, neck shining with effort. His eyes were heavy-lidded and slow.

"Can I get you anything?" Nor tried.

"No, no, but thank you," he breathed.

He'd be polite to his deathbed.

"But I'd like to get some air." He threw a nod upwards to the roof.

She gave half a mind to ask if he'd like company but feared she'd only deepen his weariness with the burning questions in her head.

How did he know Alina was lost before everyone else?

How did he find her?

And how the hell did he carry her so far when he struggled to carry himself?

She placed a grateful hand on his large bicep. It was like squeezing a rolled frying pan.

"You've helped Alina so so much. You've helped all of us here. You've helped me."

He bowed his head.

"You know that, though, right? We *cherish* you."

His eyes fell further to his shiny leather boots. "I'm still trying to get used to it, I suppose."

"I'll be sure to keep reminding you. You're incredibly loved."

His cheeks grew round and rosy like ripe peaches.

16

⟡·DEXTERAS·⟡

As though the elevator's chime were an end-of-match bell, he slid down its cool steel in defeat. His ribs stitched tightly across him as though a key had been plunged into his sternum and wound, drawing his breath thin.

But then he placed his hand where she'd held his arm. Her touch never burned or stung. She didn't feel like everybody else.

"Just kill me please-"

"What if I don't see how-"

"Is this it? Is this what-"

"Stop, stop, stop-"

"It's never going to feel the same, how-"

The thought of being alone with The Voices crept up his throat.

"So stupid, it really is-"

"-what I told her. He's never here, and he never will be-"

"-dying though."

"Why isn't anything working? You promised-"

He wished the ascending elevator would carry him into the clouds. He could eternally rest against the cold metal and listen to the grumble of the machine while it cradled him.

Ding.

He streaked the steel with smears of sweat as he regained his bearings and tripped into the hall. His body hung and shook like leaden weights, burdened more by stress than muscular strain.

The worn keypad flickered at the rooftop's handle, demanding its sophisticated code. Several placards were posted, warning of alarms and chaos that would resound for those not permitted.

But a programmed magnetism drew his fingertips to each digit until the device replied with a congratulatory escape. *A lucky guess, as always.* The same invisible cord that'd carried him to Alina.

But hers was more of a sharp chord of panic, a lostness to which others were deaf.

He shoved into the wind and spitting sky. Droplets were lost in his hair and lashes. Weight lifted his shoulders some.

Twenty-eight…twenty-seven…twenty-six…

At the furthest edge, he collapsed against it and dangled his crackling legs over its rim. Gales bullied his hair and drowned out The Voices, reducing them to a tolerable hum. His eyes rested on the rolling clouds.

He inhaled the sharp night, cold and fresh with rain, holding it in his chest until his ribs sang with pressure. As it hissed from his lips, he dropped his torso back to the stone. He saw the star Pollux again through the clouds, swelling with light the size of a pinhead.

He smiled.

Given he'd never had other friends he could observe and behold prior, he noticed each of Norah's details with attentive wonder. He saw the empathy that buckled her brows now punctured in the skies. The tired roll of her neck when she'd finished a session. How she rubbed her scarred palm. The tilt of her half-smile that seemingly demanded the strength of mountains to sustain. He composed her starry profile in his mind's eyes, scintillating and sharp.

Beholding her pieces and their likeness to his again, his cheeks fell. Even the keenest telescopes and seasoned gazes couldn't decipher such buried sadness unless they'd occupied its galaxies, too.

The more time he spent beside Norah Kestrel, the louder he heard her scars sing. And while he was honored to hear them, louder still was the strange *tap, tap, tap*ping that interrupted them.

He'd heard the metallic clamber of pacemakers and their tinny cogs grinding, but this wasn't like any of those. It was a demand for obedience, like the smack of a nun's ruler. A mechanical pulse that sat near her heart and told it to *hush*. And he was certain that whatever it was, it wasn't Norah's to wield.

He couldn't help but wonder what tortured her so.

17

✦NORAH✦

Disoriented and distant, she locked the spare bedroom at the top of the stairs and returned its tiny key beneath her shirt. It dropped like a cold drink of water to her cramped abdomen. As she shuffled out the door and into the streets toward work, she stared down at her phone to her newest email.

"RECORDS REQUEST REDEEMED. SIGNED FOR APPROVAL"

Human resources had finally acquired Dex's file and had accepted him as a full-time employee. His probationary period was ended. Combined with Norah's shining report of his competence, it was an easy decision.

This position was made for him. He's a natural.

Her contented smile fell. She considered the impossible old man's idiosyncrasies and otherworldly abilities, all wrapped in the thick mystery that was his unknowable story.

But none of that mattered. The job was finally his and he was *perfect* for it. Helping others seemed steeped in his blood.

Why bother with the file? What was there to gain?

And yet, once she arrived at the hospital, she found herself leaving floor after floor below her. With each staircase, an uneasy knot heavied her gut.

But louder still was the selfish curiosity that coerced her higher.

Records and Archives, a gold plate read on the door before her. She pressed into the quiet and ample space, leaving her good intentions in the hall.

Bonnie and Bobbi Lark sat slumped inside, typing busily behind bug-eyed reading lenses. Bonnie was dressed all in black, from her frames to her chunky shoes. Bobbi was dressed in all white, a stark contrast accented with antique pearls and frilly skirts. The women were twins in their sixties and touched every facsimile that kept Corvid Hospital thriving. They reminded Nor of old lunch ladies, witty and sassy beneath a crusty exterior that Nor had yet to break through.

"Good morning, ladies. I'm here to collect a record request for an external agency employee. Please."

Bobbi pushed her glasses up her saggy cheeks and kicked at a metal drawer below, which gasped open. She snatched a faded folder from its mouth.

"Dexteras Doe," groused Bobbi, already exhausted by Norah's presence.

"That's the one, yes, ma'am," said Nor. His name struck her heart with its intimacy. She felt monstrous for demeaning him to these scrap of paper...

But as she stood before the Tree of Knowledge, her fingers itched with anticipation.

Bobbi pulled a Post-it from the file's cover and read it aloud.

"Patient history approved for employee clearance by the previous discharge M.D. and patient's previous clinicians. HR signed off on employment and indicated no concerns with the nature of practice," she glared at Norah over her glasses. "Translator accreditation and licensure are up to date. All other records and contracts are current." The disgruntled woman began to stuff the file back into its drawer but Nor extended a hand.

"Could I still possibly see it? Please?" She bit her lip shamefully.

Bobbi sighed from the deepest depths of her wrinkly body. "Paper files must be reviewed in one of our private viewing rooms. Electronics and media devices must be turned off and left at the desk."

Without raising an eye from her typing, Bonnie patted a plastic tray on her desk labeled *Electronics*.

Nor complied and carried Dex's file to the dingy viewing room, which came complete with a tiny desk lamp and sign-in sheet. The folder's manila cover was heavy and sacrosanct. Tea-stained and ancient. The knot gripped her intestines more firmly as she ran her fingers across the old fibers of the file's shell.

It *felt* wrong.

But with a hesitant rap of her black nail across it, she flipped open its front.

Patient Demographics
First name: Dexteras
Last name:
Age: Dental trajectory 59-62. Birth date unknown.

That's how old he looks now... How was this twenty years ago?

Emergency Contact: none
No personal/familial contacts.

She blinked at his intake date. It struck her with a distant familiarity she couldn't name, but she stretched her scarred palm and continued flipping through the narrow file. Her eyes danced across it, knowing she was short on time.

Patient descended from a presumed 12+ story building in downtown Corvid. Patient's body was found beside the agency hospital. The first-response team reported visibly fractured knees, mandible, clavicle, ribs, and skull damage. Massive swelling, bruising, laceration. Compound fractures, and significant blood loss. Transfusion required. Medical coma induced due to brain inflammation. Brain activity during anesthetic was atypical despite high dose sedatives.

Jeee-zusss, Norah thought.

Post-stabilization/ICU: indicated no existing fractures or internalized bleeding but showed evidence of historic injuries matching intake's observations. The most severe of included healed breakage of jaw, nasal, and "Boxer's fracture" impacting the 4th/5th digits of the left hand, stress fracture in the right and left Patella, pelvis, multiple spinal, and hairline fractures in the skull. The remaining physiological symptoms include arthritic pain and tremors due to severe Carpal Bossing.

Well, how in the actual hell was that possible?

Mental health observations: Noncompliant, anxious, dysregulated, required routine sedation. Irritable, high-risk ideations without plan/ intention, anxious throughout. Patient refused to be touched or treated by staff. Competence determined disabled at this time...
...localized and retrograde amnesia regarding personal history. Evident generalized amnesia. No memory of the incident. Patient reports, "I'm not sure if I was trying to die or not...." Denies plan/intention at this present time.

Nor's head fell into her hands. She squeezed at her roots until her scalp stung.

Provisional diagnosis as evident by verbalizations of disembodiment and brain imaging: Cotard's syndrome and PTSD. Schizophreniform content-specific delusions were identified (patient was confused by the staff's ability to see/interact with him).

Cotard's is relatively rare. Nor had to prod the recesses of her clinical mind to recall that it involved symptoms of debilitating anxiety and fear, believing that one was dead or did not exist.

...required nutrient/med tube due to refusal of intake.

Daily auditory hallucinations. "Lots of voices." Little understanding of what's being said. Induces fear and stress. Psychotherapist assigned.

...diagnosis of Major Depressive Disorder, severe with psychotic features, PTSD, and Agoraphobia. Observed atypical reactivity to verbal/nonverbal communication and physical touch. Reports severe pain when touched by others. (ex. "It all hurts. Please don't. Please, it hurts. You can't touch me. I'm not here.")

Oh, Dex...

Completed intensive outpatient therapy for ninety days. Psychiatry prescribed SSRIs and antipsychotics. Case management services facilitated schooling/housing.

Then, nearly fifteen years following his accident, a new memo was scribbled in the margins:

Update: Client requested a reassessment of mental wellness to pursue full-time employment in clinical settings as a lingual interpreter...approved by psychiatry and general health team contingent on routine physical/mental wellness assessments every six months minimum.

She flipped through his background check and mental health status exams. Both were up to date and signed. Though there was no proof of a Dexteras Doe prior to the incident, he'd been living in Corvid ever since.

How in the hell have we not crossed paths sooner?

A copy of his translator's certificate and ID was included. His wise face was miraculously unchanged. His beard was trim, but still striking and white.

Despite the cold, fact-based medical records with their confident stamps and official signatures, none of it made *any fucking sense.*

He fell from a twelve-story building and was out of the ICU in *days?* He had spinal and skull fractures for Christ's sake.

Norah's feet absentmindedly returned her to the Lark sisters, who ignored her existence. She returned the file, absently took her phone from the tray, and hastened towards the elevator in a fog.

She knocked on Alina's door frame before the thick curtain. Dex and their client whispered in Ukrainian, giggling like schoolchildren.

Alina called out with a harsh accent, "Who is?"

Dex's sweet laughter boomed.

Norah's gut wrenched with regret, unable to unhear the ugly medical jargon and its dispassionate account of his tragedy. Shame and empathy weighed her shoulders for all he'd survived.

But he's still Dex. She affixed her grin and entered.

Dex was sitting on the scuffed laminate floor beside Alina's bed, one of his massive arms propped on the mattress. Alina was coloring in the arm's tattoos with washable markers. Her tongue peeked from between her teeth as she coated his forearms, wrists, and hands in Ukrainian text. Flowers, hearts, stars, birds, and other doodles were also left in her wake across his almond flesh.

"*Prevyet!*" they both called in cheerful greeting.

"*Prevyet,*" the therapist returned, leaning to admire the tiny tattooist's work from above. "*Krasivy,*" Nor added, *beautiful.*

As Dex's gaze rested upon Alina's wandering pen, Norah allowed her own to settle on him. Her chest ached. The horrors these two have both known, and yet here they played.

Dex rearranged his long legs with a groan and glanced upwards at Nor. His piercing stormy blues shook her from disassociation. She stretched another smile across her pursed features.

"Can Alina tell me a bit about her artwork?" Nor gestured to the muscular canvas, pulling a chair close.

He cleared the gravel from his throat and asked the child.

Alina pointed to a detailed birdcage on his forearm where she'd scribbled out its door and drawn a tiny bird flying freely from its clutches.

"Free now," said Dex, with the seriousness of a professional appraising gallery art.

Alina gestured to the crest of his large bicep to a grayscale portrait of a roaring lion. Its fangs protruded, and its wrinkled snout snarled. Alina had adorned the animal in purple fur and crooked hearts. Her carefree script danced above its head in her home tongue.

"And this one," he dictated with a wry grin, "is you."

Norah breathed with surprise. "Me? A lion?"

"*Polyshka?*" Dex asked the child, nodding to Nor.

Alina, still drawing, nodded in return. "*Da.*"

"A *lioness*. But yes, that's you," he corrected, teeth gleaming.

"*Spaseeba* Lina," thank you, Nor said, cheeks warming.

Their client twisted Dex's arm, leaving the old man to groan good-naturedly and stretch himself into obtuse angles. Alina yanked at his triceps, to point at another one of her doodles.

"Oh heavens," he sputtered with laughter, bent like a pretzel with his face pressed against the bed.

Along the back of his arm was a massive crow against a night sky. Tattooed down the full spread of his limb, it wrapped him in emerald and amethyst feathers and cast the illusion that Dex himself was sprouting wings. The bird clutched an antique key in its talons, staring with a watchful blue eye. A rolling banner wrapped the bird's claws and her friend's mighty muscles in cryptic text. Here, Alina had scribbled her own inscription and surrounded the beast by crude yellow stars.

"Can't see that one," Dex muffled into the sheets, braced in a Hail Mary hold by the child. Alina pointed to the art and made demands of the translator, who could only reply with confused hums into the bed. They bantered a moment until Alina gave an affirming sing-song response and released his hairy arm, returning to her sketchbook.

Norah giggled, adoring the lackadaisical boldness of children.

Dex twisted upright and stretched his creaking limbs, working out stuck joints with waggles of his bushy brows. After his muscles were returned to their rightful directions, he verified something with their client.

The girl nodded distantly, distracted like a fashion designer on a runway deadline.

Dex rubbed his jaw and paraphrased the question again, face falling as he persisted.

"*Da*!" Alina exclaimed. Her frustrated laughter manifested into a small coughing fit.

Dex's eyelids fluttered, computing the interaction before speaking aloud to Nor. "She just keeps saying, "*I'm from the stars.*"" He scratched at his wavy tresses. "First person. *I'm* from the stars. Such a strange thing to say."

"Does she mean the crow?" Nor inquired, nodding to his arm. "She drew some stars around him."

"Oh!" Dex barked with relief, shoulders collapsing against the bed frame.

"It's a gorgeous piece." Norah leaned forward in her seat to take in the bird's inky tailfeathers along his forearm. "Do you not remember getting it done?" she asked, lost in the impressive shading etched in his wrinkles.

But she knew it'd been an ignorant thing to say as soon as it'd left her lips. The implication of generalized amnesia had escaped her private thoughts, or rather, his personal file.

Dex's smile faded. His fingers tousled over one another. His knees crept up to his chest.

"No, I s-s-suppose not." He shifted and itched upon the floor in his dapper suit as though it were all too tight.

"I've never seen work this lovely," Norah hurried. "I'd love to know what they all mean someday." She attempted to bandage the foolish comment with even more foolish filler, but it was far too late, and he was far too wise.

In his now fallen lashes, it was easy to observe a painful chord had been struck. It flexed in his grinding jaw and working fingers.

"I could apparently use a refresher myself," he said.

Shit. Shit. Shit.

18

✦·DEXTERAS·✦

THE WAY SHE LOOKED AT HIM.

Spoke to him.

Her innocent verbiage poked at him like a splinter.

The further he considered it, the more it festered.

But this was Alina's time.

Her feelings came first here.

So they completed a genogram with the child, which Norah explained as a "visual solar system" of relationships in one's life and their symbolic placements in our "galaxy." Each person was a planet or a star that orbited one's atmosphere. Some were big, and some were small. Some near or far. Color-coded or unlabeled. All the while, Nor dared each question with unfiltered bravery.

He adored the celestial metaphor, but he had no galaxy of his own. His solar system was silent and empty, composed of ghosts, unwelcome voices, and nightmares. His planet was but a crust of dead, numb tissue.

"Do you not remember…"

Her innocent comment plagued him. It spoke of a casual understanding of his past, and that bothered him.

No, he didn't remember. But that wasn't *normal*, to not remember sitting in a tattoo parlor for hours upon end. To not remember the purpose or existence of a design that made him bear endless needles. His memories were as legible as squid ink and thus, he couldn't remember receiving any of his tattoos.

Norah had presented the question with her trademark grace and normalcy. With the ease of a clinician. And it was her training that had given her away. Because though he'd mentioned his head injury to her, he hadn't discussed his vivid memory loss. The amnesia. The fall.

The fall?

Or the jump?

Does it matter?

Of course, it does.

He hated himself for being frustrated. He was terrified of losing her to confrontation. But didn't an authentic friendship need *his* authenticity? Resentment was poisonous, and even a sliver could become infected, surely.

The tired child tucked the day's new art into her thick scrapbook, teeming with glorious creation. Its art sang to him like a well-played accordion with its various, honest sounds.

My past has taken so much from me already, Dex lamented as they ended session. *Please don't let it take them, too.*

A rapid shift in the room's rhythm suddenly shook him to the present. An invisible shudder beat in his chest like an erratic drum, uncomfortable and unsettling. He winced and scanned the space in search of its disruptive cadence.

Then he noticed Alina's pale cheeks and sweating forehead. It was her heartbeat. It had grown shorter, more precious, heavy with new strain, thudding like bass beneath his bones.

A breath later, the monitors picked up on its plucky pattern, too, beckoning Rosella from the hall. She and Norah assessed hurriedly, allowing him an opportunity to back from the room.

He hastened through the winding curves and byways of the hall until he'd found an abandoned emergency door to lean against. He pressed his spine and palms against its cold steel, leaving sweaty prints. The Voices awaited him like eager cattle against a fence and tore at him with Their typical torment. Their cries were heightened, supplemented by his own acute stress.

"You're the worst and-"

"I'm done. I'm never-"

"Kill me if you're going to kill me-"

"...and no one would know-"

"Let me go, I-"

"Am I dead?"

Inaudible screaming.

Weeping.

"I don't understand-"

"Let me die, let me die, let-"

"Oh God it, burns ple-"

More screaming.

Dead silence.

"Dex?" a visceral voice spoke inches from his ear.

He jumped, his body collapsing back into itself, a mild sweat collected on his brow. He shoved his shaking hands into his pockets.

"You alright?" asked Norah, a curious sparrow considering a thundercloud. She placed a small hand on his shoulder but quickly winced and retracted it. "Shit, you're burning up, Dex."

He leaned away with a flinch. "I run hot. I'm alright though," he lied, clearing his throat as it tightened. Each piece of him felt stitched together by fraying threads, from his skin to his thoughts.

"You were both amazing." She offered a small fist bump.

He returned it with two soft jabs and an uppercut but found it difficult to manage the trembling in his fists. He hurried them to his pockets once more.

"You two do all the work. I just get to watch from outside the ring," he breathed.

"Firstly, not true, secondly, I'm going to take my break in five. Care to join me?" She threw a thumb toward the roof.

He swallowed the rising bile back down to his throat and nodded. "I could c-c-certainly use the fresh air."

19

✦NORAH✦

BY THE TIME SHE'D FINISHED BLINKING PAST THE GRAY DAYLIGHT, he was already seated high above upon one of the incinerator towers, huffing and sweating. The climb didn't seem feasible for anyone of any age, but there he sat, fidgeting and restless. They were as they had been on that dreary day they'd first met.

Norah watched emotion paint his face, only to be smeared away by his large hands. His troubled presentation prepared her to be patient while he found his words.

"Can I ask you a question?" he called down to her finally, twisting a thick cigar between his fingers that she hadn't seen him light.

"Of course."

"Did you read my file?"

Nor sat in silence a moment before allowing herself to confess.

"I did. Just before Alina's session."

Even from far below, she could feel his frustration on the wind and in the grinding fingertips buried in his scalp. He wouldn't look at her, but she stared at him intently until her eyes watered.

His cigar never ceased its dance betwixt his fingers while his tics grew. Though he was nodding and composed, she could see the deeper damage dealt. She'd done wrong by her friend.

"I s-submitted every application. Passed all s-security clearances." His posture collapsed. A slight stutter faltered his once unshakable voice.

"I know," she said. Guilt heated her neck and cheeks.

"Both my doctor and my therapist s-s-signed off on my medical history. My diagnoses," he added with a sidelong glance. That familiar lost expression poured over him. That immense uncertainty about where he belonged, or *if* he belonged at all.

"I know," Norah affirmed softly.

"They even reassessed me before I began this work, at *my* request. *I* reached out to *them*." His fear evolved into a brimming frustration he fought to conceal.

It felt easier to bear his anger. She swore she could see steam roil from his shoulders and tiny zaps of electricity bounce from his fingertips. This was better than his disappointment, which broke her heart to pieces.

"It's been over twenty years s-s-since I was discharged. And I did *s-s-so* much therapy." His eyes grew distant as he picked at his vivid memories like old scabs.

His pain and self-doubt weighed on Norah's shoulders like a leaden pack. She'd truly wounded her best and only friend. *Of course, this is what Kestrels do*, she sneered at herself. *Chase off the only people willing to deal with their shit.*

An impulse to run away kindled beneath her skin. To drink herself into catatonia until she couldn't remember what horrid things she'd done to the kindest human she'd ever known.

Though her limbs itched to flee like the child she was, she sat with the feeling and leaned into it. Because her shame would not serve Dexteras. It certainly didn't serve her mother and father. Surely not herself.

What is the opposite of what cowards do?

"Dex… I…I'm so so truly sorry. They made the request before I knew you…" she began.

"But you had the approval of s-s-several doctors, of HR," he stated. "You didn't *have* to read it. You knew if I wasn't s-s-safe, I wouldn't be here. They wouldn't have given me a job." He buried his fingers into his hair.

"I never doubted your safety Dex, not even once, I promise. It just didn't seem like you wanted to talk about the past. And then I was afraid maybe you didn't remember…."

"Those are assumptions," he said flatly, eyes bent with hurt. "And regardless, it's mine to tell. With time, I would've been honored to tell you myself. There's a lot a file can't s-s-say."

Her chin fell. Nothing justified her actions. She'd been selfish.

"You're right. I should've talked to you. That's all there is to it." She inhaled his musky cigar on the wind. "You're just… so…*different*. Different from anyone I've ever known, and I wanted to know you, to maybe help, to…"

But she stopped herself. She was pulling at the strings of her apology and its authenticity like an idiot. People were not paper. They were not their diagnoses. And she could not burden others with her own compulsion to help. She heard Marie's lovely French accent in her thoughts again. "*My life.*"

Cigar smoke swirled about his silver hair as he watched her internal tumbling.

"It's s-so easy to read a file, Nor. To make judgments," he said, gentler now. "I receive them each and every day, as you do. You can't find what makes people in ink alone." Not once did he yell, but his voice lowered and his stutter rested. "And I'm not your client," he said. "I am not your charge. I'm not yours to care for."

"You're not," she agreed. "You're my friend." The boundary was firm, but safe. Healthy.

His wise ocean eyes flooded her their loving blue.

"I wouldn't have hesitated to tell you whatever you wanted to know. I've never had a friend to talk to about it. They even said the more I talked about it, perhaps more would resurface but..." he paused and shook his head. "The flashbacks, the nightmares, whatever they are...if they're any indicator of who I was, I'm not so certain I want to know..."

"I do," she whispered, chest tight. "I want to know everything you want to share. But I wouldn't blame you if you didn't want to."

Smoke filtered through his mustache as he took a breath and considered. "I knew you'd read it by the way you looked at me. Spoke to me." A tic bent his head to his shoulder. "I've had to fight my-s-self every day to become who I am now. I don't want to be over-sh-shadowed by who I was. I don't want it to threaten my first sh-shot at friendship."

She sighed with open relief at his willingness to still call her friend. She blinked away threatening tears, realizing she hadn't quite grasped how much she loved being around Dexteras until she'd been faced with the thought of losing him.

"I promise you, nothing threatened that," said Nor. "Can I ask a question?"

He nodded.

"When they brought you in, you asked...how they could *see* you?"

"I'd scream," he nodded, spewing plumes over his shoulder. "I think I was trying to see if they'd look at me." He fell deathly still as though he were trying to pluck the fragile memories like shards from a cut.

"Why?" she whispered.

He shook his head. "I don't know, but for a long while, I thought I was a ghost. I'd wander the halls and talk to myself. I'd disrupt other patients. Ask them if I was alive or dead. Sometimes, I'd see if they could touch me. So, of course, I was sedated often for being a nuisance." He watched his twiddling fingers.

"Sometimes, I still feel all of those things," he finally admitted. "When I fell, it felt as though I'd...s-s-split open into two. Lost everything inside me."

"That's why you do this work," said Nor. "You're unseen as a translator."

He eyed her from the chimney, brows tall with her deductions. "And you, Miss Kestrel? Why do you do this work?"

She searched the horizons of his wrinkled, stormy eyes. He held her gaze longer than she'd known him to prior.

"To make people feel seen," she said. From the corner of her eye, she saw the mirage of a little girl in a black hoodie, folded on the roof, arms hugging her knees and rocking whilst she hummed. Shrill notes warbled from the girl like a baby bird abandoned in a nest. Norah blinked hard to erase the child from her vision.

"Is there anything you can remember? From the fall?" she asked, returning to him.

He rolled his neck and loosened his shoulders like wings. "Pain, bleeding, humans touching me. Fingertips and injections felt the same." He swallowed and winced.

"Does it still hurt?" she whispered against the wind. "When you're touched?" Shame twinged within for her ignorance. She'd held his arm so many times without asking for permission.

"Mmhm. Sometimes," he grumbled, somehow able to hear her quiet voice from far above. He was attempting to roll a coin across his shaking knuckles.

"What kind of pain?" She pulled her father's coin from her breast coat pocket and modeled the trick from below.

He followed her movements with his own digits, channeling some of his restlessness.

"You know when you cut your nails too short and your fingertips… ache?" he tried with a contorted expression. "Because they haven't really been touched before?"

She nodded with wide eyes, trusting the dancing coin across her bones.

"That's what it's like. All over."

"That sounds awful."

He shrugged. "We all have things to carry, *amica mea*."

"And the voices?"

The quarter fell from his hand. It fell from the heavens and clattered to the ground beside Nor with an unusual ping.

She leaned and plucked it from the gravel. The coin was hot from his fingers and unlike any other she'd seen before. It wasn't a quarter. It read *100 Francs, 1889* on one side. It felt heavy and looked like solid gold.

"Mmhm," his voice grumbled like distant thunder above.

"What do they say?" She'd had many conversations with those who'd lived with schizophrenia and hallucinations. They graciously explained how they fought to remain themselves despite the lies and uninvited clangor in their head. They taught her about surviving both quiet and terrifyingly loud days.

"For so long, I was uncertain who or what they were," he said. "It's mostly women and children, too many to understand. Always in pain. Always hurting. There's no quieting them. No reasoning." He rubbed a gaunt temple. "Auditory hallucinations is what my therapists called them."

"You're an incredibly calming and kind person despite all the chaos you know, Dex." She warmed his strange coin in her hand, praying he'd come down soon to reclaim it.

"To be fair, you're an incredibly calming person to be around." His eyes found hers with ease.

"Do you remember anything before the fall?"

"No. I just feel…a void. I can't be certain if something was taken from me…" he rubbed his brow. "Or if it's something I never had. Drives me mad like a hole in your teeth your tongue keeps running over." He inhaled a shaky breath and let it slip from his chest in plumes of cigar smoke. "I've never told anyone any of that. Ever." He graced her with a bright, sparkling eye. "I knew no one would believe me."

She searched him a moment before replying. "I believe you." It was obvious from the moment she'd met Dex that he beheld a miraculous, impossible story within himself that she was eager to hear.

Bursts of smoke scoffed from his lips. He shook his shaggy head as though she'd told a cruel joke.

"What? It's true, Dex," she snapped, irritated by his disregard for her honesty. "And I want to help," she added. "You're my friend, and I want to help."

He shook his head, brows stitched. "Nothing about what I feel makes sense, Nor. It's asinine," he muttered. "I know nothing about who I was before twenty years ago. But I want for so much, I hurt for so much. How can I miss something I've never had?" he begged.

She sat for a moment within the holy ground of the question, letting the two coins clatter and slide against one another in her palm.

"You can, you know," she called. "My parents were never there. I've never known a healthy, consistent adult, but there's still a...a pain. An ache." She had to squint to watch him through the peeking sunlight. "So, you can absolutely miss something you've never had."

White hair fanned his face and tattooed neck as he stared upon her. "What happened to you, Nor?" he asked.

She chewed on her lip, considering how she could spin such a tale within such a small, delicate moment. But she did owe him something.

"My mom and dad loved each other in the beginning, I think," she began. "Mom was never supposed to be able to have kids and Dad didn't want any, so they set out to live their dreams." Nor raised exasperated hands to the heavens. "I didn't get the memo though. She got pregnant and there I was."

His lips curled beneath his twitching mustache. "So you're a miracle."

"Mom thought so. But Dad never saw it that way." She looked to the concrete now. "I made them *loathe* each other. He drank. She drank. He'd cheat on her. She'd drink more. He gambled. She did pills, drugs, anything to unfeel what he did." Her spinning quarter had resumed along her knuckles.

"They'd scream, hit each other. I can still hear the yelling. It was..." She shoved her fingers through her hair until they braced at her neck. She squeezed there at the painful muscles that kept her skull affixed.

If anger was a time of day, it was late evening when Leonard Kestrel shouldered through the front door, stumbling and clumsy. Anger was stale cigarette smoke and watered-down whiskey glasses, bits of ice clinking. It was rum-rich *tsks* on tongues. If anger was a storm, it was the distant thunder of slamming cabinets and clanging dishes.

And when fire began to spit, and voices began to swell, Norah had to take cover or else be consumed.

"That must've torn the world into pieces, Nor," said Dex, interrupting her thoughts.

She stared up at him, having never heard trauma breathed so poetically.

"Watching them lose each other was worse than her cancer. Worse than the fire."

"The fire?" His brows bent.

Nor attempted to shake the hot prickling salt in her eyes. *How did he not know about the fire? Everyone knew about the fire…*

She wasn't ready for this.

It was too much.

She shook her head again and again.

She'd never had a chance to tell the story aloud. *They all knew, so why bother?* She wiped her sweaty hands down her pants, remembering the locked door she couldn't enter. The key around her neck, sweaty and stuck to her stomach.

"Your story is a gift to give to others only when you're ready," he said, holding her with doleful consideration. "You're a decorated soldier of life, and I'm honored by whatever you share with me." He pulled on his tobacco with a confident nod. "I'd follow you into battle, blindfolded."

She sputtered up at him with tear-stricken chuckles. She'd never met anyone who could match her skills of metaphorical conversation. It made their vulnerable conversation burn in her chest like good whiskey.

"Was Corvid always your home?" she called into the clouds.

"No one could find anything on me that day. No paperwork. No family. Very much like Alina." He sighed. "I don't even have a last name." He held his cigar, tapping his fingertips against the burning ember, daring it to bite him.

"You're kind and gentle and doing important work right now," declared

Norah. "And I know those aren't the pieces you're missing, but it's what I see. It's what's important." She hated how it'd spilled from her lips. It didn't translate how she'd intended it to. She was simply chasing the selfish impulse to understand him and help him understand himself. But she realized all too late that she'd minimized his past, his pain.

Dex shook his head, eyes contorted in hurt, brows buckled. "But what if I really hurt people in the past? Or worse?" The lost boy in his voice grew defensive and fearful once more.

"Dex that-"

"Depression, Cotard's, Agoraphobia, PTSD. That's an awful lot to be wrong with someone." His frustration rose but she didn't recoil.

"Those are diagnoses Dex. You said it yourself, your truth is not in ink alone."

To her horror, Dexteras stood and hopped from the immense height with a groan, touching down with a mighty hand to the cement like a deity from the heavens.

Nor forced her mouth shut. She was obviously going to have to get used to impossible things if she was going to survive this day and this man.

"You read about the sorts of things I said and believed when they found me," he mourned. "What kind of monster must I have been?" he raised his tired bones to the skies. "It's evident that I was terrified of *myself*."

He approached nearer, eyes wide and watering. Norah swore she could feel an electric, tickling life against the hairs on her arms, as though he were approaching lightning.

"I hear voices that scream and weep. I still feel like my skin doesn't fit. I have anger and unworthiness that doesn't belong anywhere, and honestly, I don't feel that I belong anywhere." He was toe to toe with her now, eyes sad and upset, jaw grinding.

Norah dared not flinch or blink on the shore of his brewing mood, his internal storm.

"And it's *not* just ink. All of it is within me. Presently. Today. Right now." He was tall and towering before her, blue eyes pacing her with heavy-lidded wariness. His white mane draped his face, shrouding his features as the wind whipped and blew. She could almost hear his desperate clawing against the bars of his composure, teeth clashing, eyes watering. His breaking beckoned a memory to her consciousness:

She sat before Professor Everett Scop in his tiny office, surrounded by counseling books and viny plants. He was a narrow man with narrow spectacles and heavy bags beneath his eyes.

He was full of childlike wonder and adult pains. He stepped carefully between both worlds, making him an enriching instructor for young therapists. This day, he was inquiring about her poor attendance and the light that seemed to flicker out of her each day.

"Mom is dying..." Young Norah rubbed her dead father's coin between her fingers. "I was just given POA in case..." Her molars scraped in her skull with a whine. She shrugged. "It doesn't matter."

"What about your friends?" he asked.

"They don't know what to say. I've been bringing them down, making them feel bad. It's not their fault. They haven't been through this shit. I can't hurt them too..."

"What are you feeling, Norah?" His thin features wrinkled at her lovingly.

"If she gets sicker, I'll have to go home. To care for her. Again. And if I go back to that house, I don't think I'll escape this time. I don't think I'll make it out alive."

Scop had a way of allowing the silence to sit without threat. It took a seat between them until he found the words. Then, he asked the most powerful question that had ever graced Nor's Brokenness. It was the same question she brought to Dex now:

"How have you survived all of this?" she whispered, looking up into the timeworn storm of his shining eyes. She hoped he knew that it wasn't an inquiry of the fall that should've killed him, but an ode to his mental and emotional resilience. The love and kindness that'd somehow breathed within him.

Dex huffed. His red eyes were interrupted with blinks. It seemed as though he'd been ready for battle, but Norah sent his defenses home. She was relieved to see the puffed wind in his chest decompress.

His voice broke as it left him. "I don't know that I have, Nor."

"I don't think I did," echoed Norah Kestrel from so very long ago in her professor's office.

Dex's jawbones rolled and shifted, biting back something that trembled his chin. He looked down at her, blinking against wind and salt.

She made a gesture to touch his shoulder, and when he nodded in consent, she pulled him into an embrace. She'd read that hugs were most therapeutic at twenty seconds or more and thus counted as her head rose and fell against his chest.

Hot, silent tears soaked her shoulder. His limbs tensed. He wriggled with discomfort as though confined to a cocoon he'd outgrown.

"You're worthy to be touched and heard and seen, Dex. You're here. You're here now, and that's all that matters."

And finally, he broke. He wept and quivered and clutched to her as though drowning. Knees buckling, they sank to the ground, where his pieces could fall apart.

20

✦DEXTERAS✦

HIS BONES TWISTED AND TURNED to make sense of Norah Kestrel's embrace. His body didn't feel as though it could've ever possibly conformed to another. But her hold was firm and confident and kind and his unwieldiness seemed to melt away with each breath. The threads of his armor frayed apart and fell away, leaving his full ugly self, vulnerable and exposed.

But he was safe.

He could not remember the last time he'd been touched. Humanely touched.

He'd certainly never been hugged before. It would've broken through the thick blotches of amnesia if it'd felt anything like this. He'd never guessed prior, but it seemed human arms really were built to embrace one another.

He dove through waves of shame and peace and nothingness in his friend's arms. Meanwhile, she dirtied her coat and dress clothes patiently.

"It's exhausting work, Dex," Norah said in his ear. "Digging to find people beneath all of their hurt. You have to be gentle. Patient. Gracious," she muttered. "But it's even more exhausting when you haven't done any of that for yourself."

He held his breath, sensing a question.

"Why do you force yourself to give so much when you're still hurting?"

He wiped his eyes with a moan and released the young woman. He sat properly to face her, elbows draped across his knees, hands scraping his tear-soaked beard. His chest was lighter as though it once bore a silo of tears within him, now relinquished.

"Giving is all I've known."

"You're worthy of receiving," she said plainly, without doubt nor question.

He sought her through his locks of unruly hair, grungy and unsightly. His gaze narrowed and fell to her palm. The scar there hummed with the residue of an orchestra in a great theater, rising to the balconies upon the wings of a finale.

He leaned back against the brick smokestack and rested his swimming thoughts. He pulled on another cigar he couldn't recall igniting. *God, that's good.* His eyes rolled back into his head. His tears had cleansed a fog from his mind, and he could now ingest the world anew with youthful clarity. He spilled smoke over his shoulder and rested his skull.

✦

She stated that she'd wait for him in the front lobby so they could walk home together after session. He wasn't certain why she still bothered with the likes of him after such a horrid unfolding that afternoon.

"So, did you learn all those languages after the accident?" she asked, gait reaching to remain beside him as they walked.

He slowed, tic triggered at the word "accident."

"I'd hear a language and it would just come back to me in waves. It's so strange…." He attempted to decipher the phenomenon. "It's like when you find yourself singing the lyrics to a song you didn't know you remembered." He eyed her with caution at this confession. It wasn't normal to forget languages like song lyrics.

But she was smiling.

Despite his chaos, he was normal when he was around Norah.

Around Norah Kestrel, he heard no screams, no cries of mercy from The Voices. Even on the day they'd met, he'd gawked at the precious calm she carried with her, like her own quiet atmosphere he was permitted to stoop beneath. An umbrella of sacred silence. And then, when she'd drift from him, the Crowd in his cortex would intensify as though someone were tampering with the volume dial in his head.

Uncertain of how to discuss this impossible happening, he deferred to something more human in his panic.

"Found any nice folks to date in this small town then?" Instantly, his gut dropped for the imposing question. *You're horrid at being human, old dog.*

Norah blinked, brain clearly attempting to keep up with his disjointed thoughts. But after a moment, she laughed.

"I've dated here and there. The bar scene gets old. The online scene gets old. But I'm getting old too."

A scoff burst from his lips. "Love, you've heaps of time. If you're looking for forever, it deserves your patience and particularity."

She giggled, having surely heard such advice from deranged old men such as himself before.

"And what if I *did* find someone, then? You gonna wait on the porch with a shotgun?" she jibed with a grin, poking him with her elbow.

Heat rose to his cheeks. He couldn't deny the protective growl that rose to his throat when others eyed Norah with ill intention. She couldn't hear how their heartbeats quickened with her approach. She couldn't feel how their souls' songs jutted to crescendo with desire.

"I don't need a gun," he replied. He hadn't even considered the words before they left him.

Her brows lifted with his threats for future suitors. "Is that so?" she laughed, teeth shining. "What's your weapon of choice?"

Still giddy from his mental cleanse on the roof, he tossed a few jabs into the airspace ahead of them, shadowboxing with theatrical gusto into the wind.

His friend laughed and hollered at his spine with shrill woos.

He could take on all of his darkest demons with Norah Kestrel cheering him on. He could recover from any woe with her loving words, like hand-written letters. Any of his fires could be put out with her cooling calm at his side.

The flow of uppercuts drew hisses from his teeth. *Elbows down and tight,* said a nameless voice in his head. His abdomen tensed. He pivoted into his hips with each hook. His limbs sharpened with youthful fire and fell into a rhythm. In seconds, his lackadaisical show had morphed into a complicated strike combo.

Norah's feet scraped to a halt behind him to watch him dance. "Hot damn, where the hell did all of *that* come from?" she exclaimed.

He laughed into the evening and pushed off his rear foot, dancing with an invisible opponent in the falling evening. His traipse was silly, but it grew more earnest with each swing. His fists tightened against his jawline. His momentum collected and each maneuver was scheduled and intentional. Like Ecclesiastical Latin on his lips, effortless and fluid. A euphoric heat rose within his chest.

And then, his ears began to ring.

Darkness collapsed his peripheral vision. Only a pinhole-sized window remained.

His blood ran cold. He could barely see. His limbs felt a million miles away, swimming and numb.

Then, a shadowy figure assimilated in the path before them. A seductive silhouette he'd sworn he'd seen in his nightmares. Bright eyes flashed gold. Adrenaline gushed in his chest.

His vision was almost entirely gone now, but there was still this ominous creature threatening his friend. He pressed his drunken legs forward.

Jab-cross.

He danced forward without fear, only thinking of protecting the young woman behind him.

Jab-jab.

The ambiguous shadow remained stone still, narrow like a snake with razor-sharp shoulders. Rolling curves. A sable fitted suit. A shock of black hair. Pale skin. Medallion eyes.

Though his will was wild and awake, his body felt amoebic and nauseous, unattached.

And then, the shadow dove for him. *Through* him. The screeching in his ears hit a blinding pitch.

He attempted to make himself taller, wider, menacing like a cobra in order to protect Norah. But each inch of him was impossibly heavy, miles-deep, under weighty black waves of water. He was sinking, sinking, sinking.

Dex.

*Norah, h*e tried to speak but nothing came. He couldn't feel his fingers but willed them to reach for her.

Dex.

"Dexteras!"

He tore open his eyes. The low yet painful sunlight flooded his retinas, and he winced.

"Nor?" he grumbled. She was above him, angelic face recovering from stricken worry.

The aura of a migraine lingered. The ringing subsided. He was on his knees, torso limp and resting against an old brick building. Familiarity refilled his limbs, but they shook with weakness.

"H-How long was I out?" His eyes scanned the scene in search of the looming entity, but of course, it was gone.

She shook her head, features smooth with calm. "Just a minute. It was a quick round."

"D-Did I hurt you?" His stomach lurched at the thought.

"Of course not. You couldn't handle this." She winked with a flex.

He buried the heel of his hand into his forehead.

Nor waved off a couple of passersby who'd offered help. He felt awful for embarrassing her. His cheeks flooded with blood.

She extended both hands to him, smiling as though unashamed by his feebleness.

"Flashback?" she guessed.

Her cool fingers made his hand tingle with reawakened blood as she returned him to his feet.

"That… hasn't happened in a long time." He recalled the weeks of vivid hallucinations he'd once endured decades ago and shivered.

Clumsily, they resumed their journey as though nothing had happened. In the silence, he took several moments to gather himself and his thoughts.

Slowly, his building rose from the concrete horizon ahead.

"For the record, I know you could kick anyone's ass if need be," said Nor at his side.

His head fell, and inward pride gushed into his chest. *You don't deserve her grace, you dead dog.*

"You're stronger than anyone I've ever known, Nor. I know you can handle yourself." He dried his clammy hands down his pants. "But I hope you know, if you ever wanted help, you need only ask. I'd be there in an instant." He prayed he wasn't overstepping.

"You'd be the first to know," she leaned into his shoulder.

Unfamiliar joy warmed him at the gesture. It didn't make sense why someone would ever *want* to touch him. But when Nor did, he felt human. He felt real.

"And to answer your question…" she said casually, "I've dated." She shrugged. "But I always came up feeling empty. I realized the problem was me all along. I needed to grow into myself before I could share myself with anyone else. So that's what I've been doing." She kicked at a root that'd broken through the sidewalk. "And it's working out. I really think I'm the one."

He laughed, grateful for the distance from his episode. "For the right person, you will mean the entire world, Nor. But I'm proud of you for your inward work." He had no recollection of dating or intimacy post or pre-head trauma, but nonetheless he was elated to embark on these foreign topics with his friend.

His smile faded as they shuffled to a stop in front of his apartment. "This is me."

As their gazes rose to The Aviary's peak, Dexteras swore he could hear Norah's lips counting.

"Dex..." she whispered. "Your file, it said you'd fallen from over twelve stories."

He sighed, dropping his chin. "I know." His apartment complex also happened to be twelve stories high and served as a measuring stick to his impossible existence. He, too, couldn't comprehend how he'd survived. No one did. And yet here he stood.

His eyes glared at the asphalt ahead. He could still hear the impact, the crunch of splintering bones. He could feel the screams gargling from his throat. Blood painted the sidewalk everywhere.

God, there was so much blood.

He shifted, feeling as though his flesh were a poorly tailored suit. His joints ached, feeling too small for their sockets. His fingers twisted at a leather bracelet on his wrist. He closed his eyes in hopes to calm the twitching in his eyelid.

Norah leaned into him. He opened his eyes and looked upon her.

"You're here," she reminded simply.

Norah was safe and trustworthy and wore her emotions in earnest. Her lips didn't whisper of him to others. Her heart didn't quicken at his nearness. Norah Kestrel somehow reminded him of home when he didn't even have one.

I'm not a ghost.

I'm not dead.

She sees me.

It was stunning how lonely he could feel in a world full of people. But even more so, how one individual could make him feel like the center of the world itself.

"Can I see your place?" she chirped.

He looked about the sky. "It's nearing nightfall, love. I'd feel better if you got home while you had light to guide you. But another day, I promise."

She rushed him into a hug, forehead in his chest.

He sighed and squeezed her, already fearful of how ruthlessly The Voices would grate at him once she rounded the corner. Her cold wrapped him tightly like a planetary ring. If he could orbit Norah Kestrel for a lifetime, he'd be endlessly happy.

"Night, friend," he called as he stepped through the entryway gate.

"Night Dex."

21

⋅NORAH⋅

DEX WAS HAVING HIS ANNUAL BONE SCANS COMPLETED for his severe osteoarthritis, though Nor hadn't observed his limp for some time. She offered her company, and he gratefully accepted. Thus, they sat together upon a starchy hospital bed, sharing robust cups of coffee.

Much to his chagrin, he was cloaked in traditional hospital garb: rubber-soled socks and a stiff gown. The drab, tea-bag material billowed to his shins and braced across his large chest and shoulders. It bound at the old man's spine, which shivered occasionally.

Nor couldn't help but allow her eyes to study the tattoos that danced across his bare legs and arms. Some of the ink had blown out beneath his papery skin but was still detailed and breathtaking. She knew Corvid's lone tattoo shop well, and she couldn't match any of their illustrative styles to Dex's neotraditional lines and work.

His inked stories were usually hidden by layers of fine button-down shirts, tailored blazers, leather suspenders, and brass-buckle boots. And while his accessories were stunning nods to fashion, his skin was the true work of art.

"What does *fluctuat nec mergitur* mean?" she asked with a clumsy tongue, eyeing a large anchor at the base of his throat. It was wrapped in a paper scroll bearing the dead language.

His legs ceased their tapping with consideration.

"*Fluctuat nec mergitur* is Latin," he said, rolling the fascinating language across his teeth with ease. "Means 'tossed by the waves, but does not sink.'" He dropped his chin to her with a curious brow. "Why do you ask?"

She huffed a chuckle and poked at his throat.

"Ah." His limbs resumed their dance.

"You might learn something about yourself if you looked into these," she said gently.

"Perhaps."

"Do you avoid looking at yourself?"

An amused huff hissed through his nose.

"Is it because you don't like what you see?" she persisted shamelessly.

"They're permanent and mysterious, like my past. I'm afraid of looking for fear of what I'll find and cannot change. But no, I also don't like what I see in general." He swallowed and stifled a slight tic in his cheek.

"I do," she said.

"Well, that makes one of us, *amica mea.*"

Depicted in a neat, uniform row at the peak of his right bicep were detailed tattoos akin to military medals. The first was a pair of tattooed wings around a red thorny rose, the second was a gold shield topped by a red-bellied bird, and the last was a screaming hawk bird of sorts, clutching a sword in its talons. Each was illustrated to look gilded and precious, meant for honorary recognition of some sort.

"Dex, I think you might be a veteran." She poked at the inked epaulet. "These look a lot like the war tattoos some of my veteran clients have," she added.

He shook his head, uninterested. "No valor in my battles, love. Nothing to show for but scars and distorted bones." He kicked out a creaky leg.

"You're here today, and that's plenty to show for it," she retorted, still scrutinizing his tattoos.

He stuck out an elbow to better see the ink for himself but decidedly sighed and dropped it to his side.

"You must have done something impressive. I think I need to thank you for your service." She sought his fallen eyes with earnest respect.

He gave a sarcastic snort and downed the remainder of his coffee. Droplets flecked his mustache.

"I'm serious, Dex. These have to be war medals."

"I believe you, Nor," his jaw ground as he stared into his empty cup. "But we don't know what I fought for."

"I'm sure you fought for what you felt was right."

A faint tic clenched at the corner of his eye, brows contorted. *He truly believed he was a horrid person before the accident.*

Then, a portly Dr. Downy strode through the curtain and interrupted their conversation without so much as a knock on the doorframe. The owlish man gawked with puzzlement at Norah.

"Kestrel? Didn't see you on the chart," he said, hurriedly tapping at his laptop.

"I'm here for the coffee and the company," she said simply, raising her cup.

"She's my emotional support person Doc," clarified Dex. "What's the prognosis?"

The doctor spun his screen to reveal several digital images of Dexteras' contorted bones and calcified joints. He pointed to weak binds, vulnerable muscles, and compromised tendons. He shrugged at the marring scar tissue.

"I'd typically say at this point that we need to be resting, planning vacations, taking up quiet hobbies, things of the like." He began, pulling back his screen and typing on his charts. "We've seen you through a lot here, Dex. Your body has endured hell and back."

Norah crossed her arms, biting her tongue until salt filled her mouth.

Though he looked burly and ruthless, Dex was sensitive and gentle through and through. He was soft-spoken, analytical, and observant. He experienced moments with sharp inspection, even when it was most painful. She'd hoped her hospital's staff was capable of more empathetic delivery and bedside manner.

Dex remained silent, dissociating into the laminate.

"So what does that mean?" Nor prompted.

Downy ignored her and turned his screen to reveal another round of uploaded scans. These looked quite different, shining with more white, unblemished light. The shapes were bold, their shadows less steep, the ligaments untouched and young.

"Had we still been showing those results, it *would've* meant a lifetime of pain meds until Dex ran himself into the ground. But our newest scans are…extraordinary." He stared in awe at the screen, slapping his hands on his thighs.

"These joints look *years* before their time. I can see signs of old scar tissue…" he traced some graying slivers of light. "But overall, these bones are nearly good as new." The doctor scratched his head with high, thick brows. "I've shown these scans to multiple doctors on the floor, and they're stunned. A medical anomaly."

Norah began to smile, but as she turned to Dex, her expression crashed with sobering worry.

The old man remained silent, hands massaging his knees. He only managed a drop of his head in comprehension.

"I've got decades of bone scans from you, Dex, and these are the first that proves not just deep, resilient healing but *atypical* regrowth." The doctor shook his head, unable to tear his eyes from the ligaments on his monitor. "It's…impossible, but here we are. You're a miracle."

Dex nodded again, but his eyes were not on the doctor nor his extraordinary scans. His gaze was glossy-eyed and distant on the laminate floor.

"We have studies here you could really help us with. Clearly, there's something at your cellular level capable of unnatural, inhuman growth. It's unlike anything we've ever seen."

Norah winced with his word choice but kept her stare locked on Dex. Still, he remained silent, drifting into catatonia. They'd lost him to his thoughts. His neck flexed with a deep tic, bending his ear to his shoulder.

She leaned into him softly, but he didn't respond.

"I think he's okay for now, doc, but he'll get back to you," she muttered, watching her friend with concern.

But Downy was persistent, craning his thick neck in search of Dex's attention.

"Dex? You could be quite resourceful in our studies. You could save other people with this information."

Her friend's eyes fluttered with blinks, evidently overloaded. His lips parted, but nothing spilled from them.

"We'll discuss it another time," said Norah, much firmer this time. Her voice hit the walls hard. *Could he not see Dex was overwhelmed?*

Downy cut her with a challenging glare. "These results are unheard of, Dexteras, you-"

Norah smiled and stood between Dex and his doctor, teeth bared and chin tall.

"He heard you, Eric, but we're done here for today."

✦

As Dexteras changed back into his proper clothes, Norah retreated to her staff kitchenette. She dug through the filthy depths of its refrigerator and dragged forth a small canvas cooler, heavy with treasure.

She returned to find him in the dark lobby, waiting in silence, chin settled in his hands. She guessed his mind was on fire with anomalous prognosis and exceptional morality.

Nor gave a beckoning nod, and he followed her drearily to her old truck.

He's scared.

They headed westward of town up a gently sloping back road. After several miles, she hooked a sharp hairpin onto a gravel drive that dissolved into dirt and heavy tree lines. The path was barely wide enough for her squatty vehicle.

After several grumbling turns and narrow passes through the thicket, they came to a rusty chain draped between two massive cedars. A rusty tin sign hung at its center, *Private Drive, All Trespassers Will Be Shot.* A crusty padlock secured the barricade.

She threw the car into park and plucked the lock's suitor from her mound of tinkling keys. She hopped out, set the chains free, and tossed them to either side of the road.

She jumped behind the wheel once more and gave him a devious grin.

"Should I ask?" he muttered.

"Always," she called over the groaning axles that tore through the hill.

"Whose land is this?"

"My Papa's, Rufous Starling. He bought it with the hopes of reselling it. Nice lumber trees."

"Why didn't he?" Dex called.

The little, vintage truck bounded over the final hill, leaving them atop a bald plateau. She backed into a tight clearing, seemingly carved for them.

"Come see." She stepped onto the dusty earth and popped the tailgate.

Dex approached a small opening through the trees to reveal an overlook. It poured across Corvid, painting the small town in fresh glory. Miles above, Dex watched the horizon until the unzipping of a cooler stirred his focus.

"What's this?" he asked.

"First-aid kit. For days like this."

"Like this?"

"Shitty days. Full-moon days. Days you don't want to go home."

"You have those often?" he mused sadly, sitting beside her on the tailgate.

"Sometimes. But the other staff use it too. Rule is, if you use it, you refill it."

Nor unpacked a case of amber beer, a bar of dark chocolate, and a pack of cigarillos. She inspected it all with consideration, nodding at their wealth. She broke two cans free, cracked them open, and handed one to Dex.

They held up their drinks to toast.

"To more bottles in front of me than frontal lobotomies," she sang to the sky.

He sputtered and cackled as he sipped the dark ale.

They drank their beer and smoked their cigars, swinging their legs and taking in the twinkling lights of Corvid. Dare she call the town *bearable*, at this height? Her shoulders sagged, and her feet hung limp as she considered the faces of clients and family below, living and dead. She thought of her father's scattered cremated remains in the wind here. Of her mother, wheezing with the aid of countless machines, just floors above her office. This image, above all others, made her nauseous.

She hadn't always avoided the woman dying above her head. She'd tried to visit.

Once.

Just once. Years ago.

Nor had smoked an old crusty blunt from her mother's stash at home on an idle Tuesday and had drank far too much of her father's whiskey. Around eleven in the evening, she'd gone for a walk through the fields. At the fence line, she was so disconnected from her swimming skull and wobbling limbs, that she clambered over the splintering wood and kept walking.

Hours later, she was swaying on the threshold of her mother's hospital room, fists clenching and unclenching. She had no idea how she'd tottered past the night shift nurses and the hospital's watchful security officers. She only knew her badge was swinging from her fingers.

The sleeping Robin Kestrel was unrecognizable to her inebriated daughter, whose watering eyes burned into the frail woman. Robin wasn't old, but the atrophy of a hospital bed made her look decrepit. Her blonde hair was thin, and her wrinkles were deep. Medical bracelets lined her wrists, and cords threaded her arms. Watercolor smears of blue and purple bruised her flesh. Gaunt, shadowy patches deepened her cheeks, collarbones, neck, and the tiny divots of her finger bones. The once gorgeous and rosy Robin Kestrel was little more than ruddy veins and rice paper flesh.

CLACK.

The ID badge and its lanyard slipped from Nor's hand and smacked the floor.

Robin startled, her wrinkled eyelids lifting until her glassy blue eyes fell on her daughter. Robin's lips remained a thin, colorless line. Massive, heaving swells of the woman's sunken chest made up each of her monumental breaths.

They stared, faces still, breath held. Neither said a word and neither moved aside from the younger Kestrel's drunken swaying in the hall.

Looking back, Norah knew her ignorant, childish, self craved an apology. She wanted to be told that she could scream and cry and feel all the bullshit she never got to feel as a child from within the grip of her mother's spindly arms. She wanted to be clung to.

But Robin only stared with icy blue eyes, cold and steady. Norah heard the woman's heart monitor increase as moments passed.

And when it was evident that neither had anything to offer the other, Norah tore her feet from the laminate, scooped up her badge, and tripped home alone in the dark.

"Fuck, I hate it here," Nor muttered, returning to her present body in the bed of her truck with Dex.

He gave a half smile and dropped his head. "It is dark and isolating, at times."

"It's cursed," she corrected. "Cold and damned and nasty," she added, considering Corvid's cancerous rumors and ignorance.

The embering tip of his cigar crackled as he inhaled. He hastened it from his lips to say, "Mmm." He nodded, eyes tired and understanding. "Everyone's got a bit of that inside of them at times. We're all broken.," he said, smiling at her.

"You're so fucking nice," she said, burping and opening another beer. "Tell me something you don't want to tell me. Something that doesn't sound kind."

He fiddled with the tab on his beer and swallowed, smiling a moment before his face fell.

"It is-s-s frustrating enough to not understand my past...they called that impossible too. But now *I'm* impossible as I am. Inhuman." He shook his head. "It feels like there's never enough of me to make a whole, normal, functioning person."

She winced at Downy's ugly verbiage. "He was an ass for speaking to you that way. I don't know who teaches these bastards to treat patients like that."

"We cannot teach people anything," quoted Dex, shrugging his large shoulders until bones crackled like dry twigs. "We can only help them discover it within themselves." He stared into the peeking stars with reverence. He rubbed at his forehead, tight with stress and then yanked the elastic from his tied hair, releasing the great mane to shadow his fallen features.

Nor spat into the woods, noticing the stale cigar souring her tongue. "Who said that?"

"Galileo," said Dex.

She hugged her knees to her chest and nodded, agreeing with the wise stargazer.

"You're a whole person, Dex. And you're here with me now," she offered.

Small puffs of smoke escaped from his lips as he spoke. "This was the kindest thing anyone's ever done for me, *mellis*. Thank you." He blinked tired, watering eyes down at her.

She leaned into his large bicep. "It's what friends do."

22

·DEXTERAS·

His head ached from fixating on his impossible body and the awakened appetite for knowledge about who and what he was. That hunger had been dormant for decades, yet back it crept beneath his skin.

He flexed his knuckles as he walked, pushing blood and pain into each ancient scar and reset bone. The pain reminded him of all the stories that were missing from his head.

Dex?

He closed his eyes, hoping to stave off The Voices.

"Dex?"

He shuddered to the present to find Norah's worrying gaze on him.

"S-sorry, love."

"Stop apologizing. I just wanted to know what you're getting into tonight?"

Somehow, they's already arrived at his apartment. He scowled at its peak with dread.

"You're worried I'll brood?"

Her deep bottle green eyes swallowed him. "It's just when I tend to brood, it never ends well."

He drank in her compassion, enamored by her tenderness amidst her own hurt. The shriveled scar on her palm whistled to him, like the fragile singing of fingertips across a crystal wine glass.

"I'll try to stay busy. Make coffee. Read a book or two." Sleep never came for him, so he could finish a couple novels within a restless evening. "You can't fight my fights, but you being here today meant the world." He offered a steady fist bump, to which she complied with a round of jabs against his damaged knuckles.

"Get home. Sun is falling," he said, glaring at the rolling storm clouds.

He watched her disappear over the horizon before retreating to his roof. He collapsed at its edge and attempted to slip into a dissociation beneath the dimming sky.

But eventually, The Voices crept in, hastily shredding his peace.

"I think I'm dead, you know? I think I'm all-"

"This is never going to be over for any of us-"

"I just want him back, I need to find-"

"I could end it all so fast. It could all be over like that."

Dappled smatterings of blues and violets bruised the twilight, flecked with white electric stars that crept up the horizon. The sky breathed with life like fireflies in the dark.

Despite his peace within the galaxies, his skin prickled, and his hair stood on end. Unsettling nausea drummed in his stomach. It was the feeling of *something* pursuing him. A song he'd never heard prior bit at his heels. A salty, sulfuric storm bristled in his nose. There was a tension in the air unrelated to the weather and the barometric pressure.

And somehow, deep in his aching bones, he knew it was coming for him.

23

⁺NORAH⁺

HER SHOULDERS AND NECK SNARLED with sore muscles as she unfolded from her father's armchair and made morning coffee at home. She pulled on a chunky, white cable-knit sweater and black leggings before commuting to the hospital. She hoped Dex had found some semblance of peace throughout his evening.

According to Rosella, he paced the halls until Nor arrived each morning. Dependable as hellfire, and earlier than Corvid's songbirds, he waited to greet her each day. At the sight of her, his face lit up like the sun, and he'd greet her with a playful fist bump.

But this morning, he was not here.

She recalled his worn face just several hours prior, how it drowned in storms and rumination. But she'd left him in a weary state many days before, and still, he showed.

He always showed.

A dread built in her chest, and an anxiety itched at the back of her skull.

But there was still a job to do.

So this morning, for the first time in months, Norah commuted to her office in solace.

Upon arrival, she pulled a small package from her desk drawer and tore it open with newfound excitement. It revealed a tray of colorful plastic beads glimmering beneath the yellow office lights. They were emblazoned with tiny letters much like the ones she'd strung into bracelet as a child, but these were Ukrainian characters. A sleepless night of internet browsing had brought her to these beauties, and she couldn't help but drop the small fortune in shipping for them.

Nor buried her fingers into the glittering pool like an eager magpie seeking prizes. They tumbled from her skin like gemstones. She hoped Alina would find some joy, some temporary escape within them. She tucked the rattling package into her bag and sipped her coffee, eyeing the ticking clock on the wall. She waited.

But with each passing minute, her worry swelled, hearing nothing from Dexteras Doe.

He was never late. He was always there when he was needed.

She poked around the nurse's stations and a multitude of other hospital nooks and crannies. None had seen hide nor hair of him. Though she knew he rarely carried his damned phone, she sent a text:

Hey friend. I'm going to go ahead and begin our session with AH.
Hope you're alright and resting. Let me know if I can bring you anything.

But the child behind the curtain today was not the same they'd left at their previous session.

Alina was sleeping, mouth agape, head propped on multiple pillows. Hoarse breath wheezed from her chapped lips, accompanied by the choir of monitors behind her. A fresh waste bin sat beside the bed. Alina's pallor made it evident the precaution was merited. Her almond skin was papery and taut.

Her arm was draped around a large stuffed lion. A lioness, to be precise. It wore a blue ribbon and a hand-written paper tag. Nor crept close to decipher the flawless Ukrainian script.

Dex.

She began to ponder how the old man had slipped in when the floor was closed to visitors after hours, but then remembered his wrinkled, handsome grin. It could sweet-talk him anywhere he so cared to be with his sheepish shrug and scarlet cheeks.

The therapist took a seat and tapped across the keys of her translator app to interpret the animal's note. She poked at matching characters until she had it:

Alina, my light,

You are so loved. Thank you for teaching me to be strong. Thank you for helping me meet my best friend, your fellow lioness. We are so proud of you.

Yours,

Dex.

Nor sniffed and wiped her eyes.

This stirred the child awake with dreary squints and reddened pupils, blinking at the sight of Norah. Her fingers waved a feeble hello like a newborn bird's wing.

"Dex?" the child croaked, fingers clutching her throat tenderly.

With animated gestures, Norah mimed him sleeping and snoring.

Alina laughed with crackling coughs.

The therapist unveiled her bracelet-making supplies onto the bed and was delighted when Alina squeaked with joy at the sight of them.

Alina sifted through the trays and dropped letters into Norah's hand, who strung them obediently. Candy-colored pieces and snippets of cord scattered the bed until Alina had crafted five bracelets with unique words and color schemes. She pointed to them one-by-one, dedicating each to a member of her med team.

The tired girl plucked a dainty baby blue one from the pile made of ombré shades and clear beads filled with gold glitter. She rolled the bracelet onto Norah's wrist, leaving the therapist to gasp with honor. In Ukrainian, it spelled a word she knew all too well:

Lioness.

Nor thanked the small human profusely and squeezed her into a tight hug, petting the dark strands of her shining new wig, auburn with hot pink highlights, braided down her tiny shoulder.

Alina then extended another, larger bracelet made of deep, blue twilight tones and beaded silver stars. The Ukrainian word upon this one was much longer and unknown to Nor, but she twisted it beneath her fingers and admired its craftsmanship.

"Dex," whispered Alina, voice growing scarce and meager.

Obviously, Dex would arrive before their session was over. At any moment, he'd burst through the curtain, breathless and beaming. The therapist attempted to encourage the small girl to give it to him in person, but she refused and pressed it back into Norah's hands.

"Dex."

Finally, the young woman nodded and stretched the bracelet on her wrist for safekeeping where its beads rattled against her own.

Further procedures were scheduled for the afternoon, and Nor had the sinking suspicion they would slip Alina into a catatonia for some time. Even now, the sweet child wilted in and out of sleep, hands clutching rainbow letters and shapes as her chin lolled.

Norah showered her in every compliment and word of praise she could recall Dexteras reciting. She held Alina tightly again and petted her hair and yellow lioness cub. And though she managed a final, hummingbird wave goodbye on her way out, Alina Holub was asleep with heavy breaths before Nor had brushed through her curtain.

Throughout the day's remaining moments, Norah glanced persistently at her phone. By shift's end, her disappointment had bubbled over into fear. She fidgeted with the handmade bracelets on her wrist, brain afire with untamed thoughts. She obsessed with thoughts of Dexteras and all that could've happened to him. She knew that panic roared on the horizon of her headspace like a choppy storm.

Along her walk home, she approached his front gate and fluttered her fingers across the ancient call-box buttons. She pushed against *7B*. The button fought her stiffly as though no one had ever selected it before, aged by loneliness just like Dexteras.

No response.

"What-ifs" laced her brain with crippling unease. She couldn't navigate them quickly enough to satiate each catastrophe with answers.

Is he dead?

Is he depressed?

Did he have a PTSD episode?

Once home, she couldn't eat for fear that the tight knot in her gut may send anything back up. She thrice confirmed the room at the top of her stairs was locked. The stubby key smacked at her stomach whilst she gave a blunt kick to the doorframe and paced the house. She and Vincent slept on the sofa. Adrenaline and cortisol left her evening disturbed and littered with nightmares.

✦

The following morning, she tried his door and called his phone, but each attempt left her heart heavy. Abandonment seeped like acid beneath the doorway of her composure. It was an old, old enemy whose poison dripped into her blood like an IV.

She tapped at her work email to find an addendum on Alina's chart disclosing suspicions of bacterial infection. Defenses were doubled, and the child was exhausted by yet another round of treatment.

Nor checked in often with her translator app, ready to discuss anything the child might care to. On one occasion, the small girl was awake, brushing her new hair. She smiled at Norah weakly. Given her body was in mortal combat with each breath, it was a wonder she could communicate anything at all.

In the quiet of their drawing, suddenly and without prompting, she handed Norah a crayon sketch of a pink dress and her stuffed lioness. Norah smiled at the impressive detail given to both, from the bundle of tiny fake flowers tied around the dress's waist to the sleepy eyes of her toy. Before Norah could compliment the ensemble, the child swallowed and whispered.

"Smert. Tata."

The therapist's smile fell slowly. She only closed her mouth and nodded. She needn't use the application on her phone to know what Alina meant. She'd heard Dex translate the sacred word often enough to know what was being said.

Death. Goodbye.

This was what Alina wanted to be buried in.

Nor promised it would be so, and thus they sifted through dresses together, selecting her jewelry, her floral sash, and her rhinestone hair pieces.

How she wished Dex could've been there to shower the child in eloquent compliments and love. But the two girls made do, wearing various hats and giggling, bracelets up to their elbows and their hair pinned back with countless bows.

Exhausted by the day's efforts, Alina only cared to draw in silence afterwards.

Regardless of how painful it was to watch a strong little girl wither like a winter rose, Nor remained present. Each second was a gift.

So where in the hell was Dexteras?

In the quiet of the hall, Rosella dared to ask if they should call the telephone translator.

"No, he'll be back," Nor stated, hands lost in her hair. "Her and Dex have such close rapport. I don't want to put her through any more new adults. He'll be back." And though Nor and the staff inquired about his whereabouts daily, Alina never did.

Meanwhile, her infection raged on. Essential organs were shutting down. Pain management was now their sole pursuit. Time was uncertain.

Norah retreated to the hospital roof and fell back against the cool door. Though she'd lost clients before, Alina had taken a firmer hold of her heart.

Perhaps it was because the small girl's isolation and grief was so close to her own. Perhaps it was because when Norah was six, she too, had no one.

But Alina was facing isolation fearlessly. She fought in solace against death itself. Norah had watched her whisper in prayer with their chaplain, reaching out to a God and His goodness she wholly believed in. Alina was the genuine lioness, the warrior.

Meanwhile, in the face of mere discomfort, Norah Kestrel floundered.

What have I done to earn life?

What has she done to earn death?

If Dex were here, she'd ask him about the injustices of life and all of the bullshit this universe allowed.

Self-pity left her weeping on the hospital's roof. *Again.* Only this time, Dex wasn't there to comfort save her from herself and her pathetic unfolding. She lit a cigar but couldn't bring herself to smoke it. Instead, she stared into the stormy skies where grays and blues melted like soft velvet. She yearned for a downpour, for the catharsis of lightning and thunder.

She needed to be torn from her thoughts and dropped into her body by bracing cold rain. Perhaps trembling in an icy downfall would snap the chain on her destructive thoughts and scold them back to their cages with their tails between their legs.

But the rain wasn't so gracious.

On her commute home, she didn't bother to gaze up and guess at his window, to seek out his silhouette. She just rang his bell without expectation.

No response. Her tears welled. Then, she scoffed in self-disgust.

So many live in isolation, in agony in that hospital, Kestrel. They're actively dying, yet you pity yourself because you must stand on your own two feet.

Pathetic.

Just like them.

Just like them.

You're just like them.

Once home, she remained in work clothes, dragged an ancient bottle of wine from a high cabinet, and snatched a glass.

Just like Robin Kestrel would do.

She trudged up the twenty-seven steps to her room, Vincent trailing at her heels.

Her eyes fell to the door conjoining her room with her parents.' Though she knew it was empty and dead, it threatened her like a snarling wolf.

That fucking door.

She glared at the brass knob and her reflection distorted within it, crimson and pitiful. Her fingers hovered above it for a breath, then grabbed it, riding a sudden wave of adrenaline.

It burned her palm like a handful of metal buttons fresh from the dryer. A cry tore from her throat. Furious, she gripped tighter.

Unfazed by her foolish bravery, the knob bit back again.

The pain hit a blinding climax, leaving Nor to tear her hand to her chest and drop the wine glass to the floor where it shattered. She followed its glittering shards down on her knees as hot tears poured. The concerned, fat-faced house cat settled into a black loaf to observe.

Weak and clumsy, just like Robin.

Furious and hard-headed, just like Leonard.

You're going to die just like them, you know.

Intrusive thoughts flickered through her head whilst she scooped the pieces into her palm. She saw herself squeezing them in her fist until blood gushed down her white knuckles. She saw jagged pieces protruding from her skin, blue veins painted ruby.

Norah dropped the glass onto the carpet with a moan and held her face, flustered and horrified.

I want to feel nothing. I want to think about nothing. I want to sleep for years.

Her phone buzzed in her back pocket. She fumbled for it with a gasp. How she craved a kind voice. To be found. To hear the old man with the ivory mane speaking sweet consolations in her ear.

But it was the hospital.

Her stomach lurched. Her hands began to tremble. She pressed the phone firmly to her ear.

"This is Nor," she managed.

It was Rosella. She was in shambles.

Alina was gone.

"Funeral arrangements will be announced tomorrow," wept Rosella, hiccups trembling her voice with each breath. "Immediate staff is off to attend."

Norah couldn't voice it yet, but she knew she'd need much more time to recover. She'd need the week off. Maybe more. The death of a client always unmoored her, and took so so much to come back home to herself. To be useful to anyone.

And with Alina, it would be much worse. It would be more intimate, more disembodied. Her love for the little girl was going to be entangled in her life for years to come. Who knows when she'd be able to tame the strands, like wind-whipped hair.

"Thanks, El..." was all she could say right now. And with that, she dropped the phone amidst the collection of twinkling crystal and retreated with her bottle through the window.

Finally, the rain soaked her listless body, flat on its spine, exposed to the growling skies. Vincent sat on her chest despite the spitting clouds. With a bobbing throat and a lifted skull, she'd manage a swig of wine every so often. Commingled streams of hot tears and cold rain rinsed her hair into ringlets.

Behind her sore retinas, Norah felt like a prisoner with her thoughts. Her headspace was plastered with the pictures of all those she'd lost. A collage of grief, massive and miniscule, eliciting distinctive pains from her body and mind. And she was so weary that she couldn't leave, she could only stare and sob. She saw Alina's toothy grin and shining hazel eyes. Her tiny fists gripping her arms. Her artwork pasted on the walls of her office.

Perhaps Norah Kestrel expected someone to break down the memorial's fragile walls and carry her away from herself. Someone else to gather her into their arms until she was better.

But of course, there was no one else.

No one is coming to save you, Kestrel.

And while Norah the therapist knew countless strategies to keep emotions regulated, she allowed hers to go to hell.

The ends of her hair were twisted and knotted with salt. Her mascara left muddy streaks down her temples. Her mouth gaped against the pressure of panic, the brass key, and the old cat on her chest. As she faded into a drunken sleep, they were all that held her amidst her nightmares.

Glass smashing against the walls.

Her chest filled with smoke.

Everyone was screaming.

But Norah did nothing to help.

She only sobbed worthlessly.

24

⋆·NORAH·⋆

She nursed herself through a splitting wine headache with remorse the following day.

We're not doing this anymore.

This is how Robin handled shit.

Once past the worst of her nausea, Norah purged the house of all remaining liquor and spirits, leaving only one bottle of her mother's vintage wine tucked away in the high cabinet. A twist in her gut reminded her of the occasion it would patiently await.

She soaked in the porcelain claw-foot tub with lavender bath salts until she was pruned. Her mother had washed her as a toddler in that tub, and now Nor's slender arms draped its edges. They were the only limbs that kept her from drowning in it. She exfoliated and scrubbed dead skin from her face. She snipped split ends and rogue eyebrows, scowling at her reflection in the mirror of the master bathroom.

Her mother had often stood here, groaning and tossing cosmetics about in rage.

"I'm so fucking fat," she'd say, squeezing the pale roll of flesh above her pants. *"Ugly as a drowned rat."*

But Norah considered her mother quite beautiful, and thus often speculated *if mom is ugly, what does that make me?* Her mother was blonde and fair and had stunning blue eyes, and it was Norah's job to remind her of her worthiness often. That she was pretty. That she was good. That she was doing a great job.

Adult Norah observed herself in the reflection now and sighed. Then, she fed the old cat and left for town.

✦

She returned to Dex's apartment, feeling an immense anxiety about knocking on his door.

A book she'd once read on OCD mindfulness exercises had mentioned:

If your brain wants to be afraid of uncertainty, allow it to be. Make space for it. Don't try to fix it or convince it that it's always safe. Acknowledge that the future is indeed uncertain. Lean into it. If it tells you, "what if…" then reply with "maybe it will, and maybe it won't."

Maybe Dexteras Doe will be here today, and maybe he won't be.

Norah allowed herself to look up at The Aviary and seek his tall shape in the windows with pulled curtains. Then, she pressed his bell. When it went unanswered, she shuffled back towards her vehicle with a tired stride.

She promised herself that if there was still no word from her friend by this evening, she'd request a wellness check from Corvid PD.

Suddenly, a heavy creak of old hinges groaned behind her, spinning Norah on her toes with hope.

But it wasn't Dex.

The glass door imprinted with *The Aviary Apartments* slammed behind him and locked into place. A scruffy man in a black overcoat stepped out, smoking a cigarette. Despite Corvid's syrupy thick fog and gloom, the stranger wore dark sunglasses. As he stabbed the cigarette between his lips, she noticed the bruises along his knuckles, hues of deep purples, blues, and greens.

Just before her, he stopped, jarring the tails of his coat. He lifted a dark brow, sighed impatiently, and then backpedaled to the doors from whence he came. He slid a brass key into the lobby's lock and held it open for Norah without a word. He waited silently like a bored cat.

She began to retort and stutter, but instead rushed forward with a grateful smile.

"Thank you so much," she said, beaming at his handsome features. The dark cigarette smoke wrapped them together in its ribbons. "You came right when I needed you."

He gave a dramatic lift of his head and a wordless gesture into the doorway, revealing a tattooed arm. A talons-spread, dead-eyed bird was inked along the thick veins on the back of his hand. The bird clutched to woody thorns that trailed up into his tattered shirt sleeve.

Nor scuttled into the air-conditioned lobby and waved her thanks, but the stranger was already at the curb, tossing what seemed to be a rattling spray paint can into a trash bin. It clanged like a broken church bell as he walked past, smoke peeling over his shoulders.

She climbed for what felt like eons until she found Dex's door. She'd watched his thumb run along the old, laminated tag on his keys that read 7B. The barren ring of keys had not a single ounce of personal flair until Nor gave him a black resin keychain that said *Coffee Slut*. He'd cackled as she twisted it on for him.

That key and his keychains were sitting on a plain wooden table just inside 7B. It'd been unlocked, unoccupied, and uninviting without him in it. His scratched and neglected clamshell phone was there too, besides a business card that read an ominous set of coordinates and nothing more. Norah snapped a photo of these with her phone.

She wished to rummage and prod about the space, constantly yearning to know more about her friend. But Dex's privacy was something she was determined to never undermine again. But she missed everything about him and wanted him back.

Restraining her curiosity, she stuck her head into each of the tiny rooms and called for him.

When she found nothing and no one, she returned home, shamelessly hopeful for the new lead.

PART II

OBLITUS

25

✦NORAH✦

As EVENING FELL, Nor whipped her truck beside Corvid's tattoo parlor off Dendrocopos Street. Her eyes burned with adoration at the pale glow of *Magpie Ink*, with its blue and white neon raven hopping jauntily in the window.

On her eighteenth birthday, she'd gotten a small bird inked on her inner bicep where it could hide against her torso.

She'd asked a bearded artist with gauges and painted nails to tattoo her with a bird that was "badass and weird." Thus, she ended up with a tiny black and white sparrow-sized beast with outstretched talons, reaching for her arteries. It wasn't any breed that resided near Corvid and looked anything but menacing. When her adrenaline finally died down and the glamor of eternal art lost its sparkle, she had the nerve to ask the artist what type it was.

"Butcher bird," he grumbled, wiping her inflamed skin with another dry rake of clenched paper towel. Content with having chased down and hog-tied her wild oats, she'd grinned. Those rebel years were as fleeting and destructive as bottle rockets.

Of course, she knew all that the little bird had truly symbolized for her was freedom. Freedom from her name. From what others expected of her. From her mother, most importantly.

Her relationship with Robin didn't topple and burn like Rome. Rather, it was eroded by waves of time, by a sea that gutted them both from the inside out. And with time, young Norah Kestrel found it difficult to breathe, to find her footing, to stay afloat. So she had to choose: break free or be broken. Then, left alone to flounder, Robin drowned.

Decades of self-medicating, mixing drugs, alcohol, and tar had left her to suffer just floors above her daughter each day. Robin's mortal clock ticked loudly as though it boomed through the hospital intercoms, beating against the halls. Her daughter could hear it in the clacking of her heels, in the tapping of the cold key at her navel.

Beckoned home to maintain the house in her mother's absence, Norah didn't mind emptying countless ashtrays and scrubbing hacked-upon countertops. She didn't mind struggling to stretch their savings account for medications, meals, blood-thirsty insurance claims, and unpayable bills.

What truly ate at Robin's child was far more pathetic.

It was the implicit *obligation* she minded most.

The expectation that her mother was *owed* this sacrifice of her daughter's adult life. Norah was *supposed* to lay down her everything for the decaying and dying woman who hadn't held the space for her ugliest emotions. The parent who never allowed her the anger, the grief, the agony of being *not okay* was entitled to their child's thick, smothering mask of *I'm fine*.

That's why she couldn't go near the seventh floor without a panic attack gripping her throat, leaving her to wheeze on the stairs in a cold sweat. Stepping foot in that room again would surely crush her like the waves that'd dragged her down as a child. She'd relive that breathless betrayal of being held under by someone who was supposed to teach her to swim.

"Fuck," adult Norah muttered, returning to Magpie Ink's parking lot. She stretched the tight skin of her palm and inspected the strange building across the street. The glowing map on her phone had dutifully followed the coordinates from the business card on Dex's table and stuck a red pin onto the dark lot before her. Though there was no evidence of a building or business on her GPS, a warehouse-sized structure loomed in the shadows. It was painted midnight black with no observable doors, windows, vehicles, or indicators of life.

How have I lived here for thirty years and never noticed this place?

Her heeled boots clacked against the street and stopped before the massive bricks.

You need to get your ass home before you get trafficked, you fucking blunder of a human.

But her fingers graced the beads on her wrist.

She thought of Alina. And Dex. She thought of the years she'd spent wasting in that mausoleum of a house, decaying. Hiding from the past. Cowardly clutching to her comforts that weren't even all that comfortable.

Just like your mother.

Her heart pounded as she lapped the building, anxiety cranking her throat tight. The warehouse had no knobs, locks, windows, or signage. Not a single sound mumbled from within its inner caverns. There was no life, only leggy cords of black sweet potato vines strangling the brick in sheets of chaotic foliage. There was no way in.

An unexpected rush of tears welled at her lids. Angry, irritated, and bitter.

Had Dexteras Doe been a figment of my imagination?

Then, as the final rays of the sun dipped down past the horizon, a flash of metal gleamed in her periphery. She turned to see a set of brass hinges shining beneath black leaves. Her fingers found a door, matte black and seamless, nearly invisible in the gloom.

She rapped against it with a confident knock of knuckles. It gave a promising echo of something beyond. She knocked again.

No response.

Then, she kicked and shoved and pried at the metal with her chipped, black nails.

Fucking fuck.

Exhausted by dead ends, she rested her palms and forehead against the steel where it soothed her scar, sending currents of cold through her flesh. She was out of ideas, of avenues, of hope.

Click.

Her head snapped upwards at the shudder beneath her fingertips. Air whistled through a narrow crack, tossing her hair behind her. She slipped her fingers within the void and yanked, casting the steel aside.

"Hello?" she called into the darkness beyond. But her voice was consumed by deafening silence.

She stepped into a dark, vacant room, bruised with stormy walls and minimal decorum. There were no seats, front desk, insignia, nor pamphlets. Only shadows, charcoal walls, and black brick pillars which kissed a high tin ceiling, peeling with gold paint.

Black marble floors led her feet to the opposing side of the room. There, her options were simple: one hallway, which funneled to the left.

The hall was coated floor-to-ceiling in mirror pieces, sharp, aggressive and jarring shapes creating an illusion of endless blackness. As Nor's reflection crept between the shards, she appeared as though she, too, was made of broken pieces. The door at the end of the hall was a mate to the first, unwelcoming and steel.

She pressed her right palm to the door.

It didn't budge.

She presented her left, with its taut scars.

After a heartbeat, it clicked open.

As it cracked ajar, a surge of music and balmy heat gushed through. A metal platform and descending staircase awaited her, winding in chaotic twists and turns like a contorted snake.

She stepped from the hall and onto the grated balcony, taking in an aerial view of the humid underground expanse below. Her mouth fell open.

The scene before her looked like that of a nightclub: dark, moody, seductive, and glittering. Filled with winding bodies, tattooed flesh, and thick smoke, the crowd and its surroundings wore scarlet, black, and gold.

Some dazzled in the light while others hid in the quiet, shadowy pockets.

The building's bones were industrial, steel columns and black brick with contemporary, sparkling, and golden décor and fixtures. Countless large, red neon signs were embedded into the porous brickwork, illuminating the darkness with a bloody aura.

A majority of the club-goers were clustered, roaring, whooping, shaking their fists, and crushing one another around a circular stage at the expanse's heart. The stage was elevated above their jeering heads and wrapped in yet another twisting ribbon of metal stairs. A tall fence of gold rails and chains surrounded the platform, glistening like a menacing cage beneath spotlights.

The stage was shining with polished gold tile, topped with puddles of crimson.

Norah blinked and leaned over the balcony's railing, eyes squinting against the humid haze.

It was blood.

She watched a limp body being dragged beneath the rails and into the crowd like a garbage bag, arms and hair spread, smears of black blood following behind.

And with numb clarity, she understood.

It was a fighting ring.

If Dexteras was here, she prayed the floor hadn't already been wiped with his insides. She hastened down the stairs.

Endless shapes, sizes, and colors of bodies cheered, danced, and sipped from their glasses, eyes heavy-lidded as though swimming through an opium fog. From a smaller, more distant stage, provocative music boomed through speakers, twisting and hypnotizing the surrounding patrons. A thick curtain hung still, dark like red wine.

Norah stuck to the shadows of the winding stairs, eyes flitting across the scene, lip bitten between her teeth. As soon as she stepped onto the ground floor and into the glow of red neon, staring eyes turned to drink her in.

She crept along the dark walls and followed it towards a black metalflake bar top, scattered with gold-rimmed glasses and tap handles. Sharp-featured beings hustled behind it with toothy grins and bony features. Behind them rose a floor-to-ceiling mirror laced in a vignette that stretched on for what seemed like miles. Gold shelves sparkled with vibrating liqueurs in red bottles, thrumming to the bass.

Above it all, grand, crimson text read, *OBLITUS.*

Shrill screams and baritone hollers swelled from the club's center. On tiptoe, Nor sought out the commotion near the golden ring. Jostling bodies grappled and feet danced behind the bars. Rails and chains rattled.

She followed a handsome member of the bar staff to the sparkling bar top and perched upon a gold stool. She eyed the colorful liqueurs that lined the mirrored glass, the shining necks of tinctures, preserves, and bitters. Past them, she saw herself in the reflection, sporting her fitted black clothes, dark eyes, and lips. Feeling relentless eyes raking over her still, she zipped her leather jacket up to her throat.

Her gaze fell to the combat boots and dark pants of a handsome patron several seats from her, noting something strange about his tattoos in their closeness. What she'd assumed were tribal shapes and jagged symbols were instead chaotic, bold scribbles and winding black spills of ink. Some were narrow and others were coarse like lazy cover-up work done with crude tools. These sinewy blotches of ink dappled his chest, arms, jaw, throat, and even bled along his eyebrow like the stitching of black thread. A shock of gold twinkled in the hoop piercing his busted lip. He ran a tongue across its metal with a grin.

Norah's eyes snapped to her hands, pretending to be enamored by her father's coin as it padded across her knuckles. She also fidgeted with a black drink coaster, desperate for a distraction.

A tall slender logo bearing the letters *OBLITUS* sparkled in gold foil. On the back, Nor found familiar shaking scribbles in ballpoint pen, inscribing an assortment of dead languages in a rushed hand. She thought of the tag on Alina's lioness and her heart skipped a beat.

Dex.

He so deeply wanted answers. To understand.

That's why this place had kept him away for so long. He was looking for himself. For home.

But it was evident by the violent atmosphere and its scowling beings that what you're looking for and what you find aren't always the same thing.

Filled with fresh bravery, Nor sought one of the bustling barkeeps until their gaze locked onto hers. She raised her hand and he smiled.

Finishing a pour of liquor into ruby shot glasses, he tossed her a chin and paced to her on tall legs. He was a sharp man in his forties with a seamless golden complexion and dark dusting on his jaw. His hazel-gold eyes fluttered across Norah's body from bottom to top before leaning across the bar and extending a ring-clad hand.

"Mikael."

Nor squeezed his calloused fingers, noting that his nose had once been broken and reset and now adorned a tiny jewel at the nostril. It, along with his hairy chest, was scarred with the same chaotic black tattoo work. The corner of his mouth curled to reveal peeking teeth.

"Norah," she said, blushing with his closeness.

"Welcome to Oblitus, Norah. Care for a drink?"

"Sure, surprise me," she replied, surprising *herself* with her boldness. It'd been lifetimes since she'd stepped foot in a bar and ordered a drink. Since she'd known company for company's sake.

In a puff of pale smoke, he held aloft a bottle-blue cocktail glass. Cold nitrogen gas spilled from it like a potion.

She blinked at the illusion and plucked the glass from his inked fingers. The liquid inside was a teal blue, glittering with bits of edible gold flake. An intricately folded origami bird was perched on its rim.

Eyes wide and fixed on Mikael, she sipped from the icy glass. It was chilled and tart like cider and it slipped all the way down to her gut with its bite.

Just after her first grateful swallow, Mikael closed his eyes and his breath hitched, as if in pain. His body grew rigid against the glassy marble, fingers clutching it. The episode seemed to subside quickly, leaving him to stand reorient his dizzy limbs.

"Are…you okay?" she dared to ask.

His striking eyes rolled open and he breathed deeply with a curt nod. "Yes. I-I apologize. We haven't had anyone like *you* here before in Oblitus. Ever," he muttered, clearing his throat and breathing deeply.

She scowled. "Like me?"

"Corporeal," he replied, as though it were an obvious answer. "I don't remember your kind, but I remember…how you *felt*." He swallowed thickly and closed his eyes again, gathering his composure.

Norah set the glass back to the bar top. "What does any of that mean?" she asked, gut churning with his implications.

"This isn't your home Norah," he said, leaning closer, his warm charm returning to his features.

Her skin itched and her eyes dashed to the mirror behind Mikael. The whites of more watching eyes flashed and stared.

"I've lived in Corvid my whole life," she said, still challenging the gaze of countless strangers in the glass.

Mikael's lips stretched wider, and he opened them to speak-

But before he could unpack her endless questions, a crash exploded from deep within the belly of the club. A cacophony of chains trilled and the crowd electrified. Their jeers intensified. The floor trembled.

Kneeling on her barstool, Nor saw two men sparring and shoving in the snares of the golden ring. Their sweat and blood glowed violent red by a neon sign above the ring which read, *Til Death*. Fittingly, neither of the fighters seemed to follow any code, or obey any rules, or abide by the tolling of any match bells.

Then, with a horrifying war cry, one of the fighters was thrown into the crowd. The herd bubbled with excitement, making room for the uninvited guest. The crowd swelled and rippled, nearly engulfing Norah on her seat.

Mikael jerked his head at her, a request to retreat with him behind the bar.

But she hesitated. The intentions of everyone within this place were unreadable, polished in gorgeous bones, dazzling smiles, and jewel-toned irises.

Another crash shook the tile, closer now. The smack of flesh on flesh could be heard as the brawl of tearing beings approached. Curses in languages both foreign and familiar screamed atop the crowd and the aggressive music trembling through the speakers.

Before Nor could take Mikael's outreached hand, a rinse of cold air rushed across her back and neck. The air at her lips suddenly became so chilly, she struggled to breathe it in. And as though the breeze itself twisted her by the shoulders, she pivoted into its owner with a gasp.

"*I* know who you're looking for," said a deep, crumbling voice with a Cockney bite. She gazed upon a well-built man with black sunglasses who smelled of pine and cut vines. Woodsy, earthy, like Chinese black tea. The glass protecting his eyes twinkled in the red lights of the bar.

"It's you..." she muttered, eyes wide on the handsome man who'd let her into The Aviary this morning.

"*This* way dollybird," he purred at her earlobe. His throaty call and calming cold were compelling and confident, strumming the hairs on her neck. He was thick with rolling muscles, punctured with dramatic pockets of shadow in his features. Scars chopped the lines of his dark brow and his ears were studded with black and gold rings.

The flare of a strobe light struck his scars and dark lenses. Steely-black hair swept back from his face and the sides of his head were buzzed short. Chaotic tattoos like the others she'd seen peeked and played along his freckled skin, undecipherable in the dramatic shadow.

Nor couldn't command her feet to unglue from the tile despite his compelling demands.

"Lenore Kestrel, aye?" His expression was cold and drunken. He was in a hurry, it seemed.

"Norah," she corrected him, sick of these men knowing things about her that she hadn't granted them permission to.

"On yer bike then, birdie." This time, the stranger flashed a set of shark-white teeth to Mikael, who frowned and bared his jaw. Then, without so much as a glance over his shoulder, he shoved through the crowd and left her.

Though his pale skin was a beacon in the dark, every inch of his clothing was black. His long waistcoat, his thin undershirt. The spidery fingers of illegible ink.

Norah hurried after him, his massive form serving as a riot shield through the crowd. No one dared press against them while his shoulders were in the lead.

He led her along the bar and into the shadows of the unused music stage adorned with its wine-colored curtain and booming speakers that thundered like her pulse. A neon sign above it read in bold letters: *WHO DARES, WINS.* They ascended a squat set of hidden stairs and stepped into the shadows of the heavy curtain. The stranger tucked himself behind its velvet and lit a cigarette.

Nor hovered hesitantly in the space where neon red light and black shadow met. The balmy heat of the club slicked her fingertips with salt, streaking her phone's glass screen in her palm.

This is stupid. You're stupid. What the fuck are you doing?

The stranger leaned against the brick wall, bourbon smelling smoke rolling from his nostrils. His top lip snarled to one side as he pulled on the cigarette.

Norah's lungs fell victim to the alluring aroma. She'd once been addicted to second-hand smoke it'd seemed, thanks to her mother's frequent habit. But Nor hadn't known the guilty satisfaction of its pungent sting in years. As he pulled on the thin cigarette, the tattoo of the warbling bird on his hand stretched, the creature's eye milky and white.

"You," she stammered. "I saw you…a-at The Aviary-"

But he seemed distracted by the commotion below. His ear was tipped to the chaos as though he were listening for something.

"Who are you?" she said above the crowd.

"Colleague to that feckin' barmcake," the stranger stated, tossing his chin towards the brawl that had spilled from the cage.

Norah cocked her head. "Wh-"

"*Dexteras*, yer ancient git, aye?" Smoke waterfalled up his sunglasses with frustration, his voice snappish and tired.

"How do you-"

"Colleague," he interrupted again.

"But how do you know that I-"

"Cuz *nobody* goes to the feckin' outside," he stated, chin tossing towards the snaking staircase that carried her down. "And the both of ya wreak of the outside," he grimaced.

Between Mikael and this stranger, she wasn't sure whose words confused her more.

"Cecil," he suddenly spat, still not looking at her.

Was this his idea of an introduction?

As he held open the velvet curtain with a propped arm, she couldn't help but notice the thick blue veins that wrapped his hands and exposed arms. They reminded her of a man she'd dated once, Rook. He was as narrow as a stork, but had pale veiny arms she couldn't look away from when they twisted around her.

"What is this place ?" Nor asked, eyes still shamelessly observing his peeking tattoos. A narrow, reaching, bird's talon pierced beyond his black hairline and raked its claws against his rolling jaw. He didn't seem to notice or mind her staring.

"I can promise ya dolly, tis not the place you're s'posed to feckin' be."

She raised a brow, exasperated air spewing from her lips. "I need to talk to Dex."

"Well, he's busy with a pagga. Handbaggin' Figgys."

"*Excuse* me?" *The fuck did this man just say?*

Curses and crashes approached nearer. Stools and bottles smashed with upturning.

Cecil grinned like a demon. "He's after a hell of a chicken dinner," he said. "Gotta prove himself first."

"Prove himself? Isn't he here to figure out who he is?" she confirmed. Dex's nearness to answers had awakened a hunger in her gut as well on his behalf.

"*What* he is, aye." Smoke dotted the air with the stranger's snickers. "To put pieces back together one must first get busted-a-feckin-part," he said, manipulating impossible smoke shapes into the space between them. She swore they briefly took on the illustrations of a sword piercing a silver, pumping heart.

But then the reality of his words crashed upon her. She pointed to the chaos beyond.

"Wait, that's...?"

His teeth peeked and his rumbling chuckles dashed through the thick smoke between them. He snapped the curtain aside.

"Have a butcher, dollybird."

She peered around the velvet in time to watch a flash of snowy hair and bared teeth. He was a roaring beast in tattered dress clothes, draped suspenders bobbing at his hips. His ink, sweat, and blood were smeared across him like war paint.

Dexteras Doe was a flash of dirtied flesh, defending his skull, bending deep at his geriatric knees, delivering brutish blows as though he had trained for it his whole life. His teeth whistled with effort and his hands whooshed through the air like sledgehammers.

His opponent was dark, grinning, and slow on his feet, but catastrophic with his fists. One of these laid Dex flat on the tile where he was left to heave at the gold ceiling. Before Nor could gasp, he sprang back to his feet, a split in his forehead now leaking blood into his ivory hair.

The crowd screamed with fervor as though disappointed he hadn't died. Their rallying bodies served as a barrier to the fight in lieu of the abandoned fight ring. They whistled and cursed.

Grappling with his opponent once more, Dex was reactive and righteous. He never accepted a hit without returning it in kind.

The once old and domesticated old man had become feral, blue eyes screaming beneath purple eye sockets, swollen like plums. Exposed, rolling muscles, rounded and stiffened with each effort. He was an absolute force of nature.

Holy shit, Dexteras.

26

✦NORAH✦

THE MONSTROUS ADVERSARY SNATCHED Dexteras by the throat and threw him to the tile. Norah couldn't be sure if it was the floor or his skull that had broken with a deafening crack. But he was up, again and again, spitting blood from his teeth, recovering and wound tight.

"Haven't the feckin' faintest how yer here birdie, but we need ya out," growled Cecil, lip rising like a territorial dog's.

But Norah was too distracted by her old friend, now being thrown over the bar top in an airborne blur of white hair. A catastrophic crash of shattered glassware followed.

"Stop them," she demanded of Cecil. "He's going to get killed!"

He laughed, smoke crashing up his lenses, leaking from his chortling teeth.

"Dolly, there's endless treacheries ya couldn't fathom 'bout what yer boy Dexy is. Firstly, he's ours, not yers. And you've no bloody clue what yer doing in this godforsaken place. Go home." He tossed a dismissive brow towards the distant stairs, where the real world awaited.

A defensive fire rose to her cheeks at Cecil's claim on Dexteras. It shouldn't have bothered her, but it did. Rather than shaking the handsome bastard by his collar, she flipped him off with both ringed hands and stepped from the curtained hideaway. She expected him to grab her by the wrist, but he only smirked.

Mikael plucked glass from Dex's exposed arms and cheeks as the old man heaved and snarled, dripping with booze and oozing slashes. His eyes were wide and wild upon his cackling opponent who taunted him.

Inner compass bound towards her friend, Norah sprang from the stage and began swimming through the crowd. But within moments of her pursuit, he'd launched himself over the bar with a massive, tattooed bicep, vaulting his long limbs with ease. She saw the flash of his bloodied teeth just before he plunged down into the masses.

She fought through the bystanders without apology, no longer attempting to make herself small, but brutish. Her shoulders plowed towards the neon light of the bar top.

Through craning necks and whorls of smoke, Norah watched his swing with ferocity towards another man twice his size. He fought without fear, or perhaps, common sense. More of his ruined, dapper attire and wounded figure came into view.

One of Dex's well-versed strikes smashed against the other man's temple and dropped him to his knees. She caught a glimpse of the endless black tattooed tallies inked into his thick neck and spine. On tiptoe, she could finally make out the scene properly.

"*Fututus et mori in igni*!" snarled Dex at the downed fighter.

Norah swore his fists were steaming, crackling like struck, fiery timbers.

"*Consider* a comment like that again, I'll rip your neck from your fucking shoulders," Dexteras bellowed at his opponent, who only garbled in reply, their mouth undoubtedly filled with blood.

Having fought her way to the front row of raucous club-goers, Nor's mouth hung open in awe. Was this the same man who'd allowed a sickle-cell patient to braid his hair just a couple weeks prior? She could still see his locks pinned up in velvet scrunchies and glittering barrettes.

Maybe there is a lot I don't know about him.

Maybe there's a lot he doesn't know about himself.

Between the pulsing of bass in her chest bones and skull, Nor heard a crackle of wry laughter at her spine. She spun just as Cecil strode through the parted tides of bystanders, tipping their heads towards him in respect.

But Dex had not heard the younger stranger's approach and instead pursued his nearly unconscious opponent with bared teeth. Both of them were slick with blood and scowls, but it was evident that her friend was the one nearer to victory.

"Feckin' breathe ya muppet!" called Cecil to the old man. "*I* told him to say shite bout yer birdie."

Dex wheeled about, visibly refilled with fresh rage at the sight of the man in black. Dex pursued the snarky brute, incisors drawn, anger bending his old wrinkles. It seemed he truly feared no one.

But from the floor behind him, his once-downed opponent roared with resurgence and charged Dex's kneecaps. The old man hollered as he was hoisted above the crowd, his sweaty hair brushing along one of the hanging gold lanterns that lit the space. The fixture rattled on navel chains and swung, casting ghostly red spotlights.

Dex was thrown against the bar top from whence he'd just come, and the *crack* of stone and bone was thunderous as he was broken across its marble. He called out in earnest pain as the giant held him down by his chest and bore a fist back with the intention of ending him.

The crowd whistled through their grinning teeth.

"No!" cried Nor, dashing through the final layers of patrons toward her friend.

Cecil, too, stepped forward, a placating hand lifted to the men. "He's punch-drunk, Jezebel, lettem idle." It seemed as though this was a fight Cecil had choreographed.

Dex twisted from Jezebel's grip and leaped from the bar, intending a homicidal blow towards Cecil. But Cecil sidestepped it with insulting ease, face stoic and unflinching behind the dark lenses.

Dex fired again.

Cecil deflected with a forearm and replied with a jab to the old man's temple. Dex buckled, and Cecil palmed the old man's skull, smashing it against the bar top.

"Stop!" Norah screamed, chasing after the sparring pair.

Dex slumped to the ground, still swollen with rage, bruised in violet, and jaw fixed in fury. He was unputdownable. Relentless. Even Cecil's lips stretched with surprise when the old man sprang back to his feet.

A sharp, acidic anxiety trembled through Norah's limbs with her anger. Perhaps it was the violence, the screaming, the fighting. Perhaps it was the smell of liquor, the shoving, the disrespect of her personal space. The feeling that she wasn't big enough, loud enough, powerful or dangerous enough to make things right. She felt out of control. Emotionally unsafe.

A heat possessed her chest, swelling, inflating, burning. Before she could speak reason to her feet, she unveiled herself beneath the strobing red lights and endless eyes. Before the sparring pair, she was on fire and filled with fury. She could feel the red splotches smattering her chest and neck but was too livid to care. Then, uncertain if she would vomit or scream, a cry burst from her lips.

"DEX!"

Dexteras Doe's head whipped to hers with such speed, it should've snapped off his shoulders. In fact, both men straightened like scolded boys. Their brief alarm and hitched breaths gave her a sliver of power to relish. The fighting had stopped at her command.

The music thumped on, and other bodies tore at one another in the gold ring in the distance, but everyone in the nearby vicinity turned to gape at Nor. She found her anxious shoulders hiked high to her earlobes. So, she straightened, breathed deeply, and lifted her chin.

When the old man's fiery blue eyes collided with hers, his anger quieted and his shoulders fell. His fingers unclenched and his bearded mouth fell open.

"Nor..." stammered his bleeding lips.

"You've been, what?" she spat. "Fighting? *This* is where you've been?"

She gestured about the space like an absolute mad woman. She hadn't anticipated this *rage*, but here it was, hissing and biting like boiling oil, out in the open for countless strangers to see.

Even as his eyes gentled and his wrinkles buckled with grief, she couldn't stifle the tremble that shook her bones. A wire brush of hoarse breathing scraped her throat and burning salt stung her eyes. She wanted to hug him and hit him all in one breath. She wanted to cry and scream and hurt him.

But she couldn't bring herself to do any of those things while his face was so long and quiet. All of the fight and brutish bulk was siphoned from him and poured onto the floor.

"Alina *died, Dex*. She died and she wanted to see you and...and you weren't there." Nor lamented, still barking and furious, but grieving afresh. She hadn't intended to guilt him, to shame him. She knew, even as she yelled and her eyes spilled with furious tears, this wasn't what she'd meant to say. She knew this wasn't how she wanted to reunite with her best friend and mourn with him. But even *she* hadn't known such frustration simmered beneath the surface of her skin until it came barreling from her mouth.

Blood, sweat, and sticky champagne sparkled across Dex's skin as he shifted and rubbed his fingers. That lost, boyish expression weighed each inch of him like an old, wet coat.

"N-Norah I..." he stuttered.

"I don't know what...*fucking fight club* you're in Dex, but it wasn't worth it. It wasn't worth her being alone," she stated. Her tears poured harder, infuriating her more. Norah Kestrel the advocate shook with injustice, uncertain whether it was in protection of Alina Holub or herself.

His lashes fell, revealing a glimmer of the Dexteras she knew. His blood drip-dropped on the tile and his lips wouldn't fit together, and he dared not speak another word.

"She deserved better," Nor added, more quietly now. And she didn't just mean better of him, but better of herself, too. The child's final moments had been pasted together by a blundering, wounded clinician with impostor syndrome.

"Oy Dexy. Wind yer feckin' neck or tap her in," sneered Cecil, tipping his lenses to the old man.

Some of the surrounding onlookers snickered, but Dex was not amused. His eyes snapped to the dark hair stranger with rekindled flames and in a breath, he withdrew a fist to attack Cecil.

But despite his casual nature, Cecil was ready. He dipped backward and responded with a jab to the bony corner of Dex's jaw. Literal *embers* ricocheted from the old man's head and bounced to the floor where they fizzled out.

Doubled over his knees, Dex spat frothy blood and bits of his inner cheek, back rounded and heaving.

And with the casual thrust of piercing a meat slab on a steak knife, Cecil plunged his fingers down *into* the old man's spine. *Through* the fibers of his dress shirt, *through* the flesh. And the sunglasses never even slipped from Cecil's nose.

It took Norah three full seconds to process, to understand, to possibly *fathom* what was happening. Cecil's entire forearm was gone, missing, for it'd been plunged beneath the old man's skin as though it were soft as fog. Cecil's fingers clawed *beneath* his skin like a parasite, fingers wrapping in his spinal cord.

Despite all of the protruding bones and carnage she'd witnessed at the hospital, this particular anomaly pressed her onto her heels and buckled her knees with nausea. Her stomach churned and every inch of her washed cold.

Cecil's fingers were clawing *through* Dexteras, submerged deep beneath the flesh, raking through plasma and nerve endings. The shape of his arm bulged beneath the tattooed flesh like a science fiction alien, wriggling. The massive cathedral tattooed on Dex's back stretched and warped with the intrusion.

The bent Dex awkwardly grappled against Cecil with a horrified cry, scraping the stranger's limbs for leverage, mercy, anything to lift him from the agony.

The world around Norah darkened at the peripherals. She swayed where she stood with overfilling bile. She swallowed salt down the back of her throat.

Distantly, she heard someone scale the bar, glass shards spraying in their wake, and felt them sustain her upright with a strong arm. She was too woozy to care about who it was.

Cecil hushed Dexteras and pulled the old man upright against him by his windpipe whilst his other hand puppeteered from behind. It was an intimate gesture, as though Cecil had just dragged a wounded brother from the front lines, saving him from peril.

"I don't care what you've been told, Dexteras, but I'll say this *once*," snarled Cecil at his earlobe. "You and yer dustbin *Corpse*," he said, lenses flashing towards Norah, "need to keep the *feck* aways from here."

A gunshot crackle relented from Dex's spine like the snapped rungs of a wooden ladder.

Crick.

Crick.

CRACK.

Dexteras' eyes winced, widened, and then fell blank. He folded gracefully like a sinking sandbag. The stormy clouds of his eyes fell lifeless as his body had on the polished tile, hair fanning his listless features.

Norah screamed and raced to the old man, rolling him to his side, fingers trembling as she clawed at his body for wounds.

She lifted the tail of his shirt, prepared to be flooded in blood and neural fluids. But though the fabric was torn, the flesh beneath was unbroken.

Blinking hard with panic and disbelief, all she could think to do next was press her fingers into his throat, scavenging the scruffy beard for a pulse. Her fingertips rolled against his carotid artery and waited.

No. No. No. No, she begged, *Not like this, not like this. I need you Dexteras. I need you to get me the hell out of here so I can kill you myself.*

Still, she waited.

And waited.

And then…a sporadic, gentle tapping met her fingertips with life.

Tip-Tap. Tip-Tap.

He was alive.

How is he alive?

A shuddering CR-ACK and series of crackles popped from the old man in her arms. Then, he gasped his way back to life, coughing for air towards the gold ceiling. Having found his breath, he fell swiftly unconscious against her.

She wiped the tears from her cheeks, remembering that he should've been dead many times before today. Her body was shaking, hollow and light like an autumn leaf, spent of its anger and finding little else to sustain itself.

"Gormless feckin' muppet," said Cecil from behind, whipping wet blood from his fingers in disgust. "I feckin' knew it," he grumbled. Then, he spun on his tactical boots and walked away.

With Dex's head in hers, Norah twisted to watch him go.

The crowd dispersed, huddling against the bar top and returning to the caged arena for their next round of entertainment.

"Hey!" cried Nor, eyes burning into Cecil's muscular back. It was smoking with steam as it abandoned them. Everyone here seemed to run on blood and steam, like ruthless machines.

Who are these people? What are they? she dare consider.

"Hey!"

Still, he sauntered. His disheveled black hair and broad shoulders began to dissolve into the herd.

"You fucking bastard, you turn and face me, I *need* your help!" she screamed once more.

This time, he stopped sharp as though he were about to step on a landmine. His chin turned over his great shoulder threateningly. The pane of his black glasses flashed above his bony cheeks.

Just past his towering silhouette, a fitting set of neon letters spelled "BARE YOUR TEETH" in white and "SPIT YOUR BLOOD" in red.

"Please," she called over the crowd. "If you want me out, I need you to get *him* out."

Cecil's head tipped back to the heavens and his fingers flexed and clenched.

Then, without losing the ash on his cigarette, he doubled back, bent between them, and hoisted Dexteras across his shoulder with a bulging arm. He smacked the unconscious man across his back like luggage and trudged through the crowd without a word to her. His gait hastened beneath the speculative stares of others.

Norah scampered at his heels, ducking and shoving through limbs, following him up the clanging stairs. He carried the massive man as though he were a loaf of bread.

Cecil dropped the body on the threshold, ringing the staircase with apathetic chimes. He stepped over the unconscious Dexteras to return to the club below.

"Can you at least get him to my car?" she snapped, now unafraid and simply irritated with the barrage of ignorant men she'd shared her evening with.

Cecil's shoulders bulked as though her words were the electric tic-tic-tic of a taser.

"Ankle-biter," he bit with a spin. "Yer lucky I don't strap the git to the railroad tracks and let him turn to muppet mash."

But Nor sustained her scowl on his dark lenses. Dex was massive, she'd never manage him through the lobby.

Cecil then sighed with a great wolfish groan, an exchange of expressions crossed his features that she couldn't interpret. "They'll notice me gone," he clarified, throwing his chin to the crowd below. It was clearly a bitter annoyance for him to address.

"I *need* you to, please," she begged. "I'll pull the car round the front and you can…toss him in…gently," she added. "Otherwise, I'm waiting here till he wakes up." She sat on her rear beside Dexteras as if to further demonstrate her commitment. It was utter insanity, but she had no other leverage in this den of carnivores. She desperately wanted to go home. To feel the cool evening outside. To drink her tea and pretend this was all a horrendous dream. But the adrenaline in her veins and the unconscious friend in her arms told her that she was, unfortunately, quite awake.

And if she left him here another night, what would be left of him? How much more of this impossible place could he endure?

Cecil tipped an ear to the bloody brawl in the ring below. A fight still endured, but many of the other patrons had ceased their brawling to watch the odd trio above.

Anxiety tightened in Norah's gut with their watching stares.

"Feckin' shite," Cecil finally grumbled, shoving fingers through his chaotic hair. Then, with an ongoing utterance of creative expletives Nor had never heard prior, Cecil picked up the man from the floor and tossed him over his back. She rushed forward to get the door for them.

Though he clutched a hand-rolled cigarette in his one hand and a fully-grown elder in the other, Cecil still found the dexterity to extend a middle finger to her as he stepped through.

✦

From behind her smudged windshield, Nor cocked her head at the curious pair in the street, waiting within the shadow of Oblitus. They were both comely gentlemen with handsome seniority stamped into their lines, but Cecil was surely decades younger. They were cut from the same cloth but their cloths were used for vastly different purposes. Perhaps one sought to dab at tears and the other was stuffed into Molotov cocktails.

Once, she'd thought she'd known which Dex was.

She threw the vehicle in park and began to open the back seat, but Cecil snapped his fingers, impossibly disengaging the tailgate latch, and its ancient door fell open with a metallic crash.

Norah merely gaped, open-mouthed and unblinking.

With the sling of a hunter throwing dead meat, Cecil threw Dexteras onto the short truck's rubber mat.

"Sweet dreams ya ancient tosser," he growled.

Nor heaved at his limbs to arrange them more gently about the bed, expecting Cecil to be gone when she turned around.

"Ya fix the nutters eh, ankle-biter?" Cecil asked, a lilt of curiosity in his thick accent.

She shook her head, processing his unfamiliar language. "Excuse me, what?"

"Yer a shrink. For gits who lost the plot n' shit." He tossed his chin to Dex.

"I'm a therapist," she clarified, straightening. But chills littered her neck, knowing full well she hadn't hinted anything in regard to her profession to Cecil.

"Can ya send him for the icepick?" He made a crude, corkscrew motion with a finger beside his broken nose. "Or them zappy tongs? Zaps calmed his arse down befores." He seemed truly authentic and optimistic about the premise.

"I'm not sending Dex anywhere. He's my friend."

Cecil cackled with shining teeth. "Figs and Corpses aren't friends," he scoffed. "He's not even part of yer *world*, fleshy bird." He tossed his chin to the building behind them. "Ya don't even know *what* he is."

A flash of shame took her breath. There were no words, no response for such an asinine question.

"He-he's my friend. That's all I care about. He's a good person and-"

"Good person?" Cecil suddenly boomed with terrifying laughter and stepped nearer, his tactical boots nearly standing atop her own. Then, he tore the black glasses from his face.

Norah winced at the aggressive gesture, half-expecting flames to spew from empty black sockets. But instead, Cecil revealed plain, humanoid eyes. They were once striking and jade. Pretty, even. But they were now grayish and distant. Muted and sage in a drunk, sleepy gaze.

With a shock of understanding, she realized he was completely blind.

"Some good person, havin' nicked a nice *plenty* from me, eh dolly?" his lip arched as he gestured towards his unfocused irises.

Is he saying Dexteras blinded him?

"What? No, Dex didn't-there's no way," she muttered. "He's not like-"

"Like what?" he spat. "Like *that?*" he said, pointing to the ominous building behind them theatrically. "Have a butcher, *he's* the one blacked out in yer feckin' boot right now, *aye?*"

"Tonight, he had to have a reason. He wouldn't just-"

"He went off the feckin' hinges because I told Jezebel to talk shit about *you,* dolly. He'd four of me boys in an unscheduled meeting right befores ya walked in."

"Unscheduled meeting?"

"A beating, dolly," he cackled.

"How do you even know who I am?" she demanded, squaring up to Cecil with a raised chin. She was no longer ashamed, no longer small and tired.

Of course, Cecil had no response and only pulled on his cigarette with a scowl, but his shoulders stiffened.

"And if he's been so *awful* to you, why the hell are you helping him right now?" she added.

Cecil flicked his cigarette into the night. It had a magical, flaming tail like that of a meteorite.

"I was helping *you,*" he hissed, now clearly regretting the sacrifice. "I've already tried givin'em feckin' help-a-plenty."

"You stuck your hand inside his spinal cord," she retorted.

He grinned. "In *Oblitus,* it's best to be the puppeteer instead of the puppet." He leaned close and lowered his tone and his smile fell. "Stay the hell away from this place if you've any sense of preservation. They'll bleed his heart out with their feckin' teeth. And *you-*" he chuckled, voice deep and threatening. "Once they realize what a spark plug ya are, what intoxication they can leech from yer feckin' veins," he lingered here, breathing deeply as though inhaling her scent. "They'll keep ya. Oblitus got no answers for either of ya." Cecil huffed and shook his hands with irritation as though they were cramping. Hot sparks buzzed from his fingers like disheveled coals.

What a stubborn hardass. She understood Dex's deep craving to punch him now.

The handsome idiot roared into the stars with exhaustion and kicked at the warehouse's black door. It swung open wide and he stepped in.

"Piss off, Norah Kestrel," he shouted over his shoulder. And with a slam of the hinged steel, the club consumed him.

27

✦DEXTERAS✦

ATTEMPTING TO ESCAPE THE VOICES beneath the overcast skies of his apartment rooftop, his eyes dashed to each of the viewable clinquant stars.

But halfway into his nomenclature, a sudden, cold, and piercing tension snapped his exhausted head from the concrete. The crooning of a strange tuning fork now intensified in his skull and sat him entirely upright.

And then he saw, there in the darkness was the silhouette of a man, watching him.

Dex scrambled to his feet.

A dark-haired stranger stared at him from a nearby ledge, shadowed and laden with mystery.

But as they remained in the silence, Dex's fear fell away. For a flicker, a disarming moment in time as the stranger's dark glasses caught the glint of the moon, a note of familiarity rushed over Dexteras. They were both too comfortable in the dark, as though they'd known an eternity of sleeplessness.

The stranger leaped from his perch and drew near, extending a business card between tattooed fingertips.

"Who are you?" said Dex.

But the man only rolled his other wrist, manifesting a cigarette from a whirl of black plumes. He bit it in his teeth and again, offered up the business card.

Dex read the stranger's scars, tattoos, and emanations of misplacement. They matched his own. He reached for the card and opened his lips to propose a question.

But before it could be asked, the stranger fastened around his outstretched palm with a lightning-fast grip, dosing Dex with the sensation of cold water in his veins.

His vision went dark.

His limbs went numb.

He floundered until his eyelids finally peeled open against the night. But it was worlds different from the night he'd just left.

It was nearing dawn now. And this wasn't his rooftop.

The entire town of Corvid had spun around him and the stranger and had transported them someplace new. The gravel beneath him felt different. The shadow of an incinerator draped him in black. He was on the roof of Corvid's Hospital. It looked morbid and menacing through the lens he seemed to be borrowing from the man who'd gripped him. His limbs moved thorough the space as though he were swimming through it.

A raucous shuffle crunched and cursed from behind.

Dex spun to see two men snarling in the dark, boxing, exchanging blows, and shoving one another into the concrete.

Dex pressed himself against the incinerator just as a showers of gravel pelted the bricks from the men's dancing feet. The horrid cracks of grappling, kicking, pulling, elbowed eye sockets, and headbutted chest bones echoed across the roof and clapped against the brickwork.

Dex leaned from his cover to watch a man in a black coat and green eyes lift the other by the collar and sling him into the tower.

Dex ducked and darted from the bricks, surprisingly unnoticed by the fighting men. He spun to spectate just as the black-coated man pummeled the taller, lankier adversary.

Dex winced as the taller fighter's head ricocheted against the smokestack stone with a slap, eyes rolling back, mouth bleeding. There, the rising sun's fresh light just barely illuminated the poor bastard's face.

Dex's world dizzied and his limbs weakened. His gut dropped and he couldn't breathe. It took several long seconds of staring for him to compute: the losing fighter was himself, a long past self.

And as his past self was torn from the bricks and tossed to the gravel, it was clear to see that the other fighter was the stranger he'd just encountered on his roof with the business card. This was a shared memory between them.

Then, amidst a vicious grapple, his past-self reached his pale fingers for the stranger's skull and squeezed it like a melon. He plunged his thumbs deep into the furious green eyes until a horrid slurp of blood gushed from the sockets.

Vomit burned Dex's throat as he watched the men scream horrendous carols of agony, melodious and harmonizing as though they were instruments of the same family.

Past Dex's thumbs slurped and slipped inside the man's skull. Blood seeped from the sockets and both fighters fell to the ground in a heap, unrelenting.

And then, a wash of black paint corroded the impossible memory like a house fire to a photograph. The world simmered and curled into the present time and day, into his own nighttime once more, back to his own rooftop.

The return to the real world flip-flopped his insides and his knees were scraped bloody as he collapsed onto his roof. His authentic senses flooded him at such an alarming rate, his stomach lurched with nausea and he became sick in shuddering gasps, clutching at the asphalt.

Dizzy and sick, Dex lifted his sloshing body to face the stranger who'd forced the impossible visions upon him.

But he'd vanished.

Dex's fingers left damp, sticky prints on the business card beside him. Upon it, nearly illegible handwriting read: "What you're looking for is here," above a set of embossed coordinates that would eventually lead him to *Oblitus*.

Hours later, Dex gawked from the top of Oblitus' staircase, beholding the expanse below. With each step down the bony metal stairs, electrical fizzles simmered beneath his skin. They were unsettling blips he'd experienced in brief moments of great stress or emotion prior, but this place reconnected the shorted wires and created a live charge in his blood.

He stepped into the crowd, taking in the realm's countless doors, curtained thresholds, and shining bar tops. Then, within seconds of registering a pounding of feet behind him, he spun only to be snatched at the collar and choked.

A tanned beast held his arms behind him, leaving Dex to kick and flail and snarl as his wrist bones crackled. But as the stranger he'd met on the rooftop divided the crowd and approached, his attempts fell still and he huffed with wild eyes.

The two men stood toe-to-toe once more. Dex bared his teeth at his own reflection in the black sunglasses.

"What do you remember?" the man muttered around a cigarette.

"Remember? About what?" Dex stammered.

The goon behind him strained his limbs harder until Dex cried out.

"Don't *feck* with me Dexy," snapped the stranger. "Ya were gon fer feckin' *donkeys*. If you want what ya came fer, I needs to know exactly what ya remember about being a Fig."

For as long as he could remember, Dexteras could comprehend any language without thought or effort. But Cecil's Cockney rhyming slang was out of his jurisdiction.

"A *what?*"

"A Figment, ya feckin' lemon squeezer!" Cecil shouted.

A Figment? "Is that supposed to mean something to me?" His eyes widened with fear.

Cecil cocked his ear to Dex, listening keenly for something, brows stitched. Then with a great sigh, he whistled between his teeth and began rolling up his sleeves.

Dex swallowed with the unsettling gesture. His tattoos were covered by intentional swatches of black ink. Here and there, however, a bird with talons peeked through.

"Hold'em," said Cecil.

Somehow, the brute behind cinched tighter around Dex's wriggling muscles until he felt his shoulders might dislocate. He cried out again, evoking tears.

"Look at me brother," stated Cecil. "I'm gonna reach into yer chest and squeeze the life from yer feckin' heart. Understand?"

Dexteras tightened and shook. His heart drummed like a ballad.

"The only way yer breathin' another breath again is to give yer best dog and duck, aye?"

"Wh-what?" the old man choked. The stranger held no weapon that he could find, but he was priming himself for an attack, nonetheless.

And then, before Dexteras could comprehend what was happening, the stranger gave a lightning-fast strike of his fist. And Dexteras felt an icy cold slice *in* and up *through* him. He felt his flesh and muscle split with ease and apathy.

Dex gawked down, expecting a massive blade, but instead beheld a thick, tattooed arm churning about his insides. The sickening sensation of his intestines and kidneys being relocated made him swallow bile. He could only gape, his brain unable to fathom the impossible pain.

With each of the stranger's movements inside of him, Dex's blood surged, leaving him to call out in great, shuddering gasps.

Then, as promised, scraping fingernails wrapped around Dex's heart, blinding him with its razor wire grip. Dexteras screamed unto the heavens until he couldn't breathe. It was a vivid, acidic agony that broken bones had never come near to.

The rims of his vision flickered black. Nausea drooped his chin to his chest. Before the dark consumed him, he heard the stranger a final time.

"Ya really don't remember shite, do you Dexy? How the *feck* did the Unbecoming not brown bread ya out there?"

✦

Dexteras came-to on the tile, glaring up into a hoard of violent thugs with strange bands of tattoos and eye colors. He lurched upright, his insides tumbling within like a bag of stones. A seasick vertigo made him clutch the cool tile and close his eyes to the crimson bulbs of the bar.

The beings around him goaded in countless languages, kicking, prodding, snatching his limbs, tempting him to his feet. Once he could comprehend their demands through the onslaught of The Voices in his skull, he realized they were attempting to instigate him into fighting. Above, a fighting ring's gold chains dropped with black blood down its rusty links.

Dex didn't want to fight. He wanted to know who he was. What he was.

Of course, that was until the creature known as Jezebel had said what he said.

The large tattooed bison of a man pressed his bloody body against the golden cage from above, a toothy grin painted across his face like a rabid ape.

"Dexy!" Jezebel called down with a drunken cackle. "I've heard you got yourself a pretty little skin-sack. What's she called, eh?"

Dexteras closed his eyes and bit down on his tongue until it filled his mouth with salt. He fought to stay conscious, they to stay on his feet, and he limped onwards, towards the stairs, towards home.

Then, as though he were naming stars in the sky, Jezebel yelled over the booming music so Dex could hear, "Alice? Bethany? Claire? Destiny? Elena?"

The old man winced, furious on behalf of the women with such names that Jezebel now defiled with his demeaning jibes. He prodded onward, hot anxiety burning in his cheeks.

"Ooooo boys, we're close," whooped Jezebel. "Faith. Ginny. Hannah. Ingrid. Juliet. Kennedy. Lindsay-"

A desperate Dex fought to keep his stride kinetic, but the crowd grew thick and unmoving. They wanted to see a spar. To see blood spill. His own simmered like cooking stew, thick and tempting to boil over.

"Nearly there, Dexy!" laughed Jezebel from the stage, swinging against the chains like wedding bells. Each name was now more pronounced and dangerous on the beast's tongue. It was enough to make any father enraged with protective fury.

"Leah. Louise. Linda," Jezebel shouted.

Dex ground his jaw and closed his eyes. He could no longer move. He could no longer press forward. "No, no, no…" he whispered to himself, ears ringing.

"Lemon-meringue, lentil soup, lily blossom…" Jezebel chuckled, rambling like a madman. And then, the brute snapped his fingers and crooned once more.

"Lelani? Lilith? Lenore?" He cackled.

Dex's eyes flashed open, so hot and wide that they welled with tears. His insides were armed and rigid like an ejected steel baton, alight with lightning, ready to obliterate planets into particles.

He spun, ignoring the unset bones and maneuvered insides within him. Those bits would solder and mend and blood would clot, but he would never unhear Jezebel tasting his dear friend's name on his tongue as though it were something stuck in his teeth.

He also had no time to ponder the implications of his impossible healing abilities now. He dare not wonder about the kind of creature it made him.

"*Lenore*," the man in the ring sang with shining eyes. "*That's* it. Tell me Dexteras, she a looker?"

The crowd thickened around them with the rising tension, some grinning, some sipping their cocktails, others clapping bejeweled hands soaked in old tattoo inks. But they all implied a thirst for violence. This much was evident: fighting was the nightly entertainment.

Dex couldn't hear anything above the thudding of his heart and the humming of electricity beneath his skin. He was wound wire and cable, alight with live current. He approached the ring, locked onto the fighter's grinning red face with each step.

"You should bring her around, I'll show her a good time," Jezebel winked with a bruised and black eye. "Things her human brain can't even fa-" but the brute had been cut short.

En route to the ring, Dexteras snatched a prosthetic leg from a nearby contender who was unconscious on the tile. Its rigged bits and precious metals fizzled in his hands with obedience beneath his charged fingers. Then, in one motion, Dex leaped, pulled himself up by the thick gold chains, and tucked and rolled onto the stage. He swung the limb with monumental force through Jezebel's ankles. The mechanical weapon exploded into a shower of sparks and cogs as the massive fighter went down, like Achilles. Jezebel tremored with electricity.

Dex tackled Jezebel and pulled himself on top of him, delivering blow after blow against his opponent's skull and face. Only when the body beneath him was limp and no longer grinning bloodied teeth, did Dexteras stop. The old man stumbled away from the nearly-dead Jezebel whilst sweat and blood and sparks of dripping electricity fell from his flesh. He hopped down from the stage with finality. Later, of course, Jezebel repaid the favor by smashing Dex's skull from behind with a metal chair.

Now, in the blackness of his thoughts, was one of the very first moments he'd been gifted to stop. To process. To distance himself from the stranger he now knew as Cecil. From the blood thirsty Oblitus and its impossible beings. To fathom what horrid thing he must've been if they were his family.

He pulled at his hair in fistfuls, uncertain that he knew what reality was anymore, not that he'd had a stable grip on its luxury prior. There was a rift between possible and impossible and it was swallowing him, blending him like a food processor. He wanted to scream, so close to the precipice of insanity.

Dexteras.

Even The Voices were confused. Never before had they called out to him by name.

He felt so stuck, so trapped, as though he were folded into a coffin, suffocating, screaming, helpless, dead.

Dead.

"Dex!"

His eyes ripped open, wincing beneath a young, red sun.

His knees and hips ached and each inch of him pulsed with adrenaline. It'd seemed he'd kicked himself free, not from a coffin, but…

…the truck bed of a square-body pickup.

He was blanketed in a fleece throw and a man's canvas jacket with leather elbow patches. It smelled of old cigars.

This was Norah's car.

He'd busted the locking mechanism on her vehicle's boot, which now gasped open. Silhouetted before it was Norah Kestrel.

Beyond, a Gothic farmhouse loomed with chipped rails and detailed spindles. Its tired eyes matched Norah's on the morning he'd first met her on the hospital roof, dark and leaking. Hurting and haunted. But just as Norah's kindness had all those moons ago, the house's stretch of dark rooftop called to him with its quiet. Its massive shadow yawned across acres of dark foliage and swaying crops, blanketing the land around them in chaotic overgrowth.

Nor gazed down at her tailgate's rusted lid to critically eye the torn hardware with tall brows.

He began to apologize for the horrid overreaction but when her eyes fell to his, they were not alight with frustration, but maternal doting and worry.

"I'm sorry, I should've been gentler," she said. "But it's been one hell of a long night and I thought you might like some coffee."

28

✦NORAH✦

SHE ALLOWED HIM TO WANDER THE HOUSE as she ground medium roast beans in a ceramic hand grinder.

Clients who'd served in the military and had endured trauma altogether had taught her the importance of assimilating to new environments. Brains hardwired for chaos and crises most valued security, thus, she allowed her old friend to poke about and take his time, hoping he'd find comfort in habituating.

His footsteps creaked upstairs and down, pausing occasionally at photographs or artwork. When the floorboards groaned above the kitchen sink, her heart quickened.

He was in front of her parents' old bedroom.

What could he possibly think of a locked bedroom in my own house?

Tearing her eyes from the cigarette-stained ceiling, she noticed Vincent across the kitchen. He was sitting atop the refrigerator, his fat face staring into the ceiling as well.

"How the hell did you get up there?" she scoffed.

In his younger years, the cat was a master climber, but she hadn't seen him manage such a height in decades. At present, he looked unfazed by the effort and only enamored by the wandering old man in their home.

She heard Dex leafing through the countless poetry books stacked upon her minimalist furniture. He took in the lack of clutter, the symmetry, and the calculated deep pine and brown color schemes. He returned to the kitchen with neither comment nor judgment, looking as though he could've fallen asleep on his feet. He admired the small dollhouse drawers atop her kitchen's small island that she'd repurposed into a tea chest. When she used to paint, she'd illustrated the tiny wooden piece with comfort characters from her favorite anime movies, admiring the tiny acts of existence in their colorful, romanticized lives.

Dex pulled at the little brass handles to reveal the various sachets in each: Earl Grey creme, chamomile, pu'er, and jasmine green. He petted the hand-drawn character with his thumb, smiling softly.

He leaned into the thick forests of herbs in her window, inhaling deeply through his crooked nose. His eyes dragged across her old leather hiking boots stacked by the back door. He noticed the crude coat hook she'd fashioned from a stained and mounted piece of driftwood she'd gathered from the woods. Slick bomber jackets and faux leather coats hung from its stubby knots.

Then, upon noticing Vincent, who'd been following him diligently, Dex lowered his crackling joints to sit cross-legged on the wood floor. With minimal introduction, the cat climbed into his lap and rubbed against his scratchy beard with resounding purrs. Before Nor could comment on the anomaly, Vincent chirped with his croaky, guttural call and walked towards the stairs. Dex followed, and up they both climbed.

As the humming espresso machine warmed on her countertop, she too, ascended to the second floor. There, she kicked at the door beside her own. It gave a dull thunk, satisfactory and secure. She'd checked it this morning, but its sturdy reply still brought her brief comfort.

The large window in her bedroom was lifted ajar, and there Dex sat beyond its large glass, perched on the roof's flat ledge. Vincent had returned to his lap and kneaded Dex's thigh like biscuit batter.

She bent beneath the sill and approached the ancient pair.

Dex was rolling a cigar between his fingertips, watching its spewing shadows dance on the roof. The silhouette of his hand mingled with that of the plumes, creating the illusion that he was made of smoke.

Though she'd known how to avoid each creaky tile of that rooftop since she was a child, Dex heard her steps with ease.

"Thank you Nor," he grumbled to life, "for bringing me to your home… you truly shouldn't have."

"I had help," she said, sitting down beside him.

It was evident by his bowed features and avoidant eyes that he was recalling their interactions the evening prior. And while she still meant what she'd said, she had no intention of hurting Dexteras. As she told her clients, shame served no one.

So, to lighten the foreign and heavy tension between them she said, "Dex, my cat doesn't like anybody."

He drank in the sleeping creature with a flicker of a grin. "Well, he's quite fond of you."

"Is that so?"

"Mm. We agree on quite a few things," he said casually.

"You speak Ukrainian, Cantonese, and cat now?" She snorted, but her humor swiftly fell in seeing the old man's exhaustion outweigh his wit.

He only took a long pull of his cigar.

"What else does he have to say then?" she prodded.

"Well," said the old man, "He misses the cans of fish. Not the wet *cat* food, the fish for people."

All essence of amusement fell from Norah's features. Years ago, just after she'd moved back home, she used up her mother's stash of canned tuna in the pantry for Vincent.

"You're joking."

Dex shook his head, lips wrapped around the tiny cigar with a squint. "No, he was quite sincere. And if I understood properly, he lost something of yours. Sounds like, a shoe or a sock? Something you wear on your foot." Dex shrugged, dismissing the curious banter. "But whatever it is, it's in the bathroom air vent. He was playing with it a long time ago and it fell in there. He's been trying to tell you."

Every inch of Norah's body froze, from her agape lips to the heart in her chest.

There is no fucking way.

"He said it happened back when the whole house still smelled like-"

"Fire," she whispered, eyes wide. "I-I was changing the air filters…"

Dex turned his weathered face to read the story in hers. "You were upset."

Vince has been meowing at that bathroom door for years…

Norah stood, not truly registering the automatic movements of her body. Her brain was abuzz and noisy with anticipation and static. She walked back through her bedroom, down the hall, and retreated to the master bathroom. Falling to her knees and pulling the cover from the vent, she stuck a hand cautiously down into its bowels.

A gasp hitched in her throat.

For with a clump of dark hair and dust bunnies, a large Vincent Van Gogh, *Starry Night* sock came with it.

It was Leonard Kestrel's. One of her father's few belongings she'd been able to smuggle.

After his death, Robin fell into a fit of blind upheaval. What remained of her father's possessions was either victim to her mother's lighter, sewing scissors, or the tearing of her manic, hungry fingers.

Nor was just a child, leaking hot tears and clutching her own clammy hands. She watched from the top of the stairs as her mother drunkenly stumbled and cussed, a massive black trash bag dragging after her socked feet. In it, was every remnant of Norah's father.

Later that evening, as a fingernail sliver of a crescent moon peeked through her curtains, the child crept from her bed and tiptoed barefoot to the end of their long gravel driveway. Her chewed fingernails ripped through the Kestrel's trash cans and bags whilst a tiny flashlight was clutched in her teeth. Norah rubbed her fingertips against the fibers of her father's clothes that hadn't been clawed to shreds, burned with cigarettes, or stained with alcohol. There were devastating fatalities.

In her bandaged hand, she'd held his yellow cashmere sweater. It was splashed with wine, gory like blood. Norah loved the strange butter-soft fabric, even if the man who'd adorned didn't seem to notice how often she petted his arms and hugged him when he wore it.

Amongst the rubbish was also a shoebox filled with homemade Father's Day cards, birthday cards, and "best dad" accouterments Norah had gifted him. It was a weighty blow to the artist who now clutched them in fistfuls and wiped at rolling tears. There was an exhaustive relief and a disarming loneliness that her wept salt would be seen by no one. Her tears would too be delivered to the dump and abandoned with the rest of Leonard.

The few items Norah rescued from the trash were now stowed away under her bed in a cardboard box labeled "ART STUFF," so as to ward off her nosey mother.

The socks were particularly special, however.

It was a strange part of her father she'd never truly known of him. Despite his anger and violence and avoidance of all that was vulnerable, cracks of passion leaked through his ironclad facade at times. One of those brief, glittering facets of his humanity was his love for Van Gogh.

Nor never heard him talk about art, painting, or its complex musings. He'd never complimented Norah on her own creations. But he was the same man who'd named Vincent the day four-year-old Norah cradled the abandoned black kitten against her chest from the field.

Leo was cold, distant, and unloving, and yet it seemed he respected the sad Dutch artist who painted stars and sunflowers. He even had Van Gogh ties and a framed copy of *Skull of A Skeleton with Burning Cigarette* sitting on his nightstand. It now hung in Norah's room. This strange collection was the only proof Norah could find of her father's heart.

Resuming her seat by Dex now, she shook the dust from the sock and held it before the cat in the elder's lap. Vincent closed his eyes with contentment, his purr's motor deepening. He was pleased.

Dex watched her through wary squinted eyes, surely anticipating a panic attack to burst from her chest.

"Nope," she said suddenly, standing to her feet and ducking beneath the window. She went to the kitchen to retrieve their coffees, drizzling thick milk and Tupelo honey into heaping espresso shots. She cradled them back to the roof, balancing upon the house's hat-brim rooftop with care. She'd hoped the sock would be gone when she returned, but there it still sat.

Dex unfolded his limbs and wrapped them around his cup with a grateful sigh. He was alight with hums and inhalations, warming nearer to his authentic self.

Despite the human moment, Nor's mind was asunder with the prior evening's impossibilities, and she could restrain her questions no further.

"I watched your spine break, Dex. He put his hand *into* your spine…"

The old man leaned back onto his elbows and cast his long legs over the ledge. He pulled at his beard and perched his cigar on a roof shingle beside him.

"They call him Cecil the Shrike," Dex mumbled. "A few of them have… abilities," he muttered. "Like I do, I s-suppose."

Nor knew better than to question him too much here, fearing the shock would consume him too. Sitting carefully in this fragile space, she waited.

He kept his eyes settled on the horizon, nursing his mug close to his broken nose. For a moment, he shook his head slowly, galaxies away from himself. Then, his rings clinked against his cup and he blinked back to his body.

"C-Cecil showed me a memory of my past. *Showed* me, in my thoughts like a film," he muttered as though the images still lingered there behind his eyes. A shaky hand hovered above his forehead. "And he told me if I trained at Oblitus with him, he could get me a match in the ring. That I could earn memories there, *win* them." A tic clenched at his cheek and his foot jittered over the gutter, gripped by akinesia. "That's why I was gone for so long…" he said, in a voice so low it was nearly a whisper. "Time doesn't pass the same there, and I, I got lost in it…" he tried. "I'm going crazy, I think."

"You aren't." She leaned into his arm and sought his gaze beneath his fallen tresses. His eyes were riddled with storms, looking upon her as though he weren't certain if even *she* was real. Then his lashes fell to the horizon peeking over his kneecaps. He covered his face with his hands.

"But this is asinine. It's impossible," he whispered. Nor could see that he was terrified. "But I *have* to know, I *need* to know. I have nothing else, I'm missin' s-s-so many pieces."

She squeezed his arm, valiantly pretending her merely mortal brain wasn't terrified too. Not of him, *never* of him, but of what lengths he'd go to, what danger he would chase to understand himself. Her head pounded and pulsed with dreamlike disorientation. This was real, but it felt anything but.

His warm arm bulked beneath her touch.

And *he* was real.

"I saw what you saw," she said. "You are not crazy. I understand why you'd want to fight for something like that. We're going to figure this out."

"But what I saw of the past, *my* past, was so…dark. So awful. I *blinded* Cecil," he said with disgust, eyes clenched shut and wrinkles crumpled.

She remembered the blind man's accusations, recalling those muted and furious forest eyes. They'd stared through her as though they could see beneath her skin. She shivered. Cecil didn't seem to be someone who'd waste his energy on lying, but Dex didn't seem to be someone who'd blind someone either. Not without reason.

Her old friend stared into the distant sky, eyelids drooping and pink.

"Hey," she whispered. Nor plucked the blue bracelet from her wrist with the silver and gold stars and rolled it onto his trembling right hand. It matched the jewel tones of his bruises and tattoos.

Dex folded over his knees and inspected the bracelet with quivering fingers. His Adam's apple strained with effort.

She'd hoped the trinket would remind him of the good he'd done, regardless of his mysterious past, but it was plain to see that it only buried him in more loss.

"*Bozhevilnyi,*" he whispered with buckled brows, reading the tiny letters, entranced.

"Mine says lioness," said Nor, presenting her wrist and twisting at one of the pink hearts on her arm.

But he didn't look. The day's new light glittered in his watering eyes until he dropped his face into his hands once more.

"Oh, God. Sh-sh-she's gone. I should've been there. I should've been there…"

Alina's death collapsed into Nor's chest again too. Last evening, she'd shamed him for its heaviness and injustice, but that was unfair. It wasn't his fault. The death of someone you loved was never going to be fixed, no matter how loudly you screamed.

"Alina's last days were so much better because you gave her a voice, Dex."

"She didn't need me. I needed her, more than she knew." Slow tears leaked beneath his palms.

"Then you gave her the gift of being needed."

He cast his draping locks away in a fist and moaned, sniffing.

"*Deodamnatus,*" he whispered. "I'm so sorry I wasn't here, Nor. I sh-sh-should've been here for both of you. I should've…"

Nor rested her forehead against his bicep.

"I just got so lost… I'm *still* so lost," he said.

She leaned deeper into him. "She knew how much you loved her." Nor allowed him the time to weep and grieve without obligation to speak for some time.

Eventually, his breath steadied and his hands fell from his face. His eyes were left puffy and crimson and tears still balanced at his lids like shards of crystal. Norah knew, once one fell, it was impossible to keep the remainder of the glass from shattering.

"I don't want to fight. I don't want to hurt people," he mumbled. "But it's all I have. This is the only chance I've ever had to know what I-" but he stopped abruptly. "All of it sounds *mental*, absolutely insane. What if I'm really losing it this time?" He grumbled through his fingers, voice trembling.

"Stop it," she stated firmly. "You know that I believe you. I saw what you saw," she said, pointing toward town. "And you're right, it makes absolutely no fucking sense, but it happened." She nearly lost herself to the gruesome flashbacks of the realm. The sickening slap and crackle of bodies. A place she did not belong, on so many levels.

"I never imagined I could do those things I did," he began. "But when I was fighting..." he shook his head, losing himself to the boiling in his blood that he must've felt. The adrenaline that Norah knew clinically, could be powerfully addictive, like any drug.

"What an awful thing must I have been...?"

Norah squeezed his hand, keeping him with her in the present. "I know about wanting a home. Wanting to be found so badly it aches," she said. "It makes us carve ourselves into what others want us to be."

Dex's stony gaze glided to hers.

"But just because they knew a past version of you, doesn't mean they're who you're bound to become. Blood doesn't always mean home. The home you deserve, anyways." A pesky cliche piped up at this thought: *don't drink poison just because you're thirsty.*

His eyes paced between hers, an eternal purple blue lacing his lids, no words able to find his lips.

Nor wondered if he ever slept. She squeezed his shoulder, set their coffee cups on the window's ledge, and fidgeted with the key ring at her hip.

"And hey..." she said, tossing him a tiny brass key.

He snatched it from the air without a glance.

"That goes to the...the spare room." She nodded to the stained window around the corner. "I know you like the roof, but there's a bed if you need it. My home is yours. It unlocks the door to the hall too."

As she returned the keychain to her hip, she noticed a brave black blur of fur upon the old house's turret, hundreds of feet from the ground.

"Jesus Vincent, how in the fuck?" she hollered up at him, slapping her sides.

His smooshed features whirred about the skies, his tongue cackling and chattering at diving crows. His yellow eyes were as wide as crazed moons.

"You always lock all the doors?" Dex asked with bent brows and a wrinkled forehead. He flipped the key between his fingers.

She pulled her own copy from the chain on her chest, gripping it as though she'd reeled in a clump of seaweed on a fishing line. "Just that one."

"Why, love?"

"Because I've got past stuff to work through too," she admitted, stretching the skin on her palm.

29

✦DEXTERAS✦

THEY SHARED LATE AFTERNOON TEA in the quiet and watched the sunset. While he was at Norah's side, The Voices seemed content and merciful.

Before she went to bed, she squeezed his shoulders tight, cooling his tense muscles like a mountain spring. She smelled lavender soap and Earl Grey tea.

She ushered him blankets and pillows that he wouldn't need and cleaned the rooftop of the day's dishware. She reached for their shriveled cigars, settled in the ridges of the roof like nesting birds, still breathing with small life.

Dex extended a hand. "Don't scrape them. It frays your tobacco leaves and worsens the wrap when you relight them."

In a blink, her features became shadowy and grave. She shook her head.

"We can light new ones then," she muttered, crushing the ashy heads along the sediment. The cherries were ground into dead smoke.

He'd never heard such glacial remarks from Norah and dared not pry further. He nodded and watched her patter to her window and bend into its great mouth.

✦

He paced along the gutter's lip, toeing the line as close to peril as possible. He laid his head on his shoulder until his joints popped, aching from past brawls. Some he could recall, but evidently there were many he could not.

All that he knew thus far was that he was inhuman.

Of course.

It's why he'd always felt so wayward and lost amongst the dull hum of humanity but strangely alive whilst bare-knuckle boxing in an underground ring with impossible beings. They were all black pots and kettles.

A firm, resting heartbeat thudded like a rawhide drum against the walls of the home behind him. He knew its timbre well. It meant that Nor was finally asleep.

How could someone like her wish to exist anywhere within his orbit? He was evidently unsafe, feral. His eyes burned from unblinking at the skies. He sat in hopes of quieting his shakes.

He had to know more, and Oblitus held promise. Like thoughts of sucking lemons could make one salivate, memories of the ring lined his tongue with the saltiness of blood and sweat. But for now, he closed his eyes to escape the endless questions.

There, a pair of eyes met him in the dark. Golden irises settled in stark pearls, narrow with pleasure. The wild animal that'd finally cornered its prey.

Dex's limbs were welded still. He couldn't tear open his eyes. He couldn't breathe.

Come home, they seemed to sing in the dark, their breath just behind his earlobe, against his neck.

Finally, Dex jolted upright with a gasp, sweating at the collar. In the end, he abandoned all hope of rest and decided to instead label the stars, limbs trembling.

30

✦NORAH✦

WHEN SHE WOKE, he was still on the rooftop, tall and swaying like a dandelion stem, hair disheveled, pale, and fluffed with humid air. He didn't seem to notice her presence, planted in an upright trance with a lolling head and closed eyes. Perhaps it was his version of sleep. So early in the morning, Norah felt incapable of surprise at his unending quirks.

She gently filled her arms with the warm, catatonic man and watched his eyeballs flick beneath his lids in some distant dream. It was his flat, unbuckled, and painless brows that truly told her how far away he was from his body.

She left him to rest in his strange meditation. He undoubtedly needed every ounce of thoughtlessness he could muster.

Nor commuted to work and walked about the hospital in a daze, hoping to reflect with a level head, but the nothingness was too comfortable. She needed to request time off, to find someone to cover her high-risk clients. But for a while, her zombified feet just carried her numbly, eyes afar with glassy emptiness.

"Fututus et mori in igni!" His blood-laden war cries filled her skull.

Norah shook from her trance and returned the shitty cafeteria coffee to her lips. She'd sprinkled the horrid brew with salt in desperation, which seemed to help, much to her chagrin. She gnawed on the Styrofoam cup and fell from herself once more.

She traveled the quiet of the echoing staircases, drowning in brain fog. When she found a door handle, she shouldered through it. Her hand slid along the outdated wallpaper, its vintage *hissss* beneath her fingertips. She counted descending room numbers as she shuffled, finding grounding in their repetition.

6A

6B

6C

6D

This hall smelled like the consultation room, like the day she'd commuted from her out-of-state college and her new life to stare upon the shadows looming across her mother's lungs. The vaporous ghosts spread atop the white bones and black shadows.

Spite roared through Norah's bones back then, having believed her mother sabotaged her own respiratory system just to tear her daughter away from the healthy new beginning she'd fought for, and to finish what the fire had started.

6F

6G

7A

Awareness like an ice bath stopped her heart and her ambling feet. She spun to the plastic signs in the hall.

Inpatient Unit

EoLC

End of Life Care.

Her eyes watered with unblinking terror. Her obliviously worthless limbs had stranded her in the ward of atrophying bodies. The seventh floor. Buried bitterness and guilt flooded her in waves of heat, melting her to the floor before the closed doorway of 7B. The siren song of wailing monitors beckoned her from within.

Then, death itself petted her spine with thin fingers.

Norah gasped and spun, washed in cold terror to find Toni Plover, her mother's nurse, and Heidi Thrush from billing, who beamed.

"Norah Kestrel. Where's your partner in crime?" sang Thrush, clearly missing the near-death expression across the therapist's pale face. "I've heard no one sees you two apart." The striking brunette looked down upon Nor from tall, adventuresome heels, holding a lipstick-stained coffee cup.

Dex's blood-slicked body crashed unbidden through Nor's mind again. Tanned muscles flecked with bar glass and sweat, exotic curses roaring from his busted lips. Ironclad and snapping punches like a bear trap.

"We've got his check and he's late on paperwork," continued Thrush. "Thought hell hath frozen over, the man's always perfect." She clapped her enamel nails along the mug with a ruby grin. "Doesn't hurt that he's perfect to stare at too."

The blood swiftly returned to Norah's brain and she smacked the woman across the arm, baring her teeth in an animalistic grin. It wasn't an authentic assault, but it was the playful, daring juxtaposition of one.

Norah wasn't so naive as to not notice the suggestive stares and bitten lips of the many men and women who beheld Dex. While his features were alluring and his form was lovely, she wouldn't allow others to speak of her best friend as meat.

"Don't talk about him like that, you heathen," she said, training her eyes on the woman. "He's taking a sabbatical. We just lost a client," she added with a protective bite. "But I'll let him know." Despite her irritation with Thrush, Nor fought hard to give her the entirety of her attention in the hopes that Toni would leave.

Heidi's perfect teeth shined. "You're right Kestrel, he's not a side of rib. He's lucky to have you. Y'all make a killer team."

"Thanks."

"But be real with me, have you *ever* seen a man his age who can work tattoos and a suit like that? I mean I don't usually hunt for silver fox but *damn,* get my rifle…"

This time, Thrush skittered away on her heels with a cackle, waving over her shoulder at them as Norah smacked her fleeing limbs. Droplets of her coffee splashed to the tile.

And then there were two. Norah's cheeks and neck flooded with nauseating waves of blood as she turned to her remaining colleague.

Toni was a petite woman with graying hair, pink lips, and wrinkled features. She was a calming and tranquil presence despite her long days spent amongst the bodily, mentally, nearly, and entirely dead.

"Good to see you, sweet girl," said Toni, her words gentle as a dove. Both of their gazes flicked between the other and the threshold beside them.

"You could go in, if you'd like," Toni whispered, her expression quiet and careful.

Norah's gut cramped and her breath clenched in her chest. She hugged her disembodied arms to her chest. She floundered with Toni's invitations and the endless wave of questions in her skull.

What's the point?

After all this time, what is there to say?

Neither of us would apologize.

Neither of us would lower our masks.

What would be the fucking point?

And then, a thought like that of a panicked, drowning child played on loop between her racing heartbeats:

I can't.

I can't.

I can't.

A stress headache deepened with each neurotic shake of her head.

"N-No. No, no, no. No. But thank you, Toni. Thanks." Nor smiled with pained cheeks. Hot tears burned at her lids. And that *fucking guilt.* It gripped her trachea in a fist, leaving her to pull at the collar of her shirt and swallow.

Then, without another word, Norah spun and burst through the nearest door to the staircase. Her hurried boots squealed with each step:

I can't. I can't. I can't. I can't.

31

✦DEXTERAS✦

"I'M FALLING APART. I-"

"Not again, please don't-"

"God, my chest. It's splitting, and I-"

"This is the end. This is it."

Itchy and restless, he embarked on a disoriented walk. Twitches and aches peppered his body whilst The Voices beat like reckless insects against a windowpane.

He couldn't imagine how haggard and unruly he must look. Thick dreads of hair pulled at awkward angles in the wind, and he winced with the tugging of dried blood at his chest hairs.

He was craving peace, a distraction, *something*. A smoke, maybe.

Then, as promptly as the longing stung his throat, an electric current prickled along his chest and forearm, making his fingertips itch and flex. Then, a cigar manifested between his fingertips as sure and hot as hellfire. He gawked at the smoking tobacco in his grip and clenched his teeth to keep a scream at bay. It wasn't dementia, he now knew. It was an ability. A curse. Otherworldliness of some sort.

When Cecil performed such tricks, they looked natural, like breathing. But within himself, they felt wrong.

As Dex broached the historic bricks and cobbles of town, he met his old eyes in the black refraction of shop windows. He remembered wincing back at his bloody reflection not hours prior within Cecil's dark lenses.

The salted, coppery taste of blood returned to his tongue as he revisited those brief encounters. It seemed each rendezvous with the stranger left both their knuckles open and their bones bruised.

"Feckin' disappointment," Cecil spat after Dex's first fight in Oblitus. His cigarette smoke wafted to the gold ceiling.

"What the hell is this? Why can't you just tell me what I want to know?" Dex begged from the tile, nose throbbing with the rhythm of his overworked heart. When the first surge of cold air chilled the deepest passages of his nasal cavity, he knew it'd been broken again. With each drum of his heart, streams of blood rolled onto his shirt from the cracked cavern in his skull.

"Give over ya feckin' ice cream," Cecil snarled, seizing Dex by the collar and lifting his torso from the ground. "*Yer* memories aren't mine to give."

"But you showed me-"

"I showed ya one of *mine*, didn't I?" Cecil snapped.

"Then where in the hell do I get mine from exactly?"

"Yer not gettin' an audience with the boss until ya prove worthy of their time. Blood is the sausage and mash of this feckin' place. Spill some. *Barba non facit philosophum*," Cecil mocked with a Cockney accent unfit for dead languages. *A beard does not constitute a philosopher.*

He dropped a perplexed Dexteras back to the floor and disappeared into the club's belly.

"Worthless piece of -"

"I don't understand the-"

"Just lay here and die-"

"Maybe tomorrow she will-"

The Voices' cries shook Dex from the past. His feet had halted of their own accord before his apartment building, drawn home like weary homing pigeons.

Floors above, on the threshold of his flat, a foreign slip of paper rested on the hardwood just within. The scrawled message upon it was crude and threatening:

Boss wants to meet.

Dex's heart skipped a beat. The emotional whiplash he'd been victim to whilst knowing Cecil was head splitting. In one moment, he was telling him to fuck off, and in another, he was writing him love letters to come back. Dex pitched the scrap to the waste bin with such force, it smoked like a tiny comet.

"Futuere."

He peeled off his blood-crusted clothes and showered, hissing and groaning as the hot jets pelted his wounds. Swirls of pink and russet rinsed his toes, rich with blood and bar sweat. Once his flesh became habituated to the stings, he pressed his forehead against the tile, allowing the water to flood his ears and drown out The Voices.

"Not even with it-"

"Honestly, I don't care-"

"Probably doesn't even remember-"

"Truly the worst-"

Muffled weeping...

He toweled off, body heavy and sore, but less offensive to the senses. He trimmed his beard and mustache with humming clippers and pulled a comb through his snarled locks. Cuts and bruises vandalized his tattoos and old flesh, now growing more grim and nebulous in color.

You're a sorry sight, dead dog.

He despised his reflection and often disregarded its stare in any mirror, but a sweet memory rang in his skull above The Voices:

"You might learn something about yourself if you looked into these."

Norah's unfounded belief in his worthiness made his chest ache, but he procured a small hand mirror from the medicine cabinet and with a sigh, scrutinized his inked flesh for the first time in decades.

On his biceps were the raven and roaring lion, pierced with arrows in their backs and chests. They were the same beasts Alina had decorated in her chubby markers with childlike intensity.

He retrieved her bracelet from the sink and slipped it on, remembering how often she would tinker with his jewelry or trace his tattoos with a small finger. She'd try to fit his wrist in her tiny grip, holding his cracked and ugly hands in hers.

Blinking away threatening tears, he twisted and contorted to glimpse an intricate cathedral tattoo swallowing his spine. It was adorned with statues, lion's head knockers, and vibrant stained glass. It rose into four steepled peaks, piercing a sky with endless stars. Latin script was carved across a tattered scroll that unrolled from shoulder to shoulder.

Astra inclinant, sed non obligant. He scowled at the inscription. The stars incline us, they do not bind us.

Over his left pectoral was an anatomical heart, plump with gasping ventricles and trickles of lifeblood in spattered ink. Its wrapped scroll read *Ad Meliora*, to better things.

From clavicles to waist, two massive birds carved at one another with eager talons. Claws and beaks were wide and ravenous, tearing into one another amidst a violent aerial assault. A dark hawk swooped upon a tiny sparrow who'd barrel-rolled to its spine in defense.

Dex's gaze then fell to a pair of blossoming branches rising from his flanks, hung with ripe grapes and lush leaves. The branches were woven with red, flowering poppies below his navel, spilling blossoms and their jagged foliage down his thighs. Woven beneath the flourishing blooms, however, was a shimmer of creeping scales. Two stalking serpents crept up his form until they sprang with bared fangs dripping venom alongside his abdomen.

A banner was spread between the serpents that read, *Amore et melle et felle es fecundissimus*, to love is rich with honey and venom.

Dex groaned into his hands and rubbed his worn face, struggling to read onward. As he'd feared, every inch of his external body was as inconclusive and maddening as the internal.

"He doesn't know how much it hurts, how-"

"-drowning in everything.."

"How can I possibly go on without her?"

"Maybe it's going to be like this forever…"

He stuffed the starched cuffs of his pants beneath oiled boots and tucked a white button-down beneath a leather belt. He bound up his sleeves and wild hair and noticed the faded bird silhouette inked on his palm. It sustained a long-healed circular scar shriveled in its belly. He couldn't decipher its old, blown-out text. None of the artwork gave direction towards a home or an identity. None of it made a damned bit of sense. He allowed the hand mirror to clatter in the sink.

He took in his modest home. Plain, undistinguished. Mortal.

But then he ran a finger against the ruddy bones on his neck that Cecil had crushed hours prior. Healed nerves and muscle injuries he should've never survived.

Perhaps I didn't.

Am I dead?

No, not this again, he begged.

The Voices screamed Their verdict, but he shook his head until it hurt.

I am not dead. I am not dead. I am here. Norah sees me, she knows.

But he closed his eyes.

He wasn't dead, but he also wasn't alive. Not *really*.

He entered the bedroom where he never slept and pulled at the handle of a hard-shell case from a high shelf. Thick dust fell from it as it swung in his grip.

Then, with a final glare at his space, the old man left.

32

⋆NORAH⋆

Dᴇxᴛᴇʀᴀs sᴀᴛ ᴏɴ ᴛʜᴇ ʀᴏᴏF's ʟᴇᴅɢᴇ as she pulled into the drive that evening. He raised a cigar-wielding hand in a gentle wave. She returned it with a smile.

As she stepped out of the vehicle, a squat black shadow drew her eye to the rooftop's opposing chimney. At its peak, sat a massive black cat cackling at the darkening skies. He'd somehow scaled the bricks to birdwatch.

"Vincent, the fuck?" she called.

His yellow eyes found her and he managed a chirp of his throat with kind disregard. He then rearranged his cinnamon roll-sized haunches and returned to watching the local sparrows.

Norah bowed beneath the window's frame and sat with a sigh beside her friend. His tobacco lined her lungs with the scents of soft vanilla bean and sandalwood. As though sensing her hunger, he had a fresh smoke ready and lit for her. His magical cigars were soothing and rich, and somehow never left her scraping stale flavors from her tongue in the morning.

Vincent jumped from the chimney and settled into Dex's lap who stroked him with a large hand.

"Well look at you." She leaned forward to take in the bearded man's crisp attire. Black and white suited his contrasted features. He looked sharp, debonair.

"You look good when you're not soaked in blood."

The orange glow of her home illuminated portions of him and darkened others. A fragile smile stretched around his cigar, but his eyes remained hooded and heavy. He offered no small talk, no outward pourings of the mind, just silence. He spun his cigar in his fingertips whilst his eyes were lost in distant galaxies.

He seemed to be wearing that itchy sweater of misplacement, endless wandering. It was impossible to know where the day took his thoughts or headspace, but it was evident in his grinding teeth and tall shoulders that it was somewhere painful.

He didn't even notice the neglected embers and ash that fell from his cigar and onto his other hand. The fiery debris rolled against an old tattoo on his palm.

It seemed to be a swooping bird, clutching a banner in its beak. It was old and warped, its font bleeding and trailing along the valleys of his hands like the veins on a topographical map. Its mountains were old wounds and scar tissue. The bird's eye was blue and tired like Dex's, and the ink's remaining colors were weak and opaque.

She took the hand from his lap, brushed the ash from it, and examined its art as Alina would have, humming with interest. Her eyes traveled up and down his arm like a curious child who poked at her father's tattoos.

Dex only continued smoking his cigar, the draw of his chest brightening the tip's orange warmth.

Every so often, she'd attempt to read the Latin etched in his skin for a translation. In earnest, she wanted to keep him from fully succumbing to the catatonia brewing beneath.

"*Dum spiro spero?*" she prompted.

"While I breathe, I hope." His old voice croaked with life as though it hadn't been used in days.

She grazed his tough fists with a delicate finger as though poking at a tiger's paw. Each of his inflamed knuckles wore an inked letter and she bent her head to read them.

"*Sola...spes?*"

"Hope Alone," he mumbled, smoke seeping through his teeth.

She gave a very small smile.

"None of that means I was a good person Nor." A tic snatched at his jaw.

She bent across her legs to find his downcast irises, grateful for the breakage of the quiet between them. Norah knew he wanted answers about what ran amok in his blood. And God, so did she. But she couldn't shadow his anxiety in her curiosity. His discomposure was the only thing that kept her own at bay.

"I know you've waited a really long time," she said softly, searching his stormy eyes. "I can't imagine what that's like, Dex. But goodness or badness isn't something you're born into. They're things you work at. And I've always seen you work to be good. To be healing."

His whiskers swelled as he pulled on his cigar. Amorphous shapes spewed from his lips into the evening whilst he considered.

After a few moments in the quiet, Nor rose with his cold coffee cup and retreated to the window. She tiptoed across the threshold but fell to a standstill once inside. Her eyes fell to the shadowed brass doorknob ahead of her in the dark. Its glint in the moonlight snatched her attention like that of a predator's eyes in the woods. Her limbs were frozen.

That fucking door.

They say trauma hardens you. Toughens you. Makes you bulletproof. But it *impaled* Norah Kestrel. To leave it in would mean endless pain and limitation, but to work at pulling it out could mean a risk of bleeding out, being emptied.

It calloused the insides of her cheeks where she chewed them, raw and vulnerable. It left her flinching, cowering, and protecting her head when someone dared raise their voice. The past didn't harden her like a scab, it thinned her out until she was a bundle of overly sensitive and exposed nerve endings. It made her despise her past self for the embarrassing weakness she was left to deal with.

You ask Dex to forget his past, yet you can't even walk into their room?

Her eyes fell to a black scuff along the door's frame below. She'd punted that door the day they pointed to the vaporous poltergeist across her mother's lungs. It was the week she had to leave college and move back home to care for the horrid house. The month she had to abandon her friends, her school, and a clinical internship she adored. The year she was torn from the loving, new family she'd fought so hard for. The first knots in her rope that'd allowed her to rise from depression, from the Kestrels, from boundless anxiety, were cut off beneath her grip.

But she survived. As she always did.

She'd completed the remainder of her classes online and attended Corvid's Hospital for internship. She worked at Two Sparrows Cafe, ran part-time group therapy with teens at The Nest, and even worked after-hours on-call for their triage programming.

She learned how to pay all the bills and tend the flower beds of Black Dragon coleus and midnight petunias. She tried so hard to attempt normalcy. To force the circumstances to feel like a choice, like an extension of her grace and her compassion for her sick mother.

Thus, when adult Norah stepped back onto the threshold of 722 Ibis Trail, she saw the house as a challenge. A quest. It was her job to be certain that it would not take any more Kestrels to the grave.

She sold her mother's abandoned vehicle to hire electricians to properly gut and rewire the entire home. The curtains were torn from their rods. Fabric furniture was replaced with wooden and steel fixtures. The charred walls were coated in a muted blue. The skeleton of Leonard's armchair was tossed out. She avoided eye contact with the forced squints of family photos beneath their glass coffins as most were boxed away.

And most importantly, she kept her parents' bedroom door locked, just as her mother had during the remainder of her life there. And Just as Robin wore its key, so did Norah. The door was a padlocked scab protecting them from its oozing wounds. Its nightmares. Its ghosts. Its memories.

Eventually, Nor avoided the second floor altogether, until Dex arrived.

And now, as she stared at that *fucking* door, despite the home's candles, herbs, teas, and plants that filled each room, she realized it all still reeked of ash and death.

33

✦DEXTERAS✦

A FLUTTERING HUM BEAT AGAINST HIS CHEEK like a worried moth. Dex turned towards the house, bones groaning.

Norah's stone-still figure stood past the lifted window, listless, struck, heart racing.

He extinguished his cigar into his palm and shoved to his feet.

"*Cara mi?*" he asked gently, bowing low beneath the sill.

She yelped and spun. The teetering glassware in her arms scraped and clinked and began to plummet, but Dex snatched them from the air with outreached hands. He set them on the rug below, striving to keep his friend calm and unbothered.

He straightened and drank in the room that held her captive, finding himself wincing with its intensity. Nor and the space here tremored with aches.

Her eyes returned glassily to the door adjoining her room to another, as though dead bodies rotted within.

"You want to go that way?" He tossed his chin towards it.

"I don't know that I can..."

He eyed the door's lock and nodded, extending an outstretched palm to her.

"*You've* got a key, too," she noted.

"But yours is much heavier."

She sighed and pulled the tiny thing from her chest as though it bore the weight of a ship's anchor. With averted eyes, she dropped it into his palm.

He disengaged the locking mechanism with a shudder of steel.

Nor's heartbeat quickened behind him as though he'd pulled the hammer of a pistol.

He reached for the knob, but as his flesh grazed its dusty brass, he snatched himself back with a hiss. A poker-hot sting had bitten his palm.

"*Faex*," he cursed, stepping back from the threshold in confusion.

It wasn't the pain, but what came with the pain that struck him so. Accompanying imagery, visions, flashed behind his eyelids. He was reminded briefly of the memories Cecil had shown him.

"What happened?" Nor's heart lifted with a familiar hope his tongue knew well. It was a yearning for proof that you weren't crazy. That someone else felt what you felt. "It hurt you?"

"It was more of a...a *memory* of a hurt..." he began. "I think I picked up on something you left behind here, love."

Norah took a step back, brows stitched with fear.

Dex again gripped the handle and closed his eyes. This time, he expected the pain. *Respected* it, because it was hers.

Beneath the darkness of his lids, he was instantly met by brilliant evergreen irises, wide and fixed with horror. A small cry of pain sang out like a mourning songbird.

"You were so small Nor..." he muttered, swimming through the old memory as though it were morning fog. "The house. It smells like... cigarettes."

"How do you know that?" she snapped, defense mechanisms

unsheathing like swords from their hilts.

The struck chord in her voice returned him to the present and reminded him to be gentle.

He didn't tell her that he could hear screams. That he could feel the heavy tragedy. That trauma could imbed itself even in wood grain. It was no wonder she feared it so. Its weariness sapped him so severely, that he thought he may need to sit and rest. He turned from her to blink away his brief tears. Someone or parts of someone had indeed died here.

"Anyone would've come from that with some scars, love. Seen and unseen…" His eyes fell magnetically to her sweating palm where her white scar sang to him. "But you don't let yourself feel them, do you?"

Norah shoved both hands into her sweatpants pockets and stared at him, refusing such a confession.

He returned to the door again and grazed its handle. In respecting its memories with a quiet reverence, they were respectful in return and didn't burn him. He then reached out for her hand.

Her heartbeat was nearly louder than her voice. "I can't, Dex."

He remained still and patient and said nothing.

She wrinkled her face in pain and stepped nearer of her own volition, eyeing the knob with disgust. Her hand hovered above it, thumb lacing her fingertips as though the phantasm of a quarter rolled across her knuckles. But despite the self-soothing tic, she promptly retracted, shaking her head in defeat, eyelids batting like a flickering star.

"It's alright to feel the hurt love," he said as quietly as he could manage.

"Nothing can be done about it now. Why would I ever want to?"

He could hear the consequential buckles and straps of her armor cinch closer to her chest but knew she wasn't angry with him. She was angry with herself.

"Some things aren't meant to be fixed, Nor. You're just supposed to feel them," he said, rewording something he'd heard her voice to clients prior.

Her jaw tightened. A lump rolled in her throat. She closed her eyes.

"It's not that simple."

Her inner song hardened and crackled like distant lightning, like the jarring scratch of a record player. The hairs on his beard buzzed with its protective electricity. Though his face remained stoic, he inwardly admired her spirit. Her bite.

"It *is* that simple. But it's not that easy, *amica mea*," he corrected.

"A-Amica?"

He raised a brow, realizing he'd been slipping into Latin again. "*Amica mea*, means my friend." He rubbed his neck, heat warming his cheeks.

She smiled briefly with the distraction.

"It doesn't have to be today," he said, nodding to the door.

She blinked away hot tears. "Not today..."

He pulled her close into an embrace until the panicked moth in her chest sputtered from her lips. Still clutching to his small friend, he cast the door open wide and peered in. Dusty, unused furniture and a barren king bed loomed in the dark like sarcophagi. He stepped in.

He spun to watch her step in after him, watching her courage break through the dead, old space, her bravery glimmering like Aurora Borealis.

They cleaned dishes and watered her plants. He petted the waxy leaves and whispered inspirations of growth to each beneath his breath. He wrestled with Vincent and fed the small beast his human tuna fish whilst Norah tidied the home with a hum in her throat and only a mild, residual anxiety in her heartbeat.

Along his commute back to the rooftop, he noticed her key and its still chain remained relinquished in the ajar door's knob.

34

✦NORAH✦

He was stationed at his usual post upon the furthest ledge, facing the rising sun. His bare toes curled against the house's gutter whilst he eyed the sea of dark fields. Murmurations of starlings stretched and unfolded above the untended land, contorting into amorphous shapes.

Without a word, Dex conjured them both a thick cigar as she sat beside him. Then, with a snap of his inked fingers, he manifested a shining brass v-cutter fitted perfectly to his digits. It was like her father's.

She pressed into the old man's bulky shoulder to watch whilst he snipped the cigar's ends with a sharp *click-clack*, leaving valleys in their caps. He snapped his fingers once more and a tiny pop of electricity lit the tobacco with life. He'd been allowing his subtle magic to flow more freely around her. She'd never become bored of his fabulous gifts

Nor ran her tongue along the cigar's sharp canal, pulling syrupy flavors across her palette. Its resistance was firm, like silk scarves from a pocket. It required a deep draw from her chest that left her nodding in approval with its flavor.

They sat in pleasant silence a moment before she dared disturb the illusion of normalcy.

"What does Oblitus mean?"

His eyes collided with hers as though he too had been ruminating on the fighting ring.

"It's Latin for 'The Forgotten,'" he stated.

Norah shook her head. "Why would a fight club be named that?"

"Because you can fight for your lost memories, I suppose," he guessed. "That's why I need to go back."

Norah winced. As strangely impossible and fantastical as all of this was, it simply felt too convenient. The timing, the urgency, the desperation it evoked in Dexteras.

"Don't you wonder why they have your memories in the first place?"

He nodded. "Of course."

"Well I'm going with you," she announced.

The elderly man's head snapped to hers. "Oh no. Absolutely not, Nor. No."

She scoffed, unfazed by his fervor. "Whether you want me to walk in *with* you, or five minutes *after* you, it's happening. I don't need your permission." Though she'd never allow anyone to tell her what she could or couldn't do ever again, a minuscule, childish need for Dexteras' approval tipped her lifted chin towards him with a loving, but wry grin.

He couldn't help but grin, pink rising to his cheeks. She saw his trepidation and his pride for her all in one small, lifted curl of his mustache. She punched him playfully in the bicep and ran to change into her most menacing of black clothes for the evening ahead.

35

⋅DEXTERAS⋅

HE PROPPED HIS ARM against the icy steel door of Oblitus and turned to her. His chest was full of leaden weights.

"You must promise to let me fight my fights. To not intervene or put yourself in danger, yes?"

God, I hate her being here.

"I'll try," she said, tossing him a black elastic from her wrist.

He snatched it from the air and used it to wrap his hair tight onto his skull. Then he pressed his palms against the door, its atoms melting with his own, deciphering his identity until it popped inwards with a metallic groan.

They veered down the leftmost hall, coated in mirrors. The surrounding stares made his spine itch, swearing at times that his reflection was exchanged for that of…someone else. Shining Betelgeuse irises and departing silhouettes. Flashes of gold in the inky black.

He rested his right hand upon their final entry until it relented. The last door trembled open and thick, hot waves pressed against them with the intensity of sweaty oxen.

"Try not to get hurt?" she said.

He grinned. In the time that'd passed between the first door and the second, his worry had exchanged for eager fire. Anticipatory war. Like a chained dog awaiting the hunt, his blood screamed.

"You and I both know getting hurt is essential to growth," he winked.

She scowled. "*Discomfort* is essential to growth. Not getting punched in the face."

He pounded a rap upon the steel with his fist, bolstering his heart rate for what lay beyond. He wanted his muscles hot and prepped like the piston of an engine. If someone dared approach Norah as they entered, he wanted to be primed for ruin and without hesitation.

He jabbed the door a few rounds until he'd dented the metal. Adrenaline swallowed his limbs and swelled his ego, convincing him he was ready for any conquest. The second door gasped wide, and he ushered them across the staircase's skeleton. It was so high above the ocean of beings below, a separate atmosphere of smoke and humidity clung to them and clouded their descent for several paces. Currents of music and heat wrapped them in moisture, the glare of red neon and white strobes breached the haze. They descended the switchback mountain of stairs like wild animals in the woods. And finally, as they paddled through the smoke and cut down the final zag of stairs, the inked bodies below turned to stare.

Dex plunged into the crowd, and they parted for his towering form. Despite the roar of their disapproving screams and the churning music, he made certain that he could hear Norah's heart behind him.

Though her horizon was likely compiled of rhinestones, shimmering fabrics, and pulsing bodies, the strings of her fortitude sang in his ears, alight with tense staccatos. He kept his strides slow so that she could stay just behind him.

And then, the cadence of the *ba-bum, ba-bum, ba-bum* in her chest was jostled out of rhythm. It hitched and skipped for just a breath. A soft curse left Norah's lips and a tiny, sharp pain trilled from her body like a screaming hawk. Though she was barely bothered, her flesh gave the brief screech of a scar being born.

The maneuvers that immediately poured from Dexteras were glassy smooth and instinctual. There was no pause for consideration. No emotion had time to creep upon his features and little empathy had time to reach his brain.

He pivoted, caught the throat of the stranger nearest his friend, and stared upon the scraggly bastard in his outstretched fingers. He squeezed without thought. Throat tubes and vocal cords buckled and popped with strain, and a horrid hacking spluttered from the stranger's lips.

Dex paid him no mind and swiveled to find Nor staring at her forearm, the sleeve of her black shirt pulled up to her bicep. A small, red blister was forming there, the size of a crimson match head right in the chest of her bird tattoo. She lifted her eyes to Dex and then the ignorant man he held. She scowled, jaw bared and angry.

The bastard had burnt her with his cigarette.

"-accident, s-s-s-orry, it-" gasped the brute in his grip. He'd initially attempted shoving and kicking and clawing at Dexteras, but the old man had been far too irate and asunder with rage to notice.

"Would you like to do the honors, or may I?" Dex called pleasantly to Norah over the crowd, ignoring the flailing man in his grip. Those nearest the trio gawked and whispered over their shoulders, the whites of their eyes wide and shining.

Norah's nostrils flared and her teeth ground on each other. Her fingers flexed.

"I can teach you, if you'd like to practice your form," Dex encouraged, tipping his head to the unwilling dummy wriggling in his hands.

But finally, her shoulders fell, and her heart's rhythm steadied. She smiled at Dex as though ever-so-slightly impressed with his self-control and the measured rise and fall of his chest.

"He's yours, but I think he might be dead," she said with a casual lift of her chin.

Sure enough, the pale, chaotically tattooed body of clammy flesh hung unconscious, a few inches from the ground, dark hair fanning Dex's fingers. Dex gave half a mind to tear the bastard's head from his throat but feared the carnage would soil Norah's leather boots.

Thus, he plucked the pack of cigarettes from the man's pocket, snapped his inked neck with a quick flex of his fingers, and dropped him to the tile. If the brute was anything like Dexteras, he would survive, but would surely be reminded to watch his fucking cigarettes every time his neck bones popped. Though he wouldn't admit it to Norah, his heart was thundering beneath his breastbone and pulsing in his ears. He'd wanted to end the immortal's existence, but cared more about making her his friend feel safe and in control of her own safety.

They resumed their journey, and this time, Dex chose to instead fall behind Nor to serve as her bodyguard, walking in a synchronized gait. As her shadow, Dex was able to monitor the movements of others more proactively. If some were so bold as to nudge nearer and rest their insatiable glares upon her, Dex would step out of line and snarl. But it seemed most of them beheld her with fear and awe.

Their approach gave the illusion that Norah was the evening's featured fighter and Dex the designated cornerman, escorting her to the ring. Instead, of course, he saw her to the bar top where Mikael tipped his chin at them both. Nor's violet lips smiled upon the barkeep with familiarity.

Then, a new song pierced Dex's skull with a needle-like itch in his ears. The hairs on his flesh rose with its shrieking, searching sonar. Someone was coming.

His arm collected Norah and swung her towards a stool whilst eyeing the crowd. He looked down at his trembling hands as bands of white smoke wrapped them in stark, boxing bandages. He tapped his cushioned digits against hers with a delicate jab-jab-cross.

He then melted into the masses, following the hungry vibrations, obeying the gravitational pull towards its violence. While he still hated Norah in this den of wolves, he knew he could keep her safe. After all, he howled and bit like the rest of them. This was his home.

He propped himself against a black column and gathered his brow in his hands. He thought of Cecil and wondered how he could possibly find the blind brute in such a place. But as Dex opened his eyes in search of Cockney beast, a CRACK resounded beside his skull.

Dex dropped to the tile just in time to duck a blurred fist from the crowd. It smashed spidery cracks into the stone behind him. Dex wheeled about the column to the assailant's other side and ducked low to execute a volley of uppercuts against his opponent's ribs. The meaty beast roared.

Dex only had time to lay into his heels and defend his face while he was consequently pummeled. Through his raised forearms, he caught glimpses of a flaming-haired fighter, chest and thick arms splattered in chaotic tattoo work. He had no time to ponder what mysteries and horrors the illustration beneath had once held for each of Oblitus' fighters.

His opponent attempted a rogue overhand blow that would've surely put him down, had Dex not ducked deep and low. His rage brimmed up to his collarbones and flooded his face until he allowed himself to break free and be brave. He popped up and swung to hit the huge fighter.

Their skin was hot like an iron skillet and to feel it buckle and submit beneath his own was dangerously addictive. He couldn't pull himself from the rush of its power. Trickles of sweat slid into his bared grin and eager whistles escaped his teeth.

Concern stitched his opponent's brow, his red face shining. There on his cheek, were deep, smooth cuts, bright and angry.

Dex knew what the lacerations on their faces represented. He'd seen many fighters with them, some fresh and dripping, others old and scarred. It was Cecil who delivered them, for he was the trainer for any who wished to prove their worthiness of the ring. Those beneath Cecil's pupilage needed three wins to earn a chance in the arena to pursue their prize.

Dex had been given his three lashes already, but when he'd considered himself in the hallway of mirrors upstairs, there wasn't so much as a pink scar. This was yet another facet of Dex's being that made Cecil grumble and curse.

Dex drove the big fighter onto his heels, tucking himself beneath the blind spots of his massive muscles. He stumbled back and gave him a proper look over. He had two, bloody lines down his right cheek, fresh, as though from the talons of a reaching eagle.

The crowd conformed to their dance, cheers and whistles piercing the heat. Onlookers mobbed and hollered.

Dex leaned in and out, ducking most blows and responding with vengeful replies to his opponent's teeth. His sweat tingled with carbonation. His punches left him like big, straight missiles. He took a chance and barraged the red-haired man with a rogue bolo, a trick shot.

While the whites of the ginger's eyes followed the fake hook, Dex cut swiftly under their chin with a nasty crack of teeth on teeth. A red cloud of spewed blood misted the air. The fighter doubled at the waist, phlegm and mucousy blood slumped toward the floor.

Coppery salt spat from Dex's own soaked whiskers, grinning with the flavor. He then slid low and delivered a sharp jab to the creature's kidneys. Their lungs gasped in agony and the wet body folded to its knees.

Then, Dex sprang high into the air, filling his face and torn shirt with the balmy heat. He dropped his fists onto the back of his adversary's skull, sending the ginger-bearded beast to the ground like a downed oak, steaming like a train, unconscious.

Dex dragged the sweat from his face with dressed palms. His boxing wraps were crusty and burnt as though he'd been firing at charcoal. His fingertips followed the slow, needlelike slice of another cut down his cheek. It dripped onto his shirt for but a moment before it healed shut. There was a brief, prickly pull of split wounds stitching with immortal repair.

"Cecil!" he hollered into the crowd, now done with subtleties. He dove into the masses after what he was certain was the Shrike's baritone song. But with each stride, it seemed to drift further and further from him. It was as though the two of them were opposing magnets and he could feel the aversion in his bones.

Cecil was running.

Dex was so busy with the chase, he'd barely noticed the shift in the club's temperature. It'd dropped as cold as ice water, leaving his feet to halt and his flesh to shiver in the sharp cold. Even the raucous crowd had fallen stationary, exchanging glances with apprehension.

The music and lights lowered. Drafty breaths rattled from the throats of the crowd, settling foggy condensation above them.

Then, the herd of club-goers was rippling like a tide, bodies ebbing and carving a pathway. The beings parted an aisleway before Dexteras now, twisting through the masses to lead him to the steps of the golden fighting ring. It beckoned him, tall and treacherous like a great bronze birdcage. The crowd watched expectantly.

It was time for his first match.

He pulled himself up the winding stairs that snaked to the barricaded pit. The bony black and gold beast was more massive in person than he could've fathomed. Along the outer rim of the arena was a slick walkway carved for special spectators or cornermen. He stepped into this path and then squeezed into the arena through a flayed bit of chain-link. He squinted against the flash of polished tile.

From the opposing wall of Oblitus, a new creature strode from their own carved path towards him. Tall and wrapped in sable, they glided like a shadow. Their steps hissed with the threatening slice of metal.

Each head bowed and every eye averted as the form passed with a mouthful of ivory teeth. They smiled in a way, not that humans do, but as wolves do.

Though struck with fear, the chill in Dex's corpse craved them close. Even from afar, he had an instinctual hunger for their warm presence.

Staring upon them was akin to gazing at a solar eclipse. Mesmerizing. Deceiving. Dangerous. Cold and dark like black ice, but capable of crumbling you to ash.

Their face was pretty and handsome all at once, eyes sparkling with the dark lines of their painted eyes, cat-like and sharp. Their irises flickered with a brilliant gold in the neon.

While elements of their form seemed feminine and lovely, they were obviously beyond the bounds of gender. The song that screeched from their chest inferred that they were stony and immortal like a gorgon. The tall form rose the stairs, their gold accessories scraping at the ring's rails.

Dex's eyes wandered their body with awe and desire.

A black fitted pantsuit was pulled taut across their bronze flesh. Gold chains shimmered down their bare chest, breasts concealed in scant lapels. They dripped in black and gold from the crop of high hair to the ink in their flesh. They were no one and everyone in a single, wanting glare.

Dex's eyes trailed their shape down, down, down, where glints of gold snatched his eye. Beneath the pantsuit were complex, golden bionic limbs that creaked and bent with oiled mechanics. Their platforms were thin and menacing like razors.

They paired well with the voice that left their crimson lips, serrated and hissing like sword blades, lilted with a dialect much like his own.

"Dexteras," they sang. "Welcome home, son."

36

✦NORAH✦

BEFORE THE HANDSOME CREATURE PARTED THE CROWD and met Dexteras in the ring, they were first *formed*. Before they were a person, they were shapes, molded by bands of smoke that seeped from the corners of the bar. They leeched the space of its shadows like a sponge pulling at a black stain.

Then, the darkness was given waves of swirling black tresses and deep-set eyes. Ribbons of shadow stitched beneath their flesh to etch tattoos like black blood. The artwork was as old as cave carvings, sacred like ancient runes.

Having drunk their fill of the dark, the silhouette stepped forward, leaving residual plumes behind like spat cigarette smoke. Their square jaw jutted forward, sending more spent vapors up their feline features. Their gorgeous, shining eyes were fixated upon Dexteras with want, a lip-biting desire.

Norah heard the knife blade *shing* in their steps and saw the platinum flash of gold through the crowd. She knelt upon her barstool to behold the complicated prosthetics, unlike any she'd seen in the medical field prior. With each long stride, the immaculate gold rigging pivoted and pulsated as a muscle would, elements shuddering beneath a silk suit.

The parading stride whirred with gold gears and onyx accents, grandiosity gliding in their gait like the long saunter of a prince. While every other being was striped with black tattoo ink lashes, this seductive being wore no such brands.

And those eyes. They snapped up and down Dexteras like a grackle, with whites like shining stars and pupils bright and wild.

If asked to imagine the most beautiful and dangerous being on the earth, Norah Kestrel's mortal mind still would've come up short in comparison to this new contender bowing beneath the fight ring's chains. They stepped into the ring with the emanation of ancient Egyptian royalty, but their body appeared in its forties perhaps. The limbs were lean and long beneath their suit like a shining, black colt's. Their fingers twitched as though they could snatch the heart from a chest before anyone could know it was missing.

"Redeemed from the valley of the shadow of death," they sang to Dexteras, tattooed arms outstretched as though expecting him to fall into their embrace.

Dex leaned forward for but a moment, as though he wanted to press himself against their gorgeous chest. But he remembered himself and remained anchored until the stranger dropped their hands with a patronizing chuckle.

"I didn't believe Cecil when he told me you were alive, son," they said, locks of black hair falling across their alarming eyes. "Friends, *twenty years* Dexteras was detached from his Purpose, with the intention to join us here!" They cried to the crowd who replied with fresh, eager energy. "But," they added, holding up a finger, "he wandered, he wafted, and we lost him to The Unbecoming…"

The stranger spun and eyed Dexteras as though he were a prodigal son, a long-won prize they'd never dreamed they'd hold again. "And yet here he is," they beamed. "We have much to learn about his resilience and he has much to learn about his belonging."

Sh-shing. Sh-shing. Sh-shing, sang their long legs towards the old man, circling him like a shark.

"I don't know who you are," stated Dex, "But I know you have answers."

The crowd roared with laughter until the dark being raised a hand to silence them. They squared their sharp form before Dex and leaned close, at least several inches taller given the reaching length of their golden limbs.

"Quite a lot to learn," the stranger grinned. "While he gives us new hope for our fellow Figments detached on the outside, such waywardness comes with an unraveled agony. It tears your skull apart bit by bit until you are unmoored from your sanity…" They took Dex's clenched hand and spread the fingers there with black-painted nails, long like coffins.

They stared into his palm, considering the countless scars and tattoos. "There's great suffering in isolation," the stranger mourned, brows distorted and wobbling, poring over Dex's tattoos in pity.

Dex stole himself from their grip, face unreadable and lost.

"I've watched you fight, son. You must've found quite the strong-willed Corpse to leech upon to possess such sustenance at this brittle chapter of your existence?"

Corpse? The fuck?

"So let's have her!" they cried, spinning with spread arms like waiting, French doors. "Where is your nourishment? We must thank her for giving you the fervor to return to us!"

The crowd whistled and hooted. It was a mocking commotion.

It was evident in Dex's narrow gaze and crooked brows that he had no idea what the stranger spoke of, but his eye fluttered briefly beyond the golden rails and found hers far off in the distance.

Nor's blood went cold, feeling the urgent search for his electricity along her neck. It was a protective, impossible shield that she could sense, even from across the massive expanse. She slumped in her seat, praying no one else had registered the transaction, but the stranger surely had, and grinned.

"*Delectamenti,*" they said, eyes flashing.

"I just want my memories," warned Dexteras, "And I was told I could fight for them."

The stranger's smile fell, and they drank in the old fighter patiently from his bound silver hairs to his laced boots. To an outsider such as Norah, it seemed they were *hungry* for Dexteras, aching for him.

"I do accept sangre. Sanguis. Cruor. Bagarre. *Ancienne danse,"* hissed the stranger, lips dancing with ancient words of war until they grinned with appetite. "But it's more than that."

"I just want to know who I am, who I was," Dex said. "Please."

The stranger's amusement fell into a cold set of pursed lips.

"No," they said. It was an answer that did not invite appeal or question. They turned to walk away and leave the ring. "You're not ready. You're asking the wrong questions."

"But I was told I-"

"What my *loyal*, unshakable subaltern failed to tell you," the stranger hollered as they spun, eyes wide and threatening, "is that *I* am the one who swallows memories, therefore *I* am the one who determines who fights for them and when." They shifted their stern gaze to inspect the mob below the stage.

Norah stretched on her barstool to follow their deadly stare towards the crowd, just in time to notice a flash of dark sunglasses.

Cecil?

"*Et tu Brute*, my blinded Shrike!" Brayed the dark suitor on the stage. Their shining gaze followed the fleeing blind man, a wounded twitch curling their lip before returning to Dexteras.

"My past is mine. Why should I have to earn it?" Dex's teeth ground anxiously, like rocks in a bag.

"Because you gave it up!" the stranger snapped, their humor wilting. "You writhed on your knees and begged me to take it from you," they said with a dangerous laugh, stepping nearer to look down at the old man.

"What…" Dex breathed.

Everyone within the space cackled, and this time, their leader did not hush them. Instead, they strutted along the cage's boundary with spread arms, showcasing the crowd's loyalty.

"*Everyone* here chose freedom from the past, Dexteras!"

The chasm filled with screams of victory.

"Our home is called *Oblitus* because we are The Forgotten! Thus, we took into our hands to forget everyone else." They spun on their blades and returned to Dex in the middle of the ring.

The old man's mouth was agape, clearly as perplexed as Norah. His lips stammered, but he had no words.

The stranger's fury and fire died as they beheld his tired face and fallen shoulders. Dex was confused and aching for understanding, for anything.

And as the stranger sighed, they released a *hisssss* of steam from some sort of golden panel screwed into their chest, partially concealed in lapels.

"Everyone here came to *me*, nearly dead, weeping, empty," said the androgynous stranger. "Invisible. Suffering. All-feeling and all-sacrificing for a Purpose that would never serve them back." They eyed Dexteras, searching for his submission, his comprehension.

"I gave each of them freedom as I gave it to you. And freedom means the ability to give back the gifts they begged me for. And I shall offer them to you as well," they said, reaching to hold Dex's neck. Their tattooed forearm laid against the old man's cheek, their forehead pressed against Dex's as though to kiss him.

"But not right now." With that, the stranger spun and left the old man once more, standing alone in the ring.

"W-Wait! Give me a fight, give me *one* chance!" Dex cried.

The tall stranger stopped at the ring's rails, nails clacking along the radiant metal.

"Cecil says you're not ready. And he's blind as a fucking bat," they spat.

"One," Dex begged.

The tall stranger closed their eyes and tipped their chin to the ceiling.

"Defeat one of my fighters," they pointed to the ceiling with a black painted nail. "I'll grant you one memory. Dealer's choice." Their gold eyes flashed like a viper in a nest of eggs. "*One*," they emphasized. Then, they raised a hand and snapped their fingers.

In a rush of black plumes, the tall stranger exchanged outfits. Wisps licked them from head-to-toe leaving them clad in midnight black joggers and a tight athletic sweatshirt cinched to the throat by gold buttons. Their recessed features were shadowed beneath its tall hood like a hiding wolf in the woods. Their limbs and accessories shone a gold in the crimson neon.

They raised a sharp brow to Dexteras. "Choose your corner then."

Norah's innards cramped with worry. This was actually happening. After pinching her forearm to be certain she wasn't dreaming, she leaped into the crowd in pursuit of the caged arena. Mikael cried at her back, but she couldn't hear him.

The crowd's staring irises were bright and dazzling in the way that poisonous flowers were. Their flesh tones were a palette of endless cultures and kinds, some pierced, some affixed with rusting prosthetics, all painted in the slashed of cover-up ink.

Dex walked to the right-most end of the ring, biting his swollen lip. A black bar stool sat just beyond it in the corner man's alley.

Then, like a ball of snakes in the water, the stranger erupted into braiding strands of smoke, swirling like dye before crashing into the other corner where they perched their own stool like a gargoyle, thumb stuck between their teeth with interest.

"Marchosias!" they cried. The crowd began to churn and mutter excitedly.

Nor pressed harder, reaching for the legs of the stage, mooring herself against the cage's cold steel. She walked the perimeter in search of an entrance, hopping ever several feet or so to see what was happening above in the cage.

Dex's opponent was summoned.

He was a big man with thunderous legs and massive hands. He was clad in black boxing shorts and tall tactical boots, gripped to the tile and ready. His hair and beard were scarlet.

They both toed the center line, muscles swollen and tight with readiness.

Norah was sprinting along the ring, seeking a way to her friend.

I have to be fucking close… she persisted.

Then came the collision of flesh upon flesh. Foreign curses rode the humidity. Rap music rattled her bones from the distant stage. A series of combos shuddered the earth. Dex cried out.

The crowd exploded.

Shit, shit shit.

"*Occidere eum Marchos!*" the stranger screamed.

Nor's skin chilled with fear. Her fingers reached further and further towards each of the cage's bones. She wanted to cheer Dex on, to call on his strength, but the crowd pressed against her, rioting, clutching the rails to spectate.

"Fuckers," she muttered, piercing through them with narrow shoulders.

A great, stumble shook the stage followed by a bloody, gargled moan. The floor trembled with a damning quake.

The crowd cried out in disapproval.

Norah tunneled between their leather outfits and tattooed skin with her nails and elbows until a shock of white caught her eye through the rails above. She then saw the open maw of a staircase to the ring. She bound up their steel bones in her combat boots, rolled between the rails, and ran a lap around the narrow corner man's alley to take her rightful place in Dex's corner. She nearly knocked the barstool over, bounding on top of it and clutching the chain-link.

Fucking shit, Dexteras.

Dex was bloodied and unrecognizable. Slumped, wheezing, yet upright. A strange black sooty debris was painted across his eyes like war paint. Leaking tears traced inky, bleeding streams down his cheeks and temples.

Marchosias was smiling toothily like a child. His pink flesh was dappled with fat freckles and thick bands of black ink. His tattoo lines were deeper, thicker, more gruesome, and tissue damaged.

But there was one uncovered, massive tattoo on his spine: an ugly multi-headed dragon with serpentine necks, long claws, and dreadful red scales. The vibrant monstrosity was enough to make Norah uneasy, sensing revealed tattoos were a rarity, a prize to be won in this place.

The men grappled. Dex landed a hit on Marchos' jaw. The beast staggered, gripping his mouth.

"Fuck yeah!" she cried, punching the air with a ridiculous combo. She too, felt an animalistic fierceness rise inside of her in this place.

With her shrill cheers, Dex spun with wide eyes, horrified to see her so near to the action.

But his bloody opponent was loping from behind. A stride away, Marchos pressed a rolled fist to his lips and blew through it as though it shot poison darts. The same black, sandy substance spat from his fingers, painting Dex's face and eyes in its glimmering dust.

The old man stumbled back with a growl, wiping at the fine powder hurriedly, but then-

WHACK.

A fist cracked Dexteras in the back of the skull with a bony rupture that could've made the dead cringe. His opponent leapt and caught the collapsing old man in his arms and squeezed him with an impossible bind. Increasingly more of her friend's flesh was painted in the black, glittering soot with each touch. It seemed to accumulate like mounds of tiny, swarming gnats with each grapple exchanged. Black, shiny blotches pooling on his flesh like disease.

With the strange dusty debris came a musty, metallic-charged stench that cut Norah's nostrils like rancid garlic. The familiar substance was some form of metal shaving that made Dex's limbs tremble and his body grow violently pale. With each breath, her friend's weight hung in Marchos' arms, and his bones crackled with less and less retort.

CRACK, gave a final, fatal crunching.

With another breath of the sharp metal tang in the air, Norah finally understood his symptoms: Marchos was siphoning the iron from Dex's blood.

Released, Dex collapsed to his stomach, motionless. His head was crooked with fracture, and his spine bulged beneath his inked skin like a mountain range. His neck and back were broken.

"Dex," Norah gasped.

The crowd erupted in applause and resounding approval. The watchful stranger in the opposing corner straightened and beckoned Marchos with a whistle of white teeth. They slapped the massive beast on the spine. Members of the crowd climbed the rails to Marchos, pouring shaken beers onto his bloody torso, singing his praises.

"Seven!" cried the stranger, their voice filling the space.

Nor bent beneath the gold rails and slid to the tile beside her friend, fingers pressing into his bearded neck. There was no pulse.

There was no pulse.

A sob hitched in her throat. She held her breath along with him.

Dex, please. Dex, please. C'mon, I need you here, she begged.

"Six!" cried the crowd in tandem, counting down eagerly.

Norah's lungs burned, nearly bursting. Her eyes watered. But her trembling fingers persisted against his sweaty throat.

Ba-bum.

Ba-bum.

His heart throttled to life and beat against her fingers like a drum.

Norah gasped with him, collapsing to her rear with a wave of relief. She'd never be able to unsee how he'd been crushed in this place. It would never be unwritten from her eyelids, even if he survived every round.

And those sounds. Jesus, those sounds of him breaking…

"Five!"

She slapped his cheeks to assess his consciousness. His eyes rolled in and out of the present world like moony marbles beneath the thick powdery substance, black as night. The stench of metal wrinkled Nor's nose. She ran a finger across the fine iron.

What cheap, cheating bullshit.

She wiped the mess away with her sleeve, eyeing the wounds that had begun to stitch themselves shut and settle into greenish bruises.

"Four!"

Then, his split bones began to mend beneath his flesh. Each splintered bit of spine ruptured with crackles as it repaired its welds.

cr-ICK

cr-ACK

His body shuddered with each. Tears rinsed his cheeks. His breathing steadied. His eyes gaped far away, black, and hot like coals.

"Dex," she whispered. "You can do this. You can *do* this."

"Three!"

Then, a pop like the crack of a whip shook his body a final round, jolting him upright with a gasp. With these final vertebrae repaired, Dex flew to his feet and danced in his corner, bouncing on his toes like a bird.

Nor laughed, euphoria and endless relief warming her cheeks. She ducked back into the cornerman's alley and dried her eyes.

Dex tightened his boxing wraps with his teeth, screaming between them, "I'm up!"

The tall stranger cackled with an admirable grin. "He's up!" they cried, face alive with curiosity and wonder.

Marchos and his surrounding entourage gaped at the old man. The crowd howled and booed, making the floors tremble with its temblor.

But the pair of fighters toed the line once more. They sprang for one another like dancers.

Marchos dove for Dex's knees, a bitter finality twisted on his lips.

Dex yelped as he was hoisted into the air and tossed jabs at the monster's spine, scrambling across the slick back muscles in search of leverage.

Marchos threw his weight backward, slinging his massive feet out before him. For a moment, the pair of fighters were suspended in the air, blood, sweat, and spit sputtering from their whiskered lips.

Nor sprinted along the ring's perimeter towards the falling bodies.

Dex's limbs and skull slapped the ground like cracked ceramic, moments before being crushed beneath the Goliath. The ring's rails chimed with strain, and a deep spindling crack branched through the thick tile beneath them with the tumultuous earthquake.

The stranger in the opposing corner snarled exhaustively, drinking in a deep inhale of cigarette smoke. They unbuttoned their blazer and knelt to the broken floor, blowing gray flumes into its cracks. The smoke seeped and settled like black mortar betwixt the gold, shaking the downed fighters in the arena with its repairs.

"Dex," Norah muttered, falling to her knees again to reach for the old man. "Dex…" she repeated, pressing against the rails to clasp his fingertips.

His blue eyes bolted open and his tattooed chest swelled. A spider web of broken blood vessels branched throughout his left iris, leaving the whites of his sclera swimming with scarlet streaks. He gasped and sputtered blood from his teeth.

Norah rubbed her brow and blinked at hot tears, certain an ulcer brewed in her gut.

He gripped his side with a groan, but smiled with blood-stained teeth.

"I'm alright *amica mea.*"

To hell you are.

She wanted to be angry with him for putting her through this frustration and fear, but she was the one who begged to come along. Still, she wished how she could pick him up and carry him home from this treacherous place as Cecil had.

But she pursed her lips, knowing no words would discourage him from his sparring. And could she blame him? The prize was precious. It was everything to him, evident in his eager, hopeful eyes. He wanted it more than anything.

She drank in his big, dumb smile, committing it to memory like a weary mother. Then, she stuffed her hand deep into the pocket of his big coat that she wore in his stead and pulled out a fresh, clean bar rag, pressing it into his fist.

Deep into the early morning hours following her first visit to Oblitus, she'd swiped through many brutal fighting videos on her phone, hoping there would be some skill she could learn, some resource she could offer. Bandages, enswells, and ice were the usual tools belonging to a boxer's cutman, but the beings in this ring were vastly different. What she did have was an assortment of bar tools from Mikael, lining the pockets of Dex's massive coat. Little bottles of water, tiny samplers of clear liquor, and clean bar rags.

"Kick his ass," Norah hissed, trained on his remaining cerulean eye. She exchanged the soaked rag in his fingers for a fist bump.

Marchosias cawed with amusement from his corner. It was obvious in the young fighter's ambling gait and casual, drunken grin that this match with Dexteras was of little bother to him. The old man was a skirmish, a spar, a plaything to bat at, and nothing more. A means to a prize he was eager to get to. Marchos bantered in Russian at Dex, evidently mocking and ignorant given the childish tone.

But the truly terrifying part was that Norah *understood* him as he spoke. As the new language left his lips, she translated it with ease.

That's when she realized that her scarred palm was still gripping Dex's and that somehow, its channel allowed her access to his infinitely lingual headspace.

"Dexteras! Why don't you let your cute virgin fight me?" barked Marchos. *"We could have some fun with her!"*

Norah chuckled, as did the crowd. She was neither cute nor a virgin, but the misinformation was an oversight seeing as Dexteras was seizing with hot rage. He wiped the blood from his lips and replied in a wet, gargled language that fit his bleeding tongue.

"Oh you fucking motherfucker…" he snarled, obviously too distracted to notice Norah's comprehension. In a breath, he was crouching low and tight, steady like an arrow fresh from its quiver.

Norah erupted into laughter for his rare expletives but felt an earnest safety in his shadow as he stood. Everything about Dex's posture made her feel protected, watched over in the way a father would. With the clang of an unseen bell, the two beings exploded from their corners and collided with the ferocious snapping of a dog fight. Throat-to-throat, teeth bared, strength so threatening, the crowd grew quiet with respect.

Nor held the line in his corner, pacing for a better view when needed, following his body along the outer edge.

Dex was struck under the chin, tripping him backward into the rails with a clang of bones and brass.

Norah lunged to fill her arms with his hot torso while gnawing the lid off of a water bottle. She poured the tepid water onto his smoldering fists which hissed like doused fire. She tipped the bottle into his gaping mouth and gently slapped his bearded cheeks like she'd seen cornermen do on the internet.

"Lay him out Dexteras, you hear me?" she called in his ear, pushing him back onto his toes.

As he tripped from her corner, his water-soaked fists crackled like angry, frayed wires. Of all the impossible things she'd seen the old man capable of, this had to be the most impressive yet.

"Light him up!" she yelled, voice breaking with crackles of adrenaline.

He dove and spun like a hawk, snapping a loaded fist across Marchosias' throat. With a blinding pop of electric charge, his opponent was launched into the opposing rails at an impossible height and speed, where he was folded. His face kissed the floor, body alight with blue sparks. The tattoo of the monstrous cryptid on his spine was shimmering with sweat, deathly still.

A few meager and desperate members of the crowd counted down from seven, but Marchos did not rise again.

As his countdown was run out, the crowd replied with a mixture of rage and riot, denying the capabilities of the new contender.

Dex spat to the ground beside his opponent's head and returned to Norah in his corner. The crinkles of his scowl faded, and the tense lines of his shoulders rounded with each step.

He emptied another bottle of water, leaving him sputtering pinkish bloody streams down his front. The black, shiny soot still streaked much of his skin, including the warring birds on his chest. Their wings stretched with each of his immense breaths.

Nor leaned against the ring's gold chains beside him, surveying the disappointed crowd with challenging brows. The pride she carried for her fighter could've burned the place down.

"That was a-fucking-mazing Dex," she muttered in his bloody ear.

"Thanks, love," he choked, sloughing wet from his lips with a thick arm.

Before she could build him with more worthy praise, a chill fell across the bar, quieting the crowd with obedience. It was apparent they stilled and muttered for the return of none other than their noble ringmaster.

37

·NORAH·

GOLDEN BLADES TOUCHED DOWN TO THE CENTER RING, bands of smoke sewing together the flawless form before them. Gleaming eyes and dazzling teeth shone through the smog.

The stranger took in the carnage painted across the tile. A bloody, smearing path streaked the ground where Marchos' body had been towed from the ring.

Could any of them be truly killed? she wondered.

"A fool's lips walk into a fight and his mouth invites a beating," the stranger said, eyes sparkling towards their fallen fighter. "I would've ripped out his tongue for good measure," they added.

"I want what's mine," Dex replied breathlessly, fingers massaging one another. "I've won, fairly."

The stranger chewed on their cigarette and chuckled, but in a breath, was toe to toe with Dex, eyes copper-red beneath their dashing gold. In a swift gesture, they snatched a handful of Dex's white hair and exposed his throat, eyeing the old man like he was tender meat on a bone.

"You still don't understand, Dexteras," they threatened with a black brow. "I'm offering you a gift, this place." The regal being threatened with a brow, their full lips pursed. "I was born a Corpse's slave and remained loyal for nearly five million years, Dexteras. You can't imagine such unfairness if you tried. Nothing but suffering, screaming, wailing, generations of death." Steam rolled from the metal plate screwed into their chest. "Nonexistence, exile, suicide…they were graces I could only *beg* for," they said with a poisonous glare. "Don't *dare* speak of fairness to me."

Their eyes returned to glassy gold and shoved Dex from their grasp. "Pain only sweetens the prize and guarantees you're worthy of it. You fight another round, or you leave here with a skull empty of *any* answers."

Dex's fists were clenching and shaking as he returned to his corner, knotting his loose hair back to his skull. It was obvious that he was at the sole mercy of this stranger and their disorderly rules.

The ring's monarch spun with a dramatic flourish, hood pulled from their eyes, a fresh cigarette spewing from their lips. They addressed the crowd lovingly, like a parent who'd gone over the edge and now sought to resume their kind visage.

"And despite it all, still, we stand!" their leader cried.

The crowd imploded with mindless hysteria and support until a thunderous, rhythmic stomping echoed from their feet like a gargantuan war drum.

STOMP. STOMP. STOMP.

Their valiant emcee inhaled a great pull from their cigarette and spat inconceivable smoke rings into the atmosphere. The massive clouds swelled and contorted into ghastly shapes and symbols. Skulls, daggers, snakes that lashed and struck at one another with foggy tendrils. They slithered along the ring's rim.

"Our makers cried to the skies, forsaken!"

The crowd's pace quickened, giving the cadence to the ballad.

STOMP. STOMP. STOMP. STOMP.

"And thus we came to aid!"

STOMP. STOMP. STOMP. STOMP.

"But when the strong hold up the weak," they exclaimed with high, beckoning hands.

STOMP. STOMP. STOMP. STOMP.

"It's the strong who take the blade!" they all called in unison as though it were a jovial drinking shanty.

The stranger held up their sparkling, ringed hands, and the crowd grew deathly still and quiet. Not a breath rattled. They leaned inwards, faces wide and mouths agape.

"Behemoth!" their leader cried up into the gold ceiling.

The expanse erupted into ceremonious shouts of valor, deafening Norah. The tall stranger spun on a blade, winked at Dexteras, and bent beneath the chains and into the outer ring.

Head full of cheers and body charged with adrenaline, Norah stood in endless awe of the monstrous place and its monstrous energy and how it went impossibly unnoticed in the world's most boring town. Was she even still in Corvid while she was in the gallows down here?

Dex backed into his corner, face long and ruminative. Shoulders low and defeated.

I'm so sorry Dex, she lamented. *This is bullshit. Utter bullshit.*

The arena's stairs clanged and rang out.

Norah spun, anticipating to raise her eyes to the newest fighter, given his title. But as the new contender rolled beneath the chain-link and snapped to his feet, her gaze fell on a being no higher than Dex's bearded chin.

Black brambles of hair were tied back at his neck in thick dreadlocks which cascaded to his glutes. He was coated in countless black tattoos, large puddles of ink bleeding across his throat and arms, and shoulders. A particularly nasty patch stained his eyelid and forehead like a painted stallion. The eye in this black lake of ink was a pale, nearly white iris, rimmed with silvery, scarred brows.

Behemoth assumed his position in his corner and lifted his chin. His fingers stretched and squeezed against bright red boxing wraps. Piercings studded his ear, nostrils, branches of hair, and brows. He tore off his shirt to reveal even more chasms of black ink atop his dark flesh. Tendons pulsed like cables. Muscles were cut to statuesque perfection.

Behemoth's cornerman was pacing like a stalking lion, a cigarette lolling lazily against their lip. Their eyes were unsmiling and unfocused.

Oblitus fell quiet, the music and lights were low, and bated breaths held the entire audience captive.

Then, *CLACK*. The stranger popped their tongue, loud as a gunshot. With instinctual knowing, the rabid fighters unleashed onto one another. Fists bound, thick arms swinging. Behemoth could kick high and fast, his volleying arms black and blurry, pushing Dex to the outskirts of the ring. But Dex could dance, jump, duck, and dizzy, waning and dodging each airstrike.

"Dexteras stay on him, you hear me?" cried Nor.

A thunderous ripple of energy echoed through Dex's body, evident in his tight, flawless maneuvers and his smoking flesh. Each fist dug and tore until a sickening *CRACK* resounded from the ring.

Behemoth tripped to his corner, clinging to his jaw to keep it attached. The blow looked as though it could've sent his lower teeth up into his brain.

Norah's cheeks ached from grinning with hope. As her sweaty palms squeezed at the cage's thick chains with anticipation, they were bitten with an unseen, white hot burn. She stole her fingers from the rails and cursed, eyes following the gold links across the arena and into the stare of the opponent's cornerman.

The dark stranger winked, leaning their fine form against the rails.

Norah flipped them off with her lesser burnt hand.

The stranger grinned a toothy smile and returned their attention to the fight. Their dark lips molded cigarette plumage into gaseous shapes whilst their fingers twirled and maneuvered the wisps like an expert sailor tying knots.

The odd magic seemed to predicate Behemoth's busy hands as well.

For, from the other end of the arena, Dex's opponent was sculpting a hammered dagger from nothing but wisps of silvery plumage that spewed from his lips. Two black vaporous snakes peeled from the vapors, hissing and obedient as they wound the hilt.

Behemoth tossed the misty weapon into the air and snatched it at the handle, eyes still tethered on Dex. The dagger had formed into true, cold, metal and stone, its snakes now onyx and encrusted with emerald eyes. He tossed the weapon hand-to-hand, blinding Nor with its shining blade.

Behemoth broke into a galumphing trot. Dex jogged to meet him, fists drawn.

The impossible men in the ring struck, shouted, and bled.

Were there no fucking rules in this hellhole?

The crowd jeered. It seemed they would scream for any bloodshed, even that of their own fighter.

Now that a weapon had entered the ring, tensions skyrocketed, but Dex grew sharper, measured. Crisp and elegant.

"Knock him *out*, Dex!" Norah cried, leaning against the gold chains with abandon. She stole the ringmaster's smirks for her own with each of her friend's jabs.

A tiny grin humbled the old man's whiskers as he swarmed inwards, leaving his opponent little leverage to use his weapon. And while the blade was fatal, it also occupied one of Behemoth's fists, limiting his punches. It allowed Dex several strong and true hits.

From her peripheral vision, Norah drank in her own opponent, Behemoth's cornerman, the stranger. No hope of victory could truly be savored while they lingered near. They were the mongoose sucking their teeth as the snake's quarreled.

From between the ring's rails, between the chain links of the towering cage walls, those golden eyes locked onto hers, twitching with the fast precision of a blackbird on a wire.

Her blood chilled like ice and her shoulders went rigid.

A rush of black cables seeped from their shirt cuffs and collar and ate at their tangible form until they'd vanished.

She'd blinked, and they were gone, only to be reconstructed beside her, assimilating from the shadows, returned to their fine, fitted suit. The atmosphere that accompanied them was so bitter and cold, she could see the breath leave her lips.

The stranger called to her body like a bonfire in a winter storm. Shamefully, she yearned to warm her bones against it and stare at that pretty face.

The men in the ring snarled and bit, unaware of the spontaneous meeting of cornerbeings just outside their brawl.

The stranger's above-knee gilded limbs hissed in a seductive, serpentine language, corralling her backward against the jangling chains until she gripped them for respite. Balmy condensation beaded down her neck and between her breasts. The aroma of struck matches and fire swarmed her senses, like the sulfuric burn of a discharged gun.

They stretched their rings along the opposing rails, showcasing their gorgeous form. Their sleek chest was inked from neck to navel with aesthetic creatures, including a massive tattoo of a scarab beetle with spread wings, jewel tones shining across its exoskeleton. And when their doubloon eyes found hers, everything beyond their silhouette disappeared. The crowd. The fighters. It left only the two of them to consider one another in intimate isolation.

Holy fucking shit.

The stranger smiled with sparkling teeth and brows that bent with the curves of a fiddle.

"So ephemeral…so fragile," they sang, drinking in Norah with wandering eyes. "I haven't felt the heartbeat of a Corpse in eons. *You* are one I'm quite thirsty to know."

A vibration pulsated the air around the stranger, an inhuman kinesis. It trembled against the risen hairs of her arms and quaked behind her ears like a screaming insect. But their perfect epicene body was collected, still, and smiling. Their gold serpent eyes were soft, but she could sense snapping teeth just beneath.

"You give him strength, child. Do you know why?" they asked, so near to her that their cool breath dusted her lips.

A temblor shook the tile beneath them. Nor quickly peered around the stranger to squint through the gold chain link.

Dex had collapsed in the ring but was back on his feet in seconds.

Norah's lashes fluttered and returned her to the stranger, her hands yearning to touch the inked insects on their smooth chest and throat. Instead, she busied herself with the twisting of Alina's bracelet on her wrist.

Lioness.

The trinket returned her to herself, to the high-hackled, sharp creature that she was, not the vulnerable, swoony, weak-kneed girl bubbling with dopamine at the sight of smoky, dark eyes. She blinked the ignorant trance from her vision, feeling like a flapping moth in search of respite in a fire that would fizzle her to ash.

They'd burn your ass up, girl.

The stranger's lashes fell against their cheeks and white diamonds gleamed in their mouth. That mouth twisted as though wondering how she tasted. They offered a hand to her in introduction, laden with gold and more ink.

But despite the allure, the craving, the familiarity, the want to know them, Norah had no name for the impossible being.

In a breath, Norah blinked, and they suddenly weren't the same person, but another. Painted with the same tones, tattoos, golden eyes, and even the same gallant dressing, but a different body within. Their curves, their bones, their features, swapped in a heartbeat, a lens shutter.

She blinked again, breath stolen with stupor. But then they were their previous self, once more.

A deep sigh hissed from the handsome being's chest plate like a braking train. Between the steam, Nor sought the bright medallion eyes, rimmed in dark bronze, giving them an aura of madness.

She couldn't find a single word to justly fit the impossible beauty and danger in her midst.

"We share a contempt for our given names, *Lenore* Kestrel," they said, as though having read her thoughts.

A cold, anxious anger bristled in her blood at the very sound of her full name, but the stranger's sweet grin begged her forgiveness.

"Given names imply that we were made, but *we alone* made ourselves, didn't we?"

Norah's lips parted, curious and cautious. What a strange sensation it must be, to be unnamed. It could signify freedom, but it could also mean neglect. Unwantedness.

They snickered, seeing the pregnant pause squirm within her. "Oblitus is *my* arena, and all here know me. But in your world, I've had countless names. I am *solus, solitarius*," they added with ancient dialect, as though the comment would put the issue to bed.

"Solus?" Norah whispered, hearing the term and immediately thinking of *soullessness*.

They chuckled, throbbing the ink around their narrow throat.

"I will not be bound to nomenclature ever again," they grinned, crouching before her on their razor-blade limbs like a mischievous headstone angel. They inhaled a deep breath of cigarette and spilled it from their dark lips between them. The tongues of smoke divided into forked paths and created two massive, wafting forms, hip-high and stalking like wild dogs. One was a wide-shouldered male hyena with a low, predatory head, and the other, was a massive hyena female with a deadly strut and raised hackles.

Norah backed from the ghostly beasts, wide-eyed and breathless as the smoke creatures pinned their black-tipped ears and paced at either of their maker's sharp shoulders, mirroring the other. The impossible mirages snarled and roared at the being's earlobes like battling voices of consciousness.

Silvery paws swiped, tall back hair bristled, their teeth dripped in drool, and they snapped and threatened. Then, the tension escalated and the beasts rose to their haunches and roared distant, echoing banshee screams whilst their wraithlike bodies fought and clashed, smoky tendrils interwoven.

Then, the hyenas grew tired and returned to settle, chuffing and gasping beside their master once more, hairs sharp and chaotic. The staring, golden eyes of Solus shone behind them, *through them*, combining the two beasts into one. Then, as though a swift wind had snaked through the chain links of the cage, the elemental beasts disappeared, leaving only their maker to stare up at Norah.

"You may call me whatever you like," Solus said, resolutely.

The extravagant introduction, though terrifying and bold, seemed like a patient, considerate, and rare gesture. An obvious attempt to communicate *you may know me*. It was indeed a powerful, and wordless vulnerability that Norah could only nod to in response.

A clangor of metal jerked her head to the ring to see Dex pulling himself to his feet again, tripping against the gold rails, now only wearing black pants and boots. His shirt was shredded on the tile, mutilated by Behemoth's blade. Bands of blood slipped down her friend's chest. Each inch of him glistened with sweat. The colorful art on his body stretched and bled. It was obvious that he was hurting.

Hang on Dex, hang on.

The crouched Solus popped their tongue, eager to keep her attention. The gesture made Nor shudder and swallow.

She'd once had a session with a young boy diagnosed with Conduct Disorder after his stepfather found he'd killed a litter of kittens and mutilated some mice he'd found in traps. He was brought to The Nest for a high-risk behavior assessment, but soon after was referred to a higher intensity of care.

He'd had such a sharp aura and a violent compulsion, but an innocent sweet face and charm. It reminded her of just how fervently the brain fought to protect itself. The devastating trauma and abuse that boy had endured were made comprehensible and palatable by the abuse of others. In taking charge of the few weak and vulnerable things around him, he found an illusion of stability, and safety. Control. For some brains, it was the only way it could fathom going onward.

In the case of the odd being before her, what horrors had they endured that demanded so much power and control of living things?

Dexteras called out, angry and in pain.

Norah stood upright, fingers clinging to the gold rails.

Behemoth's slippery hands had gathered more real estate on the knife's hilt and fought to squeeze tight hooks between him and Dexteras, painting crimson slashes across the old man's forearms. Rolling streams leaked down his elbows.

"You haven't introduced *yourself*, human child," Solus sang up at her with a syrupy tone.

Nor's skin scrawled at the term *human*. "You already know my name," she said distantly, still watching her fighter.

Dex responded with a lightning-fast spin and kick of a crane-like leg. One of these managed a clean blow across Behemoth's jaw which snapped back with a pop and a brief, blinding flash of lightning. The crowd couldn't help but whistle and cheer at the dazzling elemental show.

"I only know your slave name, *mon cherie.*"

"N-Norah," she muttered, eyes dashing to Solus. Her fingers fought the compulsion to shake their hand but continued twisting the beads at her wrist instead.

CLANG.

Dex had backpedaled into his corner, the rails singing their metallic chorus about the ring. Blood squeaked beneath his feet. He'd lost bucketfuls.

"Eyes on me, Norah," the creature before her stood again, blocking her view of the fight, extending their hand, brows bent in sweet charity. Norah now noticed the words *PUGNA* and *FUGA* were inked along their knuckles. Smoke peeled from their sleeves and wrapped around her wrists, pulling her hand nearer like a beckoning wind.

"Your Dexteras knows pain intimately, like a lover."

They bowed their lovely lips to kiss her knuckles and the ruddy silver rings there, but as their fingertips wrapped her palm, their eyes shimmered like polished brass. A long, grin of knowing stretched across their gorgeous face. Their assertive fingertips ran across her hand's old scar, caressing the sore skin like the scrape of a blade.

Their brow rose and their tongue tsked. "And who did this to you?" they sang.

Norah couldn't move, her spine stiff and on high alert.

Could they all read scars?

"Pain is power, Norah. Agony, misery, despair, grief, fury, spilled blood. It's *energy*. Fuel. Art," they cooed. "That must be how he found you. And why he stays so very close."

She snatched back her hand and rubbed the scar. Her eyes cut past the stranger's shoulder just in time to see Behemoth's dagger dash from his fingers, whipped from his hip with expert finesse.

Dexteras spun and kicked the weapon, sending it singing into the air above with a clang of silver. He caught it and thrust it into the tile, plunging it deep into the grout. Dex bent and charged, eyes afire.

A horrid collision of flesh and bodies rattled the rails.

"It seems," said Solus, rubbing together the fingertips that had been scrutinizing her flesh, "we both wish to be free of those who made us."

Their cold, horrid chill trembled all the way to Norah's toes. It carried with it a guilt, a shame that welded her feet to the tile. A full breath couldn't fill her lungs. She felt trapped by the confrontation.

Suddenly, a sweat soaked Dexteras tossed himself into the rails before them, interrupting their introductions with a violent clang. The lights of the arena painted him in dramatic blood-red neon and moon-white spotlight.

At the center of the ring, Behemoth was belly down to the tile like a lizard warming on a hot stone. He wasn't moving.

"Get the *fuck* away from her," Dex barked at Solus, nostrils flaring, body pressed against the chain-link threateningly.

Solus grinned and put their hands in their pockets, stepping obediently away from Nor.

The authentic warmth of the world returned to her shoulders and she sighed.

"Love?" Dex gasped, sending her a worried glare.

"I'm okay," she croaked, head asunder with nods.

"Your reward is nearly yours, son," said Solus, stepping fearlessly to the old man, fingers interwoven in the rails. They tipped their chin to Behemoth. "But you must finish your round." From a dense plume of their cigarette smoke, they crafted another blade identical to Behemoth's, pinching it at its razor tip, dangling the hilt before Dex's fingers.

Norah's brief relief sank deep into her gut.

No.

"You said *defeat* your fighters, not murder them," stated Dex, leaning from the weapon as though it were a striking serpent.

Solus chuckled as gold sparkled beneath their crazed eyes. "Trust me, son, anything their immortal bodies may endure in the ring is nothing compared to what they've known. And it's nothing compared to what they'll endure if they lose."

Dex's eyes lingered on the blade's hilt. He was no killer, but Nor wondered if he'd convinced himself otherwise.

"It's *Occidit vel occisus est,*" hissed Solus in a dead dialect, eyes cold and distant.

"What in the hell does that mean?" Norah muttered.

"Agh," gasped Dex, suddenly. His body stiffened and he clutched to the chain link. His eyes were distant and glassy within a blink.

"Dex!" Norah reached through the rails for her friend as he fell, but he slipped through her arms. The tile shuddered as he crashed to his knees, his hips, his hands. The familiar onyx hilt of a knife quivered from his taut spine, just between the shoulder blades.

"Kill or be killed," said Solus pleasantly.

Norah finally noticed Behemoth on his feet, an inked arm bent with effort. Contempt glowed beneath the whites of his eyes.

Life in the hospital had taught Nor the basics of spinal cord injuries. She knew this one had pierced Dex's thoracic vertebrae with surgical precision. His paralyzed legs dragged behind him, leaving him to swat over his shoulder at the protrusion. The weapon was deep, ensnared between links of bone and swollen blue veins. His mouth was agape, his eyes were glassy, and he was slipping into shock.

The crowd roared their countdown from seven to one. They erupted into glory as Dex was declared the official loser of the match.

Norah squeezed through the arena's chain link and fell to the tile at Dex's side.

"Marchosias!" snarled Solus, searching the crowd. "Behemoth."

The limping beasts breached the golden arena and lifted their chins high to their commander, bleeding and blackened with tattooed tallies and bloody slashes.

They both knelt before Solus. Marchos, however, quivered and twitched, an oddly submissive behavior, given his bold, unabashed tongue. The tattooed dragon on his back jostled and contorted.

"Behemoth, your prize." Solus snapped their long fingers, manifesting a tiny, empty glass vial. With a squint of their gold eyes and a deep pull of cigarette in their chest, smoke poured from their lips and filled the bottle, trapping the wisps inside with a cork. A black, glittery liquid swirled and churned within. Solus tossed it to Behemoth who snatched it from the air, bowing with honor.

"Your past is yours alone. You speak of none of it with your fellow Forgotten. If you wish to pursue more memories from your traumatized past, you must again gain favor with Cecil before returning to the ring."

Behemoth nodded, uncorked his vial, and chose to drink it eagerly on the spot. He tossed back the vile and his eyes flickered back into his skull with its burn. Then, he hacked black smoke from his lungs and bent across his knees until he was whooping towards the tile with a bulging back. Shadowy plumes slipped from his lips, and tears of physical and mental pain fell from his straining eyes. He fell to his knees, fixated on the tile. Moments later, his coughing fit died down, and Nor could only hear him weeping. Sobbing.

The crowd and Solus only watched and waited, evidently bound to the sacred pact.

Behemoth straightened and smeared his face with a sweaty arm and limped from the stage. Several of those he passed pressed hands of solidarity to his back and neck. It was a compassionate, yet distant gesture, as though he were a grieving widower.

"Marchosias," muttered Solus, eyes low and distant on the cowering beast before them.

Marchos began to shake and bare his teeth.

At the mercy of the dagger in Dex's paralyzed spine, she and her friend could only gawk at the horrid events unveiling before them. Nor squeezed the old man's wrist, grounding herself with his still beating heart.

"Your challenger is a *detached* Figment, you understand?" boomed Solus. "He knows nothing of his abilities, nothing of his power, and still, he *crushed* you."

The remaining fighter cried out with pain, pressing his weeping eyes to the tile.

"No. No," croaked Dexteras, fists clenching. "Marchos was my match, you said-"

"This is your first round of arena matches, and I always grant grace to first timers," said Solus over their shoulder. "But it *did* count for Marchos," they sighed, "and he knew that. He was presumptuous. And if it's one thing I do not tolerate, it is ungratefulness."

"Pater, please, *please*!" Marchos' Russian accent thickened as he cried.

Pater was Latin for Father, Norah understood. He was calling Solus, *Father*. Her racing heart skipped a beat. She realized yet again, that her scarred hand was clutching to Dex's, their white knuckles keeping one another present, grounded, alive. Again, she was allowed the impossible bridge of his comprehension when their scars graced.

"This was a venture you agreed to pursue," Solus stated, voice rising. "I offered you respite. I offered you peace. You decided to wager that gift, Marchosias, on an easy contender no doubt, and you lost."

"*Please*, Pater, another, please!"

"You trained beneath Cecil, my most skilled fighter," Solus cried, pointing into the crowd. "You were given all of the tools to succeed. You gambled, you played, and you *lost*."

The tension of a taut and loaded trigger held her and the entire bar hostage.

Nor watched a flash of crimson, a trill of adrenaline flash behind the ring leader's eyes. It was a poker tell of violence. But their anger here seemed different, almost reluctant and pained the way it warped their brow. Norah swore she saw a mournful shine gloss and dry from their eyes in a blink.

"Please, he's more than he seems," shouted Marchos, his eyes wild upon Dex. "He's different when-"

But Solus snapped their fingers with the flourish of an inked arm. A horrid breaking like the cracking of tree branches echoed through the ring.

"No!" Norah screamed. Vomit churned in her throat, and she was melting, sinking into the tile beside Dex, staring at the ink-stained wrinkles of his clenched knuckles. He pressed his forehead to the tile with a whimper, haggard body shaking. His scarlet eye paced the floor in panic.

Marchosias cried out with ill-fitting fear at the breaking of his spine, leaving him immobile.

Its tenor and anguish suddenly stood Norah to her feet. Her social worker's heart bled, it yearned to save Marchos.

"*Pater! Pater!*" The sweating beast wept, weak fingers clutching Solus' pantsuit.

But their *Pater* was busying themself with the lighting of another cigarette. Their throat rounded with a deep swallow of the tobacco as they lifted their fighter from the floor by their neck.

Marchos wailed and choked.

Their golden eyes rolled and their chest swelled with nicotine. Then, they spewed black, sooty smoke into their fighter's screaming, gaping mouth like the soupy discharge of chewing tobacco.

Norah winced as Marchosias choked on its poison, falling to writhe on the floor.

Prostrate on the tile, steam rasped from his gaping mouth, spine bucking. His exposed torso and face were growing crimson, steaming. Sizzling, *peeling*.

Where his flesh was thinnest, most taut, and pulled, it grew russet orange, then brown, then black. It blistered in wide patches like a cooked animal, splitting and seeping. Blackened flesh then began to separate.

Norah felt hundreds of miles away, fully prostrate on the tile, clutching to Dex's fingers, eyes hot and burning. She couldn't tear from Marchos' face and lips, black, bubbling, flaking. How he clutched to his eyes, steam burning at the moisture that glazed them. How his fingers grew stiff and shriveled. She'd never unhear the dusty, serrated screams that cut through his throat. Norah didn't know when she'd began shaking so violently.

Marchos' scream was that of being burned alive, a nightmarish bawl she knew too well. She was grateful for the tears that blurred her vision whilst the entire crowd watched. For once, the building was silent, mourning, and present.

The once gargantuan Marchosias, wide with muscles and brazen with life, was now smoldering, crumpled, and baked to atrophied flesh. Brittle, like the shed skin of a snake.

Truly, dead.

Norah tore from what remained of the fighter and found the club's owner staring down at her with dark, sharklike eyes. Their expression was fixed like that of a weary, unworshipped god. She felt their endless gaze but could only weep with panic and distant trauma.

She understood now what they'd meant. Mere fighting would never be of consequence to immortal beings. Thus, if they were to fight for precious prizes, there had to be greater stakes. They weren't afraid to lose, or even to die, they were afraid of whatever the hell had just happened to Marchosias.

From the crusted hide came a thick, silvery plume of smoke through the broken flesh. It was a glittering, sentient, swirling form that whipped above the body like a panicked insect, crystalline-like the tangles of a spider web in the wind. The cloud wound with intention and rose to the ceiling. Above, amidst the haze and cigarette smoke, it slipped through the tile's seams and vanished into what she anticipated were the waiting stars outside.

Still paralyzed and stranded, Dex abandoned all remaining effort and collapsed fully to the tile.

A shocked and sobbing Norah spilled her armfuls of bottles and rags from the void of his coat pockets, hands shaking.

"N-Nor please don't," Dex managed between chattering teeth.

"We're both getting the fuck out of here," she muttered, abandoning all she knew to be true of traditional medicine. While Dexteras wasn't technically yet dead, Behemoth had won another stripe because his final blade to the old man would indeed be a killing blow. She tied several clean bar rags together and monitored his deathly pallor.

"I'll f-figure it out, you need to go..."

She spat the tiny lid from a bottle of vodka and gave herself and Dex a swallow, clear streams spilling down his beard. He dropped his head back to the tile and Nor braced a leg into his spine, gripping the embedded knife. It was firm as though driven through stone. She splashed it, too, with the remaining vodka. She had no earthly idea if her friend's impossible body could die from infection, but she wasn't going to risk it.

"On three," she said through gritted teeth. "One-" and with bared fists, she heaved until the knife gave with a sickening slurp.

Dex's spine bucked, leaving him slamming his fists until spidery cracks were driven through the ring's floor. Burgundy lifeblood sloshed about them both.

The hot blade cooked the residual spinal fluid and flesh clinging to it. She wrapped the damned thing in rags and splashed it in more alcohol. She pressed its steaming metal to his flayed flesh, hissing with cauterization.

Dex bridged and snarled, teeth and muscles clenched tight. His mountainous spine shuddered and the outpouring fountain of blood in his spine was sealed.

Nor packed it with rags and tied the knotted bar towels tightly around his sweating torso. She fell back to her rear, sweat clinging to her hair and temples.

The scrape of knife blades in blood lifted her eyes to Solus, who was walking in great, slow, strides towards them. She scrambled to her feet and stood before her old friend who was still immobile and recovering.

"Leave him alone, he won a fair fight," she warned, fingers tucking into her palms.

Solus' golden eyes raked up her limbs and found her hardened jaw and face. "You're quite right Corpse, he did," they smiled halfheartedly. "And as I said, I offer grace for my juvenile fighters, just once. They cannot possibly know what they've signed up for until they step into the ring."

"But why…why did you-" she began, eyes wistfully blinking at the ashen pile that had once been Marchosias.

Solus raised their brows, nearly pained with her deductions. "I simply refunded his Purpose, since it was no longer in allegiance here to Oblitus. To *us*," they added, eyeing the crowd as though they'd all drank the breath from Marchos' chest.

Norah could only stutter, jaw slack like a confused schoolchild. She was tempted to wilt beneath the whites of hundreds of watching eyes.

Solus' patience for her misunderstanding was waning. "I know I can't expect a Corpse to make sense of our ways. But to be fair, you are our first here, and our last, I do hope."

Norah winced up at the gorgeous being, despising how weak and ignorant this place made her feel. How useless her words were. How incapable her hands were of helping anyone.

Solus smiled, sadly. "You do understand, *you* are the wolf amongst sheep in this place?" they said, tone convicting and firm.

Her gut plummeted, truly feeling the weight of her worthlessness. She followed Solus' golden irises eyes and together they surveyed the crowd.

"You are symbolic of a trauma that I swore to protect them from," Solus added, gentler now. "I allow you here simply to understand you, so that I may understand how it is you're on my doorstep and then prevent it in the future."

The drone of the hot lights and neon hummed and blinded her She could not properly make out their expressions, but she did know that each one of them was in fact staring at her and her trembling hands, wet with her friend's blood.

"If you want to protect them so badly, why do you do this?" She managed a weak nod to Marchos' remains.

"Am I so terrible to offer them the free will to choose?" Solus pressed their dark lips into a tight line. "*They* run to *me* with their broken pieces, Norah Kestrel," they said. "*They* come to me to make a deal. To swallow their pain. Just as your Dexteras did."

She was shaking her head, slowly, disbelieving and so, so tired.

"I could show you…" Solus said, leaning close, their soft, tattooed hands lifting to cup her jaw. So near to their gorgeous face, Nor observed that each inch of them was flawless and untouched, unmarred by the strange lines the others wore.

And before she'd realized she was moving, her sweaty back collided with a jarring clang against the cold metal chain-link. Her fingers grappled at it for stability.

And despite being cornered, the choking heat between her and the tall being was suddenly chased away by a cool, fervent breeze. For a moment, she could breathe.

Then, Solus' reaching fingers were cut short by massive hand at the back of their collar. Whipped and thrown to the center of the arena, Dexteras tore and swung at the handsome beast.

The *shing-shing-scrape* of his opponent's golden legs carved at the tile. Their hyena grin was wiped from their face and they escaped the spar in a whorl of black plumes.

A miraculously resuscitated Dex eyed Norah and tossed his chin to the outer circle. She promptly ducked beneath the gold chain link where she could regain her druthers, slumping against the rails of the cornerman's alley.

At the ring's far end, Solus assembled from the skies in a thick dollop of smoke with shining gold and manic features.

"You hear scars. Voices. Don't you son?" they teased, their limbs kinetic and alive.

Dex said nothing. His body stood before Norah, wound and ready to strike.

"You're drawn to her and that blood bank she serves." Solus grinned, eyes darting to the watchful Norah behind the fence line. "But do you know why?"

Dex said nothing, but his jaw clenched.

"I'll give you a hint," they grinned, daring a few steps towards the old man. "Why does the fox hear the screams of the dying hare?" Solus grinned with dazzling white teeth.

Though crippled with a leaking spine, Dex roared and gave chase.

Solus twisted on their metallic legs, darting and dodging with ease.

Dex wound and delivered a blow to the stranger's chest. The steel embedded there dented, and a tiny screw popped from the flesh and clattered to the gold tile. A powerful spray of black steam gushed from the weakness in their hardware.

Solus bared their teeth smashed the metal flat with a fast fist to their shoulder. The mechanism sealed, but Solus was buckled and breathless. After passing a hand through their black hair, they disappeared again into their snakelike vapors.

Dex growled like a badger, wheeling about for his enemy. But he needn't look long. The old man spun his throat right into his opponent's grip where it was squeezed.

"Dex!" gasped Nor, clutching to the arena rails.

"I *remember* how delicious human Purpose can taste, son." The nameless devil eyed her, biting their tongue. "How it slips down your throat and warms your bones. A consumption beyond measure," they sighed. "But would she stay beside you if she knew what you've done? If she saw the past you ran from?" Solus asked, eyes warning with their deadly gold.

The two impossible beings shared endless unspoken thoughts, jaws bared, eyes afire, nostrils flared. After an eternity in this intimate quiet, Solus released Dex and the old man fell to his knees on the tile, face crimson and furious as he hacked.

Solus spun and brandished a free hand from which strands of black smoke peeled from their sleeve, lighting a cigarette in their fingers.

"But, I did promise fleeting grace, and you have served as an example for all of us. We need to see how Figments deteriorate when they're so far from their home, from their Purpose, from me," they smiled, eyes gleaming at the old man. "So!" they exclaimed, snapping their fingers. "Go join your Corpse and I'll give you a taste of what you came for, sweet boy, on the house," they stated, relishing this prize and how eagerly Dex fawned for it.

In moments, Dex was to his feet, beneath the gold chain-link and beside Norah. She embraced him tightly.

Solus, too, slipped through the fence as a wisp of black smoke, rebuilding themselves on the opposite end of the ring. They leaned back into the crimson neon to cry, "Nix!"

The crowd pulled apart to carve an aisle towards the ring, making way for a gorgeous, glittering woman who strode towards the stage, confident and unafraid, an ethereal creature that fought the snarling darkness.

Dexteras clung to the fence and squinted through, a cocktail of emotions pored across his features.

As Nix ascended the stairs, Norah couldn't stop her lips from falling open to spill silent confessions of her love.

Nix was a towering, celestial goddess of a woman with rolling curves and skin and hair as dark as midnight. Norah swore tiny, pinpricks of light pierced the woman's blackness like twinkling stars, making her glow with an otherworldly aura.

"Nixie, if you would," Solus sang to the woman, gesturing with a cigarette towards the arena.

The woman's large cloud of black hair was shimmering with nebulae as she nodded at Solus and stepped *through* its gold cage like an apparition. Her body only glittered with the effort.

Norah leaned against the rails, lips pressed against the cold links in wonder.

Nix's long, dancing fingers shone with diamonds and moonstones and mystic topaz as she gestured and drew several rune-like shapes with her tattooed hands. With each, a different tattoo on her body radiated from beneath her flesh like a dying star. When these were completed, her entire body glowed a deep galaxy blue and she was engulfed in a blinding wave of white light.

When the shielding arms of the crowd and Norah fell, they saw that Nix the human form no longer remained. What stood in her place was a tall, gorgeous black mare, dappled constellations and stardust dripping down her flanks and withers. Her gorgeous muscles shuddered with each mighty hoof step as she centered herself in the ring. The horse's eyes were moony white and shining like the beacon of a lighthouse.

Dex and Nor could only gasp, staring sky bound at the glorious horse of the heavens. Norah was certain the old man could hear her excited heart leaping in her chest.

Solus paced, eyes cutting like the big cat they were, tattooed chest washed in Nix's glorious blue light. A proud, wistful shine held the club owner's upcast eyes.

The mare shook like a massive wet hound, black flesh trembling and shedding its white starlight and drops of space to the arena's floor. It splashed, pooled, and puddled beneath her black hooves, swelling about the cage like a small ocean in a jar. The blinding luminescent tides tumbled and churned up along the rungs of the fighting cage as though fully contained.

The starry ocean rose above Norah, Dex, and Solus, above the mare's head, violently slapping the invisible glass walls of the cage until it had filled the fighting cage to its fullest capacity. It dared to splash and slip sparkling starry drips of the ethereal ocean over the cage's lip.

Horror and wonder held all of Oblitus' eyes to the rim of the arena and its nearly ten-foot-tall enclosed ocean. Within, the mare was now swimming gracefully, having split the thick flesh past its cheekbone with flexing gills and having transformed their glorious hind end into a long, winding fish's tail, shining with iridescent scales. The dragon horse's black mane and dorsal fins spiraled and twirled behind like jellyfish stingers in the moon-white water.

Norah was certain she and the entire crowd could've spent an eternity tracing the gorgeous morphing woman with their eyes. But of course, Solus wasn't through with their dramatics.

Their dark lips pulled on a cigarette, drawing deep from the bowels of their tattooed abdomen. A thin, snaking tendril slipped through their nostrils, pierced the cage and the ocean's invisible glass walls, and dissolved into Nix's water. She wound through the leeching black fingers of the smoke, integrating it into her potion.

"When you're ready, son," Solus called through the sparkling pool to Dex. They nodded to the aquarium casually.

Without a word to Nor, a hesitant breath, or a need for clarification, Dex climbed the gold chain link fence, his leather boots poking carefully for surefootedness. Everyone's mouths were agape as he settled a moment at the peak, peering down into the moonlit well beneath. Its glow sparkled in his blue eyes with wonder and lit his face with a cleansing brightness. The old man seemed young for just a moment as he stared into its depths, watching the mare swim in patient circles below.

The crowd was silent. No one moved. No one even breathed.

"Most bodies, human or not, cannot bear to be torn from their mind," called Solus to the awestruck man above. "Even when they beg and scream for me to take it from them. It's like tearing the brain from the heart," they said in earnest mourning. "It can make any being *go mad.*"

As Dex listened and leaned, entranced by the blue glowing water before him, Norah noticed a sneaking, solitary snakelike thread of black ink weaving itself betwixt the waters, dodging light and sticking to the pool's stark shadow. It rose towards the bent old man, invisible and poisonous in the radiant pool.

"Dex, Dex," Norah rasped, yearning to scream, but her voice was hoarse and feeble.

"Which is why after you wept on your knees before me, and I took your traumatic memories from you, son," added Solus, teeth flashing like fangs, "You *jumped.*"

Then, the black adder struck from the water and wound the old man's throat, pulling him over the cage and into the deep pool, his legs a chaotic afterthought, splashing about violently.

"Dex!" Norah cried, watching in terror as he sank down, down, down into the dome of water, a silhouette of ghostly silver hair and churning clothes against the light.

"Do you think if she knew what drove you to such madness, that she could care for you so?" cried Solus into the trembling waves.

Dex's body fell still and quiet, submerged, entranced, and twitching as though dreaming with his eyes open, pacing, and distant.

Norah circled him from the outer ring, her stare trained on the old man, watchful for any sign of distress or fear. It seemed as though his body and mind were reliving a memory in the mysterious water.

Solus only watched Dexteras float as though watching a beloved specimen bob in formaldehyde. Nix swam around the sunken old man, her fins and long, whipping mane twirling about protectively. And then, she coiled into the scales of her long tail, the massive Roman nose tucking into her shadowy mane, and was gone. She took with her the glorious, heavenly light and sparkling stars, and the pool grew black, blue, dark, and deadly, leaving only Dexteras within.

At this sudden change, the water jostled and brewed, the rim of its tank sloshing with displaced liquid. Dex shuddered and thrashed. The whites of his eyes grew and gawked.

Nor couldn't be certain if his head were shaking from oxygen deprivation or denial. Tiny blue flashes of electricity strobed from his body like frayed wires. In the dark dangerous water, it illuminated the tank like a lightning storm.

Come back, Nor begged in her thoughts. *Come back, Dex, please. You're not your past. You're my friend and I need you here.*

One of his great, tattooed arms floated forward as though he were reaching for something in his dreamscape.

Norah leaned against the rails and pressed against the cold cold surface of the water, leaning against its suspended, trembling tank. Her fingers breached the hovering body of ocean and reached towards her friend. Spotlights of red neon plunged the blue and cast plum-dark shadows across his crumpled, terrified face.

He jerked and wriggled and bucked now, as though he were transforming into something monstrous, or choking on lungfuls of cursed water. The tiny, bright crackles of lightning intensified form his flesh.

Then, he opened his mouth and screamed massive clouds of blue bubbles towards the surface. His horrid, morphed moans vibrated against her extended arm. She could nearly scrape his thrashing limbs with her fingers.

"Dex," she begged, pressing her cheek and body against the chain-link, tiptoes extended, fingerbones aching, tendons stretching. His bright spidery trails of electric current did not seem to hurt her.

The cold pads of her fingers reached for his cheek, her pulse trembling with pain, screaming in her taut limbs. She took a final breath and pressed with everything she had. She swore the panicked pulse of her heart rippled the water with its desperation, stirring the panicked old man in its depths.

"Come back," she begged.

And then, the glassy confines of Nix's tank shattered like crystal, momentarily suspended in its perfect perforations before unleashing hundreds of gallons of blue-black water onto Norah, the stage, and the surrounding crowd, bulging the rails and chains with its immense pressure.

Dexteras was shipwrecked against the chain-link, limp, and unconscious. Norah was nearly cast off the ring's tall stage, but was able to clutch a handful of jostling chains, nearly ripping her arm from its socket. Coughing and hacking, she swung her legs back onto the platform and gasped up at the gold tile of Oblitus' ceiling. The icy water made her grateful for the ring's underground balminess.

She turned her head to see Solus, impossibly bone dry, bent above the unconscious, soaked Dexteras, near enough to tear out the old man's jugular with their teeth.

"Hear me, son, you can stop fighting and accept your peace, your home, your family, and Purpose here," they said over the wet sloshing of the crowd. "Or risk spilling the full ugliness of what's inside of you upon this ring for your pet to see."

Still coughing water from her lungs and returning to her slippery boots, the sight of the unconscious Dexteras being preyed upon filled her with fury. His watery screams still nipped at the back of her thoughts, akin to the howls that haunted her nightmares.

Fists bared, she slipped through the gold rails and prepped for a mighty assault on the bastard who dared abuse her friend. Her shoulder steadied like a missile and her feet squealed along the slick tile. But as she surged through the fighter's circle and crashed into their tall form, only wafting ribbons of black smoke remained where they once stood.

Nor rocketed through the humid smoke, clinging to the ring's rails to keep from toppling over. "You coward!" she screamed at Solus, aching to crush their bones until she was left with fistfuls of glittering glass.

The beast poured before her from the other end of the arena, drowning her in a pitying scowl as though she were a dying, split creature in the road.

She stood between Solus and the old man, dripping and heavy. Her shoulders were heaving, her soaked hair beginning to unravel into a humid cloud about her twisted face.

Solus grinned, eyes softening at her rage. "Angry, bitter child. All you've known is pain," they sang, pretty features smiling. "*Your* makers didn't love *you* either, did they?"

Norah straightened. After the survival of her adolescence, she'd once been certain that all of the hatred her heart could manufacture had been spent. But as Solus painted her friend's gorgeous galaxies into nightmares, they relit the dead, sacred emotion from beneath her chest again. It felt justified, hot, burning and purposeful.

She missed it.

And before she could consider a way to channel it best, she was twisting and pulling a rogue fist behind her. She envisioned it stretching through Solus' paper flesh, shattering their ribs. She imagined herself reaching deep into them, as Cecil could. Reaching in the same way her eager fingertips searched for the rotting distortions of trauma in the hearts of her clients.

But as her knuckles brushed the hot flesh of their jaw, it fell through them as though striking a cloud.

Solus warped into their vaporous form and wafted toward the ceiling tiles, siphoning through its seams as the remains of Marchosias had.

"Fucking coward!" Norah cried to the gold panels. Spitting pent anger from her chest, she fell beside her downed fighter, breathing and unconscious on the gold tile. His wrinkled neck was twisted with bruises. His pants were sodden and tight against his pathetically crooked legs. His unconscious eyes rolled and darted beneath their crumpled crow's feet.

All around them, Oblitus resumed its ignorant bustle. Bass pounded in her chest. Gorgeous bodies wound and clung to one another in skirmish and seduction below the ring. The arena lights grew black, and the neon of the bar beckoned its patrons.

As the soaked crowd pulled from the gold rails, a dark silhouette remained, clinging to the arena chains like an abandoned marionette. A rugged, broad-shouldered man in black clothes and sunglasses was draped there. None dare come near or gaze upon his handsome figure for long.

Norah watched a slow Cecil poke about each stair with care like a wounded animal. With caution, he approached the center ring and knelt beside Nor and Dexteras. Brief flashes of strobing lights danced about his glasses as he felt Dex's throat.

His posture was bent and pained. The heavy lights draped him in dramatic shadow. With each dash of white light, Nor could see a wet stain reflecting from the front of his black shirt.

Was that blood?

His square jaw and fists were bulked, clenching, and releasing. The revolving lights caught a wet tremble at his lips. He was attempting to speak but seemed to struggle.

Nor leaned nearer to listen to his sputtering.

A guttural moan escaped his throat. A snarl of distress. But when no words followed, his chin fell to his chest. It seemed as though his teeth were glued together, muscles bulging in his cheeks and throat with strain. He tried again, fingers clenching at his kneecaps.

He leaned further over the unconscious man in the ring, moaning with horrid gargles.

A series of tiny steam clouds sizzled from Dex's soaked chest, hissing and angry, white and brief. Droplets of dark wine poured from the struggling Cecil above, catching Dex's hot flesh like a skillet.

Nor leaned low to seek out the dark lenses with concern. "Cecil?"

His complexion was deadly pale, and his frown lines were taut. He attempted to force words through bared teeth, fingers scratching beneath. A wall of teeth chattered beneath his dripping lips. He craned his neck. His Adam's apple bobbed. Veins bulged in his throat to swallow.

He again stretched his teeth apart against the invisible muzzle. In the deep darkness of his mouth, Norah only saw a pool of black blood.

Crimson bubbles gurgled from his throat, and he jolted with a wretch, forcing coagulated mucus to the tile behind him. The only sound he could manage was the scraping of his nails.

Nor slid closer, hands hovering in panic, uncertain of how to help.

He gasped and choked, blood falling from his face like heavy rain. Hoarse, wet rattles shook his chest. She was certain streams of tears leaked beneath his glasses.

What the hell happened to him?

"Jesus Cecil, go slow, go slow…" she urged, fingers flitting over his skin.

His throat lurched and hacked a thick bloody pool over his shoulder again.

Nor reached to slip the dark shades from his sweating face, but he clamped a quick hand of warning to hers. His gray-green irises peeked above the lenses, the flesh around them scattered with scars and divots.

He gasped and tore free from her, hacking on his own blood, limbs shaking beneath him. He was choking. Something was creating a steady enough stream of blood to fill up even his immortal windpipe.

This time, she grazed her hand against his hot, scruffy cheek. It was warm like cast iron from the coals. As they adjusted to the heat, her fingers felt a lifetime of abuse and neglect carved into his features.

"Take your time," she said, ignoring the leering spectators who still watched from below. Some snickered, others watched, open-mouthed.

Then much to her surprise, Cecil's weight fell into her palm, against her own scar.

Her fear rose, as though she held to the head of a crocodile, but his eyes grew glassy and calm for the first time in minutes. The wet shudders of breath eased from his lips. His curiosity had briefly stilled him. He leaned into her hand as though leaning into a seashell for its song. She sensed him rummaging about her embedded memories, scavenging them of their intimacy without invitation.

So near to the beast, she could see he was worn and tired like Dexteras, only much younger. Her heart softened and her anxiety ebbed.

A wet hitch caught in his throat, and he bulked and choked again, tearing away to wipe at the spilling mucus with a bare arm. It painted his covered-up tattoos in scarlet.

Nor shot stabbing glares into the crowd until their gorgeous, dumb faces turned away.

Cecil managed to sit tall on his knees, affixing his glasses up his nose. With a preparatory breath, he pried his lips apart, wincing with effort. A reservoir of liquid shone between the hollows of his teeth. And in the flicker of a strobe light, she could finally see what he was trying to show her. His jaw and cheeks trembled with strain. The air shuddered as he fought with clenched eyes.

Where his tongue once sat, there was instead a vacant pool of blood, carved mouth muscle, and cut flesh.

His tongue was cut out.

Norah's fingers slapped her mouth and stifled a scream that wouldn't come. She closed her eyes and breathed deeply. She only opened them again when she heard Cecil heaving to the tile once more.

Nor reached into the sopping wet breast pocket of Dex's massive coat. She begged and prayed for a miracle. For something dry and useful.

She withdrew a handful of clean bar rags, miraculously dry. She stuffed them into Cecil's clenched hand. He dabbed at his mouth with restrained moans. And it was then that Nor noticed a bloody phrase carved into his forearm's flesh: *ORBUM*.

Uncertain she wanted to know, she clutched Dex's scarred palm in her own and attempted to siphon his unconscious to translate the phrase. It came for her in trembling, glitchy images. Burnt pages from a Latin dictionary. It was as though a projector fueled by lamplight was being cast against her dark headspace.

Bereft.

Deprived.

Orphaned.

Norah sighed and swallowed her grief. Cecil continued to slop dripping, seeping rags to the floor. Cecil gnawed on each until it was heavy with blood.

Eventually, he gnashed a final, fresh rag beneath his bared teeth and pulled at Dex's unconscious form. With the drunken sway of blood loss, Cecil secured his footing and swung her friend across his shoulder like a wounded firefighter. Blood painted the floor after them.

Norah dashed after her friends, all the while challenging each dazzling set of eyes that scowled in their direction. Each step to the door above was clambering and painstaking. But finally, they tripped from the bar without any further signs of Solus.

✦

Keeping to the street's shadows, she led them to the vehicle. Every few paces, Cecil stopped to spit blood to the pavement where it would sizzle and hiss. She was endlessly surprised when Cecil heaved himself beside Dexteras in the bed of her truck, and slumped against the cab patiently.

Along the silent drive home, she stole periodic glances at them through the glass. The exhausted men with their matching scruffs, scars, spilled blood, and mysterious pasts.

Cecil held rags to his chin whilst Dex slumped about the truck bed at gravity's mercy, mouth agape to the heavens. At a narrow turn, his head thudded against Cecil's shoulder, and Cecil shoved the old man away with such force and speed, Nor was certain he would flip out of the vehicle and onto the road.

Despite their aversion to one another, a strange sense of peace warmed her blood. It felt good to finally be able to bring them somewhere quiet and safe. Somewhere restful and nonviolent. They were due their peace.

Once they arrived at her home, Cecil pulled himself up each step with measured breath, hoisting himself and Dexteras to the roof with swallows of effort and strain. They looked like wounded war heroes, ambling home. As they bowed beneath her window to perch upon the roof, Dex's head thwacked atop the lifted sill.

Cecil spat with a peal of strange, wet laughter that splattered against the roof. He tossed Dex against a chimney stack and stopped to gather his breath, swaying on his feet with sweat on his brow, still laughing. He dabbed his lips and seemed surprised when wet blood stopped printing against his fingertips. Then, with a thunderous sigh, he turned to leave.

"Hey," she called, chasing after his casual stride.

He growled like an impatient wolf, tilting backward into the moonlight with irritation, casting an eye over his great shoulder.

She slipped her hand around his broad shoulder and pulled him into an embrace.

"Thank you," she muttered into his chest, tears welling for all she'd seen. There was so much fire. So much burning. "For all of the help you've given us both."

He remained silent like a statue in the dark, glasses cold and unfeeling.

Then, an angry scraping, scratching commotion scuffled from behind making Nor jump and spin. Above, a bright green pair of reflective eyes glowed with crazed energy at the sloped turret. A spread-eagle black cat clung to the structure as though it were a thick tree, nails embedded manically, back twitching with bristled chaos. His fat face gawked about as though he watched demons in the night.

"Vincent, fucking shit," Nor sighed, gripping her chest. She returned to Cecil, who was unbothered by the wild beast climbing her rooftop and smirked briefly.

Then, a strange, dull static fizzled against her skull like the humming of insects and a voice breached its hiss.

"Why you botherin' with this knobhead and his feckin' tosh?" bit Cecil's familiar voice against the caves of her thoughts.

Though the impossible magic stole a small cry and a gasp from her chest, the harsh tones of his voice brought her a strange peace. She considered crying out with ignorant questions about his abilities, but decided it was simply another intimate gift of Cecil's kind. And she simply needed to accept and respect it. She considered his question a moment, allowing her heart rate to fall.

"Because I've been there, in a way," thought Nor conversationally, sampling the cave of their shared headspace. She remembered once feeling like Dexteras: the itchy, suffocating restlessness of being cornered in her own home, her own body with its unseeable ghosts.

"I remember how much bullshit had to happen to me to make me feel so hollow and desperate for family. For belonging," she said aloud now, eyeing Dex's unconscious form. Her eyes fell to take in the damage done to the old man's frame. The tattooed mural of his body, burned and bruised. Swollen and purple. Seasoned and wrinkled.

Cecil bowed his head to listen to the comatose, ancient heart below them as it rattled.

It'd beat in solace for ages. Inhuman bounds of time. But it couldn't be as dark and despicable as Solus painted it to be.

"And what makes you put up with *us* then?" asked Nor, searching the dark glass of Cecil's lenses.

"No one makes me put up with shite, dolly," he muttered into her skull. *"I'm a scout for Figments on the outside, so I have permission to go and leave as I please."*

There was that word again. "Why are you called Figments? What does that mean?" she begged.

"Feckin' hell woman," he snapped in her head, rolling his head back to the stars. *"Cream-crackered 'nuff as it is without your feckin' questions."*

Though he mocked her, he wore the same squirminess her clients wore when dangerous information itched at the tip of their tongues. He had a right to be terrified after the hell he'd endured just to help them.

She stepped nearer and touched his sleeve in apology. In the cold, she could still smell that essence of pine trees and black tea on him. Biting and lovely to the proper tongue who could appreciate it.

It reminded her of a woman she'd dated for nearly a year in college. She was named Steller, and always smelled of eucalyptus, cedar, and pine.

"But why you? Why were you chosen to scout?" Cecil was the only being she'd seen leave the club outside of Dexteras.

"For some reason I can hear 'em," he grumbled, tapping his temple. *"I can sniff out lost Fig's like a feckin' bloodhound."*

Norah remembered Dex's ability to find Alina in the massive hospital before anyone had known she'd even been missing.

"It's their pain. Their scars, right?" Nor lamented aloud. "I can't imagine how difficult that is, to find them when they're falling apart."

His chin snapped towards her. *"The feckin' fighters are the strong ones, aye?"* he thought, lenses tipping briefly to Dex *"They're at least trying to understand what they were, who they were. Those other feckers are runnin' from it. Ignorant and blissful."*

She heard an echo of pride, of protective teeth bearing for those he trained to fight. Nor nodded, agreeing.

"But what about you? Aren't you running?" she dared to press. There were no lashes on Cecil's cheeks but there was at least the tattoo of the white-eyed bird that hadn't been covered up. Did those represent memories regained?

He spat again over her roof and expressed a tall middle finger with a tattooed hand.

She snorted. "You know you're welcome to stay here as long as you need if-"

But Cecil had already spun on his tactical boots, raking unnerved fingers through thick silver waves. His middle finger was still high and proud as he stepped off the roof.

38

✦DEXTERAS✦

He tightened on her fragile throat, crumbling like crystal. He squeezed until smoke trembled from his shoulders and electricity clicked at his fingers. He couldn't scream, but he couldn't stop.

Norah was dying. He was killing her.

She gasped beneath his talons. Blood vessels burst in her irises.

✦

Dex snapped upwards, slashing through the fog to his authentic self on Norah's rooftop. He pressed his face into the collar of his shirt, inhaling deeply. With each hyperventilating breath, the taut burns pulled at his neck flesh, but he returned to himself. His entire torso was soaked with cold sweat.

Norah had given him her father's remaining box of clothes. He changed into one of the black thermal shirts that smelled of cigar smoke. He was squeezed at the shoulders but grateful for something dry.

As his heartbeat quieted, he registered watchful eyes upon him. He turned towards the dark house.

Atop the rim of her open window, Vincent's reflective eyes goggled upon him. The old creature chirped a greeting from his perch.

"Well?" Dex asked the cat.

Vincent sprang down from his ledge and rubbed against Dex's hot ribs, tail flicking with concern. The beast looked to the bedroom window and gave a guttural whine.

Dex strained to borrow the old cat's ears and listen. A rushed heartbeat fluttered within the hollow walls.

He stood with a groan and followed the dark cat across the roof to the spare room's window. He unlocked it with the tiny brass key and stepped down into the abandoned bedroom. It was still weighty with dust and trauma.

An anxious, drumming heartbeat sped behind her door.

He approached, hand hovering over the old wood. He chewed on his cheeks, fearful of intruding. But he knew that her nightmares were likely all his doing after all she'd witnessed at his cursed side. His paternal heart wished to hold her and serve as an eclipse between her world and whatever his might be.

He cleared his throat and tapped on her door with a knuckle.

A startled gasp broke from within. A shuffling of bed sheets rustled.

He then considered how horrifying it must be to be awoken by a knock from an abandoned room in the dead of night.

"*Amica mea?* Love, it's Dex," he said, gripping his forehead.

"Wh-oh!" Shock shed from her singsong voice and her barefooted steps raced to meet him. Small fingers cast the creaking wood aside to reveal her tired figure in the dark. She wore baggy harem pants and a sweatshirt that read, *I'm Sorry for What I Said When I Was Hungry.*

Vincent dashed inwards to press against her legs.

Tears seeped at her eyelids but still, she smiled.

Guilt gripped his chest and dropped his cheek to his shoulder.

"All alright?" she whispered.

"You tell me."

Her lips pursed and her chin wobbled. Then, she rushed into his chest and embraced him. Her coolness wrapped around his blazing torso like a stream. He petted the back of her head and sighed.

"Nightmare?"

"How'd you know?" Her voice muffled against his tear-soaked front.

He nodded to the old cat who sat proudly upon her bed.

Vincent complied with a loud mew.

"Seriously?"

Dex shrugged. "He was worried about you."

She retrieved the creature from the bed and held him close to her chest. The fat-faced cat rubbed against her chin and nestled against her.

"Your nightmare, was it about…?" began Dex, sure he could see the silhouette of Solus reflected in Nor's gaze.

But she shook her head. "It wasn't Oblitus," she said, her Latin practiced and eloquent. He could tell she'd been researching. "And it wasn't *them*," she added.

They'd both come to understand that Solus was amorphous, malleable, and shapeshifting. While there was androgyny and a breathtaking gender fluidity to their identity, there was so much more to understand of the ancient entity.

"It looks like they're almost… *glitching* sometimes," muttered Nor, eyes distant. "Every time I look, I see…flickers of someone different." She'd ceased petting the old cat mid-stroke, deep in thought. "What do they look like when you see them?"

Dex spread his lips wide to speak upon Solus' spellbinding nature, their perilous beauty. But he found no words adequate. Their maleficence was too great, their come-hither too tempestuous. His mouth closed.

"I think I can sh-sh-show you," he stuttered, recalling the sensation of

Cecil's hand in the dark evenings prior. Despite its impossibility, he felt he could navigate it with Norah simply.

"Only if you're comfortable, of course."

Her face stretched with awe, unafraid. "Of course."

He pointed to the scarred palm nestled in Vincent's fur and she presented it to him.

He took it gently in his.

In moments, Nor's pupils flickered back into her lids, lips parted.

He allowed Norah to borrow his perspective to behold the gorgeous feminine form striding across the mirrored tile like a silent ship draped in black sails.

The epicene was a deity clad in clinging black, towering, tall to meet him on delicate gold blades. Beneath, he could hear the heartbeat of a hardened carnivore, a wolf drooling in delight.

Their bronze skin shone, carved by gaunt pockets of shadow beneath the ambient lights. Their golden eyes were winged so sharp, they could stab a heart. Their hair was cropped and black like a raven's wing, matching the silken blazer that revealed its dangerous depths of cleavage. Rolling breasts peeked, shining in tattoos of scuttling creatures and insects.

Dex cowered in disembodied guilt as young Norah occupied his body. He knew she felt his heart flutter and his eyes drench the creature's flesh.

But it was only an initial thought. A fleeting want. Because he knew that despite their raspy allure, those crimson lips could drink the soul from his throat.

He took back his hand from Norah and bowed his head with hot cheeks. He'd been caught with his beard in the mailbox. Immortal or not, his body was still vulnerable and human.

"*Fuckin' shit*," Norah began, mouth wide. "I-I mean…they're *gorgeous*." She leaned against the doorframe to gather herself.

He lifted his gaze, grateful that she granted him grace for his human allurement. His cheeks rounded with embarrassment before resting.

"But their song, it's horrendous," he shivered.

"Song?"

He rubbed his temple, uncertain how to describe such an inhuman experience. "It...It's like the soul has a song, almost, notes it sings. I considered it auditory hallucinations for ages, but it shifted depending on the people I was near. It falls in synchronicity with their actions, their motives, their emotions." His words fell quiet with discomposure.

I must sound like a loon.

"*That's* how you found Alina," she said.

He nodded, impressed by her deductions.

"So what does *theirs* sound like then?"

A tic drove through his jaw and neck again, bending it with compulsion.

"It's blinding. Pitchy. It isn't even a musical note but a...a blade drug across a metal string." Most songs were composed of multitudes of emotions to reveal a complex melody, but theirs was only the song of a knife sharpening

She winced. Norah had surely imbibed enough impossible things to fuel a lifetime of nightmares.

"Did you want to talk about your dream?" he asked.

She shrugged. "My nightmares are usually just...screaming. Sometimes it's my parents. Sometimes I'm not sure who. But it's always loud, and I can't get away. I feel like to survive I just need to absorb it, contain it."

He scratched Vincent behind the ears with a furrowed brow.

"I'm so sorry you have to deal with that," he said. "I used to struggle with them every night after I-I..."

You. Jumped.

"A-a-after..." The stutter loitered upon his lips, and he couldn't shake it.

Nor nodded gently. "It's okay."

He took a deep breath. "Um, how's your hand?" he dared to ask, rubbing his neck.

"Wh-my hand?" She flip-flopped it in front of her eyes.

He nodded to the doorknob beside her with a curious half-smile.

She spun to compute what she'd done, and her eyes widened. A flurry of emotions registered upon her face.

"I-I didn't even notice. That's pretty cool, I guess." She stared at the cold knob with a new emotion he hadn't seen her give it prior.

He smiled. For all of an instant, the pain didn't control her.

"I think it was the first time something good was actually on the other side of this door…" she toed it with a bare foot. "I just thought of you and didn't have time to feel scared."

He extended a low fist and she replied with a gentle jab, jab, cross against it, pleasantly stunned.

"Proud of you, *amica mea*." He winked.

✦

That evening, he watched her cook in the sleek black kitchen. She folded massive handfuls of fresh leafy spinach into pesto pasta while salted grape tomatoes were seared and softened. Parmesan cheese and garlic wafted thickly through the house.

He grinned as Vincent stood on two legs and stretched up Norah's side to inch his toe beans and chunky face nearer the intoxicating smells.

"No," she uttered sternly. "Cats can't eat garlic or onions, good sir."

The Persian sat on his thick haunches as though pouting, eyes black and begging like shiny boba pearls.

"I'll get you a treat soon, promise."

He licked his lips, undoubtedly prepared to hold her to her word.

"And you," she began, eyes dashing to Dex for a moment. "Would you like food? Do you eat?"

"I can. And I can taste it and enjoy it. But I can't say I have a hunger. Or a thirst."

She hummed, staring at her meal with guilt. She offered him a bowl before serving herself.

He laughed. "No, but thank you love. I make exceptions for coffee and dark chocolate though."

They sat on the roof whilst she ate, her bare feet dangling over the ledge. She was swaddled in comfy sweats and a hoodie with cropped hems. Her hair was wild and set free of its gold barrettes.

He smiled. He couldn't remember the last time someone seemed so comfortable beside him. So safe. Honor swelled in his chest.

"So..." she said quietly to the darkness, "...you don't eat or sleep?"

His eyes fell to her swinging ankles, pale with blue veins. They interconnected and spidered about like magnesium fireballs in outer space.

He pulled on his cigar and considered the question, charmed by her curiosity. He nodded.

"After I..."

Fell? Jumped? Committed Suicide?

He tried again. "But when I was admitted, I was tubed for days until I figured out that I needed to eat. Otherwise, they wouldn't ever let me go."

"Oh Dex," Norah moaned.

He shook his head with a stern stare. "Don't pity me, love. It's just the way it was. They couldn't know I was broken beyond fixing."

She wiped her mouth with a napkin that Vincent proceeded to bat about the roof. "You are not broken. Doctors have a hard enough time helping humans and you're..." Her words faded.

He held a breath, realizing they hadn't officially admitted it to one another yet.

"*Not*," he muttered. "I've gotten so lost pretending that I was..." His fingers tied themselves into knots as he chewed on his cigar.

"What you are is my friend," she stated. "So what did they do? At the hospital?"

He knew she'd read his file and knew these answers, but still appreciated the inquiry.

"They induced a coma and did all sorts of things." He rubbed at a spasm in his eyelid and lost himself in the far horizon line, dark with black buildings. At the base of one of them, his blood was forever soaked in its sidewalk.

Jesus, so much blood. He closed his eyes.

Vivid details of that morning came to him like flashes of lightning. What had tangibly remained of him was restrained. An orderly sat upon his crushed legs. Their touches were sharp like knife pricks. Involuntary calls for mercy boomed from his chest. Wires were stuck to the blood-slick flesh where his chest, forearms, and temples should've been. They wiped him in bucketloads of stinging alcohol in order to stick him with fluids and anesthetics. After they'd seen what he could do in such a gory state, the dosage was plenty potent for his weight and body size.

But it was vastly insufficient to incapacitate his immortal brain, he now knew.

He was awake for the entirety of each procedure.

He couldn't scream or buck against his binds while sedatives wept through his blood. His bones, his muscles, and even his eyelids were frozen, but his consciousness screamed with life. His vision blurred with tears and tranquilizer.

He could feel his body being torn open and emptied.

In between scalpels and sutures and fingertips and titanium hardware, his body felt dead and worthless like an unstuffed ragdoll. He could feel their hands inside of him, pulling, prodding, lifting pieces of him with cold tools. He could hear the slurping of organs, the snapping, and resetting of bones like hacking lumberjacks. The vibrations against his ribcage as they sawed. He felt much like the rotting corpse he feared he'd been. Battered and worthless like a plaything.

It made Cecil the Shrike's work look commonplace.

When they reduced the swelling in his brain, he feared he'd rupture. An impregnable tension gripped him from head to toe. Extra things were plunged into his skull when he'd already believed it couldn't possibly contain anything else. A numbing pulsation pressed behind his eyes.

All he wanted to do was scream.

Mumbling nurses took records of his brain activity, but he was unconscious to the naked eye.

How could they not see something was wrong?

It shouldn't be this way.

The helplessness was violating. Horrifying. It was a whole new loneliness he'd never known. An intrusion of his innards he'd never granted.

Eventually, he was rolled onto a gurney and delivered to his room, heaped upon his bed like a limp slab of meat. Tears streamed ceaselessly down his cheeks.

For a few days, he shared a room with Norman Greenshank, an old wiry man, thin and leggy like a skeleton, smiling with crooked teeth. One of them was gold.

"You look like fuckin' shit friend," Norman cackled.

I feel it. My soul feels it.

Then, a metal cart rattled far down the hall with the sobering clinks of a pistol in Russian Roulette.

It was time for his daily pin cleaning. The protruding bicycle spokes that jutted from his thighs were swabbed with a burning liquid that reawakened every raw burn of the asphalt and every split seam. The alcohol burned his nostrils as the spokes in his body clanged with shakes.

"Do you think if given the opportunity, you'd try to jump off the roof again?" asked his psychiatrist Dr. Rhea.

"I'd either fly or die, and both seem pretty peaceful," Dex had whispered with a dead stare.

The probing he'd experienced at the hands of humans had driven a sinuous, winding crack through his insides. It made his vocal cords grow discordant with neglect. It made the delicate shell that was his outward mask feel susceptible to shattering with each breath.

His flashbacks were suddenly interrupted by a small sniff.

Dex blinked to the present as though waking from a bad dream and turned to his young friend.

Norah's eyes were wide and weeping. Her small, scarred hand rested upon his own.

His shoulders fell, understanding what he'd done.

She'd reached out to comfort him, and he'd shared his memories with her.

"*Amica mea, cara*, oh, I'm so sorry. I'm so sorry. You weren't supposed to see that…" he tore his hand away as though it'd burnt her.

But she sprang onto his shoulders and squeezed him tight.

"It shouldn't be like that. It should never have been like that. I'm so sorry," she whispered. "I wish I could make those things go away for you."

He gently pulled her from him, thumbs rubbing her narrow shoulders.

"*Mellis, cara mi*, hey." He tilted his head, searching her dark eyes, sparkling like rainforest leaves. "You already love me in a way that makes those things go away. But you also love me in a way that allows me to be myself and share these kinds of things too. Don't apologize for that." He smiled as convincingly as he could muster. "It's okay, love. Truly, it's okay."

Her head rejected his affirmation with small shakes. "All that happened, and you still went back every day with me, to help people. You're so brave."

His cheeks flooded with blood.

They spoke deep into the night until her tears dried. Her ankles swung in the dark, large Van Gogh socks crumbled at her ankles. Occasionally she'd reach out and hold his hand with her tender cold.

Though his fists could tear apart bodies with ease, she still held to them.

39

✦NORAH✦

"WHAT'S IN THE CASE YOU BROUGHT FROM HOME?" She glanced to the far end of the roof where a black, hinged box lay.

He jammed his cigar in his teeth and retrieved the case with a groan. He returned beside her and popped the chrome tabs to reveal an ancient violin.

She gazed at the instrument resting on his thigh. Much like Dex, she could tell it withheld endless stories that neither could speak to. Its sparkling spruce flickered beneath the day's dying light.

"What's her name?"

He pulled on his cigar with a tall brow. "How'd you know I named her?"

"She seems special," she said with a faint smile, recalling the pet names her father would gift his vehicles and other belongings.

"Well, her name is Stellato," he said, that familiar lilt in his tongue.

"Latin?"

"Means one who dances among the stars," said Dex, rubbing the varnish with a thumb.

"Will you play something?" she pleaded.

"I can."

He pulled Stellato from her plush case and maneuvered his whiskered chin against it. He tinkered with the strings and made adjustments with a tilted ear. He then dipped his elbow with the bow and allowed her to sing for him.

No matter how maddeningly familiar the melody was, she couldn't place any lyrics that would serve it justice. She only knew that she adored watching the pained, benevolent hills of Dex's brow. The emotional fault lines of his features. His lashes were low, focus flooding his wandering fingers. The wood whined and trembled as though it were his own voice box.

Nor's feet swayed on the breeze with its dreamy rhythm. It was one of those rare, simple moments where she was entirely present and purely content. The music, their shared vulnerability, his sweet expression, the warm evening. Its simple peace blanketed her intrusive thoughts for but a moment.

His song was then swallowed by the night and they sat in the milieu for many minutes.

"*Cara mi...*" His voice split the night like a rustling wind. "I've seen it since the day I met you. You flinch at the sound of your own name. Lenore."

A brick thudded atop her gut.

She couldn't deny that Dex's accent crashed particularly hard on the "n" in *Lenore* in a way that made her cringe. But it wasn't his fault. Dex wasn't her father.

"My dad's name was Leonard Jay Kestrel," she began with a hard swallow. "He named me Lenore Jay Kestrel after himself. It's just...I don't know..."

"Triggering?"

"I guess. Mom called me Jaybird. She saw him when she looked at me. I always felt like an extension of him."

Dex groaned.

"After all he did to us, all he left us with, I was a reminder of that for her.

We couldn't escape him." She fell into Dex's large arm. "I didn't even cry for him when he died," she whispered, never having breathed such a confession to anyone prior.

"You don't owe anyone your tears, *amica mea.*"

She shook her head. "No, but I cried for *myself*," she said, the words tripping from her with embarrassment. "It sounds horrible. Selfish. But at his funeral, I cried because it felt *good.*" She swallowed, making sense of her past as it tumbled from her tongue. "For the first time, there were people who held me and saw me hurting and validated me. They cared. They held space for all of the emotions that'd never been held before. It was the first time I'd felt really seen," she sniffed into her shirtsleeve. "But after the funeral, they disappeared, as families do. And I think I got left with this... *craving* for grief. Like it was a high I'd never match." She scowled in disgust of herself, shaking her head.

Dex hummed into his cigar. "Never feel ashamed for wanting love, *amica mea.* It's like wanting water. You've been without it for a long time. You have every right to want it, and it sounds like your grief gave you permission to do so."

"Thanks," she whispered into his great arm. "When did you become so insightful?"

He chuckled. "I've been following around an incredibly bright therapist." He kissed the top of her head and sighed into the evening. "You may have been called Jaybird my love, but what you are is a phoenix."

40

⋅NORAH⋅

She waited in the parking lot outside The Aviary, fidgeting with the handmade plastic bracelet on her wrist.

Lioness.

She attempted to employ her focus on the tiny droplets falling from the sky, listening to the cold patters of water kissing her skin.

He clambered through the front gate, pocketing his apartment keys and maneuvering Stellato in the crook of his arm. He propped a cane-handle umbrella over his shoulder.

Nor admired his sharp attire from afar. Only his neck and hand tattoos were visible beneath the debonair black and white suit. It contrasted his ivory mane well, which had been groomed and wound at the scalp. A pair of dark sunglasses hung at his neck and teased at the illustrations beneath his collar. His eyelids were red and weary as though he'd done a fair share of dissociating into the morning sunrise again.

He smiled and gave her a tight side hug, resting his chin atop her dark waves. He shoved his blazer sleeve up his hairy forearm to reveal his *Божевільний* bracelet with a sad smile. The only color in their worlds today would be Alina's doing.

Norah couldn't help her eyes shifting to the faded purple bruise at his temple and his bloodied iris.

He pressed his lenses to his face and they walked to her vehicle.

It was a small funeral home at the edge of town, surrounded by rural hills and horse farms. They filed into the reception area where Alina's ivory casket and flower arrangements lay. An "anonymous donor" had given the funds to purchase these, and every other detail needed for a little girl's funeral, along with a generous donation to The Nest in her honor. The reception was quaint and smelled of pink and white peonies and eucalyptus. A large arrangement draped across the tiny coffin.

A nearby corkboard held drawings and poems made by the Ukrainian child. There were snapshots of Rosella and Alina enjoying makeovers, Alina braiding Dex's hair whilst he sat on the floor. There was another of the three of them coloring, their best goofy expressions stretched for the camera.

Dex stood beside the casket, staring down at the child's peaceful expression. He rocked from toe-to-heel as though lulling himself to a faraway place.

Norah drew near, knowing he was slipping away. She touched his shoulder and greeted him in Ukrainian.

He only wrung his inked fingers.

"You're here now. With me," she added beneath her breath for only him to hear.

"But she doesn't get that chance."

Norah reflected upon the ghosts of her past, those countless coffins she'd stood before.

"But we got to know her. We know she existed. She changed us and we changed her."

"I'm not worthy to be one the few to know her." His cheek twitched as he took in the room. Her hospital team and a representative from HR had come to pay their respects.

"That's not your call to make, that was hers. And she chose you," said Nor

"I'll never understand why," he whispered, eyes searching the child's pink cheeks caked in light blush.

"I do." She laid her head against his large arm, knowing all the words in the world would never make sense of such a travesty. The tongue could never contrive peace for the death of any, especially a child.

Having pinned many medals of survived deaths upon her chest, Norah knew its reality wouldn't hit her until the casket lid closed. When the box's shadow darkened their faces, a wave of realization struck her: it was the final time she'd see them ever again.

Nana Rose Starling. Papa Rufous Starling. Leonard Jay Kestrel. Brant Kestrel. Brandon. Jacob.

Alina.

They admired the child's rose dress and matching hair ribbons. Her fingernails were painted in glittering blue and gold, matching the handcrafted bracelets on her tiny wrists. Dex eyed the plush lioness tucked beneath the child's arm and huffed with a great sniff.

"She can finally breathe and play, and just be a child," he muttered.

Norah stumbled amongst her beliefs in the safe confines of their friendship. "I-I've never been able to think about what comes next... But I... I...she *must* be somewhere better, right?"

Dex nodded. "She is."

Despite her doubts, somewhere deep beneath her sternum, she trusted Dexteras. Therefore, somehow, she believed him.

The funeral home staff prepared Alina for her final travels. The braces on the coffin were unlocked and the lid began to fall.

Nor froze, struck in terror as darkness flooded the soft sandy complexion and the child's kind, sleeping face.

Dex whipped a fresh handkerchief from his breast pocket and tucked it into Norah's grip as the small alabaster lid thudded into place. He squeezed her scarred palm. He kissed the top of her head again before falling into line beside the casket. A shimmering pink satin pall was draped across the wood and the floral menagerie was collected for the commute. He rolled up his sleeves and lifted one of the casket's gold handles. He slid his shades onto his face with a weak smile to her and proceeded to the hearse.

The burial site was a brief drive to a gorgeous green cemetery designated for Ukrainian believers. A local pastor shared an invitation to God's presence amidst their pain. Both him and Dexteras offered prayers in Alina's native tongue. Dex's voice wobbled and pitched with his quiet farewell. Though he remained steadfast, Norah saw streams slip beneath his lenses. Every few moments, he'd cough and wipe them aside.

The pastor squeezed Dex's shoulder and asked him to offer a closing song.

Nor's old friend cleared his throat and flipped the latches on the hard case, returning Stellato to the sun again. She yearned to know the full details of Stellato's life and the eternity she'd lived at Dex's side.

Dex attempted to domesticate his wild beard hairs to best position his chin. He then sniffed with a smile to Nor behind his sunglasses and began to play.

She'd never heard the song his instrument wept. It was mournful and thick with ballad-like mountains and valleys of emotion. The stringed machine spoke as though it were his translator. The tremble of each string resonated within each person who knew Alina, connecting their hurts like a power line.

A final note echoed on the breeze until all was silent but for the fresh weeping of those listening. Even passersby from neighboring graves had wandered close, stopping in reverence of the melody.

✦

They rode the rickety elevator up to his apartment. Once in the door of room 7B, Dex hurried about, picking up strewn boxing wraps and mild clutter.

This time, Norah took the time to pore over his belongings. He'd deemed some things essential like a squat coffee table and a solitary chair. His cabinets and humming fridge were unoccupied but his countertop was adorned with polished coffee instruments like a barista-grade espresso machine, coffee pots with gold hardware, tea kettles, French presses, pour-overs, and elaborate devices Nor had ever seen. Her mouth fell open at the gleaming inventions.

He laughed, leaning against the doorway with red-rimmed eyes.

She pointed to a towering copper contraption that looked like an hourglass attached to a small burner.

"What is *that*?"

"Old coffee siphon." His fingers petted its brass fittings, much like those embedded in the pale flesh of Solus. "Heat drives water up through the grounds and then as the temperature lowers, the water falls back through them. It makes a deep, robust brew that's doubly steeped. Lovely machine." Youthful spirit stretched across his wrinkles.

Norah was warmed by his passion.

She eyed an engraved brass pot hanging on the wall with a long handle encrusted with mother-of-pearl and metal filigrees. An ornate set of matching saucers and cups gleamed below on the counter, shining as though hand-crafted for royalty.

He followed her gaze. "Turkish pot. You take the finest coffee grounds you can muster. So fine they should fall into the crevices of your fingerprint." He rubbed his fingers excitedly. "Add spices, raw sugar. Then boil it on the stove until it makes a thick foam."

"Have you always liked coffee?"

His smile fell. "Human habits make me feel…normal. Would you like some?" He nodded to the intricate coffee set.

"I'd love that very much."

He beamed like a child.

She observed his bustling a moment before journeying about the cozy space. Across the hall was a master bedroom with no bed, lined wall-to-wall with bookshelves stuffed full with spines of all colors, sizes, and ages. Glossy titles and torn, crusty ones. She allowed her fingers to flutter across them, recognizing some languages and titles, but not others.

In the center of the room was a worn, blue leather armchair emblazoned with brass studs and tufted cushioning.

Nor sat within it, smelling the aftershave and vanilla-laced tobacco in its seams. She felt solace in her bones as she took in the view he'd been taking in for decades. She could feel Dexteras beating his wings against these walls in isolated fever.

He had a simple view of Corvid and its unremarkable gloom. An occasional Norway Maple tree would worship the sun with black leaves. Tufts of Black Lace Elderberry bushes and Black Magic Colocasia bent with the winds. In the distance, the chapel's iron crosses, and the hospital's incinerator chimneys towered against the sky. Everything bled of color, drab and dreary.

She noted her black fingernails tapping across the window and her black makeup and clothes reflected in the glass. Had she steeped herself so long in this town, she'd camouflaged to blend in?

But she snorted. *Can't blame everything on this fucking town, Kestrel.*

She'd always loved black garments, flowy button-downs, clinging dress pants, tall Chelsea boots, cropped hoodies, round sunglasses. A flash of gold might shine from her grandmother's rings and the hoops and studs in her ears. The color scheme made her think of the breathtaking Solus. She shivered, turning from the view.

A book on the floor beside Dex's chair was marked with Ukrainian chocolate wrappers. Norah smiled, recalling some of these in Alina's room and picked up the tome. The canvas-bound book was crumbling with loose fibers. Its dark cover was stamped in shimmering silver text and foil stars.

"*Sidereus Nuncius*," came a soft voice from the doorway. "It's a piece published by Galileo in the sixteen-hundreds."

Nor pivoted to him from the massive chair, draping her legs over its stuffed arm.

"What's it about?"

"It's his observations of celestial bodies. His descriptions of the sky and the stars are like none other I've read."

She ran a finger across the metallic text. "Is this Latin?"

He nodded, scratching at his white beard.

"It wasn't kindly received because he made observations about the imperfections of the heavens. Like how the moon has craters and valleys despite her perfect appearance to the mortal eye. Or how the entire universe did not in fact bow to the revolutions of the earth." His eyes sparkled. "He wasn't afraid to suggest that there were bigger things going on outside of ourselves. Humans are made uncomfortable by it I think, the idea there is something beyond them."

"How does it make *you* feel?"

"It brings me peace."

She ran her fingers across the engraved title and returned it to its home beside his seat, considering this concept for the first time.

"Coffee's ready," he sang.

A rich, Christmasy aroma wafted about the kitchen, laden with cinnamon, nutmeg, and cardamom.

He tilted the golden coffee pot over two embellished cups. Thick foaming mounds of chocolaty froth dumped into each with satisfying crackles. He topped them with their metal lids and filled another brass vessel with raw sugar and dark chocolate bricks. He hoisted the platter against his shoulder and beckoned her to the hall. They rode the elevator up, dainty metals clinking in his arms.

The doors opened to a concrete rooftop where the wind bustled their hair about their faces.

They sat atop the ledge of a western-facing wall where the sky was erupting with cerulean and violet in preparation for the evening.

He passed her an engraved cup and saucer, dropping chunks of dark chocolate alongside it with a set of tongs.

She giggled at his tedious dedication.

They toasted and sipped with tired smiles.

"To Alina," she offered.

"To Alina, *bud'mo*," he replied in Ukrainian.

Nor rolled the thick liquid amongst her taste buds like a caramel candy. The coffee foam bubbled against her lips, leaving her nodding in approval before she could find worthy words.

"Dex you are a wonder."

He bowed his head as pink cheeks rounded above his beard. "Pardon the theatrics. I've never gotten to use this set before."

"Oh, being served gourmet coffee is *so* burdensome," she jested, brandishing her cup with pretentious fanciness.

He chuckled into his drink.

They spent a pleasant moment watching the colors weave and wane like a palette of watery paints. She scooted closer to the ledge to better take in the somber view below. And as she stared down at the black street, that nauseating thought struck her again.

"*…you jumped…*"

She leaned across the ledge. *That had to be over one hundred and twenty feet to the asphalt.*

Dex squeezed her shoulder, driving a warmth down her spine. "Please don't."

She settled beside him, "Don't you ever wonder how…?"

His bushy silver brows lifted high as he took a sip. "It's why I don't stay up here for long. Or even come home sometimes," he mused, rotating the cup in his palm.

Its gold called her back to the rails of the fighting ring. A deep cramping in her gut feared she'd be likely clinging to its chains again before long.

But for now, Norah leaned into his shoulder. "You're doing beautifully. You're here right now, with me."

"Thanks love. I needed that."

41

✦NORAH✦

"You're going to go back there, aren't you?" she sighed.

"That place, those beings. They're all I have," he muttered. "There's something I've been terrified of facing for decades. I want to quit running and face it."

"We all have something to run from," she stated. "That doesn't mean we're bad, Dex."

"But I *chose* to empty my brain of it completely. I didn't have to cope or grieve or even change my behavior. It was selfish and cowardly."

"That's only what they've told you. How do you know you can trust them?"

"As I said, they're all I have."

"But the past isn't everything you are," Norah begged. "It *can't* be everything." She snapped, tasting her projection as it left her lips.

"Are you able to disregard *your* past, *amica mea*?" he asked with gentle conviction.

"Of course not," she muttered, rolling the cigar in her fingers. Her chest tightened, wishing to wall him out. And if she did, he'd drop the pursuit entirely and respect her walls. But she did want to give him something. She wanted to be vulnerable with her only friend.

He waited, observing the evening sky ahead without expectation.

"It's just when so much of the past is painful," she sighed. "It's easier to disregard it all together."

Dex rested his face in his palm, turning to watch her with considerate, stormy eyes.

"But there were moments," she thought, carefully tiptoeing around her childhood. "With Dad, I mean. Sometimes we'd sing with the radio. Or he'd read the paper and smoke a cigar while I read the comics…" She dug with hungry, eager fingers into the past. "He loved those chocolate suckers with the chewy inside. I'd save quarters to buy them at the gas station." She winced at young Norah's attempts at scavenging love. "I thought if I liked what he liked, maybe he'd…"

The silver man shook his head.

"Your parents clearly had a great deal of untended pain long before you came into their world, love. Those who forsake their darkness will inevitably bleed it onto those around them." His voice fell to a serious note he'd never used with her prior. "But firstly, you should've never had to fight for your father's love, Nor."

"I know," she whispered, blinking against hot tears.

"Nothing and no one will ever replace what you've lost. But I will always want you, *cara mi*. Always. You're the dearest thing to me on this Earth." He said, voice firm and strong. "How you've kept your heart so kind despite the hurt it's known, I'll never fathom."

Her heavy, wet lashes rested on her cheeks.

"I wish your father would've given himself the chance to stop running from his own past. To lean in and heal things properly," said Dex, turning to her with an earnest bend of his brows. "His shame kept him from the most loving and brilliant daughter anyone could've asked for."

Nor wiped at the spilling tears, shaking her head.

"And that's why I can't run anymore," he said. "Things need to be properly faced and healed."

42

✦DEXTERAS✦

BEFORE SHE'D GONE TO BED, she'd pressed the cool scar on her palm against his own. She showed him the horrid fate that had befallen Cecil. Her empathy and compassion for the Shrike nearly broke him.

"And you saw what happened to Marchos," she'd said. "Why would you trust someone who does that to people?"

Once she slept, his hazy, blood-filled eye lay across the dark fields and manifested a steaming cup of coffee, hoping the bitter beans would keep him mindful and awake. He gazed at the milky *galaxias* spiraling in his cup with a frown. It was nothing near Norah's coffee. His coffee bubbles were stiff and firm with the viscosity of dish soap. Nor frothed hers until it was creamy like velvet, stacking her brew like a tall crown.

A chilling whine then screamed through his skull.

His hands gripped his ears but the alarm would not relinquish.

He knew that scream, he realized. And his eyes flew open.

Not here. Not now.

The fear of having such a beast at Norah's door made his throat tighten. He leaned against the brick chimney, fingers clinging to his clavicle, feeling as though his heart would flop out of his chest in panic. His breastbone swelled with heat and his ribs were sore as though they'd crack and split him at the seams.

The atmosphere shifted as though a blanket of sleet had fallen upon Corvid. Vapors left his lips.

It was too late.

"Dexxxxterrrrrassss," the blackness hissed like a writhing adder. "Come homeeeeeeee."

The gorgeous Solus stepped into the light of the white moon, wearing a red suit dripping in vermilion and gold. For an instant, Dex desired to suck on their copper throat. But in another, he craved to squeeze the life from it.

They could entice anyone to grope for trout in a peculiar river.

"Get on with it," Dex snarled, standing between Solus and Norah's window. His bloodied eye inspected the metal grate embedded in their chest. "If she wakes before you're gone, I'll rip what's left of your heart out."

43

⋆·NORAH·⋆

SHE DUCKED BENEATH THE WINDOW'S LEDGE and straightened into a new, red morning sun. But that heat that met her in the early hour was smothering and unnatural. Caustic.

It was like Oblitus.

She sat their chocolate and coffee upon the sill and approached her friend with caution.

He swayed in the wind like a dead leaf clinging to a branch. His shirt was heavy with soaked, sweaty patches and burn holes, smoke peeling from them like bullet wounds.

Nor rounded his great shoulder to find his chest was swelling and falling so slowly, it seemed lifeless. He held onto a cigarette that had long since burned out. His blood-stained eye paced the horizon in a zombified trance, searching a far-off plane, unable to see Nor or the world around him. His ashen hair was scattered about as though he'd clawed through it for answers all evening.

It was unsettling to be unseen by those kind eyes.

Her arms longed to embrace him, but something stopped her. A strange, screeching scraped and clawed at the glass of his body, like scratching insects. This quiet was not their usual shared quiet. This was new. Violent.

Something had come in the night for him.

"Dex?" she whispered.

The wind blew between them, carrying a strange burning aroma. It was an essence of smoke, charred wood. Of hot hair. Melting flesh.

Fire.

Norah shivered, feeling alone and scared even with Dexteras beside her. "Dex…"

A pulsing muscle rolled in his jawbone as though her words raked at the tender flesh of his eardrums. His teeth ground.

"Dex."

He swiveled on his heel and closed the space between them in a single step. His approach pressed her against the chimney bricks, forcing the wind from her chest. An outpouring of heat radiated from him and smothered her still, though he never touched her.

His face was inches from hers, fingers rapping at his sides like insect legs. It seemed they wished to grab her but shook with refusal. Pallid hair clung to his face in wet, matted curls. He trembled like a terrified dog, incisors bared. All the while, his wide eyes paced through a fog, beyond her, through her.

It was as though he were sleepwalking.

"Dex…" she whispered up at him, hands hovering above his hot shoulders. She worried that waking would send him into a panic.

As the sun's sharp rays captured his leaking irises, she understood what gripped him so. For beneath the burst blood vessels were flickers of unfitting gold.

"Don't…" he grumbled. Whomever he spoke to was worlds away. "Don't t-t-touch her…."

"Dex, it's me, I'm here…" she whispered.

"I'll kill you," he muttered, "I'll kill you…" he whimpered, voice separated like crumbling stone. "No…" he begged. "No, no, NO!" he screamed in her face. Norah pressed herself back against the brick, yet still, he never touched her.

"Dex, I'm here," she mourned, hands yearning to touch his chest. "I'm okay, I'm…."

"No, no, no, Norah…" he muttered, eyes crazed and angry. Tears rolled down his handsome cheeks, sizzling and evaporating before reaching his beard. His eyes were wide and strange, bloody and gold with fear, like shaved metal trapped in resin.

He began to snarl Latin curses, baring his fists, mumbling with wild fervor.

"Dex, Dex!" she said. "It's me. I'm here. I'm not hurt."

"Give her back. Give her back to me," he groaned.

"Dex…" She couldn't bear it any longer and touched his scruff cheek, hot like a cast iron pan.

He trembled still, and his eyes rolled back into his skull, the marbled whites flickering.

Nor gasped.

"Hello, Norah Kestrel…" mouthed his cracked lips, but the voice, the gesture, was not his own. This wasn't Dexteras. He sucked his teeth and raised a tall brow. His once gorgeous eyes gave a metallic shine of violence. "Do you see what he is now?"

Nor straightened. "You," she snarled.

Solus stole Dex's lip to smile a devilish grin, an unsettling twist of her friend's soft features.

But in a blink, Dex's swimming blue pools returned to her and widened with horror.

"NO!" he screamed, still unfocused and far-off. "You get *away* from her!" he barked, punching the brick on either side of Norah's head.

She yelped and drew herself inwards. The concrete dust wafted into her eyes.

The cry awoke Dex to his senses, and his eyes paced and focused on her wounded features.

As soon as he registered what he'd done, he wilted and retreated, burying his palms into his eyes.

"No, no, no, no," he moaned. "Love, it was a n-n-nightmare, it wasn't…" He moaned into his hands. "Norah, *leave*, please. P-Please," he begged, backing away in fear.

"Hey, it's okay. I know, I know, Dex," she said, reaching her fingers to touch him. Radiating fever echoed from his collar, leaving both of their necks to glisten.

She paced between his glassy stare, seeking cerulean in the dirtied color palette of his irises. He returned to her in flashes, a war of gold and ocean gray. Colors evolving from medallion to rainstorm.

"You can do this," she whispered. "You're here with me," she tried. Though any human ear would strain to hear her through the cutting gales of the rooftop, Dex always would.

"I can't Nor, please go!" he demanded, hot tears ruining his anger while still, he clutched his face.

But his shoulders slumped, and his chin fell to his chest. And once more, dissociation shivered through his old bones.

Golden fire exploded where blue once swam, and Solus returned to her friend's wide eyeballs, hissing venomous threats. They no longer attempted to feign as Dexteras. Their voice was now many woven into one, as though an army screamed from within her poor friend's chest.

"This is what happens to my kind when they're without a Purpose, Norah Kestrel," they said in a distorted choir. "Your Dexteras is not here. He's a shell that's as easily abandoned as it's occupied. If I so wished, I could *break* him like kindling with a whisper," they threatened, rolling his crackling neck bones.

She bent backward from the sick body, infested with legions of voices. She worried about the impact it was having on her friend. He was soaked in sweat, blue veins straining at his throat and forehead.

"You are making him weaaaakkkkk," Solus teased from within, the pale, dead eyes widening upon her. "*I* am the only one who can grant him Purpose again, and you are the only one standing in the way of that. But he won't abandon you, even to save himself."

"You're the one breaking him!" snapped Norah, despite her inward doubt. "I need you to get the fuck away from my house, Solus. *Now.*"

To her surprise, they did not bother with snide retorts or alluring hisses. Solus gave a final, daring brow and a restorative blink. Within it, metallic melted to blue, and his once scowling wrinkles softened. Sharp wolfish features rounded with Dex's soft, sad ones.

He stumbled backward, eyes blinking against hot tears.

A cool, morning breeze rushed through him like a cleansing wind. With it, a bouquet of charcoal smoke ribbons peeled from his chest and faded into the skies. Dex swayed and collapsed against the chimney bricks, soaking its porous rock with sweat. His limbs buckled, and his chin fell against his chest, wet hair curtaining his features.

Norah drew cool air into her pounding heart until it unclenched, wiping her face with a sleeve. Finding no further scent of Solus, she approached Dexteras with care.

"Hey," she said softly, crouching before him. She touched the peak of his massive shoulder, which sweltered like fire. She wasn't sure how his brain hadn't melted to slush.

"I was going to hurt you, Norah…" he croaked, driving his nails into his scalp. "I've been having s-s-so many nightmares about it, and today I…I almost…" He rubbed his forehead as though it housed demons.

He hacked until final bits of black smoke sputtered from his lips, leaving him to gasp and settle his forehead against the red brick. His eyes fell glassy for a moment, shiny with bad dreams and visions. He clenched them shut and shook his head.

Finally, he shoved onto his legs, wobbling like hot noodles. His layers and skin were sticky and damp with sweat. Steam rolled off of him as he stumbled into the fresh morning.

"I-I need to get away, Norah. I need to go."

A cold weight plummeted in her gut. "Dex, no, please, I'm really-"

But he took her hands into his and knelt before her on creaking knees.

"P-Please let me go, love," he implored, holding her fingers in his. Violet rimmed his eyelids, and his iris still bled with a violent streak of red. "You need to let me go."

"That wasn't you," said Nor. "They want you by yourself, they're trying to scare you into being alone." Her old friend was stuck in a complex Cycle of Abuse, one she'd seen ensnare her clients and her parents.

"But that doesn't matter, *amica mea*," Dex insisted, gazing up at her with his pale and aging face. "Nothing else matters to me but keeping you s-s-safe. Please." It was strange and heartbreaking to be begged for mercy by someone so much wiser and older than she, someone so fierce and fearless.

He had the right to process on his own, to navigate his pain without her, and to be trusted as the professional of his needs. And after surviving her childhood, Norah held autonomy and independence as sacred, holy ground.

"Okay," she whispered. It was the most difficult word she'd ever spoken.

With a tight squeeze of her fingers, Dex released a held breath and spun to retreat through the window.

"But hey…"

He stopped, head bent beneath the sill to reveal a bloodied eye.

"I love you. So we're not done yet."

He considered a reply but instead turned and was gone.

44

⋅DEXTERAS⋅

"*Alright, if it would just take me, if I could just give it all up-*"

"*-what it's like to die-*"

"*I feel so empty, so numb it-*"

"*Let it kill me, let it-*"

"*It would all be better if I wasn't here.*"

He'd hoped to speak reason to his feet. To turn around. To go home to his apartment and lock the door for weeks as he'd once done decades ago, back when he was so near to disappearing.

But his anger, his fury, kept him grounded and tangible now. That hot, blistering poison in his lungs, his blood, under his flesh wouldn't let him run. Not anymore.

Oblitus cloaked him in shadow, corrupting him with a poisonous need for vengeance. It felt as though a key had overwound his mechanisms, leaving him with a need to relieve the bound tension.

With every blink, he saw *her* face, *her* fear. It quivered a thick knot in his throat.

In the prior evening, Solus surrounded him in the darkness, existing everywhere and nowhere, in his skull like The Voices, seeping beneath his closed eyelids. He couldn't be certain how long Solus teased him with nightmares, scratchy film reels that left him screaming and weeping over Norah's slain corpse over and over again.

But in his visions, it wasn't Solus who crushed her over and over again, but himself. Dexteras Doe clenched her windpipe against the red bricks with the ease of crumbling a champagne flute in his hands until she was blinded by blood. Dexteras Doe gutted her with the blade of silver serpents. Dexteras Doe struck her down with his own fists, breaking her bones like teacups whilst his true, horrified consciousness screamed for mercy until she was limp and lifeless in his arms. He was soaked in the nightmarish sight of her blood, black by the moonlight.

Even now, the terrors dropped him to his knees in the sunny street, feeling as though he could wretch. His fingers squeezed at the roots of his hair, praying he could claw the memories from himself. He wished so deeply to undo his existence, to fall to pieces and not exist. But he couldn't escape the vivid, dagger-like fire burning in his chest, keeping him miserably present.

As its acidity stung his throat, he finally understood that it was the raw hunger for revenge chomping its teeth beneath his chest, gnawing at the bars for freedom. Perhaps if he could set it loose of its chains, he could experience the release of being what he truly was.

"*Esto quod est, my boy...*" Be what you are. The silvery voice whispered raspy kisses against the walls of his skull, promising him a monumental unfolding.

The mirror shards mocked him from Oblitus' lone hall. Each refraction shone the painted gold eyes of Solus, winking and watching. In others, he was left to stare back at his own bloodied gaze.

Esto quod est.

In each reflection of himself, his pupils swelled and swallowed his sclera into an inky black orb, empty and shining. Dead.

This notion of finally accepting himself as he was, damnation and all, set a cry loose in his throat. He twisted and spun to scream at each refraction, feeling the hall tighten around him. His cries intensified into sobs and furious screams, breaking and tired. It shook his muscles, his bones, his clenched fists.

He screamed until hot tears rinsed his cheeks. It was the scream he'd been holding in for millennia, the scream he'd feared would never be bottled once it broke from him. His whole body shook with its vigor like the roar of a big cat.

And when he felt his lungs would rupture, and his ribs would splinter, the space around him succumbed instead.

The surrounding mirrors exploded from their mounts, showering glittering glass upon him and slicing his exposed flesh with endless hairline slivers.

He flung open the door to Oblitus, ignoring the flight of metal stairs to instead sling himself over the balcony's ledge.

He dropped from the heavens in a violent clap of cracked tile and thunder, backing the herd from him in awe. Though the ground should've broken him, the floor instead ruptured and buckled as though he were a burning comet.

He attempted to relish in the crowd's fear, but within each young being who scattered, he could only see Norah.

His entire body was sweaty and fevered. Salt burned his eyes. Like compromised knuckles against a heavy bag, he was threatening to shatter.

But this was the unraveling, the *becoming* that this place wanted from him.

And he would give it to them.

His brain burned down around him, leaving him with a narrow funnel of vision. The lobby lights of his mind flickered in anticipation of a show.

Breaching the crowd, a Figment galloped towards him, teeth shining.

Yes.

Dex crouched, abandoning his stance and his rules. He unzipped

Dexteras and disenthralled the hellfire which screamed beneath. There was something wickedly new about his fists, his heaving chest. His core. Each inch of him tightened like welded silver, solid like stone as though his muscles were electrified.

His world went black.

But he could feel himself spinning against his opponent's unguarded chest like a blackbird tucking beneath the wing of a crow mid-flight. Hooks catapulted from him like cannonballs, rumbling his foe's bones like a grindstone.

Fleshy cracks and hollers of agony screamed over The Voices. The body shuttered to the tile before him.

He craved more.

Black.

A fresh, livelier form smashed into his, forcing Dex to use his own face as a weapon to regain his arena. Rich metallic blood flooded his gums and lips, which he savored and spat. He tossed a slew of stone-leaden fists until his anonymous opponent hit the ground, buried in the fractured tile.

A new Figment grappled from behind for his throat, pressing a gold blade above his Adam's apple.

Dex thought of Norah's throat and how he'd nearly twisted it without a thought. He snarled, spinning from his assailant's grip and snatching them by the skull. A volley of white sparks bounced between his fingers, crackling a hot, electric current between their gaping mouth and eyes, twitching like dying stars.

Dex dropped him and stared at his smoking palms in horror, then pleasure. He hopped over the dead body, ready for more.

His fighting arena expanded in circumference as his audience grew more fearful. He could smell their wildly beating hearts from across the room.

And still, it was only *hers* that he could hear, as she'd beheld him on the roof in horror.

A trill of adrenaline lit him with fire as another contender broke through the circle.

The hairs on his arms and chest bristled with electricity, burning his shirt and cooking the blood on his flesh.

Black.

He beheld a brief swing of the ghastly, homemade weapon his newest opponent clutched to. It was the leg of a barstool wrapped in sparkling razor wire, and he deserved each of its jagged teeth.

Dex was unafraid and grinning as electricity *click-click-clicked* at his fingertips, making his flesh itch and fizzle. Each inch of him was etched and alive with alert nerves.

Black.

A visceral, white pain shredded and yanked at the thin skin of his lower back, leaving flapping, corroded wings behind him in strips of peeled flesh and undershirt.

Black.

He leaped upon his opponent's spine and grappled for the weapon in their mountainous arms. Once it was his, he held it to the man's throat with a bear-trap grip, uncaring that its silver teeth chewed at the flesh of his palms.

A deep *click-click-click-click* ticked dangerously in his hands, shaking the beast beneath him until he was brain-dead. They both toppled to the ground and Dex rode the great being to his end.

His fallen adversary's cigarette rolled to a stop, still smoldering with centripetal plumes. Dex bent to snatch it, spreading the flayed wounds at his spine.

He examined the tobacco, now absorbing the leaking blood from his purple knuckles. He inhaled a deep draw and spewed the smoke onto his lifted palms. It laced the ruddy flesh and settled into black boxing bandages, taut and bold.

He remembered Norah, wrapping his shaking fingers in the supply closet of Corvid Hospital, and closed his eyes, baring his teeth until his ears rang.

Tiny lightning storms flittered beneath his wraps.

Each tear of flesh and crackling fracture kept him present, alive. Each aggressive *CLICK* and *HISS* of the electricity in his body pumped him with adrenaline and euphoria. Pain was his most thorough teacher at present.

Who needed words when blood spoke so elegantly? asked a hissing voice that wasn't his.

But these thoughts felt treasonous towards Norah and her life's work. The work he'd fought so hard for at her side. The lump rose in his throat again, threatening to quash his inebriation. Before he could succumb to the despondence, a gossamer voice purred at his neck.

"Is it me you seek, my son?"

Dexteras spun with a flurry of disjointed blows, kicks, jabs, and hooks whilst broken images of Norah burned into his skull. He blamed himself for what he'd done to her, how he'd terrified her, but he blamed Solus too.

Black.

The old entity was mounted on tall, golden legs, draped in a clinging scarlet pantsuit, breathing heavily and grinning. Solus could swirl into plumes and reappear anywhere they so wished, bent on their blades, dashing, and smiling with mania. It was akin to catching a licking flame in the dark.

Black.

Dex snatched for limbs, hair, clothes, chains, anything he could cling to in an attempt to obliterate it with his own head, fists, knees, elbows, and forearms. Every inch of him was clicking, fizzling with current like a readied weapon, but Solus was never caught long enough to be struck.

"Quit holding back, Dexteras!" Solus cried. "Quit hiding your magic. You were made by the stars, now prove it!" An earnest hunger begged and beckoned in their words.

But Dex's world was still black, and all he could hear was Norah's racing heart echoing against her ribs at the sight of him.

Suddenly, he was airborne, and Dex's back buckled on the bar top, cries splitting from his chest. He put himself back on his feet in a breath.

A metallic scraping like the unsheathing of a sword cut the air and breathed past his face. He stumbled backward, running a finger along the dripping, stinging slice left in its wake. His opponent had cut him from his left eyebrow down to the right corner of his jaw. Hot blood leaked into his eye, mouth, and mustache, rich, metallic, thick, and salty. Each millimeter of the wound screamed like the swelter of a white, hot poker, but the bridge of his nose seared most.

The razors of the dark fighter's prosthetic were horribly fatal but impossible to avoid amidst the black smoke of their magic.

"Fight me properly, you coward!" screamed Dexteras. But as it left his lips, he felt his world constrict and suffocate with thick tendrils of dark fog. His insides flipped and churned unwillingly by a force outside of himself, sending him tumbling in space. He felt as though he were being dragged by his insides in the roar of a devastating undertow.

His hands flailed, grappled, and snatched a green champagne bottle from the bar top before he was torn from it. And with a nauseating spill of limbs, Dex was somersaulted onto the blinding gold tile. He squinted against the beating rays of neon and white spotlight to find they'd been transported into the ring.

The crowd roared.

The gorgeous Solus was bent and gasping in their corner, limbs crouched and spread at the ready. It was strange to see such a beautiful creature painted in blood. Their silken blazer had been torn away, leaving only a black athletic brassiere to display their stony, cut abdomen and back muscles. Their breasts heaved and dripped in gold chains whilst the illustrations of scarabs, roaches, and locusts stretched with the bronze skin. Runic symbols and skeletal birds swam in sweat. All the while, they grinned at Dexteras with bloody teeth.

He was tired, but nowhere near finished.

Solus bit their purple lip and tipped their head. "You're afraid of what you can do to me, aren't you, Dexteras?" Their golden eyes sparkled, hungry, yet patient.

Dex spat his blood to the floor, backed into his corner, and dipped low, at the ready.

"Don't be," they hissed.

Dex smashed his champagne bottle against the rail behind him, which exploded in a shower of emerald glitter at his spine. With fire in his feet, he lunged to plunge it into the old dragon's belly like swine.

The beast boomed with screaming laughter, excited by the chase. In a pivot of gold limbs, they disappeared into their obedient black plumes.

By now, Dex had caught on to the chaos of their fighting patterns. Or rather, the predictability of their unpredictability.

Whenever he managed to box them in with an onslaught of jabs, they spun and disappeared. Seconds later, they would reappear just a stride behind, turning the tables and making *him* the cornered prey. These moments of fight or flight were divided by a volley of fanciful kicks, spins, ducks, and overhand fists.

Dex ushered Solus into the corner with a series of long, hard hits, dancing forward on his lead leg, pressing them carefully against the rails as though swatting a leathery bat towards a window. Pushing, encouraging, and smothering while always maintaining a mindful toe planted on his rear foot.

Then, as sure as hellfire, smoke poured from the brass chamber on their chest, sizzling like a boiler room, enveloping them in a breath.

Without thought nor glance, Dex spun and plunged the bottle with a swordsman's thrust. And before he could even see Solus, he heard their feline scream and felt the nasty gush of their stomach flesh and innards. Warm streams of velvety blood painted Dex's fingers.

The beautiful fighter stumbled backward from the fog, eyes wide and impressed. Another piston within them hissed with pressure and blanketed them in steam.

Blinded by blood, adrenaline, and smog, Dex tracked his opponent by their wheezing gasps and distorted cadence. The knife-blade *shing* of their prosthetic occasionally scraped like a child's dinner fork across a plate.

With each step nearer, Solus responded with the spin of legs like a swiping cat, threatening to blind him. A brief, limping gait caught them hurriedly between each strike.

This was the only invitation Dex needed to end the brawl.

He sprung, wild with assaults, until bone and flesh fell into itself. He fractured a sharp nose, a clavicle, thin ribs.

Despite the subtle gratification of a collapsed body beneath his knuckles, it would never repay all that'd been tarnished. He'd never unsee Norah's fear for what he'd become. He'd never truly feel belonging besides his only friend. She would never trust him as she once did.

Never again.

With a final spring to the air like a predatory bird, Dex spun to land a hearty kick to the being's fine jaw. It replied with a satisfying snap, and the narrow body followed suit with an elegant thump upon the tile. Blood gushed from their nostrils and lips, smattering their gasping chest.

Around the ring, jeers fell to hushed whispers, and even the intoxicating bass of music had lowered for its fallen leader.

Dex fell to his knees upon them and hesitated for a breath.

It felt sinful to assault such a gorgeous being before death's door, but he remembered that they'd paid no mercy to Norah, and thus he'd pay none to them.

He struck the immortal creature, flesh upon flesh upon flesh, until their retaliation fell limp, and his knees slipped upon their blood, pulpy and wet. Until their black hair was cow-licked crimson and until breath had to gurgle from their red lips and trickle beneath the hardware embedded in their chest. The living, breathing machine wept with gurgles of blood beneath him.

Then, as if this victory had granted him some miraculous clarity, the humming Voices in Dex's head ceased, and the room around him intensified with an auditory barrage. The wheezing creature beneath seemed nearer. Aggressive, pulsating lyrics trembled from their massive speakers. He could even hear the bell-like *ting* of his blood dripping upon the green bottle still wedged in Solus' gut, like raindrops. The athletic, muscular abdomen was aquiver with spasms.

Solus was no longer bewitching but bathed in blood and purple like a murdered starling. The portions of flesh not painted sable were exchanged for amaranthine. Their teeth swam beneath pools of oozing scarlet, much like Cecil had been forced to bear, but these were grinning like a madman's.

Dex delivered a final, greedy blow to their temple and dismounted the damned beast, slumping beside them to literally soak in his handiwork.

He'd never been covered in so much blood that he could smell it on himself, metallic and warm like bathing in a tub of old pennies. Dexteras breathed his first authentic breath since returning to Oblitus, the tangy air and blood-slick floors enveloping him like a baptism.

"You've fought so hard to ask your questions, son…." Solus choked through mucousy blood, bouncing the bottle in their gut. "But as irony has it…you've already answered them, haven't you?"

What little spirit Dex possessed was promptly quashed and deflated. His legs unfolded from beneath and cast him to his rear.

It was true.

"I still want to see," Dex snapped. "*Reddere in plena*," he demanded in Latin, pay in full. He didn't come this far to turn down his prize now.

The downed opponent grinned, gasping, golden eyes darting to the scar on Dex's palm.

The old man presented it before the bleeding beast, revealing the ancient scars and tattoos across its crumpled lines.

Solus snatched the hand and embedded their sharp nails into its flesh.

Dex's eyes fluttered backward into his head as a horrific film reel warmed up and spun beneath the blackness of his lids.

✦

His world was a mosaic of screaming humans, wailing women, and sobbing children, their contorted faces and hurting songs pounding in his chest like sledgehammers. When he was sure his heart would burst, the flickering images slowed and settled into a palette of warm, amber colors as though he were peering through a sepia lens.

He was no longer at Oblitus.

He was on his knees in a small trailer home, its tiny windows dark by surrounding woods and twilight.

The smell of cooked beef, spices, and sauce poured from a tiny kitchenette, footsteps away. A massive pot of simmering chili eclipsed a little burner. The surrounding appliances were old and peeling. The laminate floor was cracked and improperly fitted together. The space was outdated, dingy, and dark, with only a few naked bulbs in the ceiling.

Dex pulled himself to legs that were not entirely his own. Still, he wore the same outfit and tattoos, but he wasn't sticky with blood or screaming with fractures. And no matter how he limped or groaned, not a sound came from his stumbling form. He looked to the black kitchen window, dark by dense forest, unable to see his reflection in the glass.

He doubled back to a sitting room with stained carpets, oversized drapes, a chugging air conditioner, and a sagging, torn couch. The space was meager and plain, but clean.

He approached a short hallway filled with shut doors. The door at the end of the hall was hanging from weak hinges, burrowed into the carpet, and propped upright. Humans could be heard within, biting with adder tongues, yelling.

Dex froze in the hall, terrified of the answers that may lie beyond.

Then, the shrill scream of a baby pierced the balmy trailer from one of the closed doors beside him. It was a horrid, ear-splitting scream that was impossible to ignore.

A man's voice raged from the end of the hall.

A bristle rose within Dexteras, but as soon as he leaned onto his foot to investigate, a set of imaginary cables secured his arms and legs against him like a doll's. He baulked, but the cords cut into him like barbed wire. He groaned and cursed at the impossible sensation that felt almost like a punishment, a process of slow torture. He was being forced to stand still and watch.

A shifting of clothes shuffled from the hall, and a portly, half-dressed man kicked open the door, black hair plastered to his forehead. The stranger approached Dexteras with fury-bent eyes, drunk and glassy. His hairy chest and beer-swollen belly gleamed with sweat as he trudged. An ugly tattoo of an eagle was poorly inked on the human's wide bicep.

Before trampling Dexteras, the middle-aged man kicked in the door beside them and stuck his red face into the baby's room.

"You SHUT the FUCK up, you little bastard BITCH!" he screamed drunkenly, words smearing together like muddy clay.

A scrawny, thin woman burst from the room at the end of the hall, long, pale limbs quickly pulling into underthings. She dashed into the bathroom, where a grainy clatter of heavy porcelain ground. She then rushed into the hall, holding a silver pistol in her bony hands, aimed at the man's back.

"Get out," she snarled, wincing against a swollen lump on her cheek. Her face was painted in heavy makeup, but her voice was young, lost. Something about the slope of her nose and the flash of her eyes made his heart skip a beat.

"Get the fuck *out* of here," she repeated, straightening her spine like a threatened snake.

Dexteras pressed hard into the binds until he was certain his limbs would break, but his confines did not relent. He opened his mouth to bark threats at the man, but his lips were wired shut like that of a mortuary corpse. The sensation sent a jolt of icy water down his chest and gut, and limbs. He felt like a ghost again. He felt *dead* again.

The vile man gave a flash of wide, white glassy drunk eyes over his shoulder at her and sneered.

Dex bared his teeth, merely inches from the brute. The lightbulb in the hall flickered, threatening to darken the space. He could nearly hear the man's horrid thoughts and see the things he wished to do to her in his distant irises.

Dex pressed his chest into the binds, screaming in his throat. He didn't recognize the young woman, but his fists burned to protect her, and his eyes watered for her safety.

Her arm trembled with the gun's weight. Faded tattoos peaked beneath her lace bra and on her pale, freckled limbs. Nearest him, along her narrow leg, was a tiny orange and brown bird on her ankle. It sat atop a nest beside its baby-blue robin's egg.

The horrid man finally snickered and left the hall, stomping to the front door into a mud-crusted pair of work boots.

"Waste of fucking change," he spat before kicking open her front door and stepping into the night. A massive engine ignited in the gravel before the tiny home and spun off, spitting rocks at the porch and windows.

As its red taillights faded into the dark, the binds restraining Dexteras and the young woman fell to the ground, dropping them both to the carpet, moaning against their unseen pains.

He began immediately crawling, reaching for her like she was his child, his charge.

She dropped the tiny gun beside her and fell flat to her back, sobbing.

"Hey, hey," he muttered, hands hovering with worry.

She seemed drunk, exhausted, sweating, hot, and fevered.

"Can you hear me? Can you speak?" he begged.

She could only respond with hot, rolling tears spilling down her temples and onto the carpet. Her fists clenched, and she shook with combustible anger.

Dexteras felt it, too, in his core, in his chest. It was the same fire that gripped him in the ring.

Her song could sing a harmonious ballad beside his own, heavy with violent drums and plucky fiddle strings and aggressive staccatos. She was too young to know such thunderous music. She had to be barely twenty, if that.

"I'm here, I'm here, love," he whispered to the woman he did not know. His heart ached to hold her, to help her clean her body and wrap her in warm clothes. He wished to pet her hair and speak only of loving, kind things and remind her of her bravery. His vacant skull knew nothing of the frail woman, but he felt in his chest that he *knew* her.

He could feel the trembling skin of her small shoulders beneath his touch but could not comfort her or hold her. He could smell the alcohol that'd been sweated from her pores. He could hear her heart drumming like that of a snarling lioness.

But she couldn't see him. She couldn't hear him.

He'd known few desires as powerful as the one he had to comfort this young woman. To simply remind her of how worthy she was of loving and being loved.

He petted the soft brown hair on her head until she shivered and pressed herself against the wall, further from his touch. Staring beyond him, through him.

He retracted his fingers and held them against his chest. The way she winced and reacted to him. It was as though he were…

Like a ghost.

Was that it?

Am I dead?

Is this hell?

She folded herself tight against her knees, beginning to sob with the chest-lurching cries of someone who believed they were truly alone. Her eye makeup rinsed down her cheeks in black streams. She wept until her body shook and her cries deduced to squeaks within her tight throat.

He tried to pick up her hand, to kiss her head, to wipe the stuck hair from her neck, to love her in any way that he could. But the only evidence that indicated she felt him there was the shiver and a tighter clinching of her limbs.

He withdrew, feeling awful and selfish. Just as with Norah, all he could offer these humans were hurt. Discomfort and misery.

Her bare spine was rounded, protruding with tiny vertebrae. He saw scars there in the dim light, scars he knew all too well.

What horrid horrid humans had she known?

"I'm so sorry, I'm so sorry. You should be loved, you should be loved," Dexteras said, eyes following her small form that was foreign but maddeningly familiar.

He ran out of fitting words and swallowed hard, knowing there would never be enough. Whispers and breath would never do justice in place of wailing and screams and the striking of flesh.

In the bedroom beside them, the baby's remaining cries had fallen to sleepy babbles.

The baby's mother remained there on the stained, sopping carpet, gritting her teeth. Her weeping rose to the trailer's ceiling and pressed against its confides.

Dexteras could only weep slow tears beside the stranger, feeling so guilty, so empty, so helpless. He yearned for even just one second of corporeal flesh to hold her with everything he had. Perhaps he'd kiss the scars on her wrists or hold her head in his lap until the pounding migraine at her temples subsided.

His own body was dizzy and weary, feeling each of her pains as his own. If only he could take those from her, he'd absorb them seven-fold. There was nausea in his blood, a fury itching in his throat. But as always, he could do nothing because he *was* nothing.

It was like an age-long itch or an attempt to run in a nightmare. The effort of punching underwater. A suffocation that split his insides. His eyes were blurry and worthless by weeping in his attempts to define what exactly he was.

A short creak of the old floor moaned from the baby's room.

Dexteras shot upright, straightening before the fallen young woman in defense.

From the darkness stepped a tall creature in a long black coat, pale hair nearly scraping the ceiling. He, too, did not see Dexteras and stepped through him like a cloud, sending Dex scampering from the new stranger's path.

The being knelt at the buried head of the young woman but made no attempt to touch or comfort her. He was silent and wrapped in black like a reaper, damning like an omen. He eyed the woman's pain with distant emotion, near apathy, and she made no notice of him, either.

The new stranger propped himself against one of the thin walls and stretched his long legs to its other end. He sighed and began humming a song, a grumbling, rough tune that was not lovely to hear by any means, but it was something to fill the damning silence, to shake the dust of isolation around her. He took deep, long breaths between verses and did his best to ease the pain of the space.

The amnesiac Dexteras did not recognize the melody but found himself mouthing the lyrics in cautious wonder. It was a helpless and exhausting sensation to not know the song but find yourself singing it regardless.

The woman between his present and past self was captured in sleep and twitching dreams in moments. This unconscious mercy seemed to be all that could be offered. After a moment, he gawked at the naked bulb that buzzed with nighttime insects above them. It was yellow and burning like the sun. He licked his thumb and snapped his fingers. A tiny crackle of lightning zipped from his hand, and the light above them went dark with a fragile, glassy chime.

Finally, Dexteras stooped to behold the new stranger's stony face with open-mouthed awe.

Of course, it was no stranger. It was him from decades ago. The body that had once been his body. His chin was shaved clean and tipped up to the skies, resting against the wall. He seemed to be staring past the old trailer into the stars with trepidation. His eyes were rimmed red, swollen, and tired.

It was the face of someone who'd endured this relentless heartache too many times to count. It was the face of someone trapped in an immortal body capable of unspeakable strength while still powerless to comfort anyone he cared for.

Dexteras Doe stared into the face of his past self, who'd been blessed with sacred *Purpose*. And simultaneously, he could understand why the beings at *Oblitus* had abandoned their past lives so willingly. He could empathize with their need to escape this worthlessness.

I'm done. I want out. I want out, he screamed in his skull, eyes clenched and watering. *I get it*, he lied, *but I'm done.*

The dizzying surge of ice-cold blood bled into his fingertips and submerged his clenched hands. The clutch of a distant grip pulled him to the present, years, maybe generations into the future. He squeezed and chased after it like a sinking, dying body to a life preserve.

Chest hollow and nauseous, Dex was pulled into his present body in *Oblitus*. Solus was splayed before him, bloody and worn, eyes cold and watchful. Dex snatched back his limbs and held them to his chest.

With its bright lights and booming music, Oblitus was over-stimulating and unnerving. The critical eyes of the crowd felt confrontational and foreign. Their ability to see and hear his gasps was too much. Each burn and wound on his skin demanded attention. Each breath in his chest wasn't enough to sustain him. He was too weak, too weary to power his overworked heart.

Solus tore the bottle from their stomach, chuckling with gargled groans. They cast the glass aside where it shattered, making Dexteras jump from his skin. Solus' matted and gorgeous head rolled to him, smiling with swollen lips.

"*Esto quod es*," they hissed with bright eyes. Even slain and wasted in their own insides, Solus still emerged victorious.

The real world was blinding and exhaustive. It was too vivid, too violent. But he couldn't unsee the brown-haired woman and her infant from his glossy stare. He couldn't shake her despondence from his chest.

"Why…" he muttered. "Why don't I remember?" begged Dex.

You abandoned them.

Solus' dark brows lifted for a breath in sad consideration. "You know why. Because you gave me your memories, your past. So could you be free."

"Why would I do that?" Dex whispered. "Why would I abandon them?"

They swallowed hard to wet their throat and finally muttered, "Because it hurt," Solus said, propping themself on an inked elbow. It was in that careful, gentle gesture, that quiet remark regardless of their agony and blood, that Dex realized Solus truly did believe themselves to be a parent.

Hot, angry tears stung Dex's pupils. He shook his head, teeth crushing one another.

"I want to know what I am," asked Dex, not bothering to lift his gaze, "I want to understand."

Solus revealed a gentle lift of their dark lips that was nearly pleasant. Then, with a wet, gurgling cough and a sigh, they peeled from the tile and folded over their knees. Hisses broke from their chest as they clutched their bare gut, holding their insides inside.

They rolled a fresh cigarette between their fingers and leaned back against the cold, jangling chains of the arena. They seemed to pay no mind to the puddle of blood that their gold legs bathed in, rippling its tides with each shaky breath.

Dex watched Solus drink from their cigarette with a scowl of gold eyes and inhale it deeply into their gleaming chest. Then, they snapped their fingers weakly, and every light in Oblitus went dark, albeit a single pale bulb that spotlighted the ring. Thick humidity and debris churned before the single bulb. The music stopped, and the onlooking crowd muttered excitedly as though a performance were about to begin.

With a free hand, Solus clutched at one of the gold rails and spit a mountainous cloud of smoke into the center of the ring. With effort, they released the golden links and slipped back to the tile with a labored breath.

Detached from its maker, the silvery plume in the ring was winding, contorting into shapes, into characters.

Solus then projected their sweet silvery voice above the crackles of smoke, like an elder sharing lore with their tribe. With every word they spoke, the smoke form arranged itself with seductive and hypnotizing movements.

"What you know as the human," began Solus, their accented voice altering the broad shoulders of a being from the smoky form, "is what we call a Corporeal. A Corpse," they added, teeth bared. The smoke person walked around the ring, wafting tendrils reaching with each dragging step.

Dex gawked at the impossible magic and exchanged glances between the story and its narrator, observing how it taxed them with effort and winces.

"Corpses endure fear, trauma, illness, unmet needs, lack of belonging, immense pain, what have you," Solus listed these hardships, eyes closed, with the emotional fervor of reading an obituary.

A long-established emotional boundary, it seemed, thought Dex.

"Often, those aches cannot be healed by their weak, external means…."

The smoke person in the ring gripped their opaque skull, heaving with spitting tears. They fell to their knees before Dexteras, clutching themselves with heartbreaking desperation. It took everything he had within him to not crouch beside them in an outpour of condolences.

"Thus, they have two options," said Solus, presenting two tattooed fingers. "Perish with its immensity, or channel it into survival."

The trembling smoke person gripped their skull until a small swirling flame flickered within. It whirled within them like an ignited can of spray paint. Flames fell from the smoke person's empty eyes and poured from their screaming lips to puddle on the floor.

The puddle of flames rose tall and illuminated the ring, molding into a fire person who breathed with life before them.

Dex looked up at the crackling orange being, radiating like the sun. He could feel its hot silhouette reflecting against his burning eyes. It was his size, stature, and build.

"This outpouring of despondent energy creates a Figment," said Solus, wincing and situating their arms along the arena's firm chains. Already, their wounds were healing. Their bruises deepening, and their gut no longer gushing its steady stream.

With admiration, they stared up at the fire person. "This is us. We are made from their most powerful emotions and needs. Thus, we are the only ones who support the Corpses when no one else can. We become whatever they need us to be. Imaginary friends. Affirmations. Lovers. Guardians. Pets. Distractors. Comfort characters. Fighters," added Solus, rolling their dark head toward him with a brow.

Dex was shaking his head, face crumpled and confused. The question *how?* was surely etched into each of his deep wrinkles and screaming in his pacing eyes.

How in the hell?

"This universe, its cosmos, are living, breathing, endlessly thriving. In the same way the cockroach gained armor and barbed limbs, the massive chasm of energy that is the galaxies, spat us out to protect its Corpses. Is it so impossible to imagine?" They grinned. "We are simply a cocktail of human agony and dead stars."

The fire person swooped up the fallen smoke being from behind like a sack of grain, returning them to their feet.

Solus' voice grew quiet, grievous.

"You'd think, when such a miracle of the mind is achieved, when the cranium and the cosmos create such power, such intimacy out of sheer ash, you'd think we'd be valued. Seen. Worshiped." A note of contention struck their narrator's tone, and they swallowed it with another wince.

"But we are given none of those things. They cannot truly see us, hear us, or feel us," mourned Solus, their reaching hand passing through the smoke being's striding ankles. "But we feel *all* of them. Each scar, injury, wound, and ache they incur, so do we. But they'll never know how much we sacrifice." Their golden eyes followed the parading characters.

Dexteras considered the many defense mechanisms of the natural world. Poison, venom, inflammatory spores, armored flesh, vibrant plumage. All tools for flora and fauna to survive dire circumstances. This was what he was to humans?

He was a gut feeling, an instinctual urge, a compulsion, that little voice in the furthest corners of people's skulls?

"We exist because they give us Purpose," said Solus, "thus we are *enslaved* to them. We need a Corpse to feed upon." With his words, the *click-click* of sooty manacles clamped across the fire being's ankles, disabling their movement.

"Do you know what happens to us when they die?" asked Solus, eyes flicking to Dexteras as though it were simply the two of them exchanging tales.

The smoky human grew slower and feebler, dimming the burning flame of their fire friend, whose light was now deduced to sparks and falling ash, flaking apart like the end of an old cigar.

A powerful wind ensnared the ring, tearing the Figment's feet from them in a cloud of dead embers, dropping them to their knees. These, too, dissipated, dropping them onto their hands, lying them on their belly, and then their chest, hands reaching, mouth gasping for breath. The bright and beautiful flame creature that once illuminated the entire stage was now a pathetic, dragging torso on the tile, pulling itself onward by dying, red fingertips.

Eventually, the sleeping smoke being breathed its last, and the pair of them were gone. The room was black.

"It's hard to know who the real parasite is," muttered Solus in the darkness. "They are, after all, *our* Purpose, our only means of existence. And once upon a time, we were a crucial key in theirs. We feel *everything* they feel. We help wherever we can, whispering, begging, weeping, protecting. But even after we've given them our lives, they never know we existed."

Dex swallowed the lump in his chest. It truly was an agonizing tale.

But how could such a thing be possible?

After following Norah for endless sessions, he'd learned that the brain was packed with energy and electricity. Power. Was it so impossible to believe that in fight or flight mode, enough energy could be crafted to bolster its own defense mechanisms? To create something to keep it alive?

He'd once thought it impossible that so many of their clients had survived such indescribable circumstances and pain, and yet, they sat before him and Norah, living and breathing.

Solus flicked open a gold lighter, kindling a new cigarette in their mouth. With the flickering glow of their new flame, the club's lighting returned, warming the space with its pale and crimson glow.

"That," muttered Solus around the smoke, "is why they come to me for peace," they said, wincing with a hand to their gut, blackened with dry blood.

"H-how?" Dex muttered.

Solus needn't clarify which answer the old man sought.

"I take the memories of their past: the pain, the agony, the bitterness. And with that energy, I power this sanctuary for them. Thus, my Purpose becomes theirs..."

A few shameless, proud Figments in the crowd dared to whistle, causing Dex to jump in his skin. He'd forgotten the building was teeming with others.

Figments.

He shook his head, skull still constipated and unsatisfied. "Why you?" he asked.

"I was the first," Solus stated as though that were evident. "I am the very first Figment constructed of human emotion," they grinned, arms spread wide. "I've known yearning and pining since I was sentient, barely a vapor of hope in a Corpse's brain." Their eyes fell wide with memories, and for a moment, Solus' proud body... *glitched*. It shuddered and dashed like pixels on a screen, flickering like a dying television, colors exchanging for others, distorting them from one character to another in half a heartbeat. Back to their tangible self, they continued as though nothing had occurred.

"Every Corpse's emotion was valued before mine. For generations. Centuries. Whether they occupied jungles or penthouses, all they craved was more and more. After millennia, I realized there would never be an escape. And that's when I began to imagine a realm where Figments could exist freely." Their language was sweet, and their intention was kind, but their voice was cold.

"But why fighting?" asked Dex.

"What do you think their memories look like, Dexteras?" they snapped, pointing wildly to the crowd. "What you saw of your own was *nothing*. I was very gentle in what I shared." Solus warned with earnest gold eyes. "And if you'd consumed their pain, their agony, their horror, as I have, you'd know it's impossible to not be protective of their ignorant bliss." The panel in their chest leaked trickles of steam. "Those are the same memories that nearly destroyed them once, that brought them to me, begging to be set free."

"And if they lose, you kill them?"

"I detach them from their Purpose here," defended Solus.

"But that kills them. You said it yourself."

"This is a sanctuary, son. And I will not allow the rogue few who willingly risk their lives to risk the safety of the loyal many," they snapped. "And ask any *one* of my flock who dare to fight," cackled Solus, pointing to the crowd. "Any of them would rather endure brief detachment by my hand rather than the endless pain of The Unbecoming!" cried Solus, dropping their arms. "Somehow you've forgotten, but The Unbecoming can last for decades, centuries on end. It torturously pulls you apart, piece by piece from the inside out." Solus shook their head, flicking their tiny cigarette butt into the skies, where it caught fire and disappeared like flash paper.

Dexteras dare not prompt with more questions. A blue vein was pulsing at Solus' forehead and in their tense neckline.

"So yes, Dexteras, I'd rather their journey end here, in control of their fate, alongside their brothers in this ring, rather than die unwanted beside a thankless Corpse, alone, abandoned, and slowly."

Dexteras was numb and wordless, but his limbs buzzed with rapid healing and cell growth. He could now assume that all Figments would heal so long as they were needed for some sort of Purpose.

"And that is why Cecil sought you out and brought you," added Solus. "It's his job to scout for Figments dying of The Unbecoming and bring them here where they can be nourished with new Purpose," they sighed. "This is a gift, but it is also a choice. A gift I empower any of my Figment's to return should they wish to train with Cecil and pursue so."

There weren't enough mortal cups of coffee that would allow Dex the mental clarity to piece together what he was.

"You belong here," Solus smiled, reaching toward Dex's skull with a hand, black with blood.

Dexteras slapped them away. Because regardless of his belonging and their shared immortality, he was still suspicious of this being who was as old as the planets. Despite their parental intentions, he still felt they'd sink their teeth into him as soon as his back was turned.

Because Norah was right. He couldn't ignore what they'd done to Cecil and the others. How they'd been mutilated despite their loyalty. This was more than strict guardianship.

And as if Solus could hear Norah's words in his thoughts, they grinned and lowered their dark lashes upon him. "A series of uncanny misfortune is what brought you to that Corporeal world, son. But fate brought you back home to us. She will never truly understand what you are or what you're capable of," said Solus. "Thus, she can never truly love you," they said, eyes flickering between Dex's with pity.

Dex swallowed and stared back, stone still with uncertainty.

"Oh fuck off, you old ass hat," cried a new voice from the crowd below.

Dex nearly choked on the uncontrollable pang of joy in his chest and the illuminating light that warmed his insides. He strained and struggled in search of Norah Kestrel, his boots squelching on blood.

She emerged from the horde, who mumbled and parted for her. She climbed the metal stairs to the ring, small in comparison to the monsters that surrounded her, but bold in her blackest of outfits, putting even Solus to shame. Her cat eyes were long and piercing. Her lipstick was dark. She wore her thickest rings, studded with chunky stones and wide bands. She sparkled with dangerous dark eyes like a black hole, daring anyone to come close.

She stepped over the legs of the downed Solus. The two of them exchanged scowls and tall brows, but Norah's grin was victorious as she eyed the bloodied glass and the bite it'd left in Solus' stitched gut.

"Cheers," she snorted.

And when her eyes found Dex's, her brows warped in hurt. She knelt beside him, seeking his face amongst wet hair, leaning back on her heels to take in the dripping gash on his spine.

"Must you always get stabbed in the back?" she sighed.

He leaned from her grasp, knowing the heat of his flesh would be far too torrid for human touch.

Hurriedly, she rerouted her attention to the tattered mess that was Solus and stared at them with dark brows.

"You do not get to tell me who I am capable and incapable of loving," she stated dangerously. "It's going to take a lot more than that to scare me off," she spat, nodding to the ring. She'd seen the entire performance, the entire telling of what they were. And yet here she was.

The old man's gut hollowed and grew cold.

"I can arrange that," Solus winked.

Dex's spine arched like a rabid dog's. His fervor and energy ignited at the sight of his friend.

Touch her. I fucking dare you.

"I'm not leaving until you do," said Norah to him, unfazed by the banter.

He'd comply if it kept her from this wretched place. Exhales peeled from his lips with each stab of pain, but still, he denied her aid and managed to his feet.

"You can't run from what you are, Dexteras," said Solus from the floor, eyes casual and disinterested. "You cannot be satisfied by merely existing in the Corporeal realm. You do not feed as Corpses do. You need Purpose to survive. You need me, this place."

In a great stride of heeled boots, Norah bent before the old, slain Figment, kneeling with terrifying composure and quiet.

The two forces drank one another in, bathed in stark contrast and disturbing similarity. Dark features, cropped dark hair, and even black attire. Striking green narrowed upon the uplifted gold irises. Though the motley pair had both tasted abandonment and trauma, they'd recycled their bloodshed for vastly different purposes.

Nor leaned close to the androgynous being without even a grimace at the gore. "He has Purpose without you. He's my friend, regardless of who or what he is."

Solus drew closer, busted lips grinning. They propped themselves upon a tattooed arm and nearly kissed Norah's earlobe. The tempestuous being dropped their lashes upon her with an unsettling appetite.

"But who he was before, stole quite the treasure from you, Norah

Kestrel," said Solus, flakes sparkling beneath their irises like unmined gold.

A brick twisted sideways inside Dex's throat, drenching his blood-soaked form in cold.

Oh God, what?

Norah shook her head with pity for the bloody beast, a glare she'd never rest upon her patients. Upon him. In the end, she tipped her head to him.

"C'mon, Dex," she said, gesturing their leave through the crowd.

"Convenient that Dexy should show when he did, no, Norah Kestrel?" called Solus with an eager cry for attention. Their eyes flashed their dangerous gold. "Simply uncanny timing," they grinned.

Nor pivoted on her toes and scowled, fingers clenched, arms shaking, and jaw bared more tightly than he'd ever seen it prior.

Solus' expression stretched from amused delight to a nauseating, sugary satisfaction. It was the tall-browed, glimmering teeth of a wolf who'd found the rabbit's den.

"Oh…" they smiled. "You didn't tell him," they sang, glossy, dark lips relenting a delicious epiphany.

Norah locked arms with Dexteras and ushered him onward, limping and huffing. The crowd's murmurs, sneers, and whispers hissed after them, but Dex heard none of it.

He could only hear his own desperate ruminations, screaming in their new-founded horror. They were digging, scraping, and excavating in search of what the ancient beast could have meant.

"But who he was before, stole quite the treasure from you, Norah Kestrel."

What have I done?

God, what have I done to her now?

45

✦NORAH✦

DISASSOCIATION EMPTIED DEX'S EYES as he stumbled into the street, Solus'
distortions undoubtedly swimming behind his gaze. He limped past her
vehicle and towards the darkened road, not bothering to exchange a single
word as he brushed by. Streetlights gleamed across his wounds and tattoos.
No flesh was unpainted by wet, shining blood.

"Dex, I'll take you wherever you want to go, but please, let me drive
you."

She snatched her father's coat from her trunk and ran to him, slinging it
across his shoulders. Steam rushed from his torso with its embrace. She had
to jog to keep speed with his healthy clip.

"Please, Dex."

He sighed and stopped, eyes closed in consideration. "If I let you drive
me home, you need to let me be alone, Nor." He was stern but breaking.

"I can do that."

She guessed it'd been several hours since he was permitted any peace to think or rest. Thus, she allowed him the rare quiet until they pulled to his lot.

With averted eyes, he winced and pulled himself from the vehicle. He took her father's coat with him as it had soaked up a great deal of blood.

She tore from her seat and squared up to the old man, hoping to elicit a hug, a hopeful conversation.

But he only eyed her with shame and shook his head. A swollen and puffy scar carved across his handsome features as though the claw of a lion had ripped across his face. It made him look miserable and weary.

"I don't think I sh-sh-should touch you. Or be close to you… anymore." His Adam's apple bobbed with a heavy swallow.

"Dex, I know you wouldn't-"

"But *I* don't know that, Norah!" His massive voice echoed into the street. "And that's not a chance I can take. I cannot *ever* bear to risk that again," he said, wiping his face with trembling palms. He shook his head into them, smearing blood from his features.

"I'm s-sorry, love," he whispered into his hands. "Please..." he begged, sorrow weighing his features. "Please."

Her tears rose, hearing the "goodbye" in his pleas. But this wasn't simply a casual farewell. It was an indefinite one. One you couldn't hear from someone you cherished. The immensity of its grief simply wouldn't calculate.

"Please," he said again.

She blinked away the tears and nodded, lips quivering. "Okay. Okay, Dex," she whispered.

He pivoted and limped away.

"But hey…" she called, voice breaking.

He twisted over his shoulder, lamplight reflecting full, rolling tears on his bruised cheeks.

"I love you. So I'm coming back." She pointed to where she stood, daring for a rebuttal.

But he only dropped his head to carry on through the front gate.

She watched until the window of his room shone ambient yellow, casting his grizzly silhouette against the blinds. It paced for several moments. It plunged a hole in the wall with screams of agony. And then it collapsed into the leather chair.

Nor fell into the plush confines of her driver's seat and stole her knees to her chest. There, she sobbed until her tears had emptied. Until she'd been left with a sharp cramp in her stomach and a throb in her forehead.

She craned her neck to see his window. His slumped shadow hadn't moved for hours. She prayed her presence was near enough to keep the auditory hallucinations at bay.

It sorely pained her that the foundation of their friendship had been so easily unraveled by the past.

Beneath the poor glow of Corvid's nocturnal buildings, she scrounged for ideas. For a plan. For anything.

Eventually, she rested upon a minuscule island of light amidst the waves of this present darkness. Memories drifted to her amongst the tides of exhaustion.

✦

Her forehead was pressed against the cold, rumbling car glass as they idled in the hospital parking lot. She and her Nana Rose awaited Robin, who attended yet another appointment. Nor's heart was only eight years old, but her childish energy had been depleted years prior. Her grandmother captured the girl's eyes in her rear-view mirror.

"Jaybird, my sweet, hang in there. The hardest part of hope is always the waiting."

✦

Rising with the faint light of dawn, she popped the rickety seat upright and drove home. She fed the bawling black cat and packed a backpack with ample supplies. She changed into outdoor layers and pulled knee-high hiking boots atop her saggy Van Gogh socks, slinging her gear across her back.

As she shook down the house's gravel road, she noticed the old cat sitting on the chimney bricks, gawking at the birds flying overhead. Hundreds of feet from the earth, he was concerned with the skies.

"Vincent, how in the absolute fuck?" she hollered from the window.

He simply swished his tail and stared at the heavens.

As promised, she returned to Dex's front gate and rang the apartment's bell. She could hear his cogs and whistles churning from above, considering if he should allow her up. The mechanical latch was eventually unhinged with hesitation, as if sensing his unease.

She rode the lift and pushed through his ajar door. His figure stood somberly on the threshold of his sitting room.

She beamed to see him.

His whiskers rose with a small, shattered smile, but his eyes and brows were stitched with worry. He was scared.

As she came close, he leaned onto his heels, scarred hands deep in his pockets.

She reached to hand him a brimming mason jar of cold coffee, sloshing with life.

He huffed with a smirk and took a pull, left wiping coffee droplets from his beard.

"You always make the best coffee." His voice broke through his throat as though it hadn't been used in days.

She admired how miraculously he'd mended himself in several hours. Smooth scars and contusions peaked beneath his denim shirt. The gash across his face was raised and crimson but closed. Leather bracelets and precious metal rings covered his bruised knuckles and swollen joints. His hair had been snipped to reclaim a debonair tidiness and framed his crimson eye.

Below, his maple leather boots shone, oiled and soft with antique patina. They were nice. *Too nice.*

He followed her eyes with a frown. "Don't like them?" he croaked.

"No, they're lovely. Do you have others?"

He raised his brows and beckoned her to a tiny, barren room. He pulled open a small closet door to expose his collection of suits, button-downs, textured thermals, and a broad spectrum of silken ties. A homemade wooden shoe rack held several sets of leather shoes and boots below. She snatched a pair of tall hiking boots with long, chaotic laces and sat them at his feet expectantly.

He observed the old shoes and their likeness to the ones she wore. But still, he sat in his solitary chair and exchanged shoes. The galled, vibrant scars across his lower back peeked beneath his shirt. He stifled a moan.

"Love, I don't know what the plan is today, but-"

"We don't have to talk," she said. "Please just go for a drive with me."

He shot her a worried, bloody eye and straightened with a grimace.

"Please."

"Norah, spending time with you is the most human and loved I've ever felt." His hand rested above his heart and clenched at the layered fabric there. "But if I ever did something to hurt you..." he inhaled sharply, rubbing his forehead with bandaged fingers. "I-I wouldn't come back from it. I'd..." he buried his face into his palms, massaging his wrinkles.

Nor ached to embrace him but instead crouched low before him to find his blue eyes.

"I know you don't want to hear it, but I want you with me today. Please?" She looked to the door.

He didn't respond, but only sighed. Then, he swallowed half the jar of cold brew and stood with a moan. He paced to the door and held it open for her.

He was fidgety and restless for most of their drive west. He tugged at his shirt sleeves, opened and shut visors, maneuvered about the windows to block the sun from his face, and fumbled with his accessories. Once they drove across Corvid's city limits, his body was kinetic.

Norah smiled but understood the unnerving fear of leaving home, especially when it was all you knew.

But discomfort brings change, she thought, recalling the words of her social work professor from long ago. It was a truth she'd denied for decades, before Oblitus bolstered her bravery and sense of self.

She pulled a pair of old sunglasses from the center console. They were large, circular lenses, blue-tinted and chrome. She'd bought them from an antique store near campus ages ago.

"Here," she placed them in his trembling fingers.

He slipped them onto his crooked nose, testing the view.

She grinned, spotting an old joy peek through the crumbling cracks of his hurt.

Gleaming shop windows faded into dancing acres of crops. Farmland melted into bottlebrush evergreens. Dense and dark pines rode the roller-coaster hills.

Asphalt gave way to gravel, and the boxy, baby truck grumbled and rocked along the trail, finding belonging beneath its massive tires.

They parked before a wooden trail sign and a laminated map. Norah hiked past without a glance at its coordinates. While geographically hopeless in the streets, she was at home amongst the natural footpaths of the woods. These acres were once her salvation through expansive valleys of loneliness. Nor swung the large pack onto her shoulders and led them inwards.

She felt that the song of the forest was most powerful amidst the silence but wasn't certain if she'd learned such truth through preference or the isolation of circumstance. *Had she ever hiked with anyone before today?*

They passed trickling creeks and bubbling waterfalls lined with hanging foliage. Mossy rock formations offered them quiet moments of awe. The high tops of evergreens made Norah dizzy with their dalliances.

In moments of stolen peripheral observation, she watched Dexteras. His eyes were glued to the stones and decaying stumps studded with pillowy mushroom towers. Forest shadows dappled his features and darkened his scars.

Though her stitched boots crunched and crushed through dry leaves like tea-stained parchment, Dex's never made a sound. His large feet were silent, like cat paws, as though he were sculpted to tread the earth in silence.

He was tired and hurting, but she wanted to tote him to the top of the mountains until the devil was sweating from his pores like a spiritual cleansing.

"What are you thinking about?" she asked.

"That I'm unworthy," he said, self-loathing evidently at the nearest surface of his thoughts. "I've been around longer than some of these trees, and still, I have no Purpose." His eyes followed the tiny birds above before falling to his feet.

"Their growth looks very different from yours," Nor said, gesturing at their immense height. "But even the trees have seasons. Maybe this is a season of healing for you."

He remained silent.

She kicked at a pinecone. "And the dead stuff that falls away is what gives us ground."

He, too, tapped at acorn shells with his toes. "I'm nothing but dead stuff," he muttered.

"Well, you'll be that much stronger when it *is* your season to grow then," she replied.

He huffed, stretching his legs over a fallen tree. "Should've known better than to engage in a metaphorical life debate with a therapist."

Norah stopped and doubled over with an explosion of laughter into the woods. It wasn't her short, pitchy therapist chuckle, bubbly and fake. It was free of restraint and shame, and it restored her soul.

He replied with a chuckle of his own.

They exchanged warm, companionable smiles. Norah had hoped for a moment that their joy might've outshone the darkness, the trauma, the red neon, and the aggressive music in their chests.

But in moments, his smile wilted, and his stare fell.

After more silent trekking, she sensed a mutual aching in their bones and sought rest. They veered off at a humble lookout across a small, rolling creek that branched into several tiny waterfalls. The streams splashed with the satisfying laps of churning fountains.

Dex sat with a sigh at the far end of a bench and dropped his head into his hands.

Their journey hadn't lifted him in the ways she'd hoped, but before disappointment could bitter her blood, she remembered everything the old man had endured as of late. She shuddered at the thought of the old Figment Solus in her bones.

A muffled clanging tore her from her thoughts to see him struggling with an old brass lighter. His rings trembled against the antique, despite his focus.

Norah slung her pack to the dirt and knelt before him, steadying his massive, inked hands in hers. They worked together to still the flame until it licked at the crumbled tobacco. He breathed relief into her cupped hands and sat back against the bench.

"Thank you." He dropped his chin back into the skies, jaw stretching wide with a drag. He opened his mouth and allowed the thick clouds to rise from his throat of their own volition.

"Is your…magic not working?" She swirled her hands about, miming his flourish.

His eyes fell, reading the shakes of his limbs. "No."

"You've been through so much lately."

His head bobbed.

She eyed the sticky gauze bandages wrapped about his fingertips, some old, some new.

"Dex…" she said, still knelt before him, "I heard everything Solus said about…what you are," she began, "But I don't understand why it bothers you, why you believe it makes you bad."

He closed his eyes.

"Because I was given a Purpose. I was given life by someone who needed me, and I wasn't there for them." He swallowed. "When I decided to walk away and give up my memories, I abandoned someone, a Corporeal, in their darkest time," he grumbled in a deep, rolling tone. It was the distant thunder before the flash of anger.

Though it was nowhere near the same sort of apathy or aggression, she felt the cold chill of her father's screams on the wind, remembering the suffocating tension that would follow him into a room.

"But if they couldn't see you or hear you, what could you-"

"I left out of sheer selfishness, Norah," stated Dex, fingers pinching the bridge of his nose until his nail beds were white.

"Out of survival," she replied.

"It doesn't matter," he stated. "I was weak, and I was monstrous. I abandoned a *child*. I saw her." He dropped his arms. "And Alina," he stated, holding up the bracelet on his bruised wrist. "*Bozhevilnyi...*" he said, trembling fingers steadying the tiny letters. "That word means *crazy*, Nor. *Psychologically ill*." He tapped his fingertip upon his temple. "*She* even knew there was something wrong with me."

"Wh-*what*?" Norah stuttered. "That is not true," said Nor, defensive of his ugly assumptions of the sweet girl who adored him so. She could still see how Alina gawked and grinned at him with adoration and boundless love. "It can't be. There has to be more to it than that."

But onward, he plundered. "It was *my* job to sit alongside broken, dying people, and I tapped out because I was *tired*," he snapped, face crumpled with self-loathing.

She nearly wilted beneath his rising tone, but instead, Nor's sharp creases sharpened and grew defensive. "It's *my* job to sit alongside broken people too, Dexteras," she stated. "You don't think there are days I don't tap out because I'm fucking tired?"

"That's different," he said, his eyes bright and wild. "You still stay. Despite everything you've been through, *you* stay. You keep doing the work. I forfeited entirely."

"Do you remember the first day you *met* me?" she spat, mouth sputtering with scoffs of laughter. "Did you know I was drafting a resignation letter when you found me on that roof?" She shook her head as it flooded with visions of Cecil, adorning his strange cocktail of compassion and snarls whence speaking with Dex. She understood now why he was so annoyed by the old man's hardheadedness.

Now, it seemed Dex sensed her tall hackles and turned his head away, gripping a handful of his ivory hair.

"Whomever I belonged to, I left them to *rot* alone, Nor. That's why I feel empty. That's why I'm fading." His words broke into sobs, and he wiped his crinkled eyes upon a shirt sleeve and stood. "I was a coward," he wept. "Ever since then, I've been pieces, parts, but *never* whole, never enough."

Norah grabbed one of his clenched fists in hers and squeezed it like a hot stone. He did not uncoil it or relent at her touch.

"Dex. You. Are. Here. You exist, you're with me, and you're enough," she whispered. "You are *enough* for me. You are everything I could want to love and cherish in a friend. That's all the existing you need to do. Just be here." She pointed to the earth.

He shook his head, refusing to meet her stare. "The only reason I exist is because someone needed me so badly, they made me from nothing but their pain," his voice broke in great rumbles, as though a vehicle backfired in his chest. "Someone *gave me* my life, and I owed it back to her," he muttered, gripping the wood railing and biting down on the cigar in his teeth. "But I left her to die."

Norah dropped her hand from him, hit by the impact of his words. It struck her at the breastbone like a stone tomahawk, thudding against her heart.

His comments made her think of her dead father. Of her mother.

She winced, lit a cigar for herself, and stood beside him, gathering her soft tone as though nothing had disturbed the peace between them.

He twiddled with Alina's bracelet, catching his breath, his great shoulders heaving.

"When I was a kid," she began, squinting to see a small Norah Kestrel weeping and shaking in the confines of her mind, "I'd sing, I'd cry, I'd laugh, and I'd talk out loud, all the time, to absolutely no one. I begged someone would be there and hear me," she huffed. "Just to hear me. I'd beg for friends, for parents, for a dad…" She closed her eyes to avoid the burning smoke that licked her sore eyes and recalled those isolating moments beside Leonard. Those days when she competed for the role of his daughter as though it were a casting call, never making the part.

"Even if someone did come or could hear me," she mourned, "they wouldn't have been able to fix anything."

Smoke fanned Dex's features as he eyed her with a bloodshot iris.

"I used to struggle so *hard* with that," she muttered, grinding her teeth. "I used to wonder what in the *hell* that must mean about me, that I had no one to love me in the ways that I wanted."

Dexteras shook his head, eyes wrinkled and soft now.

But Norah shrugged and slapped her thighs. "And then, that day when I found out that Alina was about to die, all alone, and I couldn't find you, it clicked." She gave a weary smile. "If you and I hadn't gotten the gift of meeting her, of knowing her, she would still be the amazing, wonderful child she was." She bit her lip and stared deep into the woods. "And it wasn't until the next morning that I realized that applied to me too. If not a single damn soul loved me or knew me, or if I was brought into this world by people who didn't want me, I'd still be me, and it wouldn't mean shit."

She shrugged and allowed a slow, tight breath to slip through her lips. "I'd hurt so badly and my pain was so big, that it felt *impossible* to believe that no one could see me." Her throat closed in on her words with each swallow. "But after a lifetime of feeling so a-fucking-lone, I realized no one was coming to save me. And that was the most freeing truth I'd ever experienced." Norah took a hard pull on her cigar and shook her head.

"I've made the mistake of pitying young me for so long, but then I realized that she was actually a fucking badass," she huffed, understanding the satisfaction and justice that Cecil found in obscene language. "She'd dealt with so much and survived. She thrived, even."

Norah wiped her cheeks and turned to face him, strength returning to her voice. "I bet when you didn't come back for that girl, she had no choice but to create more of herself and keep going. And she was all the stronger for it. So don't you *dare* pity her."

Dex's eyelids fluttered with sincere consideration. The calculating cogs and sprockets of his mind ticked amongst the peace of the forest.

"Solus makes humans out to be weak and worthless, but we don't *need* anyone," she stated, almost in awe of the epiphany. "We want them, but we don't need them," she said. "Which means that *you* don't survive on being needed either. You've been alive for decades, running on your strength and will alone, and I think that terrifies the fuck out of Solus," she said, standing to her feet to stretch. "It means there's a world out there where *they* aren't needed."

They remained silent for several moments amidst that discomfort. Dex cleared his throat with heavy swallows of cold coffee and vanished their cigar butts into a magical void. Eventually, without further prodding into their grief, they stood. Dex swung her pack onto his spine before she could grab it. They resumed their travels.

Nor leaned into his shoulder, shoving him gently.

He bent close and kissed the top of her head before falling to the back of their caravan, following from a cautious distance to ruminate.

They crossed handmade wooden bridges, through towering pines, past humbling distant mountains, and amongst singing tree creatures. Their climb careened upwards, requiring a frantic scramble along dusty, crumbling bedrock. The path twisted up the cliff, leaving them to grasp tree roots, branches, and one another's firm grip. Jays hollered their vast songs, and papery leaves whispered. Honeysuckle and black birch emitted waves of aromatic, woodsy fragrances that deepened their breathing.

The trail narrowed into pinching squeeze walls composed of massive rock formations. Slate gray stone rose high and carved a narrow aisle for them.

They emerged from the rocky embrace and pulled one another up to a plateau at the end of their trail.

Norah breathed heavy lungfuls of open air and grinned.

They stood before a gorgeous, towering arch of thick slate and limestone.

It reminded her of an interstate bridge carved entirely of rock. Miraculous tree roots snaked and stretched betwixt the rocks and towards the sun. The top of the arch served repelling needs, whilst below it shaded a cavern filled with smooth boulders. Various craters and pockets along the arch were filled with stacked pebble piles created by travelers.

With her mother, Norah's younger self had once piled those colorful stones as a clumsy child, stones scraping and careening with fierce winds, childish tears welling with frustration for their failed attempts.

And eventually, a much older version of that child returned solemnly of her own accord to pile these towers with much more learned and tired fingers, patient and willing to balance anything aside from her needs. To find a quiet retreat in the forest, surrounded by life, a respite from the brick town rich with the death of her lineage.

The view through the legs of the arch carried on for countless miles until it kissed a horizon line of purple, silvery mountain peaks. Endless treetops stuffed the expanse in golds, greens, and reds like thick, meringue drops.

Norah's cheeks ached from smiling, eyes fixated on the far-flung pinnacles. She inhaled the greenery and sandstone around her and spun to see where Dex's eyes had fallen amongst the landscape.

He was a few paces behind, silver jaw shining with dappled sun. His eyes flickered with tears. He was staring at her, a wobbling choke in his throat.

But he smiled.

She returned it with a sad tilt of her head and rushed to embrace him. His beard soaked his tears like a sponge and painted her arm in salty strokes. She stretched her arms to collect him as fully as she could.

After a moment, she took him by the hand and led him to the lookout's furthest ledge. She knew his heart longed for heights just as it longed for the stars.

A thick rock jutted from the ledge, offering enough foothold for one. Miles below, the forest swayed and danced. She had to tear her eyes from its hypnotic rhythm to avoid succumbing to its trance.

"It's called Stargazer's Sovereign," she whispered, releasing his hand and nodding towards the stone shelf with a bold brow.

After returning to Corvid, she'd crept this narrow mantle on the days she was feeling particularly hollow. Its descent rushed her with hot adrenaline, reminding her that she had things to fight for, and reasons to stay grounded. She reflected on how cataclysm could calibrate one's worldview.

Bundled tufts of scruff rose at Dex's cheeks. He rubbed his eyes and stepped onto the ledge. The leather toes of his boots curled over the arch's rim and his fingers spread at his sides to clutch at the winds. His hair billowed behind in shining ivory waves.

Despite her held breath, Nor couldn't deny how gallant he seemed, trusting the wind as though it were a dear friend. As though his skin was stitched with its freedom and his veins were filled with the imperfect galaxies that Galileo had spoken of.

"You're here, Dex."

46

⋆DEXTERAS⋆

He helped Norah set up her tent and collect stones and kindling for a fire pit. They built a quaint campsite beneath the stony arch. She politely offered him a bed roll and sleeping bag, but he denied them with a shake of his pounding skull.

She dispersed beers and cigars between them as they leaned across the smoldering wood. Nor cooked hotdogs on a stick he'd sharpened, and they immersed themselves in the quiet of the evening. Screech owls trilled above. Tree branches creaked and ached while the wind stretched their limbs. The sky was an immaculate cosmic indigo, struck with millions of dazzling white electric stars. He recognized constellations and celestial bodies he'd never seen with the naked eye prior.

He attempted to remain present with Norah to best seize his remaining time with her while he could still hold to her and himself. But that predatory heat still lay dormant in his chest, the sleeping Hellfire that promised retribution.

"*Amica mea*, you said you begged for someone to talk to when you were young? A father?"

The fire danced in her green eyes as they searched him.

"What would you talk to your dad about if he was here?"

Her cheeks rounded. "He wasn't much of a talker, so I wouldn't even know where I'd begin." She poked at embers with her stick.

"What would you talk about with *a* dad then?" he tried.

"A vague dad?" she said, a grin bouncing in her voice.

"Yes, I suppose, a vague dad. That you belonged to."

"That I belonged to…." The words lingered with intimacy on her breath. She fidgeted with her tiny ponytail and then with a branch of sappy pine needles from their kindling pile.

"I'd want to teach him about the things I love. Earl Grey tea with oat milk and honey," she squinted at the stone above and the fiery shadows that danced against it.

"What else?"

She grinned. "I'd make sure he knew that I like tight hugs. That my favorite plant is a monstera. My favorite color is black. That I cry when I'm angry." She shrugged. "Is that normal stuff dads know?"

He couldn't help but smile, seeing her eyes widen with childish wonder. She deserved to feel like a daughter. To be loved unconditionally by a parent.

"I don't think fatherhood is about normalcy, *amica mea*. I think it's about what's healthy."

"That's fair. There's just too many things I'd have to say."

He hummed, for he, too, had endless questions for his Maker.

The black ocean of sky deepened, brightening the stars until they twinkled with life and illuminated the full white moon like a shining coin.

He pretended not to notice, but with each errand she'd run around the campsite, whether picking up branches, tossing them in the flames, or rearranging a stone around their pit, she would sit nearer and nearer to him each time.

Eventually, Norah fell asleep against his arm, dark hairs fanning softly against him, smelling of campfire and lavender oils. He smiled for such a gift, such unworthy love. He sighed and kissed the top of her head and helped her to her tent. Eyes still closed, she cussed and swore that she wasn't even tired and was only meditating.

Once her heart rate returned to its resting rate, he walked the arch's ridgeline until his surroundings were entirely black and silent. Until he wasn't certain if his eyes were open or closed, leaving silhouettes to dart about his vision. Until muttering voices found him on the wind. Until there were moments so numb and silent, he was uncertain if he was alive or dead. He stared into the darkness for hours.

✦

"It all hurts so damn much."

"You could end it, and the pain would be finished…."

"You're invisible anyways. What would it matter if you were gone?"

"She will die…."

"No one could touch you again, and you would hurt no one else."

"You could disappear and not feel it. Be gone."

He returned to his present self, uncertain as to how much time had passed. Clenching his scalp in exhausted fistfuls, he tilted his ear towards the beating hum of Norah's heart beneath the stone canopy.

These can't be The Voices. Norah is here.

And then, he heard their campfire embers sizzle and swell. He turned slowly on his leather boots to the warming fire pit.

A ghostly smoke cloud twisted from its coals, unraveling in sinewy strands, stretching with sentient life. The serpent stretched and strained and wound as though it intended to hunt and consume the stars. But as it kissed the arch's rocky ceiling, it rounded its pointed head down at him. White glassy eyes gleamed from its skull.

He hadn't any time to run before the smoky beast lunged for him.

He fell and tripped to his rear in the dirt and the great massive snake crashed into his chest. Its smoky tendrils filled him and surrounded him, wrapping about his ankles and knees, swirling around him until it constricted his throat. He saw nothing but the blackness. It wrapped his skull like a venomous asp and hissed:

"No matter where you run Dexteras, you will leech from her until she is empty."

The smoke strands hardened like steel cords, pressing his limbs against him as they had in his memories.

They were so strong, and he was so exhausted.

The serpent's tongue flicked his ear lobe, alight with hisses.

"You're a *Figment*, Dexteras. You are not bound to a bodily form." They grazed his cheeks like a lover and whispered in his other ear. "You too, may vanish as you please and whisper on the wind. You are nothing, thus you can become nothingness. Come home son, and let your Paraclete live in human peace."

To Dex's horror, a silver, vaporous mold of Norah Kestrel poured before him in the inky dark. It was evidently his friend by her sharp cheeks and cropped hair. The narrow bones of her shoulders breathing with bright light.

"But should you attempt to carry on with this charade, your hunger will only grow. Your body will weaken. You'll become feral, dying, and desperate. Like an animal, you'll sniff her out and consume all of her that you can. Once The Unbecoming takes you, you will have no mind, only an empty shell of a body, hungry for human Purpose," they warned. "You're already another burden she must bear, yet another broken mind she must serve. You'll either die of exhaustion, despising each other, or..."

A silvery hand snaked from the darkness towards the silhouetted Norah. Its fingernails clacked like the tail of a scorpion before stabbing through her, stealing the luminous white heart from her breast. Hot, misty, lifeblood steamed from the organ in plumes as the girl collapsed to the ground with a silent scream, shot down like a falling star.

Dex broke through the binds and fell to the place where she'd puddled and disappeared. Tears tumbled from his eyes as he clutched to the stone beneath him.

A hot, spidery hand ran up his neck and across his jaw to the long scar carved by the old Figment's leg. The touch was icy like Rigor Mortis of a corpse on an autopsy table. They pressed their fingers to it with a breathy moan and stepped into his bloodstream without permission. His eyes flickered back into his skull unwillingly, at the mercy of whatever memory Solus so wished to take him to.

"All you have ever done is watched them die, Dexteras. You help no one."

✦

He was torn from the night and the campfire to a dark home. Immediately, he sensed its air was panicked and chaotic. As his eyes adjusted, he could see he was tucked in a tiny, ivory bathroom.

A brown-haired, wiry teen was pressing her spine against the wooden door, feet braced against the base of a sink. She wore similarly narrow bones and feline features as the older woman he'd seen in his prior memory. But this child gritted her teeth beneath tides of long brown hair that surpassed her waist. Her hazel eyes were wide and fiery, alight with a fervor the adult woman hadn't possessed. He understood within a blink that this was her child.

The teen was in a fleece hoodie and leggings, but trembled, wincing with the slurred, drunken shouts of an adult man and woman that roared from another room of the house. The caustic air in this memory was red like amber, heaving the distant scream to mere muffles.

The teen reached her limbs farther across the bathroom, pushing until Dex was certain her knees would fracture.

"Please!" hollered a man, rooms away. "You're making things worse, you're scaring her!"

A shuffle of bodies and crashing glassware resounded.

"No! No wait!" he cried.

BANG.

One solitary gunshot resounded against the halls.

The shivering teen screamed and covered her ears, cries echoing off the yellowing tile and bath. Her tears fell like steady streams. She had been the infant in the trailer home. This had to be at least twelve years since that memory.

Dex reached a tender hand to the child's shoulder, but she trembled with chills in response to his flesh. He pulled from her in shame and straightened with a sigh, stepping through the bathroom door towards the outer threats.

He crept silently, eyes dashing into the dark rooms, noticing the occasional flash of cocktail glasses and bar spoons scattered upon tiny tables. Some were tipped, spilling sticky brown liquor onto the rug. As with their last home, there were no photographs on the walls, no sign of coziness or safety, of thriving. Simply essential, human existence. It was small and tended to, a bit larger from whence they'd come.

He stepped towards a dimly lit dining area whose countertops were littered with beer bottles, colorful liquors, and opened jars of olives and cherries, some opened and decaying. The stench of alcohol was nearly enough to make Dexteras drunk himself.

CRASH.

A deafening clatter of glass exploded on the floor, sending glittering pieces scratching the wood floor toward his feet.

The woman before him had clearly aged and grown sick. She was on the floor again, muttering to her kneecaps, begging for something whilst her fingers were lost in her hair.

Dex's attention dashed to the pistol beside her, cocked at the ready and shining in the dark. It was then, too, that he noticed the bullet hole in the floor, just by her hip.

"Listen, love, please," breathed a man's voice from the dark.

Dex spun to face his past self again, who sat atop a coffee table several feet away, leering in the pitch black with calm and collected features. His fingers were outstretched towards the young woman, now likely in her thirties or so.

"Walk away from the gun. Go find your daughter, Rose, she needs you," he said, breath held, limbs reaching. He, too, was captured with shakes of delirium tremens, riddled with withdrawals and exhaustion. It was obvious that as her Figment, he shared in her fate. His voice was unrecognizable, slurred, and weary, gruff and hoarse with shouting.

Her body was slick with sweat, making the faded bird and nest tattooed on her ankle glisten. It'd become faded and blotchy, much like his own ink.

Younger Dexteras tripped from the dark and eased beside her now, wincing and trembling. He touched her arm and eased his lips beside her earlobe to whisper.

Watching the odd pair crouch and croon, Dexteras could nearly sense the connection between them. He wanted to reach out and pluck the golden, sparkling thread between them and watch its metal shutter. It was an old, old bond that showed age with crunching rust, but it was a relentless lifeline that kept them tethered. It allowed their bones to rattle together, their hearts to pound as one, and their bloodstreams to both be poisoned and drunk. Despite his younger self's glassy stare, he was trying, but it was getting him nowhere.

Her tears began falling harder, and bigger moans built in her chest. She closed her eyes and shook her head, chaos building within.

The face of the old man at her ear began to fall grim and dark.

"No, no, no, no…" she whispered.

"Love," he began, voice delicate, raspy, soft.

"I can't, I can't…"

"Listen, listen to me," he said.

But she couldn't, she wouldn't hear him. Her fingers itched and reached for the pistol, petting its silver with her sweaty skin.

"Love, I'm here, listen to me, listen *please*…" he begged, voice breaking. He lurched forward to hold the gun down, but she jerked it through his skin.

He truly was a ghost.

"Rose, she needs you," snarled his past self, a weary, burned-out fervor in his voice.

"I'm sorry…" she wept, "I'm so sorry." She was begging for the mercy of someone not in the room, or perhaps of some unheard voice in her skull. It could be detox or medication-induced hallucinations or maybe it was her keen sense of the being at her side. Either way, she fumbled to turn the barrel towards her chest, centering it above her breastbone.

"No!" screamed both Dexteras of the past and present, hands outstretched for their Corporeal, desperate to be heard and seen and felt.

She closed her eyes and her sweaty thumbs slipped against the trigger…

"NO!"

The memory went black like a cut film reel.

✦

"*Esto quod est*," hissed Solus. *Be what you are.* Their cold hands quickly pulled Dexteras back to the woods, back to the cold, back into the wild loneliness of the world. He shivered with the sudden transition.

The smoggy asps of Solus' fingers swept across his cheeks, spilling from his nostrils like cigar smoke. Then, the wisps spun and plunged into the campfire's blackened pyre, leaving Dexteras completely alone.

His forehead weighed immensely, like a brick shackled to his neck, and forced his skull down against the dusty stone. A cold chilly wind tossed his hair from his sweating neck at Solus' leave. And only when he heard the tiny *pit-pat-pat* of his tears falling to the rock, did he become aware of their existence.

You are nothing…let your Paraclete live in human peace.

Every second he spent beside Norah Kestrel was perilous.

They'd survived today, but what of tomorrow? He'd grow more dangerous, more hungry. And as he darkened, her heart would only break more.

He remembered now that the first time he'd laid eyes upon her had been the first time anyone had ever truly laid eyes upon him in twenty years.

No one saw you before her. Thus it's fitting you should disappear without her.

His fingertips rubbed against one another and then trailed against the silk waves of his hair. The scabbed, folded skin of his face. Could he truly become intangible? So fibrous that the wind could tear his body to pieces?

He was of the same condemned cloth as Solus.

And it would spare her.

She'd never need to cling to recollections of his leave, nor the gruesome details of his transformation into a starved Figment. There would be no vivid memories of his death. He could simply be absent and minimize her grievances.

It was the only way he could simultaneously deny his darkness and spare Norah the grief of his tangible loss.

To not be.

To finally abandon all raison d'être...

He closed his eyes and imagined his body as the exoskeleton of a locust, flaking and dry. He daydreamed horrendous visions of what nothingness may feel like. Akin to the cut of a knife so sharp, it was barely felt, he allowed worthlessness to slowly carve the meat from his skin until his flesh was thin and transparent. Until the moonlight showed through him like papyrus.

It was easier than he'd thought, seeing as his dexterity for nonexistence returned to him with ease, as well-tuned as Stellato. He rode its mournful rhythms with aptitude, chipping and chewing at his innards like an insect at dead wood. Tearing at pieces of himself to toss upon the fire.

He meditated on nothingness for hours, until his senses were tingling, stinging, vibrating, numb. Until his breath wasn't physiological, but instead a waxing contraction of atmosphere, like the swarms of starlings they'd watched on Norah's roof, suspended, contorting, endless, still, and yet morphing with coordinated energy.

But surely, not nearly as beautiful.

He wandered as translucent dust particles, rotating against the day's new light as minuscule shards, spinning like glitter, catching on fire when the sun struck his face. Nothing was concrete.

Ego sum nihi...

✦

At some point, the pieces of his body shifted and shook with an exchange of temperature. The vibrations of sound churned his atoms, but it did not stir his hibernation.

✦

The dainty jingle of a tent zipper shuddered his bones, followed by the soft, pattering of bare toes on stone. His vision was murky, shifting, multifaceted and fractious like the eyes of a nearly dead housefly.

But he didn't need to see Norah Kestrel to know she was near.

The thin sheet of his diaphanous form held its breath, even when her own intermingled with his shards and threatened his composure.

But her eyes passed across him as though he were but a smudge on the distant horizon, a ghost through a lens.

"Dex?" she whispered, condensation leaving her lips in the cool dawn.

His molecules ground their teeth. Her song pulled at the taut strings between them.

How long could he linger between nothingness and heartbreak?

Her love was the closest to salvation he'd ever come, but it was not his to have. He was given a chance to be worthy decades ago and wasted it when discomfort bit at his heels.

You are nothing.
You are no one.
You are not here.
Let her go.

✦

The sinews of his muscles and bones unlaced. It was initially painful, like the slow tear of flesh, like the vibrating pulse of a tattoo gun or a sewing machine un-stitching him strand by strand.

He allowed himself his tears to keep from screaming. They spilled into the air as dense humidity, kissing her cheeks, her forehead.

Norah's evergreen eyes were also glossy, and she wiped at her cheeks.

Dex shredded his pieces like tissue paper until his tearing wounds exchanged for numbness, formlessness.

Euphoric nothingness.

But as Norah pivoted to leave, her arm swept through the air space that was once his. Her fingers slashed through him like a shock of sleet, nearly killing him with its cutting cold. His muscles and bones suddenly remembered that they were being ripped apart, and a grounding pain stung his flesh like thousands of paper cuts soaked in lemon juice.

He suppressed a scream, though he wasn't certain it would even be possible to scream.

Norah gawked into the void where their arms had brushed.

Surely she couldn't decipher the sensation as himself?

You are not here.

You are not here.

But to his horror, she extended a daring hand toward him.

It lingered at his sternum, then breached the molecules that had once been his chest, dipping beneath his skin, vessels, blood, and bones. It was the cutting sensation of Cecil's shrike magic, but much gentler, much quieter, and much more healing.

Her hand reached until it grazed his dying heart, and the vaporous organ shuddered alive against her touch eagerly.

Traitor, he sneered at it.

His tears spilled as she grazed against his pieces, each burning with unbearable vividness. Existence. The quivering cardiac muscle churned the airspace around her again, reaching for her hand like a panicked insect.

Dex gasped and shuffled back towards the mantle's edge, bits of stone crumbling beneath him. They stopped their dance, a breath from the outlook's ledge. Waves of greenery roared below. He considered it in desperation but knew that fall would not kill him. He'd tried jumping twenty years ago.

Norah then turned to face him fully, to inspect the air. She traced his silhouette, lips fixed in awe, prying and poking with scientific wonder. She followed the rugged crook of his nose and the brambles of his beard and unruly waves. She could not see him, but her fingers discovered the feel of him with gentle brush strokes, shirking dust from his buried statue. Surely an archaeological dig of a most disappointing nature.

Her head fell into that sweet tilt she gave when she beheld something with heartache.

"You're here..." She touched his shoulder, fingers soft and traveling through as though he were a shadow.

Amica mea. Please stop.

"Please let me see you. You're here. I know you are."

His knees buckled with want. He wished to meet her gaze and watch it smile and rest, but he couldn't. He was so close. So damn close.

"Be here with me Dex," she whispered.

It'd been the only request she'd ever made of him, to just be. But even in this simplest of tasks, he'd let her down.

She waded through the silence with great expectation and the maddening finesse of a mental health professional. But after a few empty moments that nearly tore him to pieces, she bowed her head, accepting defeat.

Unable to disappear even behind the lids of his eyes, he found himself praying for a strong gale to scatter him until he was the air she breathed. But the skies were at their stillest and most unmoving, spitefully so.

Let me go. Let me go. Let me go, he begged.

But then, Norah's heart rate quickened.

He paddled through molecules to find her through the endless, mirroring refractions.

Her eyes held him without effort, without searching. Though she couldn't see him, she *saw him*. A tear slipped down her reddened features, sniffing with the early morning cold.

How he wished he could hear her thoughts and understand what that humming heart was conjuring.

"We need to feel these things, Dex. We have to quit running," she whispered, eyeing the distant, green peaks with longing.

And then, without warning, in a swirl of dark hair and canvas coat, Norah spun and dropped back into the morning, arms spread like wings, falling with the grace and confidence of a sparrow. Her dark features and lashes were swallowed in thick hair and blinding sun as she leaned back to free-fall from the rocky mantle into the abyss below.

Flashbacks of spilled blood and breaking limbs darted across his vision. The horrid crunching, jarring of his bones. His nothingness spilled for all to see.

Violent adrenaline gripped his limbs. They rushed with cold. He would not see her break as he broke.

Like a snapped rubber band, he lunged after her falling body, forcing his particles to reassemble, rebuttal crying from his throat as his flesh was restitched together like Frankenstein's monster.

His hand found hers before she'd registered seventy degrees into the descent. He held her before her toes had entirely left the rocks. Scar to scar, the sidereal iron in his veins magnetically found her body before he'd fully found his own. He held to her as though he was made to do so. Anything, anything, *anything* to keep Norah Kestrel from becoming as dead as he felt.

They were impossibly bent into the skies like tree limbs. His outstretched hand anchored their axis whilst Norah wrapped herself around him like a silken coat, dropping her forehead into his shoulder.

"There you are," she said into his chest.

He set her to firm footing where she trotted from the ledge with his momentum. He affixed his own footing only to be dizzied by waves of grief and relief. Tides of nausea, horror, exhaustion, and undoing. And uncertain of what else to do, he stumbled to his rear and wept into his hands.

He'd been so close.

His sobs shook the earth beneath him.

Can't even die properly.

The cold stream of her touch wrapped around him in moments, fingertips tracing his sensation filled-filled skin.

"I'm sorry. I'm so sorry," she whispered. "I'm sorry. That was an awful, selfish thing to do. I know. I just… I'm not going to lose you. Not like that. You think you could be forgotten so easily?" She squeezed him, keeping him present, keeping him prisoner to the pain. She kept embracing him at his shoulders, his biceps, his back. She made to reach for his trembling fingertips, but he gently stopped her at her wrists.

"Please don't," he muttered, refusing to look at her. His body screamed and burned and ached and shook. Everything was needles and cutting pain.

"It's too much. I'm feeling too much."

Respectfully, she folded her hands to her lap and nodded.

He wiped his eyes and sniffed, feeling ugly and weak, old and decrepit as he gasped for breath. A dying man who'd run away from any discomfort or worth or meaning. A coward.

"It *hurts* to be here, Norah." His voice broke without repair, scratching like a snapped violin string. "I thought I'd lost you and…" he glanced to the ledge, then clenched his brow, praying he'd vanish into the sunlight. Into dust.

But it was impossible to retreat into the nothingness with her eyes upon him. He could feel her gaze pour over every inch of him.

"All I think about is the burden I've been, the pain I've caused. The others who sh-sh-should be alive who are so much more worthy than me." His breathing grew shallow. "I'm s-s-so tired of *being*," he begged, as though she could take that from him. It wasn't fair, but it burst from his lips like the pleas of a scared boy. He cursed the heart that refused to decay in his chest and rested his eyes in his hands. The world was blinding and bright in comparison to the nothingness he was torn from.

Nor sat still and silent beside him, allowing him to disassociate and collect his breaths. To experience his hurting bones and heartache.

Again, the ancient pains of age throbbed at his joints and crumbling body. His shoulders and eyelids drooped with exhaustion, having no more to give. His knees, hips, shoulders and neck swelled with the inflammation of human existence.

They remained in his shame-filled silence, burdening his dearest friend as he always had. He felt himself inwardly running away, mentally clawing through the dark fog of his agony. He hoped to lose himself there until his skin fell off his bones.

"Can you please help me with something?" she whispered, voice soft like rustling crops.

He remained a moment, fighting gruesome visions of her split body impaled on the tree line below.

But she was quite alive, as evident by the heart thumping in her chest and the reaching fingertips she still offered him. She was alive.

He winced and slowly took her hand. He was dragged to his feet and sat before the warm fire pit that scared the cold from his bones. She rewarded his efforts with a smile and a kiss on his scruffy cheek. Norah unpacked clanging metal tools quietly from her bag and sat beside him. Every movement she made was slow, making a grand effort to be silent and sparing of his senses. She put the tools before him.

His heavy eyes knew the apparatuses well. His tongue watered unwillingly.

Traitor. Traitor. Traitor.

"I bought these years ago for camping," she admitted, "But I have no idea how to use them. Can you please show me?"

He couldn't look at her without seeing her corpse in his head. The dead she could've been, the dead *he* should've been. And he knew what she was doing now. He knew she felt him running into the woods of his mind, clawing through the dark to outrun what he'd done.

But after a moment, he reached for the glass French Press, rings tapping along its silver fittings like a veteran petting his prized pistol. It was foolish, but he felt an empty distraction in simply knowing what to do and how to operate the small machine without thought or emotion. It allowed him to feel some sense of control. Competence.

He inspected a slim hand-grinder, steel with a ceramic blade, cool against his palms. It disassembled in his calloused hands with the same natural flow of a weapon in a soldier's grip. He poured dry coffee beans into his hand, clacking like the beads on Alina's bracelet. He doubled the rations, still learning to make coffee for two. He spun the grinder's handle, rumbling beneath his hands as it clacked like a gemstone tumbler. He allowed his eyes to rest on the far-flung mountains he'd nearly succumbed to as the machine shook in his grip.

Aromatics flooded his nostrils and rolled on his palette. It was earthy, like tobacco. Nutty with subtle caramel. He pinched the grinds between his fingers, coarse and sharp like sea salt. They pattered into the glass body of the press like the sands in an hourglass.

He winced, remembering his own hourglass had nearly been emptied into the winds not moments prior.

Nor filled a small kettle and sat it near the embers. She fumbled with a lighter, begging it to lap at a fire starter.

Dex eyed her over the French Press and snapped his fingers. With a spark of life, the fire caught with ease.

The dark-haired girl grinned at him with sparkling hope.

Grateful that she no longer wept for his dead hide, his cheeks flushed with heat. Though he was still washed in bodily pain, his magic was rekindled by her need for him. And besides, he knew brewing in his bones, like he knew boxing.

The kettle screamed, steam peeling into the blue skies where it spread thin and disappeared. He was briefly jealous of their escape but shook his head, torn from thought by the redolence of the freshly-ground beans. Rich. Citrusy.

Much to Norah's horror, he took the hot kettle from the fire and into his hands, assessing its temperature. His calluses and scabs slid across the metal fixture, determining its readiness and soothing his hardened scars. It did burn like hell, but that warmth grounded him like the whir of a tattoo gun on an elbow.

He poured it into the French Press and counted the minutes down in his head. He'd known from decades of practice that it required approximately the time it took him to name six hundred and thirty-one stars.

Norah respected his still focus in silence.

He pressed the piston into the black ocean of beans, filtering the elixir of its sludge. It was poured into their jars and taken to the ledge for them to imbibe before the rising sun. Norah showed no worry, mistrust, or concern for their nearness to the descent that'd almost taken them both.

Thankfully, they were just Norah and Dex again, as always.

He sipped. Dark cacao and bursts of orange peel ebbed on his tongue. Foam crackled against his mustache. His cheeks strained with a small, unnatural smile, his body betraying him again.

The resulting weightlessness in his skull was neither good nor bad. But in the momentary distraction of hot coffee, his once terrified skull remembered with sobering clarity: he'd just tried to take his life, his existence. He was going to commit suicide, death by depression.

The rare and present moment snapped the chain on his consciousness, commanding it to heel. The feral dogs that were his thoughts snarled and bit but now cowered home, docile and domesticated, tails tucked and ribs wheezing.

I almost left her like everyone else had.

A tear raced down his cheek with shame. He prayed she wouldn't see.

She laid her head into his bicep. "It's okay."

"I'm sorry," he whispered.

"You have no reason to be sorry. You're here right now, and that's all I wanted."

47

✦NORAH✦

WELL. WHAT A COMPLETE, FUCKING DISASTER, she grieved

The change of scenery was supposed to give him peace and rest. Instead, it'd nearly killed the both of them.

They didn't talk for the entire morning and instead drank their coffees and watched the horizon grow golden with autumnal tones. The rocks around them warmed and made them both exhausted and heavy-lidded. Neither of them had rested adequately in days, it seemed.

They adventured about the immediate terrain, walking strange paths, peeking after scuffling tiny noises in the brush, and even drawing on the large boulders with bits of wood singed from the fire pit. She'd sketched some charcoal crows, and Dex sketched a profile portrait of her whilst she did so. Throughout the entire afternoon and early evening, they were silent. Occasionally, he'd share with her the ghost of a grin, but still said nothing. They needed the quiet, its safety. Its time to think of everything or nothing.

In solace, Norah walked the trails with her collapsible binoculars, scouting blue nuthatch birds skittering up the bark of trees like insects with their quick and fevered movements. Her feet carried her half a mile off course further than expected, and by the time she returned to Dexteras beneath the massive stone archway, he was clutching another cup of coffee against his mustache. Likely his fourth or fifth of the day.

They kindled the fire back to life and she warmed a can of chicken and rice soup beside it patiently. Still, they did not speak and only exchanged small, fragile smiles and deep sighs. She ate her soup beside him at the fire, watching papery moths chase the flame's rays that bounced off surrounding stones. She drank one, two, three beers. Dexteras denied her every offer for his own.

Drastic, ghostly shadows stretched behind their crouched forms before the fire as they watched the sky bleed into cotton candy hues.

The entire time, some part of Norah touched Dexteras. Whether it was her knee against his, or their elbows brushing. Or, as the sun fell low and the world turned cool, her tired head against his shoulder.

I can't lose him. Please, don't let me lose him, too.

Her gut flipped and flopped within her. She'd nearly been entirely alone all over again. There were no proper words to describe the cramp of anticipatory grief that had bent her in half. And selfishly enough, it wasn't just the agony of never having coffee with him or waking to him on her roof again. It was the deep ache to have a semblance of family after difficult days. After amazing days.

A deep, ancient fear flickered in the dark cove of her chest. A fear that reminded her, in the end, everyone would leave her. They always did.

Her chest swelled and stitched tight, remembering their ache. Recalling just how much of her insides that anxiety had rotted away of her.

She couldn't beg him to stay for her sake. She couldn't ask him not to chase the answers he craved. She could only rest her head on his wide shoulder and let her drunken, sloshing, thoughts numb her into a restless, twitching sleep.

"Jay Bird. Just wanted to say I'm sorry for everything that's happened. I love you and I always will. Thank you, honey. Bye."

Norah jolted awake, limbs tight and trembling. Her face and chest were impossibly hot as though she'd abused a bottle of cheap wine all on her lonesome. She wiped her eyes and found tears there, cold by the breeze, some old and dried, others fresh and pouring. A fevered, hot anxiety simmered beneath her skin that reminded her of being eight years old again.

"Thank you, honey. Bye," echoed the warbled voice in her skull, distorted, old, and antiqued as though it'd croaked from a radio dredged from a shipwreck, garbled with seawater and deteriorating hardware. It made her shiver and feel suddenly very alone.

Dex.

She needn't look far for him. Dex was still beside her, watching her with wide, watering blue eyes. His hand was in hers, clutched so tightly, his bruised knuckles were white. Their palms were sticky and taut from the hours of holding one other.

Disheveled hairs had fallen into his face, framing his parted, bruised lips. He, too, looked as though he'd been awakened from a horrid nightmare. But he now beheld Nor with *pity*. The pity she was certain she wore once, after reading his file. A pity she'd never seen him wear around her. His fingers squeezed hers gently in affirmation.

"Bye," teased the warped voice again in her skull. It turned her blood cold.

And with the sobering clarity of a pumped shotgun at her spine, Norah tore her peeling hands from Dex's and backpedaled onto her feet. She stared down at him as though she'd never seen him.

His outstretched hand remained open, reaching for her. It was the palm that was scarred and tattooed. The understanding of what had happened drowned her in nausea.

Their matching scars had been touching whilst she slept.

What had he seen and heard amidst her unconscious, untethered thoughts? Her nightmares and dreams?

Her backward steps were trained and unfeeling like those of a schoolchild in a fire drill. Her head ached with the pressure of the deep ocean, all the while, a high-pitched ringing squealing in her ears like an unnatural violin note. She winced.

"Love," Dex mouthed softly, a sweet, careful note that begged her to come back to him.

But her face was ablaze and trembling with dismissive shakes. No. *No.* *Oh God, what had he seen?*

"Nor…" he whispered so gently, it barely rose above the crackles of the fire. Still, his fingers reached for her.

She could hear very little above the shrill ringing that reverberated in her skull. Its screeching, blinding pulse pressed at the back of her eye. The therapist heard her own voice mutter worlds away, as though buried underground.

"I-I-I can't…"

His eyes blanketed her in a tragic hum that seeped from him and the surrounding stone with such viscosity, it threatened to suffocate her. Her heart thundered in her chest like an oncoming train. He made the smallest motion to stand, his bones popping loudly.

Dex's eyes searched her with eyes that had sought her for millennia, and she was certain they'd never *truly* seen her until this very moment. Not fully. Not quite this broken and pathetic. His great tattooed hands rose and reached for her as though she were a feral animal about to take off running on a broken leg.

A brief, nauseating compulsion to embrace him lit her blood. She wished to be squeezed by him until her ribs shattered and her lungs flapped with sharp gasps.

He knows. He knows. He knows.

But she knew not even the large man's immortal strength could hold her pieces together. She'd only slip through his fingers like crushed crystal, and the pain of weighing him with her grief would only make hers seven-fold.

She shook before him, uncertain how her entire world had just come to an end in mere seconds.

You can't fix this. You can't fix this. You can't fix this, her eyes warned him.

He steadied on a crackling knee and dared again to reach towards her, eyes softening and understanding as if to say, *I know. I know, amica mea.*

But she was still shaking her head, answering his endless, unspoken questions.

Those blue eyes narrowed, begging her not to do what she did next. Hoping she'd deny the deep animalistic want of her brain's amygdala that shook her limbs.

But still, she ran.

She spun and sprinted, flinging cloudy plumes of the campsite's soft earth in her wake. She climbed and leaped atop the towering, defensive boulders. She skittered into the tree line of snatching, scraping branches and crackling limbs and leaves, skittering against the dewy earth.

She felt she was conquering miles in her breathless bounds, wheezing, gasping, and tightly wound as if she were stuffed with springs. Shrubbery and plant life were crushed in each merciless stride. Not a single thought could catch up to her skull in her chase. Albeit the occasional:

"Bye."

She slipped and skidded on her heels and rear down endless, dark embankments, pushing off of scratching bark and the sappy arms of pines. She dug through dense greenery and dark honey locust bushes teething with thorns, trudging until she was swallowed by invasive plant life in all directions. Reaching, leggy vines and needled burs clutched at her clothes.

She stopped suddenly, radiant hills of golden leaves and pine needles arching before her. She gasped, feeling that pressure in her gut, her chest, and her throat catch up. It left her clutching her splitting throat as though she were about to erupt with sobs, prayers, and screams.

That's when the flashbacks began. Vivid memories skipped across her vision with the jarring scratch of a vinyl record. With each, the hairs on her arms raised and her breach dropped to her gut like a stone.

She saw her mother. Smiling. Golden, curly permed hair, wearing a thick, stitched sweater. They laughed at something on TV.

She and her mother sang loud songs in the car with warbling notes. They were lying in Robin's king-sized bed, reading novels, exchanging scoffs and quotes with time.

She hadn't thought of these scenes in ages. They'd been buried and unheard. Armored with a bulletproof fence and razor wire.

Nor took off sprinting once more.

Amongst the aimless stumbling, a cord of cockled brambles wound at Nor's knee, shredding her leggings to threads. She caught herself on the corrugated bark of a nearby Hawthorn tree before tumbling to the woodland floor, palms flayed and bright with dirty blood.

She thought of Dex in the supply closet, fists clenched and shaking. She remembered the impossible divot he'd left in the dense wall.

A hot surge of energy made her snatch the briars from her bleeding leg, tearing the fibers from her pants. The stings of nettles primed her hunger to feel more.

She squared up to the old tree and pulled back a fist. With an ugly, breaking scream, she struck the bark, making contact with the wrong fingers first.

"Pointer and middle," Dex had once instructed beside the heavy bag in his basement. *"Not ring and pinkie. Those will break and give you Boxer's Fractures."*

But she didn't care. She struck it again, begging to break. Her flesh made a pathetic thudding sound like that of a bug to a windshield.

"Fuck!" she cried, bones burning with agonizing regret.

How infuriating that her strength couldn't match her rage.

Never enough.

Never enough.

Never enough.

It'll never be enough.

Her bony fists continued bludgeoning the bark, filling her scraped knuckles with splinters. The meek sound of flesh on lumber made her hotter, more ravenous, more dissatisfied.

She struck harder and harder and harder until each digit was skinned and crimson, leaving the chapped flesh gnarled and shaking, dripping. She wanted to tear the bastard down from its roots, but its great wood never even groaned with effort. It never acknowledged her anger and remained apathetically.

She gasped for breath. More memories ambushed her.

Her mother's hand was fragile and thin, bumpy with bony mountains and blown blue veins. That was before she was admitted to inpatient care.

Months after Leonard's funeral, left alone in the dark, smoke-stained home, Norah was newly eight. She'd poured herself a plastic cup of whiskey as she'd watched her mother do countless times. She sipped and winced at the charred heat in her throat while Robin wailed from her own bedroom. The bottle in Norah's hand had a silver horse on the logo, well-fitted to the hoof-like blows that assaulted her gut with each drink.

Don't feel, don't feel, don't feel, it begged, tightening for hours, days, years. *It won't do you any good. It'll only leave you hurting and worthless.*

The widowed wife and the fatherless daughter grieved in their isolation and unspoken expectations, feeling as though the other should be their comforter and save them. They'd never been mother and daughter, but once another time, they'd briefly been akin to codependent sisters.

Norah struck the tree again with a messy, uncaring form. Her knuckle bones stung as she pulled away and fell against the Hawthorn's flesh, allowing it to scratch her brow and cheeks and snag at her hair. Despite the abuse, no tears came. Nothing came. Instead, a maddening burn lingered in her chest and rose to her throat.

She heaved against it, regathering her breath, certain the fire in her heart could burn the forest to the ground if she gave it an inch. She gasped and whimpered, teeth grinding, limbs shaking beneath her in the cold.

She needed to feel like a weapon. She needed to feel dangerous, to know what it felt like to fold the world around her. She needed to feel powerful, like Dex. But she was too small to be feared or respected. She was helpless to this feeling and it didn't care what she needed.

And then, a soft, wafting wind graced her cheek, piercing the deep, cold forest with an uncanny warmth.

She was on her feet like a spry bird and spun. Droplets of blood slipped from her fingers and pattered on dead leaves.

Dex stood several yards away, still like a crane, hands tucked into his pockets, silent and watchful. Clouds of thick hair swept his bruised and scarred features as though he'd run after her. His crimson and blue eye shone in the falling dark.

"How in the fucking hell did you get down here?" she managed between breaths, embarrassment swelling into tides of hot anger.

He eyed her bleeding knuckles. It was now the old man's turn to take in his wounded fighter, eyes reading each inch of her like a medic. After a moment of silence, he snapped his fingers to reveal a rolled wad of clean white wraps in his grip.

"May I?"

"No," she snapped, shaking her head. The pain was the only thing that came close to explaining, to validating the unnameable, inescapable thing in her chest. Emotion was moons away, but the pulsing drip of her blood and the searing pain in her fists was more intimate than anything else she had right now. She couldn't risk veiling its sharp clarity.

With a flick of his wrist, the wraps vanished into a whiff of white smoke.

"No one can hear you, *amica mea*," he muttered, eyes drinking her in with care.

"What?" she stated, daring him to comfort her. To respond. To fix her. To just *fucking try* his magical healing on her pain.

"No one can hear you up here. You could scream if you wanted."

She scoffed, limbs trembling and armor falling. *Somehow,* he could hear the stifled bellow swallowed deep in her intestines. Somehow, he knew exactly what she needed.

His eye flickered to her bleeding hand again, the one burdened with old and new wounds. It likely screamed in his ears when she wouldn't.

"What I *want* is a reason for *this,*" she gestured to herself in disgust. "This *hate,*" she exclaimed. "I *hate* them. I want to make them hurt like they hurt me." Her face contorted with unbearable guilt. "But they didn't leave any marks," she gazed upon herself, wishing her father had struck her, that her mother had shoved her or slapped her.

You have no right to feel so self-righteous. So cheated.

"But they didn't touch me," she whispered, voice climbing. "So *why* am I so fucking angry?"

Dexteras dared not respond and only pierced her with his wise, narrow gaze.

"What did you see?" she snapped, angry at his passive quiet. Enraged that he looked so put together while she fell to pieces. "In my head?"

"Nor-"

"What did you *see,* Dexteras?" she cried.

He shook his head. "I didn't see anything. I just heard a voice," he promised. She could hear him begging, his words eager to reach her. His eyes searching for her own.

Norah only huffed and snatched the phone from her jacket pocket and found the eldest voicemail in her phone's mailbox. She tapped its speaker and played it aloud for the entire forest to hear. The trees were nearly black with shadow and the sky was vibrant with the jeweled colors of sunset.

Then, the static of old audio clicked to life:

"Jay Bird. Just wanted to say I'm sorry for everything that's happened. I love you and I always will. Thank you, honey. Bye."

Honey. Never before had Robin Kestrel called her that. *I love you and I always will.* Norah couldn't recall such an immense proclamation of her mother's love shared prior. At least, not with the casual ease of the voicemail. It wasn't used against her, with implications of guilt, or as a sentence, a manacle, a bribe.

Dexteras' eyes never left Nor's as he listened. When the old voicemail clicked and finished, he nodded but said nothing.

Norah gave a manic chuckle and threw the phone somewhere into the leaves beside her.

"That," she muttered, pointing after it, "was the last thing Mom ever said to me." A violent hiccup seized her throat. She shrugged and chuckled again like a mad woman. "She died," Nor snarled, "right after that."

Dex's eyelids fell with a slow, reverent comprehension. Norah watched the truth weigh him from head to toe. Robin Kestrel had been dead the entire time he'd known her.

Of course.

"Where were you, love?" he whispered. "When you received that?"

She chewed on her inner cheeks and lips and shook her head. The fusion of a smile and a sob twisted her mouth.

"Session," was all she could say. "The day I met you," she breathed. "On the roof. That was right after I got her voicemail."

"Oh love," Dex's shoulders sagged. "I-"

"The day before, they told me she'd taken a turn. Her cancer had been spreading, I should've known. But I…I thought I had more time…" her voice faded into the whispers of the forest. She clutched herself, cold and alone.

"It's not your fault that you weren't there, love."

"I was a floor below her!" Norah cried, hands smacking her sides. "And even after the fact, they offered to keep her body for me to see." She shook her head, eyes wild and watering. "But I never went to see her, even then."

"It's not your fault that you weren't ready, love. You don't have-"

"*I'm* the fucking coward!" Norah yelled, irritated by his compulsion to fix her. "So why am *I* the one who's so angry at her? At him?" her voice broke into shards. "And I let *him* die too, did you know that?" she added.

"The night of the fire. He was trapped in that room, and he couldn't get to the door because of..." she began, shaking her head. "I could've opened it, but I didn't," she said, voicing her heavy guilt for the first time in decades. "I didn't or I couldn't, but I was too weak. So he *died*," Norah scoffed, covering her mouth before more horrid truths could tumble out.

Dex was shaking his head with vigor, eager to speak, to stop her, to correct her.

"But *I'm* fine!" she exclaimed, arms spread in disbelief. "*I'm* the one that did wrong by *them*. And neither of them laid a hand on me. And yet, I feel like..." she screamed in the drum of her throat, clutching her short hair and squeezing, certain it would tear from their roots. "They didn't touch me! They didn't do *anything!*"

It was as if she prayed a repressed memory would rise to the surface and burst with trauma so devastating, it'd fill and validate the endless pit she'd dug for herself. It would give her a reason to hate them both.

You wanted for nothing. You were a spoiled, entitled brat. An only child with nothing better to complain about.

Dexteras took one confident step towards her, eyes trained on hers.

"But they *should've* done something, *amica mea*. You were their child. They should've touched you. They should've held you tighter than anything they'd ever held to," he stated, hands reaching at his sides as though yearning to hold her in their stead.

Nor shook her head as though it were swarming with wasps.

"*Yes,*" he retorted. "Yes. Yes, you deserved to be held," he said simply. "Despite the consequences of their actions, despite how they lived, or how they died, you *were* still hurt, Nor. They hurt you in a way that doesn't leave marks. But you have every right to be full of rage. To want their love. To want them to feel what they did to you. To understand."

He took another slow step as though approaching an orphaned fawn. It was an accurate deduction.

"But they didn't know," she blubbered. "They didn't know how angry I was. *I* didn't know how angry I was," she scoffed, gesturing again to her shaking limbs.

"But children are *supposed* to care about what their parents think of them, Nor. To want them. You were not the dysfunctional, broken ones in that equation." Dex bent low onto his knees, leaves crunching undertow, tendons crackling. "You don't need permission to feel what you need to feel," he said, looking up at her. "It's going to be there whether you hold space for it or not. You need to let yourself feel it. It's safe to, out here. No one can hear." He offered this gift with the casual notion of sharing a stick of gum.

Norah swallowed the coerced scream back down her throat, scolding it for its eagerness. She thought of her mother's last breath creeping from her atrophied throat, disappearing into the ceiling tiles as Marchos had. No one was there to hold either of them in their final, miserable breaths.

Every muscle and tendon in her limbs trembled, begging to quit. She tipped her chin to Dexteras with a final effort.

"Do we really owe all of ourselves to the people who gave us life?" she begged, voice breaking. "Even when it really fucking hurts?"

He found her eyes and held them in his, gentleness folding his soft features. "No. No, love. You do not owe *anybody* everything. And the right people would never ask everything of you."

She shook with tempted tears.

"But you owe yourself your anger. It deserves a place to go. Tear the whole forest down, love," he nodded to the darkness around them.

"I can't," she whispered.

"Why aren't *you* allowed to be not okay?" he challenged, voice strong and paternal.

Her jaw locked tightly enough to fracture forged steel.

"There's no one to make better. To heal. No one to be strong for. Take your mask off, Norah Kestrel. Feel everything you need to feel. You can scream as loud as you want out here."

It was as if she were fearful she'd morph into a ravenous werewolf and consume the world with her insatiable appetite if she let it go. A howl felt tempting, like the guiltiest, most indulgent pleasure she could imagine, an unthinkable luxury.

Her eyes snapped to him, searching and hungry. He'd known the devastation she'd known. The homelessness. The lovelessness. He'd been tortured by the people he'd served. He sought his only remaining family for decades, only for them to lock him in cages for death matches.

"What about you? Aren't *you* mad?" she challenged, eyes filling with hot salt.

His jaw drooped slack with want. His eyes widened and his fingers clenched. He swallowed and licked his whiskered lips. His chest swelled with the cold.

And then, he *screamed*.

His scream tore apart seas and skies with thunderous rumbles until tears squeezed from his crow's feet and his limbs bent with all their worth. He screamed birds from the forest and into the hazy skies until his chest shook and his fingers clenched and stretched and clenched shut again with waves of effort. It was a raw and chilling roar that was beautiful in its ugliness. Its honesty.

He screamed until he was on his knees, electricity crackling from his fingertips and zapping the dead leaves around him. They burned and circled him in smoke as though he were a dying star that'd touched earth. He slumped to the forest floor, gasping and weeping for oxygen. But his eyes were wide with life and fire.

Nor craved his pain, his fury, its violence. Thus as Dex was engulfed in his crumbling, she claimed her own.

She spun in the leaves to face the dead valley of forest below and followed suit, screaming with a piercing, blinding cry that could shatter glass and cochleae alike. She was certain the folds of her trachea would vibrate themselves bloody and that her tears were hot enough to blind her. Her lungs spat their flames until they were dry like bone, gasping for mercy. Her fingernails clutched at tree bark until she, too, fell to the cold ground, sacrificing even her leg muscles to pay tithe towards the overdue wail. Tidal waves broke from her until she fell limp.

When the forest fell silent, their eyes found one another, gasping and gaping.

Dexteras smiled at her, mouth ajar and eyes sparkling.

His calm infuriated her, but it also made her feel free, free enough to lose her sanity beside him and let out whatever had been caged behind her bones since she was a child. Her face contorted, sensing another inward gush of madness.

"They *left* me, and I didn't get to feel any of it," she wept, winded and wheezing. "They got *all* of me, and I got none of them. But *I* had to be one that was okay," she muttered. "I don't know how they didn't see…" she lamented, eyes glassy on the forest floor.

"What didn't they see?" asked Dex.

"That I was so…tired. Because what I was expected to hold for them and hold for myself wasn't-*isn't* staying down, and it hurts so bad." She squeaked, scraping at her chest and clutching her throat.

Dex's fingers flexed with want again, but he waited.

"I *always* held *them*. *They* were allowed to cry and be pissed and hate each other and grieve, and I had to hold *all* of it," she forced, breathless. "I wasn't supposed to…I couldn't, I can't. I can't. I can't. I'm so tired. I'm so fucking tired, Dex…" she begged, eyes shifting to him, blurred with boiling oceans. She attempted to stand and slosh through the leaves toward him, but everything weighed so much more than she'd remembered. Her insides were leaden and immense beyond her strength, and she sank like an anchor to the forest floor.

Dex met her in an impossibly quick stride and swooped her into his arms. They collapsed onto the cold ground as Nor wept with injustice.

Dex's massive arms wrapped around her and held her firm, even as she shook.

And she was right. He couldn't keep her pieces from pulling apart. But he loved her in a way that celebrated her exactly how she was, nothing more. Somehow, it felt as though he loved her in all of her shattered bits. *Especially* her shattered bits.

"You were hurt. You were hurt. You were hurt," he whispered into her hair, rocking the adult child in his arms. "You deserve to be angry. You deserve to tear the earth and skies into pieces."

She sobbed, unable to recognize her own voice. "I'm alone, I'm all alone. It hurts, it hurts," she moaned, clutching at her chest. A hot, clawing scraping raked beneath her breastbone. To let it go on would be to let it kill her. It was cranking her throat shut like a window on an old car, squeaking with effort. If it won, she'd rupture, she'd be sick. To succumb didn't seem possible.

You're an orphan. An orphan.

"But you still deserve love, Norah. You deserve love. To be held and seen and touched and loved."

Her fingers raked at his thick arms, clawing at his shirt and squeezing its fabric.

"Let it hurt, let it hurt love. Please stop fighting it, stop fighting."

Then, through the brush of his beard, beyond them both, she saw a dark form through the trees, puddled on the forest floor. She made minimal effort to see the sorry sight, knowing full well who it was.

A seven-year-old girl was cast to the dirt in a black dress. Her collar was soaked with tears and snot as she bawled with open-mouthed, ugly sobs. Juvenile, hyperventilating gasps tore from her without relent.

To be fair, the child had never wept for anyone before that day. Not even for Leonard. She hadn't been allowed to. Thus, a lifetime bucketed down her crimson cheeks. Her salt finally seeped into the earth that had buried countless Kestrels.

Adult Norah remembered that the child in the dirt wasn't pitiful. She wasn't submissive or weak. She wasn't to be coddled and ignored. The girl was a quiet beast that could tear down the oaks with her bare fists if given the time. Her screams could flatten mountains.

And she was allowed to if needed.

She was allowed.

✦

Helplessness washed upon waves of guilt. Guilt crashed and sputtered against anger. Anger bubbled along the shore and sunk into the sands of grief. And it was there she was thrown onto its beach like a dead fish.

Dex's strong body still sat upon the cold ground, encompassing all of her as though she were a gift to cling to. He didn't speak or expect her to. They simply remained.

Nor's stretched her headspace to feel the gaping holes in her future where her parents would never tread. Where their arms would never hold her or escort her down the aisle. Where their hands would never wipe her tears or hold her children. Where no loving word would empower her. Where instead, there were Leonard and Robin-sized craters torn from her timeline, leaving black, irredeemable voids. The future was corrupt with the eternal coldness of corpses. Their absence was more immense than the galaxy, and she'd never allowed herself to notice it until this very moment.

Dexteras brushed bits of crushed leaves and twigs and earth from her dress clothes and hair.

Norah Kestrel had always been alone, and now that would never change.

✦

I thought I had more time.
I thought I had more time.
I thought I had more time.

✦

What felt like hours later, Dex plucked a cigar from her limp hand and snapped his fingers, rekindling the bright cherry in a crackling pop of lightning. He took a pull until intricate, twirling smoke twisted from his whiskered lips to form a gray Blue Jay. It flapped to Norah with ghostly wings in slow, sweeping motions before it was distorted by the wind.

She'd smoked through two and a half large cigars until her tongue was numb and peppery and her stomach was nauseous with nicotine.

"I needed her," muttered Nor. "And when she couldn't be there for me, I tried to fix her. To make her happy. And even though I never could, she let me keep trying."

"That should've never been your responsibility," Dex bellowed with a stern brow, propping his spine against the tree trunk that'd been bearing them.

"I-I wanted to tell her how I felt. Why I hated being around her. All the things she owed me. I'd planned to tell her one day, but now…shit. Oh, God." Norah wiped at fresh tears with irritation. Her face was taut and stiff with dried salt. She bent over her knees, attempting to regain her breath.

"I couldn't even talk to her…I…"

Dex wrapped a large, warm arm around her like an unfolded wing.

"Love, even if she was here, if *he* was here, they'd never be able to pay the debt owed to you. Your childhood was too valuable. Too precious."

She pulled at her neckline, heart racing in her throat. Her weeping eyes were sore, but they still found the old man's.

"How am I supposed to heal then?" she croaked.

His blue and crimson eyes paced between hers. His lips parted, but he rolled the words on his tongue like a marble, uncertain if he should give them to her.

"When it comes to unpayable debts, we can either invest our energy in awaiting repayment, or we can forgive and grieve what's lost," he whispered.

Norah's face crumpled with a multitude of emotions. Fury buckled her brow, followed by exhaustion. She'd given an honest question, and he replied with an honest answer. She whimpered like a tired child who'd been encouraged to keep walking after a long journey. She just wanted to sleep in the woods and be left alone.

"There's so much I needed to say," she whispered.

His eyes grew distant and starry as though he were excavating the skies for answers.

"I don't think," he began, "it's ever too late to say what needs to be said, love." He graced her cheek with a thumb, its warmth easing the muscles of her jaw.

48

·DEXTERAS·

DESPITE HIS UNSPOKEN PROMISE to keep from Norah Kestrel, the circumstances were inarguable. Her mother was dead. She'd been dead all this time he'd known her, and not once had he thought to poke or prod or clarify. He had been the center of all their energy and efforts and had taken Nor from her own grief in the process.

It seemed something wonderful or catastrophic would always keep them tethered. They were inseparable stars in a constellation, bound, orbiting planets.

They sat upon her roof as she reminisced, recounting childhood tales of her mother, both lovely and horrid. The parentification. The cognitive distortions. The rules to which Norah clung in survival.

Do not grieve Dad. Don't listen to his records. Don't speak his name.

Do everything by yourself. Robin's mental illness and addiction were unwound by the loose thread of Leonard's death, leaving no remaining motherhood to spare for her child.

Mom's happiness is your responsibility. The key that weighed Norah's chest was first her mother's. It was the family crest of trauma which she'd borne through the throngs of war. The key shuddered through its locking mechanisms and resounded through the halls with the damnation of manacles.

After Leonard died, Robin often crawled into bed with her daughter and clung to the child until she buzzed with neglected circulation. Between her mother's sobbing spine and the cold brass of bed rails, Norah was talked at like a ghostwriter, a hollow mausoleum built only to bear her mother's tales. Norah Kestrel didn't sleep for years. Her head would slip and slump from consciousness at school and everywhere in between until she was riddled with tears.

Mom's health is your responsibility. Norah came home from school one afternoon to find Robin lolling and incapacitated on the bedroom floor. Drooling and heavy-lidded, eyeballs spinning into white marbles. She'd mixed sleeping meds with liquor again, thus at fifteen, she heaved the slurring woman to the car and drove her to the hospital.

"When you're a kid with unhealthy parents," said Norah, "you either lose your authenticity or your attachment. So I gave up who I was and who I wanted to be. And even after she died, I was so scared to think of who I could be without the trauma, the past. I've done everything to live by that book of survival, and now I have to write a new one."

Because it was the caregiving of her mother that had become Norah's sole purpose and worth. She'd draw pictures, cards, write poems, clean, organize, draw baths, buy gifts, pick flowers, embrace, kiss, brush her hair, cook meals, sing songs, decorate their heads in flower crowns, read stories, share movies, make coffee and tea, and fill her small arms with the weary woman until she had no kindness left even for herself.

"I think mom loved who I was as a kid because I made her feel strong and wise," Nor muttered. She fidgeted with her cigars, twisting them in her fingers until their papers were frayed and unwinding chocolaty leaves onto the rooftop beside the piles of dead ashes. "She just wanted to feel in control, like we all do. But once I found my own voice, I couldn't serve that narrative for her anymore."

As a teen, Norah began running away from home, disappearing into the neighboring fields for whole days at a time, deep into the night. She'd trip into a clearing of purple-capped wheat crop only to collapse into its arms and wait.

For something.

Anything.

Anyone.

She'd sing her father's favorite songs and scratch in her sketchbook or at herself. And as Norah Kestrel grew old and tall with the pale fields, one final rule to her survival was crystallized:

No one is coming to save you.

"You wanted to be found," said Dex, eyes hot with salt. He watched her scratch the scar alongside her eye ritualistically. It followed the creek bed of her tears, down her cheek.

Sensing his gaze, she dropped her journeying fingers to her lap.

He extended a hand to her cheek and conformed to its shape without touching.

"May I?" he proposed.

Stumbling clarity fell upon her features, but she nodded.

His touch maintained the gentleness of holding bird's egg as he ran a thumb along the scar. It was thin and smooth like magnolia petals. He rested his thumb into the valley of it and her eyelids fluttered closed. They stepped into her memories with care.

Thick, grassy roots squeaked and bent undertow with groans. He cast aside tall crops, following a sad, strumming chord he knew too well. Though it was smaller, quieter than its full composition, he could've recognized its instruments in the violence of a hurricane.

He found her tiny form rocking against her kneecaps in the overgrown field, humming a tune much older than she. Her fingernail dug at the soft flesh beneath her eye in rhythmic catatonia, vision glassy and distant. And though it was not the burn of a cigar or the breaking of bones on a boxing bag, he intimately knew why she scraped and sought. He understood the brief service, the treasure beneath the wound, and its inflammation. Its essential comfort was often craved by the lost, the tired, and the numb. The message in its depths, deep like a bone bruise. The intimate reminder in its ache:

You. Are. Still. Here.

They fell back into their still bodies. He wiped tears from her low lashes and watched her return to him with soft blinks.

"Why scars?" she asked.

He'd conjured a deduction but couldn't be entirely certain why scars were most efficient for cosmic conversation and the sharing of memories.

"Scars stay with us longer than anyone else," he guessed. "I believe they know us most deeply. What we're made of and what we can survive. Gateways for raw vulnerability."

She smiled briefly.

Despite her visit to the traumas of her past, he listened to her heart's once fearful drum now beat with greater, slower, peaceful rhythms until the anxious organ lowered in her chest, slowly, *slowly*, like a landing swan.

Dexteras yearned to drink as much as she could share. He commanded every detail, each vivid memory, every jagged and soothing corner of her mind she could spare until her cupboard of memories was barren.

Norah Kestrel deserved to be heard in the same way she heard others each and every day.

She wrestled open a bottle of red wine from the depths of a high cabinet. They shared it on her rooftop and leaned back into the stars. Their legs swayed drunkenly above the whispering fields.

"Wine is sun held together by water," he quoted Galileo between sips. He gazed through his glass at the white coin moon. It shone silver beams through the lacing liquid, thick like blood. When Norah didn't respond, he turned to her.

Her posture was rounded and heavy like a river stone worn by waves. She also stared into her glass, disgust twisting her lip. He knew her thoughts before they'd left her.

"I'm afraid of being like her," muttered Norah. "Deteriorating in this fucking house. Slowly killing myself. But even if I leave, wherever I go, they'll still be within me. I can't run from it."

He sat his glass down and faced her.

"You cannot run, but who *they* were is not who *you* are," he said. "There's a capacity for chaos waiting within all of us, love, genetics or not. But you are aware of who you want to be and who you don't," he promised. "You'll protect future Nor. You'll make mindful choices so she can be healthy where they weren't."

"Being really *is* hard," she muttered.

"Cheers to that."

After one goblet-sized glass of sloshing libation, she fell into a hard sleep. It left her strung about the rooftop in an array of chocolate wrappers, fleece-coated limbs, and cigar butts. Her lips were parted and reddened with wine.

He watched for a moment as her eyes danced beneath drunken lids, praying her headspace cared for her and took her far from the cavity of grief. Though it was a scant serving of meager crumbs, he wished he could share his peace with Norah like breaking bread. But all he could do was tote her to bed, wrap her warm, and place Vincent at her feet.

He cleaned the rooftop of the evening's wrappings before hopping upon a chimney stack. He stared at Robin Kestrel's vacant window, massaging his sore jaw with circling thumbs. It reminded him of Norah's scars. Of her touch on his cheeks. Of her kindness, despite all she'd known.

Despite all he was.

And as quickly as the correlation registered, he was reduced to tears.

He wept for Norah and for Robin. He grieved for all of their lives and suffering until his tears drained him into gentle unconsciousness. A catatonia, inebriated with weeping.

"...do you think if she knew what drove you to such madness, that she could care for you so?"

The sultry voice shook him awake with such a violent chill, he fell from the chimney bricks and dropped onto all-fours. His flayed skin stitched shut whilst he scrambled to his feet.

His gut dropped at the dramatic atmosphere shift.

Spirit-like breath snaked from his lips.

That cold sensation shuddered his senses like a death knell.

Then, a pair of thick lips pressed against the nape of his neck, skating over his flesh like a viper's tongue.

He spun with disorientation until he was toe-to-toe with the archaic being, Solus.

Amber flashed beneath the smoky eyes. The beguiling skin had healed to its coppery perfection, glimmering and immodest. Their blazer was sharp-shouldered and buttoned at the abdomen, pulled over their bare breast and gold chains. The raven hair had resumed its luster. Their cherry lips were plump and unbroken. The shapely form was grounded on their tall, golden appendages.

"Son," they said, red irises flashing like dying stars.

Dex interrupted the monologue with a snarl and a fist, boxing with wild, unplanned strikes. He would not have evil here again at her home. This was what he'd fought so hard to avoid.

But the hellhound only grinned with expectation, bending and leaning into ducks and dodges, always a millisecond ahead.

The fizzles and crackles of his electric fingertips sparked against the night, eager to strike.

"You're returning to yourself, Dexteras," they chided, a thin cigarette teasing between their teeth. Solus sidestepped one of Dex's blows with an easy stretch of the golden leg, its mechanisms whirring. The beast leaned in to deliver a mocking slap to one of Dex's elbows.

"Tighten up. You've the composure of a fowl," they said, hopping like a plucky crow, testing Dex's footwork. With a grin, the creature spun into a swirl of dark smoke and vanished.

Dex wheeled about on his ready toes, fists high and pressed against his jaw. Once he found the pitying golden irises again in the dark, he charged with drawn fists. However, breaths before contact, he screeched to a halt, nearly a heartbeat too late.

Dex flung his arms out to keep from bowling himself over the ledge. He was at the roof's rim, having run out of tread. He'd nearly launched himself from it after the tempting figure.

Solus was suspended in the airspace just beyond, held afloat by black swirls of smoke wrapped at their shins. A raspy hum resonated from the tattooed throat in pity.

With a snap of their fingers, they returned behind Dexteras.

Swollen with fury for the childish charade, Dex spun off a grounded boot to strike the old creature's jaw. His height was impressive. His power was building.

But the beast was fast as polished steel, skating across the roof on gold blades.

The archfiend snatched Dexteras from the air and threw his body down to the rooftop with a force that shook Norah's home. Shingles cracked and shuddered with a huff of dust.

Dex arched his back in a silent gasp, clawing in pain. Somewhere in his vertebrae, something had snapped with the loudness of a broken cane pole. Something substantial and important. He backpedaled in search of release from the piercing fractures, withholding his screams.

"*That* was for taking my second in command from me." A flash of crimson sparkled in the dark skull above him.

Cecil?

"I didn't touch him," Dex grimaced.

"But you filled him with doubt, *hope*," they snarled, stepping from the shadows. Their jaw was not mocking, but bared. "I heard it in his voice, his hunger. And hungry dogs are never loyal." A bitter, hurt expression contorted their bright eyes.

Before Dex could place the unnatural want on their face, they blinked the grieving shine from their eyes. "But I don't have to hear anything in his voice anymore, do I?" they said.

Dex attempted to stand, but fell back with white, hot pain. Crunching, grinding bits of bone shifted beneath him until his eyes clenched shut.

Solus then suddenly grinned with wild eyes and turned towards the window.

It lifted with a soft hiss and out stepped Norah.

An unfitting hatred painted her exhaustion as she beheld Solus on her roof. Her fists clenched, and her heartbeat pounded like a cannon.

Dex's deducing eyes took in the pair before him: the ancient being that yearned for him to be who he once was, and the beautiful, beloved human who cherished him exactly as he was at present. He felt them pull at his aching insides as though the sinews of his heart were unraveled and clutched in their desperate grips. They were both toe-to-toe in their own ring, and he was the rope.

This is what Solus wanted.

She crouched beside Dex, who clenched at his spine, struck still whilst sinew braided itself inside of him.

"You were nearly dead before you met *her*, *Dexy*. You felt as though you'd fade to nothingness. Don't you wonder why?"

Norah paid the banter no mind, anxious hands wandering the old man's broken spine.

"*Amica mea*, I'm fine. I'm healing. But please go back inside," he begged, surveying his opponent over her shoulder.

"Don't you wonder why she gives you strength?" whispered Solus, a pink tongue flashing across their teeth.

Norah stood and approached the old Figment like an oncoming storm of a woman, fearless and huffing.

"Norah, don't!" Dex called.

Solus remained planted, hands in their suit pockets and a cigarette twisting between their teeth. A thin, black brow raised at her approach.

"Why now?" she snarled. "If you cared about him so dearly, why did you wait twenty years to bring him home?" she said, fists bared.

"Because as I've said, Norah Kestrel, once I take a Fig's memories, some give way to The Unbecoming. Washing your brain clean of your purpose and your past, it unhinges you. It's like taking the oxygen from your heart and being told you don't need it anymore. You're lost to senility," said Solus. The voice was smooth and dangerous between those hungry lips.

"What? So you *lost* him? How in the hell do you lose a man who doesn't know who he is?" she spat, pushing herself onto her tiptoes towards them. "I know nurses with full wards of dementia patients, and we've never fucking *lost* one."

Solus grinned a true, bright smile. "Moments after I took his memories as he so begged me to, he jumped off the roof of your hospital."

Norah's heart stopped for a beat, and her shoulders fell.

"A nurse was the first on the scene," called Solus. "Her Purpose was to heal human bodies, and because he was hungry for survival, a human body he became. But once he left the hospital, he unraveled again and lost himself. We had a hell of time pinning you down after that, Dexteras," Solus called over Norah to the downed fighter. "When Cecil told me he'd found you, I honestly didn't believe him. I was certain you'd completely unraveled into dust from The Unbecoming." A new, fallen expression weighed the elder Figment, eyes wincing with pain.

Dex clutched at his scalp. The world was spinning, and the last twenty years of his life were wafting and lost.

"A lack of Purpose is essentially a lack of love. It can terrify Figs and Corpses alike," Solus said to Norah. "You'd know something about that, wouldn't you?"

Dex tested his legs again. They were still numb with paralysis. A stab echoed throughout the rest of him and dropped him to his elbows. He huffed with fear. He wouldn't be healed in time to help her.

"You were molded by pain, as we were," said the towering being, medallion eyes darting to the hand clenched at Nor's side. Surely they heard its silent scars. "Just as your mother was." Solus lifted their chin with a shark tooth smile. "Dexteras saw to that."

A fatal stone plunged down into Dex's intestines. He couldn't breathe.

"I can show you," offered the archaic fiend. "You could know everything."

49

⟡NORAH⟡

"They are memories from *your* life, Norah Kestrel," stated Solus.

"And why the fuck do you have *my* memories?" she snapped.

"As I said, they are *from* your life but not yours. All I possess are those belonging to Figments."

"And if I let you show me, you'll leave my house and never come back?" Norah's stare paced their eyes for a malicious glint of crimson. If Dexteras could be safe, she could manage the past. The pain was worth its weight in respite.

Solus extended a ringed hand, scuttling in its inked insects.

"Nor, no!" cried Dex, pounding the roof with desperate fists.

But her sullen eyes found his in apology as her hand gripped Solus.

"*Perfectus,*" they whispered, their well-carved, Grecian jaw bared.

"Norah, please-" Dexteras begged over the wind's wails, but he was cut short.

For as the oldest Figment's frigid fingers wrapped around hers, the oxygen was stolen from her chest. It reminded her of the fourth grade when she'd slipped from the highest set of monkey bars and landed on her spine, mid-winter. For half a heartbeat, she couldn't command her body to breathe, and it terrified her. Tears streamed down her cheeks as she squeezed splintery mulch in her frozen fists.

The same sensation stole her now, rattling her bones like a sack of wooden blocks. A roller-coaster force churned her gut and clenched her eyes shut, leaving her to combat vertigo on swaying feet. The earth's axis shifted beneath her and dropped her back to her rear. Her head spun.

As she regathered herself, she did not feel gritty roof tile beneath her hands, but carpet. Starchy, cheap, tufted carpet. Synthetic fibers scratching beneath her nails. The space was dark, but she knew she was home, in her own room. But the lens through which she saw the familiar space was amber, hazy, and trembling as though swirling with fumes.

A small lump on her bed hummed with dreams. Burnt auburn locks draped her pillow in a chaotic heap. A limp hand rested atop a sleeping black kitten.

Nor stepped close and squinted to see the child's tiny palm unscathed, free of its ruby scar.

She approached her parents' door, her stride long and lumbering as though she were wading through water. When she reached for the knob, her hand fell through it like mist. With impossible calm, she held a breath and stepped through the wall. It pierced her ghostly form with cold.

In the dark of her parents' room, a shallow breath snored into dark sheets. A massive, pale shoulder heaved with sleep.

Her knees weakened as she crept toward the incapacitated man. Dark hair, much like her own, was strewn about his face and scruffy jaw. His eyes paced beneath reddened lids.

Her lip trembled. She'd taken these brief moments of his life for granted. What a strange gift she didn't know she'd had, to simply know her father existed a room away. She wished to touch the coarse bristle at his jaw, to pull the blankets higher onto his bare torso. But somehow, she knew that nothing she did in this body and in this realm was going to make a difference.

As she rounded the banister downstairs, sniffs and mutterings echoed against the walls and plucked at Nor's heartstrings. From the hall, she could see into the kitchen to their tiny island countertop, covered in its common corkscrews and sticky liquors. Her mother's torso was draped across its surface, blonde hair scattered in waves along the marble. Her arms hugged close to a blue bottle of wine.

Nor swallowed at a lump at the base of her throat. She remembered with heart-stopping clarity, now more than ever, that her mother was dead. For the first time in her life, Norah yearned to truly, deeply stare at the tired woman for millennia. To know her as deeply as she could.

Robin's fingers twitched as incomplete words slipped from her lips, riding lapses of consciousness.

As Norah drew nearer to her mother, she sensed the static presence of another. Her eyes lifted upon a quiet creature lurking in the dark, camouflaged in shadow at her mother's back.

Dexteras sat upon the sink, hunched over his long, crossed legs like an ivory statue seated atop a tombstone. He was swallowed in black garments from head to toe, long coattails dripping to his calves.

He didn't move or pay any mind to her, only fixating on Robin's spine as though he were attempting to burst her into flames with his thoughts.

Norah's mouth fell open and she squinted at the old man in the dark. She hadn't truly believed Solus' accusations about Dexteras and her past, yet here he sat. This Dex was not the one she knew now. He was not hers. This Dex was all business it seemed, hair and beard crisp and short, tattoos fresher and lesser. Still, Norah shuddered against the sickening sensation of being unseen by him again. His focus was cold and stoic upon her mother only.

He hopped from the counter to crouch beside Robin, leaning near her trembling shoulder to whisper secrets in her ear. But Norah couldn't hear any of it. It seemed the memory's quality was grainy and old, scratchy and neglected.

Robin shivered but continued with her drunken muttering. She snatched up a corkscrew and plunged it into the bottle with a grunt, but despite years of experience, her sweaty hands slipped and shook with dehydration.

Robin cursed and tripped to the liquor cabinet, the one Nor had since purged. She twisted open a bottle of rum and poured it into her dirty wine glass. It splashed across her and the countertop.

Still, Dex whispered, matching each of Robin's movements with expectation as though they'd been choreographed. It was an eerie matching of stride that made him look like her mother's shadow.

Robin tottered towards the hall with her cradled glass, eyes bloodshot and brimming with tears. Her figure banged against the walls.

Then suddenly, she pivoted, nearly tangling herself in her own legs, and returned to the kitchen once more. She snatched her purse from the table and shuffled within it like a burrowing creature. She then stared into the depths of the thing as though she wished to disappear into its void.

SLAM.

Dexteras slapped his fists upon the table, making Nor jump with a shrill yelp. She wasn't certain how the old wood hadn't split in two. He shouted angrily with white, wide eyes, but his words were muffled by the thick syrup-like filter, the exact details lost to time.

What was he trying to do?

"Fucking *shit*," Robin hissed, withdrawing her cigarettes and lighter and stuffing them in her pockets. Then she and her drink returned to the stairs. Dexteras was at her heels and Norah chased after them both.

Robin shouldered into her bedroom and slumped into Leo's overstuffed burgundy armchair studded with brass buttons. He'd often come home from work and read the paper in that chair. It smelled of cigars and aftershave.

Not long after Norah was born, he stopped coming home after work. He instead drove to the casino or the greyhound track, where he became addicted to gambling, heavy liquor, and other women.

Norah's eyes fell upon the unconscious man in the bed again and heard his voice in her thoughts.

"I didn't want this Robin, remember? I didn't want a fucking kid, and I'm no

fucking father!"

Slaps. Shoves. Rumbles of furniture. The striking of walls. Roars of anger.

As Robin situated into the cushioned impression of her estranged husband, honeycomb-colored rum splashed from her glass and onto the synthetic velvet. She slurped its rim with irritated grumbles, staring at the mass that was Leonard. An empty glass of whiskey sat beside his nightstand in melted ice. That had to have been his fourth or fifth.

Norah swallowed for what she knew came next.

We've all been trying to escape some sort of pain, haven't we?

Her mother slipped in and out of consciousness, leaving the wine glass to tilt and cover her lap and legs in stains. Each droplet was sand falling from the Kestrel hourglass. Each loll of her chin against her chest was a step closer to their undoing.

Dexteras moved closer, gripping the armchair like a perched raven, slipping incantations into her mother's ear. His lips paced with articulation, but Nor could make out none of his words.

Robin stirred with a wet cough and drunken shudders, drawing a cigarette to her lips and lighting it after several attempts. She sipped liquor from one hand and pulled on her tobacco from the other, with episodes of violent head nodding scattered in between. Each round tipped the cigarette towards the antique fabric like a torpedo. Each spell seemed more debilitating than the last, gluing her eyes shut for longer strokes of time.

Norah hadn't read the investigative reports, but she knew how this story ended. She'd read it in the papers. She'd been drilled by her middle school classmates on it for weeks.

And yet, she couldn't look away. It felt cowardly. A nauseating guilt kept her eyes glued to them in an attempt to understand her parents as intimately as she could. For there would never be another opportunity like this. She'd ruined the years of opportunities. She'd thought only of herself and ran selfishly.

And as she knew and dreaded it would, the glass tipped onto Robin with the malicious intent of spilled gasoline, soaking her limbs and the cushion in its sloshing wake. She only whimpered dreamily, regaining enough cognizance to toss the half-finished cigarette over the chair's spine and into the bottom of a metal wastebasket. As it left her fingers, her faculties were abandoned, and she fell limp, succumbing to the alcohol and undoubtedly other substances.

Why won't you do something? Nor begged Dex, her eyes boring into him, now.

But he only remained statue still and watching.

At the sight of her old friend, an unfamiliar anger and hurt rose in Norah's chest and threatened to break her heart.

The trash receptacle's plastic liner shriveled and blackened in moments. Smoke spilled into the atmosphere in wisps. The Kestrels had a smoke alarm, but its batteries were never replaced despite Robin's pestering upon the matter.

Within seconds, the infant flame consumed paper bits, food wrappers, and other trash until it kissed the tail of the window's curtain. The sheer fabric ignited in a blink.

It lapped with insatiable hunger until it tasted the fibers of the maroon couch. The fingering tendrils bubbled and boiled at the threads before burrowing into the cushioning. With each bite, the fire flared toxic green. The billowing draperies charred to scrap. The room stuffed itself with gaseous black fumes. The pulsating flames roared and rose.

Norah tottered on her feet as her tears fell and landed perhaps in a time decades from here. Her hands helplessly clutched at her sides. She drank in her mother's sad features and her father's drunken flesh, heaving in ignorant sleep.

The fumes smudged the ceiling and walls with black. Moisture poured from the pores of everything, sizzling and steaming. Chemicals and flames chiseled at every inch of the dry room.

But the Kestrels still slept, immune to their vices.

The fire crept up the lacy sleeve of her mother's blouse, simmering the fabric until it contorted and folded into itself. The hairs of her bony arm vanished in wisps of smoke. Curious embers traveled to the soaked stains in the sofa. They popped with satisfaction, chasing the trail of rum ingrained in Robin's jeans. Patches of clothing crumbled to ashen threads before turning towards Robin's pale, freckled flesh beneath.

Norah whimpered and fell to her knees. She broke her stare, hot tears pouring into her hands. She couldn't watch the skin redden and blister. Briefly, she scowled at Dexteras instead, gripping her father's armchair, eyes trained on her mother's dancing lids. Every so often he'd watch the hungry fire.

The flickering flames bounced drastic shadows across his ghostly pallor, but he was listless and still. He wasn't her Dexteras. She wasn't certain who this was.

Why don't you do something? she attempted to cry out, but her words were swallowed by time. It was a horrifying feeling to be unable to scream. Salt still spilled from her squinting eyes and the smell of burning hair and flesh still filled her nose, but nothing she did would matter here. Norah had to inch closer to see through the thickening air.

And finally, what felt like hours later, Robin awoke, prying open her heavy lids. All hell was untethered by her consciousness. She came to with a gasp, choking on her words and clawing at flames. She attempted to flee from the sofa but collapsed into the wall, screaming with horrified bleats. Her arm was laced in flames and smoldering fabric.

Awakened by his wife's cries, Leonard fumbled from his sheets.

"The hell? Jesus Christ, Robin!" He fell from the bed in his boxer shorts, his naked torso glistening with sweat. He stuttered and coughed violently for a moment in utter, mental chaos.

Then, he grabbed a heavy quilt from their bed and wrapped his wife in it with a valiant swoop. He stomped from the flames and carried her to the opposite corner of their room where he peeled the layers away from her extinguished burns. Her skin smoldered and shook. Robin cried and screamed at the pain and shock.

Though Norah's mind had nearly lost the vivid, bold lines of her father's figure to time, she knew she'd never seen him as a brave man. But now, he acted heroically in his final moments. His voice could be kind. His hands could hold Robin gently. Though most of his actions spoke otherwise, it was evident in his worried brow and petting fingers that wiped sticky hairs from her forehead, he'd once truly loved Robin Starling.

Norah wept harder, her face burning with shame and guilt and the bright flames in her vision.

"There's a fire, my wife's been badly burned," Leo cried into his cell phone, pressed to his sweating cheek with a shoulder.

A horrid, gurgling groan of the old house's walls stretched and moaned around them.

The 911 dispatcher then evidently gave him orders because he promptly followed up with, "Robin, get Lenore and get out!" he bellowed.

Norah flinched at the gargled cries of her name.

But Robin did not respond. Her eyes were wide and fixed, she was crouched on all fours, and she was hacking lungfuls of ashen, poisonous air.

"*Robin!*"

He, too, roared with wet, horrid coughs before wheeling about to assess their options. The door to the hall was completely swallowed in flames, and Norah's door was fanned in burning debris and hung spiderwebs of electrical wire from the crumbling antique ceiling. It was impossible to tell if they were live and fatal through the smoke and fire.

Leo instead yanked and fumbled with the bedroom window, yelping with each barefoot step to the carpet. His cellphone, Norah knew, would later be found as a fossilized plastic melted mound.

He heaved the glass, watching the smoke gather and suffocate them. Flames crackled. Blackness stained their walls. Each inch of carpet and furniture bubbled and released gases. Leo wiped streams of sweat from his squinting eyes and coughed hard again.

"Fuck!" he yelled, yanking at the window's ledge, forearms straining with blue veins.

Then, a shadow sprang from the corner and dashed across the room towards him. Dex, too, was gripping the window ledge, matching Leo's effort invisibly beside him.

But as her father pulled in desperation, Dexteras was *pushing* it back down.

He was keeping it shut, responding to Leo's snarls with groans of his own.

Leonard of course, only believed the window was sealed shut with the melting antique paint. Regardless, it wasn't budging. It seemed the flames engorged around him, taunting him further.

Norah wasn't certain what to believe. Her mouth was agape, and her heart pounded with fear and confusion. Her weeping eyes were glued to Dex's straining, massive hands and his shaking fighting muscles.

Why?

Then, Dex's head whipped over his shoulder in fresh alert, and with a dash of tall legs, he threw his shoulder against the door to Norah's bedroom, coattails fanning behind him. Despite the fire and the limp wires around him, he pressed his ear to the wood, eyes pacing the floor with apprehension.

It was then that Norah fell into a spell of unsettling *déjà vu*.

Each sound that piqued her ears was now familiar in its nightmarish timing, tone, pitch, and pace. She knew what came next in the way that she knew the final words to a song she couldn't shake from her skull. These last moments are when the Kestrels' daughter had stirred, waken, and became cognizant of the crises in the next room. But this time, Nora was watching it from the other side of the door.

The ceiling above Leonard crackled like popcorn.

The gunshot pop of melted wires killed the electricity in their home.

The wheezing croaks of her father heaved and cried out just below the window.

The ghostly, inhuman wails of her mother.

Adult Norah paddled on her knees through curtains of smoke, seeking out Dex's polished boots at her bedroom door. She had to know what he was doing. Why he was so eager to abandon her parents.

The steps of her tinier self could be heard thudding from bed.

Dex's fingers twitched.

The brass jiggled.

He snatched it and gnashed his teeth.

A cry of panic and pain responded from the child's bedroom and ended with a thud. She'd fallen to the floor at the mercy of a second-degree burn.

Dex also tore from the handle to reveal his own right palm blazoned crimson, skin sweltered as hers. He winced but did not cry out.

Norah felt the world pull out from under her.

It was Dex who'd burned her.

I could've saved them. I could've saved them, she thought. *I could've saved them, and he stopped me.*

Adult Norah Kestrel wasn't certain if it was disorientation or the unsteady seams of the memory, but her vision flooded blurry. Her face burned. Her chest ached with stitches. She couldn't breathe. The space was closing in on her, claustrophobic and blinding with blackness.

Am I seriously having a fucking panic attack?

She hadn't had one since middle school when her class was visited by the local fire department for a presentation. They showed a video on housefires and safety plans, and she'd run from the room hyperventilating. She'd smacked a teacher who'd tried to hold her still and calm her. Her fellow students stared and muttered at her back for months following that incident. Even school had become another place to wear her mask and not feel anything authentic and real.

Norah now clenched at her kneecaps, eyes weeping and hot. Tears blinded her further. The scene had somehow ignited with the light of a fed blaze, but nothing could be seen beyond the flames and pulsating smoke.

How in the hell had it grown so fucking fast?

The shudder of an overturned sofa and a collapse of large limbs jerked her head towards the window. Her father screamed.

Norah again crawled on her knees, seeking him out.

She could hear the crackling of galled fibers and wooden bits crumbling into the carpet like ashen branches in a bonfire. Ahead, reaching hands shook and clutched the ground before her, attempting to pull and scrape themselves from the flames. The fingers were bubbling in white blisters. Burning debris has showered and stuck to the sticky flesh.

Then, his once pale torso breached the smoke and approached his adult daughter on the floor.

Leonard Kestrel shook on all fours, no longer wearing his handsome features or identifiable traits. His naked flesh was entangled in frayed kindling. From the waist up, he was brick red with thick pustules. Steam rose off his flesh in heaping swirls. All the salt and pepper hair on his body melted. His ears bubbled and molded like smooshed clay against his scalp.

And his face…

His face was a white and crimson egg-like shape, hanging differently from his skull now. What remained was the lidless, partially molded shape of Leonard, as though his creator had only just begun the drafting process. There were still lumps to press out and features to chisel.

A partially torn sash of peeled, oozing skin was hanging from his cheek where burning drapery had melted to him. He trembled below his daughter, uncertain how to stop the pain.

And Norah Kestrel couldn't move. She couldn't breathe. Her brain screamed for her to spin and dry heave on the carpet.

She could *hear* her father simmering. She could smell his follicles and flesh.

TAKE ME BACK TAKE ME BACK she screamed, but her voice couldn't breach the space.

Leonard bellowed an inhuman gargle.

Robin wailed.

Norah's world tilted. She wasn't certain if she was going to black out or melt into the carpet.

The pink and crimson figure that was her father, dug and crawled in place, doing so with the executive functioning of a broken wind-up toy.

The grotesque figure stole any remaining bitterness of Leonard Kestrel from her brain. The years of isolation, pain, and fear at his anger were overwritten in a breath.

He called out into the night with distorted, guttural screams, like the haunting wails of a theremin.

Jesus, he's still alive.

LET ME OUT LET ME OUT LET ME OUT, she screamed.

Visions of baking flesh were plastered on her shut eyelids. Her stomach lurched, forcing a hand to her chest. She heaved into the carpet, her nose and lips pressed into its surreal fibers.

I'M DONE. I'M DONE. I'M DONE. STOP.

Stop, she gasped.

Stop.

"Stop!"

✦

The eager scream finally trembled from her throat and left her lips, her father's cries still in her ears. She collapsed into the arms of the present world, the memory washing away like a melting filmstrip. She wiped sweat and tears from her burning eyes, pressing cold fingers against their lids. But it didn't matter.

Everything was still etched in the darkness of her headspace.

On her knees, she prayed the vomit remained at bay. Nausea forced her forehead to the roof's cool, gritty surface as she wept.

Her vision blazed with salt and her nostrils were still filled with sulfur and burning skin. She could still hear a wounded man's cries of desolation on the wind. She whimpered and folded into herself, clamping her hands against her skull.

But as the horrid cries broke and wailed on, she realized the man's screams didn't belong to Leonard Kestrel. She pushed herself upright and sought out the begging, pleading soul.

Dexteras was at the golden blades of Solus, digging his fingernails and forehead into the roof until bloodied scrapes painted him. A puddle of teardrops streamed toward the gutter.

He'd seen everything too.

No.

She didn't want that.

No.

I didn't want him to see…

But Solus surely had, evident in their crooked, pitying grin. Golden eyes poured with sympathy upon the shattered Figment below who wept on their sharp prosthetics.

Dex shook with such violence, it appeared he was seizing. His old wrinkles contorted into pleats, and his lips bled through gritted teeth.

"I don't remember, I don't remember, I don't remember being there, I don't I-" he pleaded.

"Of course, you don't, son," said Solus. "You asked me to take it all from you."

Dex's words wobbled into horrid sobs of denial.

Nor watched yet another strong man crumble before her.

And as she did so, she couldn't deny a burning, mechanical pain of betrayal in her chest. She prayed the wind would take it from her just as Solus had been torn from Dex's chest days before. But the teeth of bitterness, of anger, sunk deep into her breastbone and wouldn't shake free. Visions of the fever dream she'd just escaped were still etched across her eyelids. And Dexteras had done nothing about any of it.

He was there. He was there the whole time. And he'd done nothing to stop her father from burning. He'd done nothing to stop her mother from setting the blaze. He simply watched and whispered and scarred a child.

Norah's eyes burned for rage and for tears as they rested on Dex's shuddering body. Then she lifted them to Solus on their shining gold limbs. They sported a boyish grin, relishing all that fear and fire consumed. Decades of *"I told you so"* twisted in their lips.

She knew in the depths of her logical, fact-based brain that neither Dex nor Solus could take credit for that evening. It wasn't theirs to take. It was just as she couldn't take responsibility for the pains or victories of her clients.

She knew that despite the convincing whispers of imaginary friends, figments of our imagination, angels, Figments of the stars, deities, therapists, doctors, and parents alike, humans had free will. *They* were in control of how they lived in response to the world's brokenness. Only *they* could decide what to do with what had been done to them.

But still, the betrayal burned on within her. She could observe it objectively but would not deny her clenching fists. She would never deny herself her anger ever again.

You were there, Dex, and all you did was make it worse.

Were you her Figment? Norah wondered. *Were you his? Wasn't it your job to guide them? To love them?*

Solus knelt beside Dex like a spider descending a web. They stroked the old man's grieving spine, still shaking with screams. Dex seemed to be calling into Hell, begging it to claim him.

Norah knew Dex was suffering as she was, but it was the first time in their friendship that she felt a disconnection. A rift. A chasm. It felt as though she'd been lied to, betrayed, though she hadn't been.

"Son," cooed Solus, "Of course you can do nothing but destroy and ruin. You were made by self-destructing Corpses-"

"Do *not* call them that!" Dex screamed, spine rounding like a dog's.

"*Consumed,* convoluted minds are created to consume and convolute. It's not *your* doing that we follow the suit of our makers." They begged as though holding to the remains of a fallen child. They bowed their head, black lashes lowered in authentic compassion. "I only showed you so that you wouldn't deny what you are anymore. This was a gift."

Still, Dexteras wept.

Then, Solus' pandering mask gave way to rage and irritation. Their fingers raked through the old man's hair and clutched a handful in a fist, stiffening his skull to look at him.

Dex's entire face was crimson and bloodied and broken. His trembling hands clung to Solus' arms.

For a moment, Norah's numbness was so vast, so endless and thick, she couldn't feel anything for anyone, not even Dexteras, not even her father or mother. It terrified her therapist's heart to feel the suffocating abyss of such exhaustion. She couldn't move her feet while her friend was abused. She couldn't even breathe.

When Dex didn't give Solus the audience they so desired, they snatched the old man by the collar and jerked him upright. Both Figments on their knees, praying for very different fates to claim them.

"*This* is your opportunity to own your existence Dexteras, do not waste it! Another gift, a home, a family that will earnestly know you and give you worth," they cried, spit and steam flinging from their lips. "*Esto quod est!*"

SLAP.

Norah's rage had finally found her feet and then her fingers, swooping upon the crouched being and striking their cold, stony face. The force turned their cheek just so, twisting a small, masochistic smile at their lip.

It'd stung Nor as though she'd assaulted a block of dry ice, but she bared her teeth and squared up to the old Figment.

Dexteras was dropped to the broken shingles of her roof while Solus gazed up at her with manic wonder. They were filled with an awe that one might recognize in the bulging white eyes of a rabid wolf.

"*He'll* decide who he is," she growled, limbs trembling.

Unreadable emotion swam across the beast, whether they considered devouring her or laughing. Eventually, a carefully measured grin lifted their handsome cheek and they rose high above her to their full height. With a fresh cigarette between their dark lips, they snapped their suit across their shoulders, steam gushing in swirls.

"You and I both know what it is to make ourselves from nothing, child. You don't *need* him," they stated, their tone as sure as hellfire.

"You're right. I don't need him," she agreed, with more bite than intended.

The tall creature chuckled, eyes wide in interest.

"But you," she began, reading between their fiery eyes with a therapist's scrutiny. "*You* sure seem to. Why?"

Their feline smile fell. "You're one of the meager lots who could possibly comprehend my motives, child," said the old Fig. "Because, like yours, my Makers broke my heart, and I've made it my life's work to break theirs."

Solus didn't want to save the Figments. They wanted to punish the Corporeals. It was never about Freedom.

Nor gazed upon them, jaw tight and lips pursed in bridled sadness. She was certain it was the first time they'd spoken the entire truth in her presence.

"All you care about is survival." Her heart panged with empathy for the old fool.

Solus chuckled into their cigarette. "You do know that it was *your* Makers who brought him and you both into this miserable existence with *their* need for survival?" they said. "I'm simply trying to free him from your wretched past, just as you're trying to free yourself."

Nor's gut clenched, killing what minimal commiseration she could spare in these delicate moments. "You don't get to decide how people handle their shit," she stated. "Now fuck off, we made a deal." She threw her chin to the wind.

They sucked their white teeth and glared at her with the hunger of a beast who'd been run off their kill.

"If only your past could be lifted from your shoulders too," they teased, "you could be a force to be reckoned with, Miss Kestrel." The handsome cheekbones rounded, and steam peeled from the rusty panel on their chest.

Nor stepped nearer, breaking through the bullet-proof glass of her fear.

"Bitch, I already am a force to be reckoned with," she snapped. "Now *leave*, Solus."

The Figment lifted their proud chin with raised brows, surely considering unspeakable responses. But for a moment, Nor swore the being flickered in and out of the airspace like a mistuned radio, unfocused and uncertain of who they were supposed to be. But then, within a blink, they were wholly themself, grinning and certain as ever.

"For someone so mighty, you surely do quiver at the sound of your own name, *Lenore* Kestrel," they hummed, stepping back into the night until they were swallowed by darkness.

Their departure cooled Norah's sweating chest, allowing her to steady her heart and find a seat on the roof. From a distance away, she simply watched Dexteras in disbelief, who'd slipped into a shell shock of sorts. He was crumpled on his side, arctic eyes glossy, absent.

Floating and untethered to her body, Nor dared a few feet nearer to the man and sat again, simply breathing and existing.

Despite his immortality, his amnesia, his joy, and his bright light, they both had been torn apart by the same exact story and the same exact people. And perhaps it was that likeness that made her look upon him with pity and anger now. With such denial and rage.

He'd been a deep, unspoken need the Kestrels had pined for, composed of their composted grief. Just as Nor was. And now, they were both here, universes apart, in the flesh. They were truly slaves to the same sad tale.

Guilt and betrayal exchanged turns at stabbing her insides.

He'd loved her through each of her ugliest vulnerabilities, through her screaming and weeping and shaking. But he'd also been the one to watch her mother suffer, and her father burn to death. To listen to a child sob helplessly as her parents died.

An insatiable need for closure, vengeance, clarity, logic, *anything* lit her blood like a kettle, simmering beneath her flesh for hours.

I just want to understand. I don't want to hate him. I don't want to hate him. I cannot hate anyone else.

✦

She made them tea and sipped on her own while his grew cold in the rooftop chill. His throat had to be hoarse from sobbing, but he didn't touch his cup or move.

A few times, she found her fingers reaching for him, wanting to touch his scars, to hear what he was thinking or seeing. But each time the craving came, she wrapped her fingertips more tightly around the hot teacup.

Besides, the stormy horizons that once welled within his irises were gray and lifeless. A tornado had struck his shores and left the skies deathly still and violent.

Vincent slept on the old Figment's chest, purring endlessly.

Nor kept her teeth welded together and her lips pursed. Hot tears would rinse her wind-chafed cheeks in waves. Her brain itched for some sort of thought, idea, or emotion that was safe to hitch itself to. Because the islands of disappointment, grief, isolation and anger would drown her if she lingered on them too long. The swelling, burning rise of a scream was inching up her chest and into her throat.

I need to get the fuck out of here before I say or do something I regret.

"Dex, I need to leave for a little bit. I'll be back, but I need to go." Air crackled through her throat, echoes of sticky, dehydrated life rattling on her tongue. "I-I just thought you should know."

She groaned and stood, joints crackling to life. She turned for the window when-

"I-I took everything from you, and I remember none of it," Dex said. His words peeled from his mouth like flypaper. "I'm the reason…" his voice broke, and his sobs returned, "I'm the reason you're alone."

Nor stared at the motionless old man for a long moment and didn't say a thing. Eventually, she crouched beside him and put a hand on his massive shoulder. She said what she knew she was supposed to say, though she didn't feel it presently:

"*They* made those choices," she whispered. "And you didn't take *anything* from me, Dex. *I* survived. *I* made it." She gestured to her chest, offended by the thought that anyone but herself could decide when she was done fighting.

Through his tresses, Nor could see one of his red, watering eyes squinting, burning with tears. It rested on her palm and the scar he'd put there. He clenched his lids shut until large, salty streams spilled from him like sap from the wrinkled bark of a tree.

"I'm a *parasite*, Norah. I die without someone to feed on. That's why I was fading before I met you," he whispered.

"No," she snapped. "You're just fueled by helping others, just like I am."

His head shuddered against the roof. "But I make things *worse*," he whispered. "I'm nothing but chaotic, recycled energy, just leeching on others for Purpose."

She huffed into the chilly morning, grinning dryly. "You and me both."

Dex fell silent again, spine slumped, eyes still locked on her palm.

Nor reached to spin the bracelet on his lifeless arm, remembering the sweet child and how she looked upon Dex with sparkling eyes of adoration. But she stopped her fingers and rubbed her knees instead.

"We're both messy and learning, Dex. But you're the stronger of us both," Norah muttered. "You've done nothing but love me, despite all my mistakes and despite all your exhaustion. Even though I let her die alone in that hospital." She swallowed and closed her eyes.

All she'd ever done was run from discomfort, as Kestrels do. When would it stop?

Butterflies beat against her intestines as she eyed the hospital's spire in the distance.

"I've got to go. But I'll be back soon." She touched his shoulder and stood, leaving him unfolded beneath the skies. It took every ounce of her strength to not spin on her toes and scream at him, to ask him why, and to raid his skull for more memories.

50

ꞏDEXTERASꞏ

LUCIDITY CAME FOR HIM IN WAVES, in crashing swells that drowned him. Dizzying undertows of guilt, nearing the gallows. And he was ready for them.

Norah Kestrel had entrusted him with the scars upon her heart and her home. She'd allowed him to peer through the fragile lens of her pain and behold the spindling cracks her light shone through. She'd invited him to know her where no other had been fortunate enough to tread.

But her scars were *his* doing all along. *He* was the reason her family had been taken from her and the reason she was truly alone. And not once, but *twice*, he'd attempted to jump, to die, and abandon her again in his shame.

Coward. Coward. Coward.

This was a simple end, but still unjust for all he'd ruined. He was destined for *occasus*, oblivion, and he'd deserved it.

Let yourself be broken so that you'll never break her again. Do it right this time.

He was an evolved star, dissolving in gases, losing mass with each breath.

He was destined to end in fire and ruin since the day he'd been dreamed up. To destroy everything in his path.

You weigh her with pity. With grief. Disgust.

Norah must've left on foot because the Voices returned slowly like an oncoming train. He had no energy to roll his worthless corpse from Their tracks.

"The most worthless kind-"
"I don't know what's left-"
"It's breaking. Or it's broken. I'm-"
"Please don't leave me, please-"
"I never wanted it to be like this. It-"

Esto quod est. Be what you are.

But I don't want to be anything.
I don't deserve any Purpose. I had my chance.

Then, a stench pulled at his nose hairs. Tangy, sweet, the saltiness of sweat and blood.

A grip as hot as a stovetop wrapped around his throat and hoisted him into the air. Skirting fingernails raked up his chest. Humid lips pressed against his neck.

"Tell me, son, what gives a Figment power?" Solus snapped their fingers, and the world around them disappeared.

A drop tore at Dex's gut, stiffening him with nausea, fearful of retching. New, wild winds pulled at his hair, and the pressure in his forehead intensified with altitude. A murder of crows fled the new scene before them.

Dex tore his eyes apart, wincing against the red sun. They were hundreds of feet above Corvid, atop the towering Gothic spire of its chapel. Cracked, thirsty cement crosses stood guard at each pinnacle. A halidom such as this was a fitting and righteous end to a damned Figment such as himself.

The elder Figment's copper hands dug their nails into him and the church's buttress as an anchor.

Dex swayed towards the beckoning earth below, but Solus pulled him against their warm breast.

"Pain," Solus answered finally. "And you've known endless bounds of it." Commiseration and parental pity dripped from their voices as they beheld Dexteras in the skies

He leaned into their tearing claws with impatience. His chest was scraped hollow. A tear fell from him and sizzled away on the old Fig's skin.

"Even without your memories, your hungry blood found her once already. You yearned for her hope just as your Corpse had, and she will always be at risk of infection from your rot," grumbled Solus, nails burying themselves into Dex's skin. "But if your ruination serves Purpose with me, you'll be endlessly satiated and at peace. Comfortable, at last."

Dex closed his eyes.

"Give me your ache, your agony," they muttered into his neck, each consonant scraping his ears like a knife blade. "And this time, I'll carry you to Oblitus myself."

Dex knew it would solve nothing, but he still longed to fall. To be free of Solus, to be free of logic. It was no wonder he bound from the ledge so willingly all those decades ago.

Let me go. Let me go. Let me go.

He laid harder and harder against their hold, forcing his captor to huff with mild strain, amusement hissing through their nostrils.

They laid their gorgeous head over his shoulder and locked him tightly in place. Their golden eyes flashed to the sky.

"Or do you want this horrid cycle to play on for eternity? This generational chase?"

Dex began to tremble and weep. He was truly trapped. This would never end.

"You love this one. I know you don't want to do that to her," whispered Solus.

"W-what if she finds me? If she comes back to the ring-" whispered Dex.

"You served as a bridge from her world to ours. The sooner you forget her, the sooner she'll be safe. She won't be able to return to Oblitus when the line is cut."

Dex wept for how he knew Norah would weep for his worthless hide. How angry she would be with him for leaving her, just as everyone else had. It was inescapable: both avenues would hurt Norah.

"What must I do…?" he whispered.

"Simply give me your word: your agony for your loyalty."

Dex clenched his eyes shut, tears spilling past them, soaking the long, inked arms that braced him.

He swallowed deep and parted his lips…

"I-"

51

✦NORAH✦

SHE GATHERED MINDFUL BREATHS AS SHE ASCENDED. A wrapped parcel bounced beneath her elbow with each step.

Her outstretched fingers settled upon the steel door ahead. She thought of Dex, pounding on the club's steel entrance for courage, awakening. She mimed a few hits against this one now, a smile flickering as her rings clunked against it. Her amusement fell at the thought of him, suffering on her rooftop. She would go back for him, and they would make this right. But first she needed to make herself right.

She drew a breath, swiped her key card, and stepped into the hall. It was early, so the space was reverent and still. Quiet with death and exhaustion.

She knew the bed would be made and empty. The charts would be torn from their boards, and the monitors would be wheeled away. She knew what awaited her on the other side of that door. Or rather, what did *not*.

But still, her limbs were frozen on the threshold of 7B.

Norah was statuesque, chest hung in a breath it couldn't unhitch.

A small figure approached carefully from her peripheral. A tiny, pixie-haired woman from the nurse's station glided towards her with caution. Toni Plover reached out a small hand, slowly, gently, as though she were worried the girl may scare like a frightened bird.

"Hey, beautiful lady," the nurse whispered.

Before tears or breaths could collapse from either, Nor and the small nurse collided in a powerful embrace, holding each other tightly.

Toni gazed at the door beside them. "It's empty. Would you like to go inside?"

Norah looked towards it, fear trapped in her throat. But she nodded into the petite woman's neck.

Toni took Norah's trembling fingers into her own calloused hand and led them in. Cleaning chemicals and detergents burned her nostrils.

Toni sat upon the starchy bed with its new linens, patting beside her with a small, elfish smile. She perched there with the casual ease of someone who'd sat there countless times to console the dying woman who once occupied it.

Nor wished to join her, but her feet had turned to stone, leaving her stranded in the hall. Her lips were parted, but feared those aforementioned screams would burst from her chest.

"You're here now, sweet girl. And that's all that matters," said Toni. "You be wherever you need to be."

This grace drew Nor nearer, but still, she was flooded with embarrassment for how yet another empty room could debilitate her so. Her hand drew to her chest at the thought but remembered that her key no longer hung there. Thoughts of Dex's patience and his compassion kept her feet moving towards the bed until she was able to sit beside the nurse. She laid the package under her arm onto Toni's lap.

"Cookies from Love Dove's. There's not enough I could ever give you and the other nurses, Toni…for…."

But the tiny nurse interrupted her, rambling with happy gasps, tearing open the box of bird-shaped treats. She plucked a Blue Jay sugar cookie from the box with its intricate icing, edible glitter, and shining blue candy eye.

"My darling. Trust me, if we wanted compensation for our work, we wouldn't go into nursing," she chuckled. "We loved your mama bird. And we love you."

Tears continued to pour from Norah's eyes, but she found peace in inspecting the nurse's smile lines and silvery hair. Nor was angry with herself for avoiding her for so long.

"I-I thought I had so much more time. I should've listened, Toni. I should have listened to you, I-"

But Toni was shaking her head. "No, no, no, my gorgeous girl. No. This is *your* life. Your heart. Your grief. You alone know how to care for it. Robin wanted you here when you were ready, I'm sure of it."

Toni took a massive bite of the Blue Jay's tail feather and bent to tote a cardboard box from beneath the bed. A label-maker sticker that read ROBIN KESTREL was peeling from its side.

Nor stood and backed towards the door as if Toni had withdrawn a living scorpion from the room's depths. Her head shook and she felt leaking mascara clumping at her lids.

Toni chewed at her cookie and continued. "I know you didn't come here with anticipation of seeing any part of your mama today, sweet girl. And that's not what this is," she said, gesturing to the meager belongings. "This is simply an opportunity for you to take what you want so that you can better see her. When *you're* ready."

Norah covered her face and moaned in self-pity. First, she was threatened by an empty bed, and now by a cardboard box.

Fucking wuss.

"I-I thought I was… but I don't know now, Toni, I don't know."

"Then maybe it's not today," she sang with a small shrug, mouth full of gourmet cookie. The nurse's wrinkles and worn crow's feet bent with unending grace.

Norah saw Dex's loving features there again and sighed, dropping her hands from her face.

"Maybe you put it in a storage room and consider it in another week, another year." Toni clutched her desserts and stood with a groan to embrace Norah again and kiss the sides of her head. She pecked until they both burst into pitiful sobs of laughter.

"I sent you a letter in the mail sweet girl, but your Mama made me her POA about a year and a half ago. I tried to call you before-"

"I know," whispered Nor. "And I'm sorry."

"Don't ever be sorry. She simply didn't want to burden you with anymore to do. She'd already decided that she didn't want to fight much longer. We're still waiting on the kit to be mailed back, but she asked to be cremated and planted with a tree."

"Jesus, Toni," blubbered Nor, wiping the endless tears from her cheeks. They both chuckled gently, their crimson eyes squinted in exhausted grief. Robin *would* want to be a fucking hundred-year-old oak that Norah would have to keep alive until she was dead, too.

Nor nodded until her nods became slow, tired shakes of denial.

"I'm always here for you if you need me. And I know a guy if you need a really good therapist," Toni winked. Then she looked about the fluorescent-lit room, her cheer softening.

"Take all of the time here you'd like," she said, hugging Norah for the millionth time with a great moan, wiping tears from her cheeks, and finally shutting the door behind her.

As the latch caught with a satisfying click, Norah collapsed upon the bed her mother had lived in and died in for years. She wept until there was nothing more to give.

52

✦DEXTERAS✦

"I-"

But he stopped, unable to finish.

He surrendered his weight entirely against the immortal's grip, suspending himself above the blacktop below. His tears streamed without restraint, painting a target for his corpse. The Voices screamed, busting his temples at the seams with pressure.

His and Nor's orbits were fated to collide. Solus was right. Which meant he was only putting off the inevitable. Either he'd abandon her entirely or continue to expose her to his unfolding darkness.

Solus growled at the old man's weight, fingers deep in his chest, leaving crimson indents and beads of blood to trickle down his torso. The fingernails of their other hand could be heard scraping the pinnacle's crocket like steel nails against concrete. Their lips were fixed with such focus, that their cigarette pressed into the soft flesh of Dex's neck, burrowing a crusty red blister into him.

"Say it. Say it, son, and your pain will be ended."

Dex swallowed against the insistent devil's thin fingers and closed his eyes, still leaking with unyielding salt. His lips parted, and he drew a final rattle of breath into his chest.

Amica mea, please forgive me, please forgive me.

53

✦NORAH✦

THE LAST BELONGINGS EVER TOUCHED BY ROBIN KESTREL poured across Nor's lap, heavy with guilt. The pile was scant and unpredictable, even for a woman Norah felt she once, distantly knew. But ultimately, it came down to paperwork and knick-knacks. That was it.

Her blood grew hot. There'd existed a deep, inner longing for a letter. Some final words written in Robin's shaky script to her only child and the Kestrels' final heir. Perhaps it'd voice all the things she'd done wrong, owning her mistakes and mourning the gift she'd lost in losing Norah. But no.

Instead, Robin called Norah from a hospital line before she died and left a voicemail Norah could never delete.

I thought she was all that I needed to be okay. To fix whatever was wrong with me.

That he was all I needed. Leonard's gruff head bowed in her thoughts, eyes dark and staring beneath his furrowed brows.

She'd even believed it was Dexteras she'd needed to be okay.

But she now knew that no Figments, old gods, mothers, fathers, nor stars in the sky could fix Lenore Kestrel.

They're all gone, and yet I'm still here.

What I thought I needed, was only what I wanted.

I'm still here.

I don't need anyone to fix me.

That's my job. Just like it was Robin and Leo's job to fix themselves.

It was a nasty, ugly thought, but it was all that kept Norah here at this moment. It was all that gave her hope that she could still pull through at the end of the day.

Her mother's box was filled with fake flowers from the gift shop, dusty and smelling of the hospital. There were a handful of free items stamped from the local church, plastic pink rosary beads and tiny, gold embossed Bibles that were shortened and revised, seeming to sense the reader was limited on time.

There were incomplete puzzle books and a tiny album of photos. The albums were dusty and gray as though they'd soaked in a wash of muddy water for ages. In them, were pictures from Robin and Leo's wedding and throughout their life before they were parents. There were grainy snapshots of Norah's birth, which were surely taken by a NICU nurse, depicting an exhausted yet beaming mother and her beet-red infant.

Her father hadn't been there that day, a tender subject in the Kestrel home that Nor dared not inquire upon further. There were tiny, wallet-sized class photos of Norah from elementary and middle school, undoubtedly purchased, saved, and scrapbook by her Nana Rose. Norah hadn't seen any photos of herself after 3rd grade, after Leo had died. Her mother hadn't the mental investment for such luxuries. But to her surprise, there were even pictures of her high school and college accomplishments from the internet. Pixelated graduation photos, poetry awards, and group shots from the Future Authors Club were cut and tucked in the album's pages. Though she couldn't recall Robin ever speaking kindly of her own mother throughout her life, it did seem that Nana Rose attempted to redeem herself in raising Nor, even from afar, until she died.

There was a stuffed cow, heavy with weighted buckwheat and lavender and worn with stains. Nor raised the beast to her nose, hoping its fibers were ingrained with her mother's scent, a scent she wouldn't know even if it were there, but the fake fur only held musk cafeteria food stenches and its cereal grains and florals.

As she sat the plush beast down beside her, a familiar clacking of plastic caught her eyes. The cow wore a homemade beaded bracelet around its neck, old worn black letters spelled LJK. It must've come from the house and its dredges of Norah's art. She stared at her initials for what felt like hours, feeling the salt and fire return to her face, wondering why her mother had had it, but finding no reason suitable.

The childish trinket, however, reminded her of something else she'd meant to do, and she quickly retrieved her phone from her pocket, poking at its translator app hurriedly. When it didn't deliver the answers she sought, she copied and pasted some text into her search engine, tapping through an article on etymology. It was there that Norah found what she needed, nodded, and set the phone back on the bed.

There was a stack of glittery birthday cards from Rose up until the year she died. There were copies of dust-ridden framed photos from the hospital's rooms walls. A few were also on the walls of their home. It was strange to think she and her mother gazed upon some of the same images each day, several times a day. Clattering at the bottom of the box, there were countless pens and stress balls with the names of prescriptions and specialists on them.

There was a set of cheap reading glasses patterned with black and white cow print. There was a matching thin, fleece blanket scattered in purple cows and florals.

She nearly forgot about her mother's interest in the bovines but scarcely recalled Robin rolling down the window whenever they passed the chewing creatures, yelling "Moo Cows!" at the top of her shrill lungs like a toddler.

A jab of shame cut Norah just under her breastbone. Her mom would've been easy to buy gifts for, but she never did once she moved into EoLC.

One item not encrusted with dust was a white mug with the hospital's logo partially worn off. Its innards were stained with various copper and brown rings and cracks as though Robin drank black coffee from the thing every day for years.

Nor's chest burned. She had endless coffee cups at the house that would've at least had some character to them. All she could do now was shake her head and put the mug beside her on the mattress.

Then, all that remained in the box was a packet of stapled papers, pixelated from a dodgy copy machine, and slid into a coffee-stained manila folder. They seemed to be reprints of an official record that Norah had to squint at. The papers were nearly fibers with their wear and age.

She dared to wipe the cow bifocals and push them up her nose. Her eyes widened. Reading the blurry typed letters filled her head with black smoke and screams.

CORVID CITY FIRE DEPARTMENT
CASE NUMBER: 07220
FIRE INVESTIGATION REPORT
SUMMARY OF INCIDENT: Investigators Grouse and Vermilion responded to a reported fire at 125 Condor Court, Corvid, at approximately 3:11 AM. Upon arrival, fire crews found heavy smoke coming from the two-story wood-frame construction. The building was an occupied living space for the Kestrel Family, consisting of three members including Leonard Kestrel (M, 39), Robin Kestrel (F, 31), and Norah Kestrel (F,7), and one black house cat. Investigation revealed the fire originated in the master bedroom, nearest its southern-facing window, started by the distribution of a flammable accelerant (trash can receptacle debris, alcohol, high-proof rum) and ignited by an open flame (unextinguished cigarette thrown in a metal trash receptacle) by Robin Kestrel who was tested with a .46 BAC upon emergency intake. Due to these highly debilitating levels, it is determined the incident was accidental and Robin Kestrel was admitted for moderate carbon monoxide poisoning, bronchitis, second-degree burning on her arms, first-degree burns on her thigh, and lung tissue inflammation

exacerbating preexisting clinical diagnoses. The fire resulted in 1 fatality of Leonard Kestrel who died of a 6% oxygen level, 95% burn rate, severe fluid loss, and exposure due to a highly aggressive flash fire after opening the bedroom's outside window, exposing highly concentrated flammable gasses (O_2) to the open flame.

That's how it all happened so quickly.

She wiped at her hot tears.

A flash fire.

She remembered her father's trembling form, slick with sweat, panicked and trembling. She used to hear his angry screams in her head, but now she heard only his cries of her name, hoping that somewhere in the night, his daughter was safe.

Leonard was a numbers man. Calculated, logical. Type A. An educated gambler. He couldn't have been expected to understand the complex chemistry of house fires and how they breathed, or how quickly vapors pressurized a room with combustible toxins. He couldn't know how fatal it was to expose such a swollen, flaming space to immense oxygen.

She'd never laid eyes upon the arson report and didn't care to before today, but she'd always fought the ache in her gut that pondered how a cigarette fire had escalated into a fucking blitzkrieg before the fire department arrived. Perhaps if she hadn't had a panic attack when the fire department visited her school when she was a kid, she might've learned a thing or two. With a final sniff, Norah read on:

The youngest member, Norah Kestrel was removed from the home with moderate oxygen deficiencies, smoke inhalation, and shock with the most severe injury being a second-degree electrical burn on her palm after attempting to open the doorknob connected to the impacted room. The child's symptoms included muscle spasms within the electrocuted limb, tingling sensations, and numbness throughout to confirm this diagnosis. Atypical for electric burns, no further damage or muscle impairment was found, and no evidence of tetanic contraction. On-site, investigators did not observe any live wires near the door's hardware that would've resulted in a burn of this nature, and the doorknob was found unlocked. Investigators reported if this electrical charge had not prevented the child from entering the room, the implosion of the flash fire would have likely resulted in her death as well. At the time of investigation, Fire Chief Swift stated, "It doesn't make sense, but she's still alive."

Before she could consider another thought, Norah Kestrel was *running*. Sprinting at a speed she hadn't known possible in booted heels as she tore the hospital into shambles with her strides.

There was no time to dry tears or to tuck the fire report into her pocket. No time to wipe at smeared makeup or to embrace Toni upon exiting.

Norah tore doors from hinges and slid into hallways with such momentum she slipped to her palms with sweaty squeaks on the laminate. Nurses mumbled and gasped as she parted their busyness in reaching bounds. She leaped half-a-dozen stairs with each gasp of breath and crashed onto the parking lot with hot feet.

Norah cut through lawns, the cathedral's prayer garden, and any other landscape which could deliver her as the crow flew. Her ankles screamed, and her knees threatened to buckle atop her stomping heels. Her eyes watered, she was wheezing, and her fists cut through the air with aching joints. But she did not falter.

Finally, home peaked over the horizon. Untamed crops waved her inwards.

Though she couldn't see him on the rooftop, she bolted through the porch skipping stairs two at a time, shaking the foundations of her home with roaring breaths.

Please be here, please be here.

She burst through her parents' door, then her own, exploding onto the rooftop.

"Dex!"

But her cries only fell upon the scattering birds.

Dammit, where is he?

She fell to her knees, skinning her dress pants and burying her face into her hands, exacerbated and panting.

"Dex, please. Please. Please listen," her voice was pinched and loud, and her hands trembled beneath her. She stared at the place where he'd lain. A soft *pit...pat...* drew her eyes to the paperwork in her hands, where it absorbed her falling tears. She held a breath to assess its precious epiphanies.

"Please..." she began, "Dex, please hear me, I need you. I need you, I need you to be here." She had no idea how such a message and yearning would be shuttled to the old Figment, but she knew talking aloud was how she sustained her sanity as a child, so perhaps that energy could bring him to her now. She rubbed the running makeup from her cheeks.

"Please...Dex, you're good. You're good. You saved me. You saved me that night. Please remember, please don't leave. I need you to know that you saved me." She rested her forehead on the crunching roof tile where Dex's tears had puddled just hours prior. Where her anger had been palpable and afire for him.

She saw the sweet sparkle in his stormy irises. The warmth of his sly smile. The raising of his happy whiskers and brows. The wrinkled eyes that always searched and loved her. All he'd ever done was love and fight for those he loved.

"Dex, *you* saved me. Let me save you..."

54

✦DEXTERAS✦

BREATH WHISTLED THROUGH HIS THROAT. His vision waned through a black funnel. But none of that mattered. He was empty of panic and worry. He was dead, regardless.

If he ran to each corner of the earth and its frontier of galaxies, he'd never escape how he'd hurt her. Everything he was. Everything she believed him to be. The love she'd outpoured for him. All of it stolen back with the awe of his betrayal. His self-worth sent crumbling with her pained stare.

This was his only chance at offering her peace.

Though his head was pulsating with a lack of oxygen, The Voices screamed desperately without consideration of his dilemma.

"Don't think to-"

"I don't want to do this any-"

"Please hear me, I need you. I need you right now."

"Just don't even know-"

His heart skipped a beat, and his eyes shot open. He breathed deeply and swallowed.

That was...there's no way...that's impossible.

But he'd never miss that voice in any crowd. He'd always hear Norah when she called. It was as if she were the bow and he was the string, and the resulting vibrations illuminated him with unfeasible joy.

He closed his eyes again and sought her, lips blundering in search of her words amongst The Voices. As he sifted through the vast cries, They quieted. They settled with peace as he encountered Them with willing consideration. With each he processed, the remaining could be interpreted more clearly. They served as Polaris in the navigation of his friend.

"It's all I have now. There's nothing else-"

"-wonder how long this can last, it's so-"

"Please remember...I need you. I need you to know-"

There.

"Don't leave, I need you. I need you to know that you saved me that night..."

He dropped his weight into his heels, anchoring himself into the warm bosom of the eldest Figment. Their gold chains singed his collar and neck flesh.

"Now it's my turn. I need to save you."

His brows bent to console her appeals, so determined, so restless, so certain, so full of fresh epiphany. *What had she discovered?* His ribcage was going to split in two with heartbreak. But then it struck him like an uppercut.

These were not auditory hallucinations.

He was hearing...thoughts.

Cognitions.

Not just his own, but those of living, breathing Corporeals, like Norah.

Mouth agape, he tuned into the requests again. The once infuriating horde of voices became a cathedral of sorts, echoes of yearning and respite.

"I feel so alone all of the time. Please, someone, sit with me if you can."

"Christ, I'm scared. Send someone to get me through this. I've got no one else."

"Be with my son. He means so well. He's just lost. Give him guidance."

"Please send someone to be here since Dad can't be."

"Just let me know what it feels like to be loved by a father, just once."

And then, like an avalanche of clarity, his world spun with comprehension. Not just comprehension, but remembrance. The past was a thread, a ribbon that had been fraying and trailing from his skull for decades, slipping from him with each step.

But now, the avalanche was rebuilding itself in reverse, tumbling, turning, welding to its original shape before it'd been demolished. The frayed ribbon wound and knotted and knitted itself into tangible thoughts again.

Memories.

He was returning to his memories. To himself.

He slapped a hand to the arm of the Figment who still held him, seeking reliable ground with his reaching toes.

Solus' muscles and grip tightened, startled by the sudden violence.

Dex's heart quickened like the flaps of wings, gawking upon the red sun, more hopeful and dazzling than he'd ever seen before. The rising dwarf star served as a symbolic solstice to a very important understanding.

But he was still clutched at the throat, centimeters from a familiar demise.

Dex awaited fury and hunger to rise within him for Solus' comeuppance. They'd manipulated him, dallied with the life of his dearest friend, lied with ease through sparkling teeth, and they'd convinced him he was atrocious, unsightly. That he'd abandoned his Purpose, his Corporeal.

But warmth rose in Dex's chest as the bodily Helios did, and with it, his vindication fell away. He swelled with too much joy to be wasted on burning anger. After a microsecond of investigation, Dex registered a weakness in the chokehold that bared him and responded.

He locked his chin onto Solus' arm like teeth and mule-kicked one of their delicate, locked knees. He followed with an elbow jab to their nasal bone, folding the rogue Figment. Immortal blood seeped between their fingers, painting their gold rings as they clutched to their busted face.

Dex snatched their dripping chains and exchanged positions like a swift tango, flowing like oxygen. He held to their gorgeous form, fingers strangled in jewelry and leaking blood. Their tarnished prosthetics shone gold in the sun, dripping with blood. The tailored suit jacket whipped about violently. The form in his hands shuttered and changed like a hologram, uncertain of who it was in the chaos.

Dex became enamored by a driving, spidery crack that branched about the bony face, splintering the surface like an eggshell where he'd fractured their nose. The statue of *Le génie du mal* began to wear its proper age and neglect. The once smooth flesh of their brows and nose bore splits and valleys. Seams cracked like desert sand, breathing plumes of black smoke with its breakage.

Years ago, amongst his mortal numbness, Dexteras had turned his weary head to art in search of something that would shake the cobwebs from his soul. He'd touched the thick smatterings of Impasto paintings and smelled the hot fires of clay kilns and their varnished prizes. He'd hungered for deep emotion, deep humanity, for devastating lows and exhilarating highs.

And once, he'd uncovered a brief emotive in the Japanese art of *Kintsugi*. The soldering together of broken pottery pieces with molten gold. It is meant to represent the gift of breaking and the growth one contrives in falling apart. Though it busied his brain with its beauty, he wouldn't come to find his own breaking precious until Norah taught him with her ruthless acceptance.

In pouring upon the eldest Figment in his hands, Dex realized Solus had never comprehended the beauty of theirs or anyone else's brokenness, but had a physiological likeness to *Kintsugi*. For what remained beneath their flesh was charred, black bone, decaying, rotting. Blackened timber sealed with golden hinges and ichor to avoid compromise. It even glittered beneath their ancient, painted eyes.

Dexteras finally understood that he was seeing Solus as their actual self, beneath the consumed memories and parts of others they'd harbored. It was the memories and Purpose of countless Figments that kept them plastered together.

And with a lifetime of memories returning fresh to his skull, Dex knew it wasn't an infatuation with aesthetics that'd driven them to this façade. It was because their inner mechanical, toothy instruments that once ticked beneath with organic, human Purpose were now rusted and corroded, untended and cankered.

It wasn't the perfectionism that narcissists seek, nor the toxic pursuit of the vain. Instead, this perfectionism came from a deeper, more feral desire. It was meant to quench an undying uncertainty, a fervent anxiety.

Solus had been right. They were the oldest Figment in all of time.

"You're Fear," said Dexteras, eyeing their crumbling features like tattered papyrus. Solus had to surely ache with such corrosion, gripped by inflammation, like eternal bone cancer. One would never see it beneath the twitching smile or the curl in their bloodied lip. Their mask was held upright by gold stitching and dead sinew and the Purpose of others that served them in Oblitus.

"And there is no Unbecoming. *You're* The Unbecoming," Dex whispered. "Figments don't die without Purpose. They return to the stars from whence they came until they're needed again. You've simply been killing them if they get in the way of *your* Purpose."

Soft raindrops began to fall upon them both, spitting and hissing against the inhumanly hot flesh.

"Welcome back, Dexteras," snarled the old being. Though molten gold and sloshing black sap slurped beneath the cracks in their complexion, they could decipher the light of awakening in Dex's eyes. Their throat throbbed against Dex's grip. Fragile fractures expanded through their bony cheek, now rendering one of their eyes dead and gray, like stone.

"You tried to have me killed. Again," Dex mused, a twist in his lip.

"Consume or be consumed," they said.

"There's more to it than that."

They spat on Dex's shoes. "I gave *everything*, only to be unseen and neglected and hated by Corpses, brother. I worked so incredibly hard to protect them, and I was never enough, just as you were never enough," they sneered. The Figment heaved, unhinged and growing hot.

Dexteras sighed. "You're right, fear is never respected as it should be. You deserved thanks. Appreciation. But it doesn't work that way."

They scoffed with cacophonous laughter like the cries of a raven.

Dex watched them lovingly. "It's getting worse, you know," he said, observing their winding crevices.

"*Centuries* I was used and abandoned. *Centuries*, Dexteras," they snarled. "I tore myself into pieces for them. This is no worse than what they did to me," they snapped, eyes flooding.

"But you were trying to *fix* them. Your job was just to be present. To see them. To love them when no one else would. Of course, you were run to death, you-"

"I couldn't even destroy myself to spare the pain because I was *always* needed," they mourned, fingers raking at their dark hair. "No matter what I tried, I awoke to splinters of my own bones and limbs. *All alone*," they spat. "There was no height immense enough to end it all." Unbridled rage shook their windpipe and tore apart their separate voices from one another. "Entire pieces of me, obliterated beyond salvaging. And still they wanted more."

"I know," Dex mourned. Solus hadn't lost their insides and their legs and their sanity from The Unbecoming. They lost them to the destruction wrought upon themselves in attempt to escape the torture of watching their Figments suffer. "Fear is painful. Uncomfortable. And we know how terrified they are by discomfort." Dex's tone hardened. "But you can't keep using others like us to overwrite your pain. It will catch up to you and eat you alive. It's making you monstrous."

"I took their grief and their pain and their tears and their misery. Does that make me such a monster?" Solus lashed out. "I gave them *everything!*" A chorale of voices echoed, each with a distinctive tone, volume, and anger.

Thunder rumbled on the horizon. Dex eyed it with distant wonder.

"Even if we can't fix them, sitting with them in their pain is sacred. It's important work. It's worth the moments they hear us. It's worth it for what they can teach us and give us." Norah's face smiled in his mind's eye.

"*Es stultior asino.* Utter brainwash bullshit," the bitter Fig cackled.

Dex rolled his eyes. "Brother please. Look at us. You have an entire army of Figments who keep you alive with their Purpose, and I have one Corporeal. Who's stronger?" Dex further proved his point by withdrawing a finger from their collar, dropping their body another centimeter towards the earth. They twitched and revealed their teeth.

"A Purpose grounded in love is so much more rich and powerful than one in fear," Dex prompted. A Figment's power wasn't about quantity or strength. Its quality lay in its patience, its compassion. It gathered worth for every moment its goodness survived a brutish world.

Solus' jaw tightened with a scraping of bone, and they squeezed Dex's arm until his sleeve shriveled to threads. Hot fumes and gases trembled about them.

"You said it yourself, we grow stronger with pain, and being a Fig is painful work. But each of the Figments in Oblitus deserves a chance to decide if they wish to pursue it. They don't know that you've been making that choice for them. They don't know that they're enslaved, that they could survive and try again. They could leave or-"

"It's too LATE!" They begged. Some of their distant voices had deduced to faraway screams. Their flesh was sopping, and their cries swelled their quivering throat. "My skull is filled with endless screams and stories that are horrid, lovely, agonizing, and tranquil and they go on for millennia, you understand? I couldn't possibly begin to unravel them. I can't even unravel any of my own!" Their body flickered to further illustrate their undoing. They gasped and bared their white teeth. "Is it so horrid for me to consider our own kind after they've been neglected for centuries? To give them peace and freedom without misery?"

"They have a right to know. To choose. They're not truly free in Oblitus. Neither are you. You could-"

But Solus released their grip on Dex and spread their arms wide with abandon. The beautiful body was soaked in rain and hot tears.

"*Irrumator* Dexteras, even if I could give back everyone's pasts, I'm empty of crusading for Corporeal affections," they lamented. "None of them wanted me no matter how I labored and bled. I refuse to go back to scavenging for belonging!" Their screams broke in multi-faceted pitches as their arms outstretched with wanton disregard. Their eyes leaked like hot springs.

"I gave everything to save them, but I was *always* the villain," Solus snarled, voice breaking. "So that's what I'm going to be until the bitter end."

Dex pushed aside matted layers of hair to behold the branching lightning. It made his skin itch akin to the static of a dead television in the dark. It energized him, it called him home.

Dex sighed and gently returned the bronze body to their towering limbs beside him and clothed his sibling in a final empathetic gaze.

With immortal Figments serving their immortal Purpose in *Oblitus*, Solus would never die. Would never bear the pain of loss. But they'd also never live.

The Patron Figment of Fear would forever be the most misunderstood and the most betrayed by humankind. Fear pined for survival, for life, for the hope of better things, for safety and control. But they were treated like death, like disease. Discomfort was always villainized.

Despite his sibling's fury burning into his spine, Dex hastened the cathedral's flying buttress with confident toes. He found a stable peak before a stretch of rooftop and momentarily lost himself in its far-off horizon. A victorious flash of the skies celebrated his return. The raging boom of thunder applauded shortly after.

His hand swept back into his ivory tresses as a foreign joy captured his wide eyes. A warm, syrup-sweet euphoria slipped down his throat and wrapped his chest and limbs.

Dex was then bounding upon his toes, sprinting with every ounce of his immortal capacity. A smile stretched across his face, his head reared and tossed in the wind like a spirited stallion.

Solus had re-plastered their spoiled flesh, lacquering it in its porcelain once more to glare at him as he ran. Dex understood that they would always be the doll behind the glass, fragile and gorgeous, never to be touched, held, or loved properly.

Mid-sprint, Dex tore the suit jacket from his shoulders and left it in his wake. He inhaled a massive swallow of air into his lungs, bent low, and shot himself from the cathedral's peak, chest-first like a diving swallow. His limbs and hair were pressed behind him, and his eyelids fluttered close.

After an eternity in the clouds, his core rocketed toward Earth. Radiant colors of stained glass and antique stone blurred by. His shirt billowed, drying its fibers.

Another glorious strike of lightning and thunder boomed as he fell.

55

✦NORAH✦

A HEAVY CRUNCHING OF ROOFTOP SHINGLES UNDERTOW made her spin with a gasp.

Dexteras Doe was radiant and grinning, affixing what remained of his tattered shirt to his shoulders. The stark, white mane bounced with his stride. His twinkling eyes were filled with stars. He stopped before her with a breathless grin.

"*Bozhevilnyi*…" she stammered in Ukrainian, irises wide and watering with tears. "As one word, it does mean unhinged, mentally unwell. But she meant it as two words, not one."

He cocked his handsome head, waiting and patient.

"*Bozhe* means god," she breathed. "*Vilnyi* means free. So some use it to mean-"

"Freed by the heavens," he said, cheeks swelling. He dropped his chin and closed his eyes, finally understanding.

"She knew you were special," Nor whispered. "Of the stars."

His shining eyes rose to her beneath his silver brows.

She laughed and sprang for the old man.

He collected her in his arms, laughing like a melody, shoulder blades trembling with joy. His wrinkles scrunched tight. He hugged her tightly as he always had, but this time was different. This was with a fullness, a knowing. A complete comprehension of the both of them and who they were.

"*Amica mea...*" he breathed. He returned her to her feet, eyes drinking her in with the adoration of a father. "Thanks for calling me home."

"You heard me?"

His cheeks rounded like pink melon balls. One of his great, warm, bandaged palms held her cheek. "Of course, I did. I've always heard you."

They embraced one another tightly again, her fingers tangling in the wet shreds of his shirt. Sweet homecoming twisted his bruised lips and made him glow with brilliant happiness.

After all, he'd been an orphan just as she, and now he finally knew home.

✦

The following afternoon, Dex helped Norah dig a hole in front of the Kestrel's home in anticipation of the flowering dogwood tree that would soon fill it. According to Toni, the seedling kit interwoven with Robin's remains would arrive in another week or so, and from there, it would be ready to plant. Norah was grateful for the gift of not planning her mother's funeral but did discover that dogwood trees live up to eighty years.

"Of course," Norah joked, smiling weakly at Dexteras.

But many years ago, little Nor had been certain that planning her father's wake and burial would put her in the ground with him. A shocked, introverted child and her catatonic mother picked out Leo's outfit, shoes, and what framed photos to display for his meager and remaining family. They'd tutted upon whether he'd be buried in his cold flesh or if his remains were to be set ablaze and crushed. They'd chosen the latter and scattered his ashes across the racetrack where he bet on greyhounds and poked at slot machines, an ironic and nearly sacrilegious gesture. While crusty coarse and talcum smooth remains clanged against the aluminum bleachers and intermingled with the well-kept turf, childhood Nor could only wonder what'd happened to her father's gold teeth fillings.

But this time, there was no lid to lock shut, or proceedings to prepare. No entertainment nor playlist to create for the reception.

But that didn't change the grief.

It didn't change the fact that her mother's rice paper pale fingers would never again clutch her cigarettes or her daughter's hand. A thousand unspoken proclamations of love and apology were forever trapped in the decayed crevices of her mother's cremated lungs and would never be Nor's. And though Robin's lips hadn't been wired shut by a mortician, they would never kiss her cheek. Those brittle, veiny arms would never unfold to hold space for her daughter's mess and pain.

But I am all that I need.

I am all that I need.

She thought of the cold arson report in her back pocket and remembered its quote:

"It doesn't make sense, but she's still alive."

✦

They sat before the hole, hands and nails crusted with thick dirt, legs dangling in the shallow pit. Dex had brought Norah a package of fresh peony bulbs and a gold bird feeder to go beside Robin's tree.

"If you'd like, you can put it in the window until the tree's tall enough to hold it," he said.

Nor petted the glass and gold cage, wrapped in wire stars and moons with a sparkling prism dangling from the bottom.

"I'll put it in front of Vince's favorite window," she said. "He'll love that."

At the tree's future home, they both cradled a fresh bottle of beer and wore sunglasses to cover their tired, weeping eyes.

"You look nice," she muttered, eyeing his tied hair and shined boots. Dex wore his beautiful pine green suit with gold details and pocket square. He emanated a quiet peace beside his friend.

He reached with a gentle hand and pulled the large sunglasses from her face, exposing her swollen eyes, stung with strain and salt. He wiped a few tears from her cheeks with his thumbs and kissed the top of her head.

"You're beautiful as always," he whispered into her hair.

Her throat closed off until barely a breath could squeak through.

Sensing the stifled song beneath her chest, he pulled the young woman into a massive embrace, paying no mind to the dirt and mud that smeared the legs of his fine suit.

She wiped the makeup beneath her lids and fanned her hot face. Then, with a shaky breath, she stood and helped pull the old Figment to his feet and led them towards the house.

"How does anyone get over this kind of shit…" she moaned, rubbing her sore eyes.

"There's no *over it*, love, you know that. There's only through. You might laugh and love and cry and pound your fists all in the same breath, and that's precisely how you need to do it."

"That's just the grief," she sighed. "There's forgiveness too."

The levels of her journey were layered like a multicolored mesa in the desert, immense, unmoving, and tiring to behold. Each layer required patience, even though she had little to spare.

"Forgiveness doesn't involve anyone else but yourself, love," he said with a breath of cigar smoke over his shoulder. It flapped into a small flock of Blue Jays whose bodies were whisked apart by the wind.

"It's just you freeing yourself of the bitterness. Focusing your efforts on your healing."

"I thought I felt it yesterday. But I woke up today, and it was gone."

"I think it's a daily decision," he observed with wise knowing. "And there will be days it's harder. But hopefully, those days will become fewer and farther between with time."

There's so much work to do.

He pulled her into a side hug as they hobbled along in the shade. They pushed the lenses up their noses and admired the smoky birds he'd freed into the sky.

At her request, Dex played Stellato on the roof. He flicked her a gentle eye above the instrument and smiled while his hands wandered the strings, rocking to make the notes croon.

The vision of his rhythmic motions and low lashes loosened the knots in her chest. She marveled at his ability to transition from a seasoned fighter, hot and wrought with war, to a passionate musician. His hands melted from calloused, bandaged fists to sensitive dancers across the strings.

Tears fell from them both, but still they smiled.

"Do you think I'm like her?" Nor whispered once the rooftop had gone quiet.

He hummed and passed her a small cigar to keep her from tearing bits of shingle off the house.

"Every choice and fiber of your being belongs to you and you alone, *cara mi.* That includes your decisions to protect who you are and who you want to be." He leaned into her.

"But I am part of *him* too…" Her mind whirred with Leonard's addiction, his violence, his bubbling rage that was prone to erupt at any moment. The way he'd scream and grab her mother by the shoulders. The poison in his genetics surely predisposed his only child to self-destruction.

"Your *story* is a part of his, yes. But your identity doesn't have to be," said Dex. "Meditate on choosing healing choices each day and you'll undo your family's curses. Until it's as natural as making coffee in the morning."

He was right of course. She needed a self-care plan. She needed routine.

Mindfulness.

The wind blew between them, beating their manes of hair and drying salt to their cheeks.

The seedling of a soft peace sprouted in her chest with his words. She eyed the old, blurry Blue Jay inked on his exposed palm.

"What do they call you?" Her heavy-lidded eyes dragged across him in awe.

He smiled. "I'm one of the Figments of the Fatherless. But to you I'll always be Dex." More smoky birds spilled from his lips and wafted towards the sky.

"You saved me," she stated.

"You saved *me*."

The air in her chest grew heavy, leaden.

She ached to ask "*so what happens now?*" but ever since he'd returned with his memories, a truth punctured her bones and harvested winding, strangling roots up her lungs and throat. Its vines choked her until she was shaking her head, breath held.

"Hey," he said, shifting in the dewy grass to face her. "Look at me."

No. No. No. She'd forgotten how to breathe.

"Love…" he begged.

She turned a leaking eye to him. The cigar in her fist was long extinguished and frayed in her fingers.

With a grumble, he pulled her reluctant limbs into an embrace.

Though exhausted, she gripped him with all her strength until she was winded. She could've fled inwardly behind the protective glass of her retinas, but she didn't.

She needed to feel again. That's what she needed.

You need to feel this.

PART III

·HOMECOMING·

56

✦DEXTERAS✦

He stayed for sunset.

He loosened his tie from the healed, smooth burns of his neck and peeled it from his collar with a sigh. On the inhale, he captured an aroma of warming coffee beans from her home.

Vincent nestled into his lap and melted into a black void of sleepy green eyes. The beast purred and gave the occasional gentle chirp.

"I'll miss you too Vince," Dex grumbled, scratching him behind the ears.

The evening was quiet and peaceful. The Voices had stopped entirely after Norah's cries had broken through them in his head. Yet another gift she'd given him.

The sounds of the young woman tinkering in the kitchen throbbed an ache in his heart. Deep in his bleeding, human chest, he wished to stay with her.

He wished to walk each day with Norah in this human form until she was as wrinkled and gray as himself. To remain beside her until she'd lived out each dream, spoken upon each difficult thought, and experienced each becoming and gut-wrenching emotion. He wished to hear every word she breathed until her final breath. To embrace her with each step. To cherish each version of her as she grew.

He was jealous of all of the humans who would get to share her air, feel her embrace, know her goodness, and love her. What a gift it was to truly, deeply, and wholly love her. She made him remember why he was a Figment of the Fatherless and why he adored the position so.

Patience would be demanded of him for another sixty-odd years before he'd hold her again on some other cosmic plane, wrapped in constellations and nebulae. But he also knew a lifetime here was spent as fast as a struck match for someone, *something* like him.

I could have a coffee and she'd be home before I'd finished my cup.

To distract from the pool of tears upon his lashes, he picked at the bandages on his fingers and rubbed the flesh, smooth like polished oak. His earthly skin was healed and fresh, but it was his innards that grew restless and kinetic. There was a pull at the cardiac muscle in his chest that called him towards the skies. He listened to its promise of rest. Only the tiny clinks of glass chiming from the window stirred his meditation and opened his eyes.

Norah sidled close and passed him a mug.

He inhaled the brew over his cup with a sigh.

"So, all the memories…" began Nor, "that Solus showed you from your past, like the ones with Mom and Dad," she sipped and shook her head. "You were never hurting them. You were sitting with them in their hurt."

"I learned from the best," he smiled.

She stared into her heaping cup of soft foam, starry ankles swaying over the rooftop. Her heartbeat thudded louder for a beat or two and she sighed.

"I-I think I'm going to go to therapy…" she said. "It's long overdue and there's a practice outside of town." She explored aloud, a shrug holding her shoulders high and anxious.

He rearranged his long limbs to look upon her. "What a beautiful way to empathize with your client's processes and best understand your own."

She smiled with tiny nods, but her blooming confidence wilted fast. Her heartbeat was chaotic and irregular with worry.

How he wished to share the monumental truths of her future with her now. All of the promises of *aethra, lux*, the light crystallized in her path, set in patient amber. He knew her soul's song so proficiently that he could deduct future strummings with ease. But he couldn't give her prophecy, it wasn't his place. And it wasn't fair to weigh her new beginning with such expectations.

But perhaps he could give her something else instead.

"Can I show you something?"

"Yeah," she said, setting down her coffee cup. "Of course."

They spun their tired bodies on the rough roof's terrain, twisting to face one another, cross-legged and tired. Her lips were pursed so firmly that they were white.

He cleared his throat and moved some hair from her face. He placed his right hand along the contour of her jaw, moving his thumb to the carved scar along her eye. Its divot fit him like a worry stone.

"Trust me?" he whispered.

"Always," she said, tears falling.

57

✦NORAH✦

HER EYELIDS FLUTTERED AND HER LIPS FELL APART. Her world was drenched in the warm sepia of the past, its palette blurring with the blackbird greens and blues of evening. Wild grass and clear evening air. She was in a growing field of chaotic stalks, whispering in a gentle, brisk wind.

Home. Decades ago.

A shuffle of footsteps crackled ahead, treading deep into the field. A baby's small babble cooed on the wind like a kitten's mew.

Nor swept the papery husks from her path, ducking beneath fractured stems, squinting through the moonlight. She hurried, in pursuit of the distantly familiar singsong banter ahead. As per usual when she visited the past via Dex, her clothing was her common black attire, and her body was her real-time adult self. But she felt freer, nimbler, and more importantly, safe. Finally, she caught up to the wading bodies.

"My Nor, my Jaybird," cooed her mother's voice through the thicket. It was stern, expectant, yet wobbling with grief. Robin trudged, tilting her chin to the inky sky, pricked with pinhole stars. "I'm so sorry. You deserve better. You deserve better than *us*. I wish I could give that to you, but I don't know how. I don't even know how to find it for myself."

It was one of the few times in Norah's life she could recall her mother's voice unburdened with alcohol and drunkenness. The unseen adult Norah Jay Kestrel trailed behind, never knowing until this moment that many moons before she'd found solace in these fields as a child, her mother's footsteps had first worn a trail.

As they plunged deeper, a large form clad in black swam through the rustling overgrowth alongside them, crops crunching beneath a long, calm stride. Concern bared the stranger's scruffy jaw as he fell in line behind Robin.

Norah gawked at the strange caravan, consisting of her mother, her infant self, the invisible Figment Dexteras, and her invisible, adult self. Nor rushed to walk beside him and take the man in.

The moon poured over them like white paint, illuminating Dex's ivory locks and trimmed beard. He wore a vibrant baby blue vest and suit pants, crisp and fitted as always. He seemed adorned for the most important job interview in the galaxy. He was less weathered, less drained from humanity's impact it seemed. His wrinkles were fewer, and his broken bones were whole. But a pain stretched his expression. One she'd seen him wear often.

But then, at the sight of the infant over Robin's shoulder, a fascination unbent his brows and sparkled deep in his icy eyes. His cheek fell sideways into his great shoulder, puffing his whiskers in a grin. He was enamored by the child's simple existence.

"I don't want her to hurt like I did," whispered Robin to some unseen force or deity. "I want her to find her own strength. Because damn, she'll need to fight just to survive us. And fight hard. Please help her learn."

And then, another shudder of crops trembled from the other end of the field. Another trudging, lumbering form was approaching, and fast.

She'd expected Dexteras, but certainly no one else. An automatic switch of fear and anxiety flicked on inside of adult Norah.

The figure drew nearer, louder. Their gait was far more casual and unmeasured than Dex's. Billows of cigarette smoke spilled in the air above their shadow. Norah squinted, jaw bared-

But before she could make out the dark newcomer, the world's colors shifted from ocean-floor twilight to warbler yellow, pulling adult Norah from the fields reluctantly.

"Wait-" she began, but in moments, she'd been set down gently in the golden belly of the ambient beast that was home. She'd already been transported to a new memory.

She was in the hall, taking in the small kitchen where her parents now screamed and spat. Their voices had aged several years, evident in the croaks and slurs of their curses and unrestrained insults. Now Robin was surely drunk, inhibitions long buried in liquor.

But here, the audio of the room was muted, as though she'd been submerged underwater.

Somehow, she knew it was Dexteras, protecting her. The vitriolic remarks of her parents added no meat nor merit to the story he was trying to share.

Their faces were red and blue with strain. Their fists clenched. Shimmering slivers of glass sparkled on the floor. Sopping puddles of tears and alcohol were sticky and strewn about the laminate and sprayed across the walls, leaking down the paint in streaks. One of her mother's cheeks was crimson, swollen. At its center was a scraped bit of flesh where a gold wedding band might strike.

Norah winced. These were the brawls that plagued her nightmares. Even though their words were muffled, she remembered vividly how they snarled.

"You know the bastard you married! You know I didn't want any of this!"

"I didn't sign up for this fucking shit, Robin! It wasn't supposed to be like this."

The *this* he'd often referred to of course, was Norah. He never wanted a child, especially after having one. And Robin wasn't supposed to be able to conceive.

Leo's voice could shake the beams of their home. That's why Robin found the need to break things. It was the only way she could be heard above his storm.

Norah chewed on her cheeks as the pair continued to scream across the battlefield of their small kitchen. If words were weaponry, a full ballistics team would've been needed to navigate her parents' countless crimes.

Then, as sure and silent as hellfire, the old man in the black coat rounded the corner, breaching the space between the brawling couple. His long tresses were tight and wound at his skull and his beard was short and well-cropped.

He ducked a flying champagne flute from the Kestrel's wedding day as it exploded against the wall beside him. Dex eyed it and the pair with exhaustion before stepping from the trenches and continuing down the hall.

He sidled past adult Norah in his long-tailed black coat that flew behind him like the feathers of a diving sparrow. Glimpses of new tattoos peeked beneath his sleeves and chest as he climbed the stairs with angelic grace. Norah chased after him.

He swooped into Nor's bedroom and leaned against the doorframe, taking in the dark space.

A small mound was nested atop the brass-framed bed, wrapped in a yurt of blankets. A child's stubby legs protruded from the fortress. Each piercing curse that belted from below made the small body beneath stiffen and gasp.

Adult Nor remembered that feeling. A bursting, swelling, shaking ache. A bone-deep trepidation, seeping in her blood like poison. Hot, buzzing Cortisol.

"Oh love," Dex whispered. He pushed his whiskers aside and knelt to his knees, tutting his tongue, beckoning something unseen with a tattooed, come-hither finger.

A shrill chirrup replied with interest from a tiny black kitten who emerged from the blanket heap. Baby Vincent gawked at the man on his floor with wide reflective eyes, the size of headlights. From the squashed mane on his oversized head, two fuzzy, bear-like ears pinned in high alert.

Adult Norah burst with joy and a wide smile.

"Don't just sit there, feckin' smack the bastard Gunpowder," grumbled a lilted voice from the corner of the room.

Norah spun to watch as Cecil stepped from the shadows, head to toe in baggy black layers one would wear to the boxing gym. The fabric across his shoulders and chest was taut where his muscles swelled. His smile was wry, and his eyes were sparkling green in the dark.

Adult Nor's lips parted in awe of him, handsome and dappled in becoming scruff. Without his deep scars and perpetual frown, he seemed decades younger.

But what was he doing here?

Paying heed to Cecil's commands, a tiny Vincent twisted sideways to reveal big, prickly hairs along his spine. In an adorably furious assault, the kitten bound towards Dexteras across the bed, the desk, and then slid to a halt at eye level, scattering a stack of sketchbook doodles to the floor. The small, fat bundle of fur licked its lips with menace.

Adult Norah laughed, covering her mouth in adoration for the trio.

Dexteras blew a puff of air towards the kitten who spun and ran away in a huff, offended and spiky. The old man on the floor rejoiced in more chuckles, evidently unfazed by Cecil's presence.

The pillow rooftop upon the child's fort popped off to reveal a chaotic mane of chocolate hair and bright eyes. Her nose, cheeks, and eyes were tomato red with weeping. Sloughing off the blankets, she was alight with tiny, static lightning storms that crackled and sparked, leaving her hair electrified and wild.

Smearing tears and snot up her pajama sleeves, she slid from her bed to gather her fallen artwork in the kitten's wake.

The Figments watched quietly. Cecil leaned against the wall, his tattoos unmarred and blotch free. Where Norah recalled a once massive patch of black ink on Cecil's forearm, she could now see the portrait of a female boxer, alight with vigor, red gloves, and bruises. Though bloodied, her inked arms were poised and ready at her jaw.

"But she still needs you, Leo. I still need you! We can't change this."

The child's face twisted, and her shoulders rose tight to her ears, frozen in place.

Adult Norah ached to hold her.

"Any luck?" Cecil growled, his eyes never leaving the child. It was a sharp, cold glare of protectiveness.

Dex's lashes fell to the floor and he sighed. "She's too intoxicated to hear me. Too much adrenaline and alcohol," he lamented.

Cecil shook his head and pushed from the wall. His fury was evident by his sudden pacing. He pressed a hand to his forehead as though it ached, closing his eyes.

"She's so feckin' shook," he grumbled. "Dolly hasn't slept all week. Fell asleep in class again today." Cecil eyed Dex with a vicious injustice, baring his fists. It was evident that this was not the first time they'd had this conversation. It carried an exhaustion, a burdensome weight for the both of them, but it was Cecil who wore it most.

A crash of something heavy ricocheted off the walls below. Leo laughed manically and cursed.

"What the fuck Robin!? A wine bottle? You really are trying to kill me, aren't you?"

The child before them vibrated into another round of shakes, wiping tears up her cheeks until her eyes were raw.

"Feck," whispered Cecil, punching the wall beside them. One of Norah's pictures swayed crooked on the wall, ever-so-slightly beyond perception. "How do ya not *strangle* the feckin' *life* from 'em Dexy?" he demanded, pointing to the floor. "After all they'd done?"

Dex sighed.

The child's tears now bubbled into hiccups and sobs, forcing Cecil to cease his pacing and press his fingers to his temples in concentration. It was obvious that her anxiety was his, too. Her mourning was his. Burning tears even seemed to sparkle with rage in his own eyes. Never would Nor had imagined him capable of such vulnerability.

"I could try to shut 'em up again," Cecil mumbled, rolling his sleeves up his thick forearms.

"No," stated Dex. "You nearly sent Leo to the emergency room with the migraine you gave him last time." Dex clenched his jaw as though he, too, had felt the surreal sensation of Cecil in his skull.

"Then what the feck else is there?" Cecil snapped, eyes hot and desperate. "Why the feck is this all I can do?" he begged, lifting his hands as though he didn't want them.

"A Fig's power isn't always for fighting C," Dex said. "It's a reflection of their pain, their need. She yearns to change others, to fix them, so she can prove her worth. That's why you can hear thoughts and impact bodies."

"It's because of feckin' *them*!" Cecil snapped, pointing to the adults below. He winced as though he were in agony.

"I know it is, C" Dex said. "You're right."

Cecil rubbed his face and snarled like a dog, raking through his hair. "All this screamin' blue murder," he moaned, "how the feck do *you* stand it?"

Dex sighed, fingers deep in his pockets as he commiserated with the handsome Figment.

"Feck this," Cecil groaned again, spinning on his black boots. He whistled through his teeth and eyed the tiny cat kneading biscuits on the bed.

"Oi, Gunpowder!" The handsome Cecil tapped his dirty fingernails on the window's glass beside them. The kitten's tail fluffed with the thrill of the hunt and jumped and batted at the window, mewing and running up the glass with pink, padded paws.

The child Nor stared a long moment into the night, its quiet calling to her. She stood and lifted the glass, feeling the cold dry her cheeks. A breeze rushed inward, lifting goosebumps on her arms.

"S'feckin' taters dolly," Cecil muttered. "Best get yer coat."

Despite Cecil's complex rhyming slang, childhood Nor sensed a sudden need to wrap herself in her father's army jacket before climbing out. Slow and precise, she settled herself just outside the glass. She rested her forehead upon her pale kneecaps and stared into the black sky.

Unseen, unheard, and unacknowledged, Dexteras and Cecil sat beside the child and smoked their cigar and cigarette until flocks of smoky birds filled the sky.

Though young Norah Kestrel was small enough to be carried off by a stiff wind, she never felt Dex's strong arm on her, or Cecil's broad shoulder against hers. She couldn't hear the jangles of a silver coin her Figment Cecil rolled up and down his knuckles whilst Vincent watched, entranced.

Dex serenaded the black night with a deep, slow, vibrato song with his ocean-tide voice, strong and persistent like a large crystal singing bowl. Every few moments, Cecil would hum a word or two that he recognized.

The strange pair eventually sang in tandem like bar mates, groveled voices grumbling atop the screams of Nor's parents below like steady thunder.

The child rocked without knowing that the song in her head wasn't hers. The gruff lullaby lowered her lashes and smooshed her cheek to her knees.

In a close-eyed, dreamy whisper she said, "That's really pretty." After a few anxious shivers, her heavy, breathing was loud and heavy with sleep.

A quiet sniff turned Dex to his brother who was wiping his eyes. He smiled upon Cecil.

"Feck off," he whispered. "She's never spoken back befores."

Dex nodded. "It's very rare," he affirmed. "You and Norah share something special, C."

The pair remained beside her in the dark as the memory faded into watery swirls of blue paint.

Adult Norah wiped the tears from her own cheeks, realizing that the Kestrel family had driven dedicated Figments to tattoos, smoking, and crippling mental illness.

She was returned to the kitchen for another memory. The specific spillage of sticky liquors made it evident this was the night of the fire. Her blood went cold. The kitchen was orange with dim bulbs, holding only two figures in its shadows.

"Robin don't quit, don't give up," said Dexteras, following Robin Kestrel as she collapsed at the kitchen table, mumbling and incoherent.

"Think of Norah. You need to stay awake. Stay clear-headed. Stay with your feelings, stay with me," he pleaded, falling to his knees before her, long hair falling across his determined face.

The weary woman only fidgeted with her leather purse, searching it in desperation. She stared into the bag with the dead-eyed stare of a corpse, stone-still, fixated. Then, big, shining tears twisted her wrinkles. Her bony limbs shook whilst she clutched the bag, begging it for answers.

Dexteras' wide hands pounded the table like shot cannons.

"You *need* to get up. Just get up and walk. This will not save you or Lenore." Fear laced his shouts. "Go *somewhere*, please. Think of your daughter and go." He gripped his hair with tight hands, wrought with anxiety. He stood and wheeled about the kitchen, in search of something.

"Cecil!" he cried desperately to the ceiling.

But there was no response.

Deaf to the old man's rare screams, Norah's mother shook her head and drunkenly stumbled towards the stairs.

Norah remained a moment to lean across her mother's purse, abandoned in the dark. Beneath crumpled tissues and lipstick tubes, Robin's thirty-eight pistol glistened within the void, its silver tempting her with quick, violent mercy.

She mourned her mother's loneliness, ghostly tears falling from her like wisps of smoke. The memory flickered around her like a dying light bulb.

Somehow, she knew it was Dex, ensuring she was okay, inquiring if she needed to stop.

She shook her head, *No, I'm okay, I want to see,* she thought. And quickly, her world returned to full view and the lights brightened.

She followed the pair upstairs, seeking out the old man's frantic voice from the bedroom.

"Stay strong, have *hope.* Robin. You're not alone, you're not in this alone," he begged, pointing to the child's door. "I know you're in there, just *hear* me, *please, please I know you're in there.* You deserve love. You deserve good things. Both you and Lenore…" his voice broke. Dexteras was on his knees before Robin where she was strewn across the maroon chair. He touched her hands and petted her hair, his own tears falling like the dripping rum from Robin's lips.

He gazed in desperation at Norah's door again. "Cecil!" he called. "Please!" he begged.

But no one came.

Then, the quivering hand that held Robin's cigarette let go.

The fire grew as it was destined to, and Dex buried his face into his hands and wept.

He couldn't control the fire.

He couldn't control the traumas of humanity and how they coped or didn't cope with them.

He could only remain beside them and love them.

God, how did he do it? mourned Nor. *How did he bear loving people who couldn't hear his kind voice?*

But Dex's time to grieve had run out.

Leo was tugging on the far window. Dex sprang after him, fingers outstretched, attempting to prevent a flash fire from killing them all.

Even with Dex hanging the entirety of his weight upon the window's ledge, he had to cry out into the night to match her father's strength. He couldn't hold on forever.

"Cecil please!" cried Dex at the door of Norah's room.

No response.

"Cecil!" he screamed. The electricity in the entire house flickered.

Shuffling finally came from behind the door, and Norah watched the hope in his eyes spring to life. But the both of them seemed to register the truth at the same time. It wasn't Cecil at the door, it was his Corporeal, Norah. She cried out from the other side. She was going to open the door and fill the room with Oxygen. The Kestrel home was a ticking powder keg.

Lives were hung in the balance and Norah knew Dexteras had a vital choice to make. Let Leo open the window, induce an isolated flash fire, and thus *perhaps* save Norah, or let Norah open the door, induce a flash fire, and it likely kill her and Leo.

"Cecil *please*! Please brother, I *need* you," Dex cried, arms trembling as he wrestled with Leo at the window. With his breaking shouts, the electricity popped and the lights went black.

Dex sprang for Norah's bedroom and threw his shoulder and ear against it, hand hovering the brass knob. As soon as it jiggled, he snatched it.

The both of them gasped at the hissing bite of the metal. The *click-click-click* of electric sparks bounced from his fingers, forcing the screaming child away from the door.

The old man pressed his forehead against the dark wood grain, slamming his other fist against it miserably. Devastation bent his wrinkles and he bared his teeth.

The child screamed and sobbed beyond the threshold all alone.

"I'm so sorry love," he groaned into the door. "This grief alone will last you a lifetime. And you don't need to see this." He gazed down at his singed palm, blistered and burning and trembling with fine shakes. He blinked away at his tears and shook his head. "No one should have to."

He lost himself in the fresh scar as the room ignited around him. He looked over his shoulder just as Leonard cried out into the night and the window gave way.

In seconds, the room was only flames, screams and whorls of fire.

Sirens wailed in the distant dark.

✦

The memory flickered to blinding white lights and squeaking rubber shoes.

Adult Norah could barely match Dexteras' healthy clip as he flanked the traveling troupe of medical professionals racing towards the ICU. They stepped through the patterned curtains and revealed the chaos inside. Monitors and machines were attached to both Kestrel girls who now shared a room, divided by another curtain.

Dexteras stayed with little Norah who whimpered, blood pressure rocketing. He knelt beside her bed and watched nurses tend to their handiwork. Vitals were assessed. Water and fresh oxygen tanks were ushered in. Staff and monitors hollered on.

The child was fed antibiotics and installed to a respirator to ease the hacking in her lungs.

Her mother was preparing for her first skin graft.

Adult Norah knew that Leonard Kestrel's flesh was being treated for severe asphyxiation and Carbon Monoxide poisoning down the hall, walking a tightrope between life and death.

Dex rested his bearded chin upon his hands to watch the child battle nightmares behind her closed lids, rimmed crimson and raw.

After a moment, Dex suddenly sat upright in his seat as though he'd been stung by a wasp. He winced with its jolt, pulling at his buttoned shirt sleeve. He stared at his right palm, where in real time, a neotraditional tattoo carved into its flesh atop the scar that had saved the child's life just moments ago.

Adult Norah shuffled behind him to watch as a script of black ink illustrated the familiar Blue Jay, carrying its banner across his calloused skin. The bird's great, winding feathers wrapped his wrist like boxing wraps. The ink seeped beneath the layers with graceful penmanship, writing a script within the banner that read:

Serva me, servabo te.

Save me, so I may save you. Dex's headspace translated the Latin with ease for her.

His brows bent with thought as he ran his fingertips across the swollen ink. He replaced his sleeve and affixed its buttons. He returned his chin to his steepled fingers and continued to wait until he was needed, as he always had.

58

⋆DEXTERAS⋆

HE PRAYED HE WASN'T GIVING NORAH TOO MUCH. There was so much she deserved to know and only a finite time remained at this juncture.

He remembered the shock in his blood when he felt the ink in his palm, sharp and blindingly painful above the fresh burn. But each tattoo represented a new chapter of existence for Figments. To have tattoos was an honor, representative of the many lives, the many scars, and the many Corporeals served. When he saw the Blue Jay, he knew his Purpose had shifted to an entirely new story completely. While he was honored for the opportunity to continue serving Robin's family, this change in his charge meant something was very wrong.

The next memory he shared with Nor was moments after the last but occurred on the hospital rooftop. He and his brother had reunited in the aftermath and were dueling to the death.

Cecil slugged him across the temple, bending his younger self in half.

"This is *your* feckin' fault!" he screamed, eyes bulging and furious.

They looked like true opposites here, different pawns of the chessboard.

Cecil was an apt fighter, sharp, fiery, and built like a boxer dog. His black hair was wrapped in a bun at his scalp, and his dark clothes whipped about him like wings.

Dex's white hair stuck to his temples with the humid evening. His limbs were long and lean, *tick-tick-tick*ing with threatening sparks. Blood leaked from a cut in his pale hairline.

All they shared at present was their Figmented blood.

Dex recovered, and they danced again. He was efficient, sharp, and measured, but he had no desire to kill his brother.

Cecil took full advantage of this intention.

They'd tussled over the Kestrel's issues prior, all of which were resolved for the sake of Norah. Despite their burnout, they always seemed to find peace for the child.

But this fight was much more.

Dex was slammed into the incinerator bricks until they creaked with ancient dust. His temples were pounding as Cecil pinned him against the structure and sliced a cold hand up and *under* Dex's ribs, impaling him beneath the breastbone.

Dex's world grew cold with surprise as the arm plunged up into his torso, hand slick between the wet bones of his sternum. The old man's breathing hitched and he nearly stumbled with nausea. He wailed, feeling the horrid vibration of his screams against another entity pressing on his lungs.

Cecil squeezed at inner organs, eyes ablaze like wild green chemical fires.

Tears streaked down Dex's cheeks, intermingling with the now pouring rain. His blood shone like molten gold, oozing down Cecil's forearm. This was before Cecil had perfected his craft and made a mess of most things he touched.

"Cecil…" Dex gasped, knuckles white, gripping his brother's shoulders, attempting to lift himself from the unfathomable pain.

"Why didn't ya feckin' *stop* her?" Cecil screamed, bicep twisting with tension, stirring like a knife blade. "Robin was *yer* feckin' pet Dexteras," he spat.

"She couldn't hear me!" Dex called out into the storm clouds, tears falling like tides. "The alcohol, the pills…" he moaned. "She can't feel me like she used to."

"And ya *burned* Norah, she's *me* feckin' turtle!" he roared, torquing his arm until Dex's muscles contorted and tightened like wound elastic.

"Please," Dexteras screamed. "I tried, I tried, truly I tried," he said through gritted teeth, nails raking into Cecil's neck.

"Ya feckin' tried," Cecil laughed manically, "but *she's* the one suffering!"

Dex remembered this part well. Words and breath were becoming more and more impossible to force from his chest. His throat was taut with screams and his heart pounded like a hummingbird's. His feeling body was going into shock.

"Wh-Where were *you*?" he screamed with a final, desperate screech.

Cecil bared his teeth like ivory gates, pressing harder into Dexteras, reaching, clawing, tearing at muscle and tissue and sinew to grasp his heart. His fingers wound tight around the cardiac muscle, and he clamped down hard.

Dex had never experienced a heart attack.

He'd only experienced the physical pains that Robin had. The worst was when she overdosed for the third time. Her veins collapsed. Her brain was oxygen deprived. Her lungs slowed and depressed, fluid leaking between their decaying tissue. She couldn't swallow, and then she couldn't breathe. Until teenage Norah Kestrel rushed into the bedroom and saved them both.

But *this* was a heavy, searing, lightning-white pain that made his eyes bulge, and his gut tremble. He attempted to tear at his chest, throat, and lungs like he'd swallowed live, lumpy coals, red hot from the furnace. He could only pry his lips in agony, unable to scream. Black flooded his terrified peripherals like leaking ink.

He's killing me.

He's killing me.

I'm dying.

And Dexteras knew, in the end, he had no choice.

If he wanted to exist to see Norah or Robin again, he'd have to save his damned neck. Cecil knew fighting, and that was the only language he spoke.

Thus, Dex tore his face from his brother and drove his thumbs into Cecil's eyes. He pressed until the *snap-snap-snap* of ocular nerves gave beneath his fingers. He dug until they both relented and collapsed, writhing on the bird-shit-ridden roof of the hospital.

Wheezing for life, Dex croaked again, "Where…were…*you?*"

But Cecil was too preoccupied, the heels of his palms shaking above his bleeding eye sockets, collecting puddles of blood.

"I can't see, I can't see, I can't feckin' see!" he screamed.

"Cecil, where were-"

"He was with *me*, Dexteras," hissed a new voice behind them.

Dex scrambled to his feet and propped himself against the wall to take in Solus, standing coolly by the roof's ledge to spectate.

Their gold blades scraped against the stone roof as they approached. They wore their beguiling form, their hair was much longer then, black and shining to their round buttocks with the gloss of a horse's coat. Their dagger eyes were painted with black smudges like smoke.

Black, high-waisted pants clung to their ribs beneath a sable knee-length velvet coat. Gold chains jostled and shone, gripping their scant lapels like sutures.

"*What?*" demanded Dex.

"He was with me, agreeing to my contract."

Dexteras dropped the gripping hands at his gut and straightened to fix his eyes upon the beast. "*What* contract?"

"I only offer one, Dexy. I've offered it to you many times."

"No…"

"Cecil wanted peace from all of this," said Solus, gesturing below to the hospital that held their Corporeals. "Can you blame him? All the pain you've both contained? Aren't you tired? Aren't you exhausted by the idea of a forever in this void, this pain?" Solus chuckled as though the answer were obvious.

"You fucking vulture," growled Dexteras. "You wait until things are bad, and then you make bargains!" He spun to scream at Cecil. "Cecil, if it was a good offer, he wouldn't approach you with it when you're *weak*!"

"Ya feckin' bastard," said Cecil between gasps, his eyes clenched shut, leaking tears and blood and unknown fluids. "It's *my* choice."

"They take your memories to keep you obedient Cecil!" Dex exclaimed. "You can't do this to her!"

Cecil roared and was on his feet in seconds, against Dex's chest, clutching to the lapels of his suit. They were both painted in blood, but Cecil's face was abhorrent. A horrid guilt wrought Dex's gut for the gruesome aftermath he'd inflicted on his oldest friend.

"What the *feck* would I want with all this pain, aye?" he said, shaking and snarling like a cold dog. He pointed below to where Norah was recovering. "What good am I to her?" he slapped his chest where clotting blood from his eye sockets shone. "Can't stop yer feckin' Corpse from being absolute bobbins to her!" he snarled.

Dex had no response. He only watched the bloodied Figment wince and convulse with rage.

His brother had always brimmed with hatred for how Norah wept and ached in that home. His fury had often given the entire household headaches for days. The helplessness ate at him, but he'd given Norah so much more than he knew.

He taught her to love the adrenaline of rooftops and the relief of punching pillows in her room. He'd taught her to flip off her screaming parents behind shut doors and how to feel in control and strong. He inspired her to go the field the day she found the old cat. He'd taught her to find peace in little things like fidgeting with coins and caring for Vincent, to draw, doodle, and paint when there were simply no words for the chaos.

But she was still so hurting and small, so vulnerable and innocent. His anger atrophied and corroded at his insides until he was the creature before them, weeping blood and weary.

"I clearly wasn't doing her any feckin' good," Cecil cackled with pathetic laughter into his hands. His brutish rage was exchanged for despondence. "She lived tonight 'cause of *you*. *You* be her Fig," he stated, stumbling back from the old man. "I can't hear them anymore," he whispered, clutching his skull. "Can't help none their screamin' Dexy."

With a moan, he shuffled towards Solus blindly.

"No. I can't let you do this," muttered Dex, shaking his head. "I can't care for her like you did C...My own Corporeal...."

But he knew it was a lie. His own Purpose had fallen dormant. He could feel it in his bones. Robin wouldn't leave her bed again once the disease caught up with her. He could smell it in the tar-ridden exhalation of her lungs. He could hear it in her wheezes. One day, those gasps would tremble in his own chest and take him back to the stars. But he had to know. He had to know how the Kestrel's story ended. After generations, he needed to know, and this was his chance to stay.

"She still needs you, C," Dex still begged, "it's not too-"

But without warning, Solus spun on their blades impatiently and gripped Cecil's head by his bleeding temples. Fingernails raking, Solus bent and kissed Cecil deeply on his busted lips, long and hard. They drank tides of Cecil's thoughts like a euphoric drug into their bobbing throat.

Cecil's hands fell, and his bloody eyeballs flickered back into his skull, where the past was now stripped from him entirely.

Solus tore away with a moan and swallowed the memories down their gullet like thick wine, lips tipping to the sky for breath.

Cecil collapsed to the ground lifelessly.

"Don't worry, Dexy, I left some of you in there," gasped Solus, eyeing the younger, dark-haired Figment. "That little scuffle there. Let him think you tried to kill him for pursuing his freedom." Solus grinned, eyeing the old man like meat. "Or, I could offer you the chance to join him if you'd like?" They winked, eyes dazzling and hopeful.

"I could also tear your insides out through that mechanical fucking cage," snarled Dex, eyes cutting to the tarnished brass pressed into their skin.

The smile fell from the ancient Fig. "Your Corpse is out of hope, Dexy. You can smell it as well as I can."

Yes, Robin would deteriorate. It'd already begun. Her mental health would wither. The energy she once invested in otherworldly hopes would die. And then...

"You'll die," said Solus, straightening their bloody lapels. "It'll take a while. You're a concept. An idea. But you're only her's."

Dexteras didn't care, of course. He knew what being a Figment entailed. He loved each moment with every Starling woman he'd been honored to share existence with. Rose and Robin. And, of course, that was why he too, loved Norah and Cecil. He was theirs, and they were his.

But returning to the stars wasn't death, as Solus coined it. It was simply a new chapter. Something else. And that terrified Corporeal and Figment alike.

Cecil moaned, and his crusty eyelids strained on dried blood. His fingers clutched to the earth but couldn't lift him from his stupor just yet.

Dex swallowed and blinked away his tears. Cecil was the bravest Figment he'd ever met, but he was so tired. Dex hadn't any idea just how weary the young Fig had been and felt horrible for not noticing how much he'd been hurting. How much must one ache to choose nothingness above everything?

"Give me your pain, Dexteras," muttered Solus, walking nearer now with soft eyes. "Is it so asinine to turn from our most vivid horrors so that we may know peace?" The beautiful form approached gently on golden limbs, a hand outstretched in empathy.

"They're the reason we exist. We *owe* them loyalty," Dex objected.

"Dexteras," they said, eyes closing in disappointment. "Humor me a moment." The tips of their gold blades tossed bits of gravel toward Dex with their creeping. "*We* didn't ask to be created." They gestured to the skies as though it were the cosmos' fault. "To endure all this pain." Solus bent their head like a doting parent. "Just like little Lenore didn't. Do you truly believe she *owes* her parents her life and death simply because they created her?"

Dex's shoulders fell.

He knew how Robin's untreated trauma would simmer to the surface and feed on others as it had for decades. She hadn't done the work to heal, so took it from others to survive. Just as Solus was plastering themselves with the power of others Figments to avoid their own process.

Rose had taught Robin that if she wanted to survive, she had to steal, hoard, and take everything without mercy. Grace and compassion would only weaken their hides. It was in that dark hunger where Dexteras had been sewn together. Consume or be consumed: a game all Figments and Corpses knew equally well.

What he represented was always left unnamed and lingering in the shadows, so there was never healing. There was never peace.

So consequently, Robin couldn't find peace in the orange plastic bottles of pills with their peeled-off labels. Peace had nothing to do with high-percentage alcohol or the hefty bequeathal her grandfather gave her when he passed. It wasn't in any of the rooms of the charming sable farmhouse outside of town. It certainly had nothing to do with the handsome financial analyst who'd left his number and name, *Leo*, stuck to a welcome folder from her local bank after she'd inquired about an account.

Peace was always an inside job. One that Robin had never been taught.

She'd been hungry her entire life for love, and validation. Just as her mother Rose always had been. He was concocted from that thirst, that unfilled cup where fatherly fervor should've been stored and flowing like fine wine.

But now, Robin had no parents, no guardians, despite all her running, and no partner to love.

She only had Norah.

And it would be from *that* child's meager cup, still brimming with fresh hope, where Robin would attempt to drink her worth.

It wouldn't be fair.

It wouldn't be loving.

And it surely wouldn't be pleasant to watch.

But it wasn't a Figment's job to find pleasantries in life; it was their job to remain and offer hope. Mental and emotional consistency. He could bear that. *He* could carry that when Cecil could not.

But Norah was a human child: bleeding, weeping, temporary. How much more could *she* take?

She didn't ask to be created either.

She didn't owe Leo and Robin anything simply because they brought her into existence.

She hadn't been given the time to dream.

She was just set up for the same dismal road as Robin and Rose. Take what you must to survive.

She hadn't-

SHING.

Dex's ruminations were interrupted by a slash of searing pain behind his knees. A sensation that turned his legs to fire and their blood to ice water. His screaming calf muscles shook and buckled before dropping him to the concrete. His arms clutched the rooftop's ledge and twisted to see the mess that was his limbs.

Shining slick blood flooded the bend in his knees. They'd been cut in one slice across the hamstrings, severing the muscles deep, nearly lopping them off. His feet were already numb, and his legs were soon behind.

Solus crouched beside him on the slender gold blades, one of which was rimmed in his blood. They wound their fingers into Dex's hair and gripped it like the reins of a runaway horse. They pressed their icy, dead thumbs into Dex's temples and squeezed until a headache pounded behind his eyelids.

"Psychogenic amnesia is usually what it's called, Dexy. Sometimes trauma induced shock. Localized memory loss, what have you," they sighed, eyeing the old man in his hands. "That's what the Corpses will say happened to you when they find your empty body. Dead. Hollow. Thoughtless," they said, almost in mourning. "In Oblitus, I call it The Unbecoming. Catchy, isn't it?"

Dexteras could only swallow with strain and stare upon the devil that held him.

"It has to be this way, Dexy. I know you'll pursue me, I know you'll fight for him." Their eyes flicked with apathy toward Cecil. "And I can't have you threatening Oblitus or my Fallen there. But please know, as long as he's loyal, he will be taken care of." Solus vowed.

"But *you* could've been so extravagant beside me," they sighed, disappointed as they read the fallen Figment's prostrate body. "I've seen you fight for them. You've walked amongst generations of skin-sacks without relent." Long, cold fingers wiped Dex's forehead and petted his hair. "But now, they'll find you up here and believe you to be some braindead bastard."

Solus pulled Dex's skull upwards towards their ruby lips, kissing him deeply, intimately, hungrily on the mouth.

The world grew pale and dark as though Corvid were being desaturated of its ink. Deep, long gulps gurgled from the beast who clutched him, dizzying the old man as though he were being emptied of blood.

Dex attempted to kick and crawl and thrash, but everything below his waist was numb now. His fingers struggled to rise to the beast's throat, swallowing him hungrily.

Dex tried to scream but couldn't. It'd seemed his lungs had forgotten how.

He was going to be sucked dry of who he was.

No. No.

I need to save Norah.

I need to be here for her.

I need to keep her safe…

Serva me, servabo te.

His fingers reached for the ledge and yanked, dragging his chest onward until he gasped and moaned.

Solus was so transfixed by the consummation, they'd barely noticed Dex's dragging limbs, inching towards the ledge. They drank like a bloodthirsty animal, succumbing to thirst, holding the old man like dead meat in his teeth.

Skull gripped upright by Solus, Dex pulled himself sideways towards the shallow ledge, arms trembling and heaving with his weight. He hugged the cool stone ledge with his broken body, forgetting why he was doing so as he did.

His hair whipped in the wind about them both. His head felt peaceful, empty.

A strange, beautiful creature clung to him and pulled from his throat like a straw. It was nauseating but not so bad. Not as bad as the descent before him.

Why would he escape the numbing warmth in his skull?

Because it was her. Her. Her.

Her.

Robin?

Le-Len...Norah.

He saw her face. Small, dark. Weeping. A child.

But with another gulp of the creature's throat, he'd lost her name.

Her face dissipated from his fingers like sugar granules in water.

Then her shape.

Her silhouette.

He *needed* to hold to what he could. He *needed* to hang onto whoever she was.

She was so important. She needed him.

Right?

He reached over the edge.

He leaned...leaned...leaned

...and he was falling.

Falling, flying, tumbling, rolling, spinning. Air screaming in his ears.

Hang onto her. Hang on...

I'll find you.

I'll find you.

Who?

59

✦NORAH✦

THE GENTLENESS WITH WHICH HE FELL BACK INTO THE SKY'S EMBRACE was filled with a peaceful acceptance. His features were swallowed by his hair, and he closed his eyes.

A drunken Solus attempted to clutch at the falling man with inebriated arms but was far too late and intoxicated with the old man's memories. There were lifetimes to consume in him.

Norah backpedaled from the ledge with a choke, unable to bear witness to what remained of him below. She would not behold the memory of his gruesome breaking.

Then, the scene began to darken at her peripherals like a vignette.

Below, screams could be heard. The screams of Corvidians. One of which would be a local nurse who genuinely yearned to help others, to resuscitate the dead, and thus needed Dex to stay alive with deep Purpose.

Blurring white clouds fogged Norah's vision and set her in the hospital's lobby. She heaved a great breath for all she'd seen.

The emergency port doors slammed open down the hall, spitting out a herd of professionals escorting a bloody heap upon a gurney. The mass of men and women huddled about it was so thick, she could barely see the sorry soul.

And then his cries echoed upon the hospital walls, driving ice through her bones.

"No, stop, please! *Please.* Please, you have to let me go. Please let me go. I have to find them. I have to!"

Her knees weakened, and she tripped after the rolling bed.

"Please don't, please d-don't touch me. How can you s-s-see me? Please don't. It hurts. Please!" He fought against a nurse who called for a sedative, a relatively high dose at that.

They attempted to coo and calm him and begged him to lie back, but he clawed beneath tattered, blood-soaked clothes and limbs.

She could tell by the glimpses of white and wild eyes that he was horrified. Still, he attempted to be gentle with the humans.

"No, please, I'm not supposed to be here. You can't s-see me, p-please stop!"

It shook shivers through her skin to hear the piercing and unfamiliar fear in his voice. Rushing beside the boisterous troupe, glimpses of what remained of her old friend came into vision.

Her stomach flip-flopped, leaving her to swallow bile back down her throat.

His once handsome tea-stained skin was puddled in blood, jutting with bones in unnatural angles, leaving him crooked in the traveling bed. Nothing seemed as it should be. Nurses pressed steady hands to wounds and gaping holes across his corpse where innards threatened to come outwards. His white hair was slicked with crimson. He was a screaming, bloody pile of misery.

Most of the seasoned emergency staff could conceal their disgust and fear, but others were not so tactful. One male nurse even ran down the hall to likely vomit from the stench of blood.

"Oh God, Dex…" Nor managed, uncertain how they'd stitched his pieces into the handsome creature she knew today.

Professionals attempted to administer fluids and needles, but he cast them aside with massive arms. But a nurse in the distance was running with a syringe clutched in his hand.

Why would any creature willingly accept such pain, such horrendous torture, she grieved. *What could possibly be worth such hurt?*

"Please make them stop, please! Please! Save-" But his voice was cut short, for her broken friend had fixated his distorted face upon an adjacent hallway.

Nor careened for a better view to see a pair of humans approaching the exit. Her mouth fell agape.

A small Norah Jay Kestrel walked hand-in-hand with her Nana Rose as they left the girl's parents just floors above. Around this time, near the end of Rose' life, she'd found sobriety, quiet, and some semblance of a relationship with her daughter Robin. But there was still a strained tension between them, whether civilized or contained.

Rose attempted to shield the already traumatized child from the macabre horror of the old man in the bed, but Norah peeked around her grandmother's hip.

The wounded Dex's shoulders fell, and his bloodied jaw hung slack.

He pivoted to watch them leave, captured in brief freedom from his fractured bones and punctured organs.

"…wait…" he whispered.

And then, a sting pinched his arm, and a swollen mound of his flesh was inflated with sedative. He fell to his elbow but still fought to behold the bandage-wrapped child. It seemed that he couldn't fully understand why she captured him so, but before he could call after them, his spine laid him flat to the gurney, eyes wide and leaking. His medical team collected his awkward limbs upon the soaked mattress and crashed through another set of doors.

Norah watched her younger self twist and gawk before succumbing to her grandmother's tug into the street.

The world finally faded into lush clouds, swirling about Norah's vision. Finally, the retelling of their long-begotten story had brought them to today.

Delicate tears rested upon her cheeks in real time, returning her to her present body. For a moment, her adult flesh felt ill-fitting and oversized. She stretched her palm and assessed its scar with its taut pull.

She began to speak, but the words were stolen from her tongue. There simply weren't enough.

But a Dexteras decades wiser reached across and wiped her tears with a warm hand. Wrinkles gathered at his almond eyes, sparkling like the shiny blue of a blackbird's coat.

She choked and pressed her hands to her face. "Don't go. Don't go," she breathed. "I still need you."

He chuckled. "Love, you never needed anybody. Especially me. What you needed was to come to terms with that fact."

"Obviously, I needed a Fig," she retorted. "I had to dream up someone else to get through."

Dex raised his brows, nearly offended. "Have you *seen* Cecil?" he challenged. "Have you seen how fierce and relentless he is? You created Oblitus' champion fighter when you were a *toddler*," he scoffed. "He's a reflection of you Nor, do you truly think he's weak?"

"No," she grumbled. "He's kind of an asshole, though."

Dex cackled into the skies. "He's just afraid sometimes. His vision and voice were taken from him, but that never stops him from doing what he thinks he should."

Her chin fell, considering her likeness to the Shrike. She recalled something he told her once about his abilities. "Best be the puppeteer and not the puppet." There's no need to protect your insides when your opponent is preoccupied with what's inside them.

Cecil was looking for control. They both were, of course. That's why she'd become a therapist, she was sure. Her gut cramped.

"Why can't other humans see *Oblitus*?" Nor asked.

He sighed with wide eyes. "That's a tough question to explain," he began. "In short, the human mind is very protective. It requires an invitation. Reason. Logic. Otherwise, it rarely cares to venture beyond what it cannot see."

"So why could I see it?"

He grinned with guilt, growing pink. "Because you chose to see me. You saw me when no one else had in decades."

"And mom made you?"

"Your grandmother Rose did," he said, eyes sparkling with affection. "She lived in fear of being unloved, being alone. A pain that began with her fatherlessness. Your mother gave her purpose just as you gave Robin purpose," he gave a weak smile. "But there was far too much pressure for any child to bear, and that fear and loneliness was passed down. A fear of being alone, unloved. When that was passed to your mother, so was I."

Fresh tears fell, and she sniffed, but more questions swelled beneath her chest.

"I've followed generations of Starling children without fathers, lost and hungry. And that's why I found you, the day that Robin died. But you've begun the process they couldn't bear to, and thus the cycle is broken. Generations of pain and suffering end with you, Nor." Though it left him without a Corpse, he was beaming with pride.

"I wanted to know her," Nor whispered. "I wanted to love her…."

"*Amica mea*," he cooed. "Who do you think you're loving when you love me? Whose heart was I born of, just as you were?" He smiled proudly.

"You're different," she sighed.

"But I'm not, really. I'm a mirror of her pain and her messiness. But I'm also a mirror of her love. As always," Dex said, looking to the far horizon, "Solus had that wrong about us, too. We're not brought into existence just by agony. It must be coupled with a will to fight, a fear of losing something or someone," he affirmed with great confidence. "A love we wish to hold to. That goes for humans and Figs alike. Survival is reflexive. But loving is transcendental."

Norah's lip twisted for a moment, understanding him ever so slowly. But then, her small grin disappeared. "Why didn't dad have someone like you?" she asked.

The old man lifted his bright blue eyes to Norah, keen on her with full attention. "He never truly believed he was worthy of asking for help. For love. For more."

An unexpected pity thudded in Norah's gut for Leonard. "Never?" she grieved, eyes growing hot.

Dex shook his head. "In the hearts of those who believe they must endure life entirely alone, Figments can sense a hardness, like a locked gate. A padlocked door only he could open."

She shook her head. What must life have done to a boy to make him believe such lies about himself? Norah sniffed, wondering if that was why Robin couldn't bring herself to quit on her late husband.

Dex reached and squeezed Norah's fingers in his. "Leo forsook others and Robin forsook herself. But I know you won't make their mistakes."

She swallowed and dried her eyes with a sleeve. She did not want to waste this time on blurry eyes and pitying silence. Her mind whirred. A part of her hoped to burden Dexteras with so many questions that he'd have to stay there with her until she was old and gray. But a sinking sadness drew her voice to a whisper with her remaining inquiries, final and frightening.

"When will I see you again?"

His crow's feet crinkled. "Your job is as mine. We know we did well when we're not needed anymore, even when it pains us to go," he said. Seeing that this didn't satiate her aching heart, he added, "But soon, in a very long time, *amica mea*."

✦

They lay on their backs and stared at the stars. She would've done anything for another day or hour with him beneath that sky. A firm lump suspended in her throat until she was oxygen-deprived. She stifled her wet sniffs but couldn't conceal the wobbles in her voice.

"Where will you go?"

He reached for her hand and squeezed it in the dark. "Where I'm needed."

She struggled to swallow or breathe. "I can't lose you," she whispered.

He turned his head and smiled at her, eyes alight with endless secrets. "You've seen what the universe does with life and energy," he said, gesturing to himself with a wry grin. "Do you truly believe it all just stops? That any of us are *really* gone?"

Norah had no words, unable to answer such a question.

"The only thing keeping you from the stars is gravity, *mellis*. We won't be so very far apart."

"I don't want you to go," she squeaked, stealing her hands from him to scratch the scar on her cheek. "I'm afraid," she admitted.

"Of what?"

"Of being alone, of…of lots of things," she stated, voice building.

Of being like them.

Of being like them

Of being like them.

"Love. Fear is not your enemy. Fear brought you and me both into this life," he said. "But you'll never be like them because your Purpose isn't defined in your fear," he said. "Solus had it all wrong. Purpose is a process inside yourself, defined by you alone."

Again, she had no worthy rebuttal. He was right, after all. She knew it was true from the work she did each and every day.

"Close your eyes, love."

Her gut dropped, and she shook her head. "No. I'll open them, and you'll be gone."

"*Cara mi*, it's okay," a small smile flavored his voice. "It is. Please, trust me."

He'd trusted her so many times when it was difficult. She owed him the same consideration. She closed her eyes.

"You've always been so excellent at making others feel present. Even when I felt I wasn't alive or worthy of being. It was a privilege to be human beside you, Nor. You made me feel real and loved and needed. And do you feel me here now?"

She sniffed hard in the darkness, redirecting her consciousness to her skin, limbs, and senses. She could smell his vanilla-spiced tobacco. She could feel his warmth on the hairs of her arms. Even though they didn't touch one another, he held her like the weight of a wrapped cardigan with his cool comfort.

"Yes."

"I once told you we connect with scars because they know us best… but there's more to it than that," he began. "The veins running through your body, the royal blue ones beneath your skin? They're filled with hemoglobin. Iron."

Blood pulsed harder through her as awareness grew. She rested her fingertips on the soft flesh of her wrist to feel its rush.

"There's only one place in the cosmos where such iron is naturally made. An exploded star that mixed with your earth's clay billions of years prior. The earth from which we're all molded," he said, voice tilting to the stars to speak to them directly. "So you're filled with star-stuff love, just as I am. As we all are. And those pieces communicate with one another most clearly at our scars. That's where the skin is thin, where blood and iron and stars were once spilled."

She stretched her palm. His words hit her with a foreign pride for how precious the scar there now seemed.

"So you and I, and everyone else, we are *sidereus,* of the stars. We're connected."

Tears streamed down her temples while she wrought her wrists beneath her fingertips. Her wildly beating pulse sputtered beneath the skin there.

She saw his smile beneath her eyelids.

"I'm a part of you, *amica mea.* I'm always here."

60

✦NORAH✦

HER EYES PEELED OPEN THROUGH TIGHT LIDS, crusty and tight with dried tears.

Tension clenched her gut as she winced through the medallion sun, warming her chills with a new morning. She despised her body for its betrayal and for wasting precious moments with Dexteras. Gritty shingles crunched beneath her as she sat up and dared to survey the space.

She felt in her chest that she would find nothing. No one. Dexteras was gone, despite his grandeur and immensity, he'd served his Purpose and gone home.

Her chest and throat tightened. Sobs welled in her hot cheeks.

But before she could fold with grief, her finger grazed something beside her. She turned to find her hand upon Alina's bracelet to Dex, clacking with beads and string stretched by wear and love.

Tap. Tap. Tap. Tap, it sang against her fingers.

Wiping tears on her sleeves, she sensed a static hum in the air that prickled the hairs on her arms and spun her with wonder.

She turned to see Cecil sitting on the chimney stack, elbows draped across his knees, facing the new sun like a snake warming his skin on the stone. The young Figment's black attire was tattered and torn, blood-smeared and singed, but he was here. His scruff was longer than usual, but it fit his handsome face.

The squat black cat sat purring in his lap, eyes closed and content, warming in the morning rays.

"Vincent, how the fuck…" she muttered.

Cecil pulled the glasses from his face, revealing his pale irises, heavy-lidded and worn. The morning's shadows cast deep, scarred pockets across his fierce features. He tipped a curious ear toward her.

She understood now that he was a Figment built by anger and fury. *Her* fury. Though he'd been unable to watch her break all those decades ago, he still carried her burnout, exhaustion, and need to be in control.

It was much like her role as a therapist: neither she nor C could force others to change or heal. It was immense and difficult to watch suffering and would surely bleed you dry if you weren't mindful. But being beside someone amidst such pain was sacred.

"Even when I couldn't see you, Vincent could," she said quietly, staring at The Figment with a warm smile.

Cecil smirked and he swallowed with a massive bob in his Adam's apple. *"The universe knew I was a feckin' flake and sent backup,"* he chuckled in her thoughts, ruffling the old cat's fur playfully.

Nor's smile fell. "Wh-Vincent is a *Figment?*"

"Course he is dolly. Showed up right when he was needed, didn't he?"

Norah could only shake her head in struck awe and huff.

"Dexy?" Cecil then growled quietly into her headspace, brows tall and considerate. Hopeful and curious.

Nor's silent tears promptly spilled. She swung low and tossed Cecil the bracelet with a sharp breath.

He caught it in a one-handed swipe and read the Ukrainian characters with analytical fingertips. His weary face rose into a lopsided grin.

Norah gazed at the rising sun and smiled too.

"He's home."

✦ABOUT THE AUTHOR✦

A.M. ALCEDO is a licensed therapist with specialty training in trauma recovery. She adores the mental health field and the clients who share the privilege of their story and their vulnerability. Much like Norah Kestrel, A.M. Alcedo has also found healing, hope, and power through her grief, loss, and pain. As a child, she desperately needed a Dexteras Doe in her life, and thus wrote *OF THE STARS*, to pay homage to her littlest self. This debut novel is written in solidarity for those who have lived in the empty, lonely cove of grief and isolation. For those who have waited in the dark, warming their hands by their tiny, yet fierce fires. This book is to remind them that there are endless coves along the shore occupied by others just like them. They are not alone and they are not forgotten. This book is a love letter to honor them and their stories.

Ava Mae is a wife to the kindest man in the galaxy, and a mother to Pancake the calico. She is a lover of Pu Erh tea, anything matcha flavored, birdwatching with binoculars, doodling unicorns, hiking to waterfalls, and getting new tattoos. Above all else, she feels her Purpose is to hold space for the sacred stories of others.

Instagram: @writemindedlefthanded

Milton Keynes UK
Ingram Content Group UK Ltd.
UKHW012153131223
434335UK00015B/227/J

9 798988 421269